O. HENRY MEMORIAL AWARD
PRIZE STORIES
OF 1941

O. HENRY MEMORIAL AWARD
PRIZE STORIES
OF
1941

SELECTED AND EDITED BY
HERSCHEL BRICKELL

DOUBLEDAY, DORAN AND COMPANY, INC.
GARDEN CITY *1941* NEW YORK

PRINTED AT THE *Country Life Press*, GARDEN CITY, N. Y., U. S. A.

CL
COPYRIGHT, 1941
BY DOUBLEDAY, DORAN & COMPANY, INC.
COPYRIGHT, 1940
BY THE ATLANTIC MONTHLY COMPANY
COPYRIGHT, 1940
BY WILLIAM FAULKNER
COPYRIGHT, 1940
BY MARY O'HARA
COPYRIGHT, 1940
BY HEARST MAGAZINES, INC.
COPYRIGHT, 1940
BY CURTIS PUBLISHING COMPANY
COPYRIGHT, 1940, 1941
BY THE F-R PUBLISHING CORPORATION
COPYRIGHT, 1940, 1941
BY STORY MAGAZINE, INC.
COPYRIGHT, 1941
BY CONRAD AIKEN
COPYRIGHT, 1941
BY THE LOUISIANA STATE UNIVERSITY
COPYRIGHT, 1941
BY THE VIRGINIA QUARTERLY REVIEW
COPYRIGHT, 1941
BY STREET AND SMITH PUBLICATIONS, INC.
COPYRIGHT, 1941
BY EDITA MORRIS
COPYRIGHT, 1941
BY VINCENT SHEEAN
COPYRIGHT, 1941
BY JAMES STILL
COPYRIGHT, 1941
BY HARPER AND BROTHERS
COPYRIGHT, 1941
BY EUDORA WELTY
ALL RIGHTS RESERVED

FIRST EDITION

CONTENTS*

	PAGE
INTRODUCTION. By Herschel Brickell	vii
DEFEAT. By Kay Boyle	3
A WORN PATH. By Eudora Welty	17
EIGHTEENTH SUMMER. By Hallie Southgate Abbett	31
THE VISIT. By Andy Logan	49
HELLO, TIB. By Conrad Aiken	61
A BOTTLE OF MILK FOR MOTHER. By Nelson Algren	71
RETREAT. By Sally Benson	93
I'M GOING TO ASIA. By John Cheever	105
HOOK. By Walter Van Tilburg Clark	113
SEVEN BOYS TAKE A HILL. By David Cornel DeJong	139
THE OLD PEOPLE. By William Faulkner	155
THE SNOW GOOSE. By Paul Gallico	173
THOSE ARE AS BROTHERS. By Nancy Hale	197
I'D GIVE IT ALL UP FOR TAHITI. By Paul Kunasz	213
AFTERNOON IN THE JUNGLE. By Albert Maltz	223
CAPUT MORTUUM. By Edita Morris	235
MY FRIEND FLICKA. By Mary O'Hara	247

*After the prize stories, the order is alphabetical by authors.

	PAGE
THE CONQUEROR. *By Vincent Sheean*	273
THE PROUD WALKERS. *By James Still*	289
MY PIGEON PAIR. *By Dorothy Thomas*	307
APPENDIX	323

INTRODUCTION

IN THIS, the twenty-third annual volume of the O. Henry Memorial Prize Award Stories, appear twenty examples of the work of American short-story writers, chosen from American magazines published during the year ending in July 1941. They were selected by the editor as representative of the best work in this ever-fruitful field of literary endeavor, and as worthy to honor the memory of the master craftsman whose pen name distinguishes the collection.

THE PRIZE WINNERS

Four of the stories have been awarded prizes by three noted authorities on the short story, acting with the editor.

They are:

"Defeat" by Kay Boyle, of Nyack, New York, from the *New Yorker,* the first prize of $300.

"A Worn Path" by Eudora Welty, of Jackson, Mississippi, from the *Atlantic Monthly,* the second prize of $200.

"Eighteenth Summer" by Hallie Southgate Abbett, of New York City, from *Story,* the third prize of $100.

"The Visit" by Andy Logan, of Candler, North Carolina, from *Redbook,* a special prize of $100 for a first published story.

The judges who assisted in making these awards were:

Harry Hansen, literary editor of the New York *World-Telegram,* lecturer and author, and from 1933 through 1940 editor of this anthology.

Edith Mirrielees, professor of English in Stanford University, author of *The Story Writer,* short-story writer, and member of the staff of the Bread Loaf Writers' Conference.

Blanche Colton Williams, former professor of English in Hunter College, biographer, author of several volumes on the short story, and from its founding in 1919 until 1933 editor of this anthology.

A STATEMENT OF POLICY

As the new editor of this collection, which has made a secure place for itself in the twenty-three years of its existence, it seems fitting that I should make a statement of policy. Perhaps the best way to do this would be to point to the examples of my judgment in the present volume, since they are bound to illustrate my principles of selection.

But there are a few general comments that may be made as further indicative of my attitude toward the short story. First of all, I shall try to keep the flexibility and catholicity of taste that have been characteristic of the selections of stories for inclusion in preceding volumes. I believe the short story to be a living organism which cannot, except to its detriment, be bound by hard-and-fast rules, and which should even be left free of definition, except in such loose terms as are used in Somerset Maugham's admirable introduction to his anthology, *Tellers of Tales.* All he asks of the short story is that it be a "piece of fiction that has unity of impression and that can be read at a sitting." This fastens only the lightest and most elastic of fetters upon a form of expression which because of its inherent limitations needs to be as Protean as possible.

Again I agree entirely with Mr. Maugham's opinion that the short story must be entertaining, must be "moving, exciting, or amusing." In other words, that it must arouse a definite emotional response in the reader. I hold, too, with Poe that everything in the short story should contribute directly to its effect, which is merely another way of saying that conciseness is an essential virtue. The short-story writer has no more time to play around than the etcher, although if he be clever enough he may trick the reader into thinking that he is making an indirect and leisurely approach to his goal. Otherwise, I attach great value to originality in theme and treatment, and to style, which seems to me of supreme importance in the brief narrative. The very nature of the short story demands the best qualities of writing.

The distinction often made between the story and the sketch is significant, I think, only if we are careful not to be too rigid about it. The story must have conflict to make it dynamic; the sketch, on the other hand, can be, and usually is, static. But the emphasis laid upon the so-called sketch, as opposed to the plotted short story, by the late Edward J. O'Brien, had a decidedly liberating effect that has been of the most genuine importance to the artistic quality of our short fiction. It is greatly to be desired that someone like Mr. O'Brien will always be on hand to help shatter whatever mold the short story falls into and to see that it maintains above everything else its vital freedom of form.

Finally, I should like to quote from an essay by Robert Frost, reprinted in the admirable quarterly, *American Prefaces,* and called "Education by Poetry," because it describes clearly one touchstone I hope never to lose sight of in undertaking to pass judgment on short stories:

"Every time a poem is written, every time a short story is written, it is written not with cunning, but by belief. The beauty, the something, the little charm of the thing to be, is more felt than known. There is a common jest, one that always annoys me, on the writers, that they write the last end first, and then work up to it; that they lay a train toward one sentence that they think is pretty nice and have it all fixed up to set like a trap to close with. No, it should not be that way at all. No one who has ever come close to the arts has failed to see the difference between things written that way, with cunning and device, and the kind that are believed into existence, that begin in something more felt than known. This you can realize quite as well—not quite as well, perhaps, but nearly as well—in reading as you can in writing. I would undertake to separate short stories on that principle; stories that have been believed into existence and stories that have been cunningly devised."

My preference is strongly for the stories that have been "believed into existence," as I feel a number in the present collection have been. But I do not altogether scorn the "cunningly devised," either, and they are naturally far greater in quantity than the superior variety which arise from the "inner compulsion" that is the source of all true art.

At this moment, when my first year's work is just completed, I am peculiarly aware of the amount of time and effort on the part of previous editors that has gone into making this anthology an institution. The average quality of the volumes has varied somewhat, of necessity, since no amount of prayerful diligence on the part of an editor and his assistants can provide masterpieces when none has been printed, but the record stands for itself, and I shall be altogether satisfied to try to maintain it.

The two former editors not only served as judges this year, but also made interesting comments on the state of the short story. Dr. Williams, who has seen a tremendous quantity of water go over the short-story dam since she helped to establish this collection in 1919, with the backing of the Society of Arts and Sciences, said she was most impressed by the present dominance of the influence of Tchekov and his disciple, Katherine Mansfield, with Mr. O'Brien as their prophet. This influence, she said, was all toward the "starfish design," or "the creation of a tiny candle to light up a room or a life." She recalled the days of the "vertebrate structure" of the short story that followed the O. Henry period, and warned that many writers thought the apparent lack of form in the prevailing mode made it easier to do, when exactly the opposite was true.

Mr. Hansen said "experiment no longer dominated the short story" and that we were now in a period when there was "a firm determination among the youngest writers to think the problem through, to give a genuine expression to their ideas, and to enjoy the satisfaction that concentration on a work of art gives." He declared that the present collection "reflected a more earnest attitude of authors toward their material," and a strong tendency on their parts "to emphasize the hidden facets of human conduct." He also said that he believed continued experimentation was essential to the healthy progress of the short story.

The Stories of 1941

Some general observations may be made on the stories in this year's collection. All three judges thought them of superior average quality, and Edith Mirrielees, whose article in the *Atlantic Monthly* early this year, "What Is Wrong with the American Short Story," struck a distinctly pessimistic note, reported that reading the collection had made her feel much more hopeful.

Since the present-day short story is likely to lie closely to the very bone of life, either in dealing with larger topics of consequence, or with the more intimate aspects of human affairs, it is not at all surprising to note that six of the stories selected are concerned more or less directly with the war. (The 1940 volume had only one, Kay Boyle's "Monsieur Panalitus.") Four of the half-dozen, the prize-winning "Defeat," Nancy Hale's "Those Are as Brothers," Paul Gallico's "The Snow Goose," and Vincent Sheean's "The Conqueror," were singled out by the judges, and a fifth, Paul Kunasz's "I'd Give It All up for Tahiti," was selected as an exceptional "short-short" by Dr. Williams. John Cheever's "I'm Going to Asia" rounds out the six.

I report also as a curious coincidence, perhaps without any deeper significance, that not since 1935, when Kay Boyle's "The White Horses of Vienna" won first prize, and stories by Dorothy Thomas and Josephine W. Johnson second and third prizes, have women writers swept the field as they did this year. In fact, since 1935, when Sally Benson's "Suite 2049" won second prize, all the awards have gone to men. In the twenty stories chosen for this volume, however, eleven are by men, and several of these were close contenders for the awards.

The judges found difficulty in reaching an agreement on the prize stories because, they reported, so many of the selections seemed to be of almost equal merit, although Miss Mirrielees thought Nancy Hale's "Those Are as Brothers" "far and away" the best story in a good lot, and Dr. Williams was equally emphatic in choosing Paul Gallico's "The Snow Goose" for first place. In spite of these two enthusiastic judgments, Miss Boyle's skillfully done and deeply moving war story was finally settled upon because Mr. Hansen and I agreed on its merits, and because, further, both Miss Mirrielees and Dr. Williams thought it as good as anything in the competition, except their first choices. Miss Boyle's stories during the O. Henry year just closed were all on war themes, and all excellent. One of them,

"T'en Fais Pas," in *Harper's Bazaar,* was an extraordinary and unforgettable sketch which gave place to "Defeat" only because the latter seemed more of a story, and I am sorry it could not be included also. Miss Boyle has kept to a very high level of excellence in her short fiction for years, and "Defeat" seems to me one of her finest stories. Mr. Hansen called it "a superb handling of the unreconcilable psychological forces revealed in the situation."

One of this story's most notable virtues is that it shows how fiction, given all the appearance of fact, may actually be much more effective than the best reporting. Mr. Maugham observed, in the introduction referred to earlier, that it would be the death of the short story if it could be beaten at its own game by the naked truth. The short story is in no danger of death from this cause so long as writers like Miss Boyle are alive.

Of the other two stories appearing in first place on the judges' lists, Miss Hale's "Those Are as Brothers" was liked by both Mr. Hansen and Dr. Williams, while Mr. Gallico's "The Snow Goose," one of the most-discussed short stories of the year and published in a separate volume after its appearance in the *Saturday Evening Post,* was considered "prolix" by Miss Mirrielees and "definitely lacking in genuine artistry" by Mr. Hansen. I thought very well indeed of Miss Hale's story, which was easily the best specimen of her work currently available, but felt that it was somewhat too mechanical in conception and execution—too "contrived," to borrow Robert Frost's word—to receive a prize. As for "The Snow Goose," it is possible to acknowledge the criticisms of the two judges who did not care for it especially, and still to consider it a story likely to be long remembered because of its appealing theme of heroic self-sacrifice and the vividness of some of its pictures.

Miss Welty's story was given second place by Miss Mirrielees, and Miss Abbett's third. Mr. Hansen simply reversed the order of this judgment. Dr. Williams placed Miss Abbett's story in her first grouping after the prize awards, and gave it this excellent characterization, "It is as strong and delicate as a cobweb." Her comment on Miss Welty's story was that it seemed too slight, unless judged separately as a "short-short," while Mr. Hansen thought its brevity a definite advantage. Both these stories seemed to me to be done just about to perfection. I cast my vote for Miss Welty because of the freshly original beauty of her writing and because of the effective use of the hidden motive for the conflict upon which the story turns. It is a stronger story because the reader does not learn until the end why the old woman is traveling the "worn path." It is also, as Miss Mirrielees said, "touching without being mawkish." Two others of this writer's stories in the *Atlantic,* "Powerhouse" and "Why I Live at the P.O." were seriously considered, the former a strange, highly original, and somewhat forbidding translation of a jazz band's music into words. A collection of Miss Welty's stories, "A Curtain of Green," with an introduction by Katherine Anne Porter, has been recently published, and bears sufficient evidence of the remarkable versatility of her fine talent. She was represented in an earlier O. Henry volume by "The Petrified Man."

Miss Abbett is a discovery of *Story*. She won a prize in a Junior League contest conducted by the magazine. Miss Mirrielees said of her prize-winning story, "It has a very delicate and clear characterization, a situation so natural that any reader has seen it happen, and yet few readers would have thought of its effect upon the group." She also spoke with admiration of the "beautiful restraint" that marked the handling of the story. Mr. Hansen thought it "A fresh,

Introduction

genuine record of adolescent behavior, revealing completely what Jean, the principal character, feels." He added that it reminded him of Maureen Daly's "Sixteen," included in a previous O. Henry collection. I agree with these high opinions and consider the story one of the best I have ever read by a young writer. Its characterization and atmosphere are notable, it is done with both warm sympathy and deep understanding, and the ending is as skillful as all the rest, which is the final test of a story's quality.

The special prize, which went to Andy Logan's "The Visit," is an innovation. It is to be given to a first published story in a recognized magazine which pays for the use of its material, although the exact terms of the award are subject to modification to meet special circumstances, since its real purpose is to recognize new talent. Miss Logan wrote her story when a sophomore at Swarthmore, where it was printed in the college magazine, and later selected for reprinting by *Redbook*. Among its competitors were E. S. Forgotson's "My Name Is Mike Daniels" and Frederic J. Lipp's "And the Soul Turning," both taken from the excellent quarterly published at the University of Iowa, *American Prefaces*. Miss Mirrielees voted for Mr. Forgotson's story as the prize winner, saying she thought the handling of Miss Logan's opus fell below its possibilities, but Dr. Williams, Mr. Hansen, and the editor voted for Miss Logan, whose story, in spite of certain flaws, remains a remarkable piece of work for a beginner.

Other stories nominated for prizes included, on Dr. Williams' list, Vincent Sheean's "The Conqueror" and Mary O'Hara's "My Friend Flicka." Mr. Hansen also thought well of Miss O'Hara's story, although he said "the ending is conventional and the last few lines tacked on, as if the storyteller had to run for a train." (Maybe Miss O'Hara was merely running for a typewriter, since the story has already been made into a novel.) Miss Mirrielees thought this story split in its intention after an excellent beginning, and that it ended lamely. I agree with these criticisms, especially the reference to the weak ending, but still like the story. If its possibilities had been fully realized, it would have been a stout contender for a prize. As for Mr. Sheean's story of a Frenchwoman who won her private battle with the Germans, a direct contrast in theme to Miss Boyle's "Defeat," Dr. Williams gave it second place, Miss Mirrielees did not comment on it specifically, and Mr. Hansen objected to it as being "Robert W. Chambers in his most opulent mood," suggesting that Mr. Sheean be forced to read, for penance, Madame Foucault's "A Château at the Front." This is a good example of how judges can disagree on the merits of a story. I did not find it at all unconvincing, and I also admired its fair-minded attitude toward its antagonists.

David Cornel DeJong's "Seven Boys Take a Hill" proved to be one of the most popular of the stories with the judges, and also stood well up on my own list. It is a finely turned bit of adolescent drama by one of the most consistent of our better short-story writers, and that it did not receive a prize is less of a reflection upon its obvious merits than a revelation of the obvious fact that there are not enough prizes to go around. It is a pleasure to have Mr. DeJong's work once more in a collection where it has so often appeared before.

William Faulkner's "The Old People" was rated as "one of Mr. Faulkner's best stories" by Mr. Hansen, but Miss Mirrielees considered it lesser Faulkner. I thought it had a good deal of the peculiar Faulkner magic in it, and that it was particularly interesting because it was so different from most of this Mississippian's short fiction. Also, Mr. Hansen

Introduction xvii

gave a high mark to Sally Benson's "Retreat" and to Albert Maltz's "Afternoon in the Jungle," two typical short-short stories from the astonishing number of good ones published in the *New Yorker* year after year. Both these stories show uncanny insight into the workings of alien minds, and both, like nearly all the *New Yorker* stories, are written with a skill and finish that borders on the miraculous. (Read the collection, *Short Stories from the New Yorker,* for convincing evidence of what I mean.)

Conrad Aiken's "Hello, Tib" was praised by Dr. Williams under her short-short grouping, and Mr. Hansen also called it "an excellent example of this author's mature writing." I liked it especially because of its effective combination of the objective and subjective and because of the fine style. Nelson Algren's "A Bottle of Milk for Mother" gave Mr. Hansen concern because he was puzzled by the author's "confusing attitude" toward his central figure. It was not liked by the women judges. I considered it a peculiarly vivid piece of characterization, a successful and sympathetic effort to show the plight of a muscular young man with little else except his muscles to enable him to deal with the complexities of our civilization. I believe it has sharpness and vigor as well as originality.

John Cheever's "I'm Going to Asia" was selected, after long consideration, from a large number of Mr. Cheever's good short pieces available because it seemed of larger significance than most. It struck two of the judges as trivial, an opinion with which I am wholly unable to agree, because it seems to me the undertones are exactly the opposite of trivial. I found it packed with suggestions of the effects of the war on a middle-class American family, liked its irony, and gave it a high rating among the shorter stories in the collection. Walter Van Tilburg Clark's "Hook," the life story of a hawk, applies the biographical pattern so often used in the novel to a short story, and is filled with minute and fascinating observations of nature. Mr. Hansen observed, with reason, its freedom from the anthropomorphism that usually spoils stories of this variety. Paul Kunasz's "I'd Give It All up for Tahiti" is a neatly turned small piece about a war bomber, which sticks curiously in the mind and which says much in a few words.

Edita Morris's "Caput Mortuum," a strange tale by an author whose work has appeared in the past in the O'Brien collections, found favor with only one of the judges, but I thought it most effectively done, a hauntingly tragic bit of life, handled with a kind of airy deftness that gives it marked distinction. James Still's "The Proud Walkers" is first-rate folk stuff, which charms by its expert use of mountain talk, but which is also good because it is written about the building of a home, a universal theme. Dorothy Thomas's "My Pigeon Pair" is one of the best of Miss Thomas's many stories, a tale of our own times which rings wholly true, and which is filled with a tender understanding of youth in love frustrated by economic circumstances.

The absence from this collection of the work of some of the better-known short-story writers may be noted by some readers, who will wonder if it has any significance. It has not; it merely means that a good many of the recognized writers produced nothing within the time limits of the volume, or that what they produced seemed to fall below their own high standards.

Thanks are due, and are hereby tendered, to all who have generously helped to make this volume what it is. I am especially grateful for the help of my assistant, Muriel Fuller, a veteran at the job; for the suggestions that have come from many directions, all of them most welcome, and to the authors and editors who have given their permissions for the inclusion of stories. Without their friendly cooperation this anthology would be an impossibility.

HERSCHEL BRICKELL.

Ridgefield, Conn.
15th July, 1941.

DEFEAT
By Kay Boyle
From the *New Yorker*

KAY BOYLE

who has lived in Europe for years and who from that distance has kept her place year after year in the top flight of American short-story writers has only recently returned to this country to live. Her many fine stories of the foreign scene reflect the history of the troubled period of her residence abroad. She was the winner of the first prize in the O'Henry Memorial Award Prize Stories of 1935, *with "The White Horses of Vienna," and her "Poor Monsieur Panalitus" from the* New Yorker *was included in the 1940 volume. Like the present prize winner, it was a story of World War II.*

Toward the end of June that year and through July there was a sort of uncertain pause, an undetermined suspension that might properly be called neither an armistice nor a peace, and it lasted until the men began coming back from where they were. They came at intervals, trickling down from the north in twos or threes, or even one by one, some of them prisoners who had escaped and others merely a part of that individual retreat in which the sole destination was home. They had exchanged their uniforms for something else as they came along—corduroys, or workmen's blue, or whatever people might have given them in secret to get away in— bearded, singularly and shabbily outfitted men getting down from a bus or off a train without so much as a knapsack in their hands and all with the same bewildered, scarcely discrepant story to tell. Once they had reached the precincts of familiarity, they stood there a moment where the vehicle had left them, maybe trying to button the jacket that didn't fit them or set the neck or shoulders right, like men who have been waiting in a courtroom and have finally heard their names called and stand up to take the oath and mount the witness stand. You could see them getting the words ready —revising the very quality of truth—and the look in their eyes, and then someone coming out of the post office or crossing the station square in the heat would recognize them and go toward them with a hand out, and the testimony would begin.

They had found their way back from different places, by different means, some on bicycle, some by bus, some over the mountains on foot, coming home to the Alpes-Maritimes from Rennes, or from Clermont-Ferrand, or from Lyons, or from any part of France, and looking as incongruous to modern defeat as survivors of the Confederate army might have looked, transplanted to this year and place (with their spurs still on and their soft-brimmed, dust-whitened hats), limping wanly back, half dazed and not yet having managed to get the story of what happened straight. Only, this time, they were the men of that tragically unarmed and undirected force which had been the French army once but was no longer, returning to what orators might call reconstruction but which they knew could never be the same.

Wherever they came from, they had identical evidence to give: that the German ranks had advanced bareheaded, in short-sleeved summer shirts—young, blond-haired men with their arms linked, row on row, and their trousers immaculately creased, having slept all night in hotel beds and their stomachs full, advancing singing and falling singing before the puny coughing of the French machine guns. That is, the first line of them might fall, and part of the second, possibly, but never more, for just then the French ammunition would suddenly expire and the bright-haired, blond demigods would march on singing across their dead. Then would follow all the glittering display: the rust-proof tanks and guns, the chromiumed electric kitchens, the crematoriums. Legends or truth, the stories became indistinguishable in the mouths of the Frenchmen who returned—that the Germans were dressed as if for tennis that summer, with nothing but a tune to carry in their heads, while the French crawled out from under lorries where they'd slept maybe every night for a week, going to meet them like crippled, encumbered miners emerging from the pit of a warfare fifty years interred, with thirty-five kilos of kit and a change of shoes and a tin helmet left over from 1914 breaking them in two as they met the brilliantly nickeled Nazi dawn. They said their superiors were the first to run; they said their ammunition had been sabotaged; they said the ambulances had been transformed into accommodations for the officers' lady friends; they said *"Nous avons été vendus"* or *"On nous a vendu"* over and over, until you could have made a popular song of it—the words and the music of defeat. After their testimony was given, some of them added (not the young but those who had fought before) in grave, part-embittered, part-vainglorious voices, "I'm ashamed to be a Frenchman" or "I'm ashamed of being French today," and then gravely took their places with the others.

There was one man, though, who didn't say any of these things, probably because he had something else on his mind. He was a dark, short, rather gracefully made man, not thirty yet, with hot, handsome eyes and a cleft chin. Even when he came back without his uniform and without the victory, a certain air of responsibility, of authority, remained because he had been the chauffeur of the mail bus before the war. He didn't sit talking in the *bistro* about what he had seen and where he had been, but he got the black beard off his face as quickly as he could, and bought a pair of new shoes, and went back to work in stubborn-lipped, youthful, almost violent pride. Except one night he did tell the story; he told it only once, about two months after he got back, and not to his own people or the people of the village but, as if by chance, to two commercial travelers for rival fruit-juice firms who were just beginning to circulate again from town to town in the Unoccupied Zone. They sat at the Café Central together, the three of them, drinking wine, talking about the anachronism of horse-and-mule-drawn cannon in Flanders and the beasts running amok under the enemy planes, and saying how they had all believed that the French line was going to hold somewhere, that it wasn't going to break.

"At first we thought it would hold at the Oise," one of the traveling men said. "We kept on retreating, saying the new front must be at the Oise, and believing it, too, and then, when we dropped below the Oise, we kept saying it would hold at the Marne, and believing it, and then we thought it would be the Seine, and even when we were south of Paris we kept on believing about some kind of a line holding on the Loire...."

"I still don't know why we stopped retreating," said the other commercial traveler. He sat looking soberly at his glass. "We can't talk about the Italians any more. I still don't see why we didn't retreat right down to Senegal. I don't see what stopped us," he said. Then the quiet-mouthed little bus driver began telling them about what had happened to him on the fourteenth of July.

He had been told, he said, that in some of the cities the enemy hadn't taken, or had withdrawn from, processions formed on the fourteenth and passed through the streets in silence, the flagstaffs they carried draped with black and their heads bowed. In some of the villages, the mayor, dressed in mourning, laid a wreath on the monument to the last war's dead while the peasants kneeled about him in the square.

"I was in Pontcharra on the fourteenth," said one of the traveling salesmen, "and when the mayor put the wreath down and the bugle called out like that for the dead, all the peasants uncovered themselves, but the military didn't even stand at attention."

"By that time none of the privates were saluting their officers in the street anywhere you went," said the other salesman, but the bus driver didn't pay any attention to what they said. He went on telling them that he'd been taken prisoner near Rennes on the seventeenth of June, and that there he saw the tracts the Boche planes had showered down the week before. The tracts said, "Frenchmen, prepare your coffins! Frenchwomen, get out your ball dresses! We're going to dance the soles off your shoes on the fourteenth of July!" He told the commercial travelers exactly what use they made of the tracts in the public places there. He was more than three weeks in the prison camp, he said, and on the night of the twelfth of July he and a *copain* made their escape. They went in uniform, on borrowed bicycles. They kept to the main road all night, wheeling along as free and unmolested in the dark as two young men cycling home from a dance, with their hearts light, and the stars out over them, and the night air mild. At dawn they took to the side roads, and toward eight o'clock of the new day they saw a house standing alone, a little in advance of the village that lay ahead.

"We'll ask there," the bus driver had said, and they pushed their cycles in off the road and laid them down behind a tree. The house, they could see then, was the schoolhouse, with a sign for *"Filles"* over one door and for *"Garçons"* over the other. The *copain* said there would be nobody there, but the bus driver had seen a woman come to the window and look at them, and he walked up to the door.

The desks were empty because of what had happened and the time of year, but the bus driver said he knew it must have been the schoolmistress who was standing in the middle of the room between the benches, a young woman with fair, wavy hair, eying them fearlessly and even sharply as they came. The bus driver and his *copain* said good morning, and they saw at once the lengths of three-colored stuff in her hands and the work she had been doing. They looked around them and saw four French flags clustered in each corner of the classroom and great loops of bunting that were draped along three sides of the room. The first thing the bus driver thought was that she ought to be warned, she ought to be told, and then, when he looked at her face again, he knew she knew as much as or more than they.

"You ought to keep the door locked," he had said, and the schoolmistress looked at him almost in contempt.

"I don't care who comes in," she said, and she went on folding the bunting into the lengths she wanted to cut it to drape across the farthest wall.

"So the village is occupied?" the bus driver said.

"Yes," she said, but she began cutting the tricolor bunting.

"There's one thing," said the *copain,* looking a little bleakly at the two others. "If you give yourself up, at least you don't get shot."

The schoolmistress had put her scissors down and said to the bus driver, "You'll have to get rid of your uniforms before there's any chance of you getting through." She glanced around the classroom as though the demands of action had suddenly made it strange to her.

"Take them off and put them in the cupboard there," she had said, "and cover yourselves with this stuff while you wait," and she heaped the blue and white and red lengths upon the desks. "In case they might come in," she said. She took her hat and *filet* off the hook as she said, "I'll come back with other clothes for you."

"If there would be any way of getting something to eat," the bus driver had said, and because he asked this, the tide of courage seemed to rise even higher in her.

"Yes," she said. "I'll bring back food for you."

"And a bottle of *pinard,*" said the *copain,* but he didn't say it very loud.

When she was gone, they took their uniforms off and wrapped the bunting around themselves, doing it for her and modesty's sake, and then they sat down at the first form's desks, swathed to their beards in red, white, and blue. Even if the Boches had walked into the schoolhouse then, there probably wasn't any military regulation made to deal with what they would have found, the bus driver had said to his *copain*—just two Frenchmen in their underwear sitting quietly inside the colors of their country's flag. But whether he said the other thing to the teacher as soon as she brought the bread and sausage and wine and the scraps of other men's clothing back, he didn't know. Sometimes, when he thought of it afterward, he wasn't quite sure he had ever got the actual words out, but then he remembered the look on her face as she stood by the tree where the bicycles had lain and watched them pedaling toward the village just ahead, and he knew he must have said it. He knew he must have wiped the sausage grease and the wine off his mouth with the back of his hand and said, "A country isn't defeated as long as its women aren't," or "until its women are," or "As long as the women of a country aren't defeated, it doesn't matter if its army is"—something like that, perhaps saying it just before they shook hands with her and cycled away.

That was the morning of the thirteenth, and the bus driver told how they rode all day in the heat, two what-might-have-been-peasants cycling slowly hour after hour across the hushed, summery, sunny land. The war was over for them, for this country the war was over; there was no sound or look of it in the meadows or the trees or grain. The war was finished, but the farmhouse they stopped at that evening would not take them in.

"Have you got your bread tickets with you?" the peasant

said, and even the white-haired sows behind his legs eyed them narrowly with greed.

"We're prisoners escaped. We've got a bit of money," the bus driver said. "We'll pay for our soup, and maybe you'll let us sleep in the loft."

"And when the Boches come in for the milk they'll shoot me and the family for having taken you in!" the peasant said, and the bus driver stood looking at him bitterly a moment before he began to swear. When he had called the man the names he wanted to, he said, "Look here, we were soldiers—perhaps you haven't got that yet? We haven't been demobilized; we were taken prisoner, we escaped. We were fighting a little war up there."

"If you'd fought it better, the Boches wouldn't have got this far," the peasant said. He said it in cunning and triumph, and then he closed the door.

They slept the night at the next farm (the bus driver told the commercial travelers), eating soup and bread and drinking red wine in the kitchen, and when they had paid for it they were shown up to the loft. But they were not offered the side on which the hay lay; the farmer was thinking of next winter and he told them they could lie down just as well on the boards. They slept heavily and well, and it was very light when they woke in the morning, and so that day, the day of the fourteenth, they did not get far. By six that night they were only another hundred kilometers on, and then the *copain's* tire went flat. But a little town stood just ahead and they pushed their bicycles toward it through the summer evening, and down its wide, treeless street. They hadn't seen the uniform yet, but they knew the Germans must be there. Even on the square in the heart of town they saw no sign, but still there was that unnatural quiet, that familiar uneasiness on the air, so they pushed their wheels through the open doors of a big garage, past the dry and padlocked gas pumps, and stood them up against the inside wall. There, in the garage's half-security and semi-dark, they looked around them; twenty or more cars stood one beside the other, halted as if forever because of the lack of fluid to flow through their veins. Overhead the glass panes of the roof were still painted blue; the military and staff cars parked in the shadowy silence still bore their green-and-khaki camouflage. The war was over, everything had stopped, and out beyond the wide-open automobile doorway they saw the dance platform that had been erected in the square, and the dark, leafy branches twined on its upright beams and balustrade, and the idle people standing looking. There were no flags up, only this rather dismal atmosphere of preparation, and it was then the bus driver and his *copain* had remembered it was the fourteenth.

"It's a national holiday and we haven't had a drink yet," the *copain* said. He stood there in the garage with his hands in the pockets of the trousers that didn't belong to him, staring bleakly out across the square. Even when two German soldiers who were putting electric wiring up in the dance pavilion came into view his face did not alter. He simply went on saying, "We haven't had the *apéritif* all day."

The bus driver took a packet of cigarettes out of his jacket pocket and put one savagely on his lip. As he lit it, he looked in hot, bitter virulence out to where the Germans were hanging strings of bulbs among the fresh, dark leaves.

"'Frenchmen, prepare your coffins!'" he had said, and then he gave a laugh. "They've made only one mistake so far, just one," he said, and as he talked the cigarette jerked up and down in fury on his lip. "They've got the dance floor and the decorations all right, and they've probably got the music, and maybe the refreshments too. So far so good," he said. "But they haven't got the partners. That's what's going to be funny. That's what's going to be really funny."

The bus driver sat there in the Café Central telling it to the two commercial travelers, perhaps because he had had more to drink than usual, telling them the story, or perhaps because it had been weighing long enough heavy on his heart. He told them about the dinner the garage owner gave him and his *copain:* civet and fried potatoes and salad and four kinds of cheese and armagnac with the coffee. He said they could scarcely get it all down and that then their host opened a bottle of champagne for them. That's the kind of man the garage owner was. And during the dinner or afterward, with the wine inside of him, it seems the bus driver had said it again. He had said something about as long as the women of a nation weren't defeated the rest of it didn't matter, and just as he said it the music struck up in the dance pavilion outside.

The place the garage owner offered them for the night was just above the garage itself, a sort of storeroom, with three windows overlooking the square. First he repaired the *copain's* tire for him, and behind him on the wall as he worked they read the newspaper cutting he had pinned up, perhaps in some spirit of derision. It exhorted all Frenchmen to accept quietly and without protest the new regulations concerning the circulation of private and public vehicles.

"Without protest!" the garage owner had said, taking the dripping red tube out of the basin of water and pinching the leak between his finger and thumb. "I'll have to close the place up, and they ask me to do it without protest." He stood rubbing sandpaper gently around where the imperceptible hole in the rubber was. "We weren't ready for war and yet we declared it just the same," he said, "and now we've asked for peace and we aren't ready for that, either." When he had finished with the tire he showed them up the stairs.

"I'll keep the light off," he said, "in case it might give them the idea of coming up and having a look," but there was no need for any light, for the illumination of the dance pavilion in the square shone in through the windows and lit the rows of storage batteries and the cases of spare parts and spark plugs. From outside they heard the music playing—the exact waltz time and the quick, entirely martial version of swing.

"Somebody ought to tell them they're wasting their time," the bus driver had said, jerking one shoulder toward the windows. He could have burst out laughing at the sight of them, he explained, some with white gloves on even, waiting out there to the strains of music for what wasn't going to come.

The garage owner shook out the potato sacks of waste on the floor and gave them the sacks to lie down on, and then he took one look out the window at the square and grinned and said good night and went downstairs. The *copain* was tired and he lay down at once on the soft rags on the floor and drew a blanket up over him, but the bus driver had stood a while at one side of the window, watching the thing below. A little group of townspeople was standing around the platform where the variously colored lights hung, and the band was playing in one corner of the pavilion underneath the leaves. No one was dancing, but the German soldiers were hanging around in expectation, some standing on the steps of the platform and some leaning on the garnished rails.

"For a little while there wasn't a woman anywhere," the bus driver told the commercial travelers. "There was this crowd of people from the town, perhaps thirty or forty of them looking on, and maybe some others further back in the dark where you couldn't see them, but that was all." And then he stopped talking.

"And then what happened?" said one of the traveling men after a moment, and the bus driver sat looking in silence at his glass.

"They had a big, long table spread out with things to eat on it," he said in a minute, and he didn't look up. "They had fruit tarts, it looked like, and sweet chocolate, and bottles of lemonade and beer. They had as much as you wanted of everything," he said. "And perhaps once you got near enough to start eating and drinking, then the other thing just followed naturally afterward—or that's the way I worked it out," he said. "Or maybe, if you've had a dress a long time that you wanted to wear and you hadn't had the chance of putting it on and showing it off because all the men were away—I mean if you were a woman. I worked it out that maybe the time comes when you want to put it on so badly that you put it on just the same whatever's happened, or maybe, if you're one kind of a woman, any kind of a uniform looks all right to you after a certain time. The music was good, it was first class," he said, but he didn't look up. "And here was all this food spread out, and the corks popping off the bottles, and the lads in uniform, great, big fellows, handing out chocolates to all the girls. . . ."

The three of them sat at the table without talking for a while after the bus driver's voice had ceased, and then one of the traveling men said, "Well, that was just one town."

"Yes, that was just one town," said the bus driver, and when he picked up his glass to drink, something as crazy as tears was standing in his eyes.

A WORN PATH
By Eudora Welty
From the *Atlantic Monthly*

EUDORA WELTY

is a native of Jackson, Mississippi, and was educated in the public schools there, at Mississippi State College for Women, the University of Wisconsin and the Columbia School of Business. Her first stories were published in the Southern Review, *where her work attracted the attention of Katharine Anne Porter. A collection of her stories, "A Curtain of Green," including this year's prize winner, has recently been published, with an introduction by Miss Porter. Miss Welty has been a Fellow at the Bread Loaf Writers' Conference and has also worked at Yaddo. She is a painter and a noted photographer of Negroes.*

It was December—a bright frozen day in the early morning. Far out in the country there was an old Negro woman with her head tied in a red rag, coming along a path through the pine woods. Her name was Phœnix Jackson. She was very old, and small, and she walked slowly in the dark pine shadows, moving a little from side to side in her steps, with the balanced heaviness and lightness of a pendulum in a grandfather clock. She carried a thin small cane made from an umbrella, and with this she kept tapping the frozen earth in front of her. This made a grave and persistent noise in the still air that seemed meditative, like the chirping of a solitary little bird.

She wore a dark striped dress reaching down to her shoe tops and an equally long apron of bleached sugar sacks, with a full pocket: all neat and tidy, but every time she took a step she might have fallen over her shoelaces, which dragged from her unlaced shoes. She looked straight ahead. Her eyes were blue with age. Her skin had a pattern all its own of numberless branching wrinkles, and as though a whole little tree stood in the middle of her forehead, but a golden color ran underneath, and the two knobs of her cheeks were illumined by a yellow burning under the dark. Under the red rag her hair came down on her neck in the frailest of ringlets, still black, and with an odor like copper.

Now and then there was a quivering in the thicket. Old Phœnix said, "Out of my way, all you foxes, owls, beetles, jack rabbits, coons, and wild animals! . . . Keep out from under these feet, little bobwhites. . . . Keep the big wild hogs out of my path. Don't let none of those come running my direction. I got a long way." Under her small black-freckled hand her cane, limber as a buggy whip, would switch at the brush as if to rouse up any hiding things.

On she went. The woods were deep and still. The sun made the pine needles almost too bright to look at, up where the wind rocked. The cones dropped as light as feathers. Down in the hollow was the mourning dove—it was not too late for him.

The path ran up a hill. "Seem like there is chains about my feet, time I get this far," she said, in the voice of argument old people keep to use with themselves. "Something always take a hold of me on this hill—pleads I should stay."

After she got to the top she turned and gave a full, severe look behind her where she had come. "Up through pines," she said at length. "Now down through oaks."

Her eyes opened their widest and she started down gently. But before she got to the bottom of the hill a bush caught her dress.

Her fingers were busy and intent, but her skirts were full and long, so that before she could pull them free in one place they were caught in another. It was not possible to allow the dress to tear. "I in the thorny bush," she said. "Thorns, you doing your appointed work. Never want to let folks pass—no sir. Old eyes thought you was a pretty little *green* bush."

Finally, trembling all over, she stood free, and after a moment dared to stoop for her cane.

"Sun so high!" she cried, leaning back and looking, while the thick tears went over her eyes. "The time getting all gone here."

At the foot of this hill was a place where a log was laid across the creek.

"Now comes the trial," said Phœnix. Putting her right foot out, she mounted the log and shut her eyes. Lifting her skirt, leveling her cane fiercely before her like a festival figure in some parade, she began to march across. Then she opened her eyes, and she was safe on the other side.

"I wasn't as old as I thought," she said.

But she sat down to rest. She spread her skirts on the bank around her and folded her hands over her knees. Up above her was a tree in a pearly cloud of mistletoe. She did not dare to close her eyes, and when a little boy brought her a plate with a slice of marble cake on it she spoke to him. "That would be acceptable," she said. But when she went to take it there was just her own hand in the air.

So she left that tree, and had to go through a barbed-wire fence. There she had to creep and crawl, spreading her knees and stretching her fingers like a baby trying to climb the steps. But she talked loudly to herself: she could not let her dress be torn now, so late in the day, and she could not pay for having her arm or her leg sawed off if she got caught fast where she was.

At last she was safe through the fence and risen up out in the clearing. Big dead trees, like black men with one arm, were standing in the purple stalks of the withered cotton field. There sat a buzzard.

"Who you watching?"

In the furrow she made her way along.

"Glad this not the season for bulls," she said, looking sideways, "and the good Lord made his snakes to curl up and sleep in the winter. A pleasure I don't see no two-headed snake coming around that tree, where it come once. It took a while to get by him, back in the summer."

She passed through the old cotton and went into a field of dead corn. It whispered and shook, and was taller than her head. "Through the maze now," she said, for there was no path.

Then there was something tall, black, and skinny there, moving before her.

At first she took it for a man. It could have been a man dancing in the field. But she stood still and listened, and it did not make a sound. It was as silent as a ghost.

"Ghost," she said sharply, "who be you the ghost of? For I have heard of nary death close by."

But there was no answer, only the ragged dancing in the wind.

She shut her eyes, reached out her hand, and touched a sleeve. She found a coat and inside that an emptiness, cold as ice.

"You scarecrow," she said. Her face lighted. "I ought to be shut up for good," she said with laughter. "My senses is gone. I too old. I the oldest people I ever know. Dance, old scarecrow," she said, "while I dancing with you."

She kicked her foot over the furrow, and with mouth drawn down shook her head once or twice in a little strutting way. Some husks blew down and whirled in streamers about her skirts.

Then she went on, parting her way from side to side with the cane, through the whispering field. At last she came to the end, to a wagon track, where the silver grass blew between the red ruts. The quail were walking around like pullets, seeming all dainty and unseen.

"Walk pretty," she said. "This the easy place. This the easy going." She followed the track, swaying through the quiet bare fields, through the little strings of trees silver in their dead leaves, past cabins silver from weather, with the doors and windows boarded shut, all like old women under a spell sitting there. "I walking in their sleep," she said, nodding her head vigorously.

In a ravine she went where a spring was, silently flowing through a hollowed log. Old Phœnix bent and drank. "Sweet gum makes the water sweet," she said, and drank more. "Nobody know who made this well, for it was here when I was born."

The track crossed a swampy part where the moss hung as white as lace from every limb. "Sleep on, alligators, and blow your bubbles." Then the cypress trees went into the road. Deep, deep it went down between the high, green-colored banks. Overhead the live oaks met, and it was as dark as a cave.

A big black dog with a lolling tongue came up out of the weeds by the ditch. She was meditating, and not ready, and when he came at her she only hit him a little with her cane. Over she went in the ditch, like a little puff of milkweed.

Down there her senses drifted away. A dream visited her, and she reached her hand up, but nothing reached down and gave her a pull. So she lay there and presently went to talking. "Old woman," she said to herself, "that black dog came up out of the weeds to stall you off, and now there he sitting on his fine tail, smiling at you."

A white man finally came along and found her—a hunter, a young man, with his dog on a chain.

"Well, Granny!" he laughed. "What are you doing there?"

"Lying on my back like a June bug waiting to be turned over, mister," she said, reaching up her hand.

He lifted her up, gave her a swing in the air, and set her down. "Anything broken, Granny?"

"No sir, them old dead weeds is springy enough," said Phœnix, when she had got her breath. "I thank you for your trouble."

"Where do you live, Granny?" he asked, while the two dogs were growling at each other.

"Away back younder, sir, behind the ridge. You can't even see it from here."

"On your way home?"

"No sir, I going to town."

"Why, that's too far! That's as far as I walk when I come out myself, and I get something for my trouble." He patted the stuffed bag he carried, and there hung down a little closed claw. It was one of the bobwhites, with its beak hooked bitterly to show it was dead. "Now you go on home, Granny!"

"I bound to go to town, mister," said Phœnix. "The time come around."

He gave another laugh, filling the whole landscape. "I know you old colored people! Wouldn't miss going to town to see Santa Claus!"

But something held Old Phœnix very still. The deep lines in her face went into a fierce and different radiation. Without warning she had seen with her own eyes a flashing nickel fall out of the man's pocket on to the ground.

"How old are you, Granny?" he was saying.

"There is no telling, mister," she said, "no telling."

Then she gave a little cry and clapped her hands, and said, "Git on away from here, dog! Look! Look at that dog!" She laughed as if in admiration. "He ain't scared of nobody. He a big black dog." She whispered, "Sick him!"

"Watch me get rid of that cur," said the man. "Sick him, Pete! Sick him!"

Phœnix heard the dogs fighting and heard the man running and throwing sticks. She even heard a gunshot. But she was slowly bending forward by that time, further and further forward, the lids stretched down over her eyes, as if she were doing this in her sleep. Her chin was lowered almost to her knees. The yellow palm of her hand came out from the fold of her apron. Her fingers slid down and along the ground under the piece of money with the grace and care they would have in lifting an egg from under a setting hen. Then she slowly straightened up; she stood erect, and the nickel was in her apron pocket. A bird flew by. Her lips moved. "God watching me the whole time. I come to stealing."

The man came back, and his own dog panted about them. "Well, I scared him off that time," he said, and then he laughed and lifted his gun and pointed it at Phœnix.

She stood straight and faced him.

"Doesn't the gun scare you?" he said, still pointing it.

"No sir, I seen plenty go off closer by, in my day, and for less than what I done," she said, holding utterly still.

He smiled and shouldered the gun. "Well, Granny," he said, "you must be a hundred years old, and scared of nothing. I'd give you a dime if I had any money with me. But you take my advice and stay home, and nothing will happen to you."

"I bound to go on my way, mister," said Phœnix. She inclined her head in the red rag. Then they went in different directions, but she could hear the gun shooting again and again over the hill.

She walked on. The shadows hung from the oak trees to the road like curtains. Then she smelled wood smoke, and smelled the river, and she saw a steeple and the cabins on their steep steps. Dozens of little black children whirled around her. There ahead was Natchez shining. Bells were ringing. She walked on.

In the paved city it was Christmas time. There were red and green electric lights strung and crisscrossed everywhere, and all turned on in the daytime. Old Phœnix would have been lost if she had not distrusted her eyesight and depended on her feet to know where to take her.

She paused quietly on the sidewalk, where people were passing by. A lady came along in the crowd, carrying an armful of red-, green-, and silver-wrapped presents; she gave off perfume like the red roses in hot summer, and Phœnix stopped her.

"Please, missy, will you lace up my shoe?" She held up her foot.

"What do you want, Grandma?"

"See my shoe," said Phœnix. "Do all right for out in the country, but wouldn't look right to go in a big building."

"Stand still then, Grandma," said the lady. She put her packages down carefully on the sidewalk beside her and laced and tied both shoes tightly.

"Can't lace 'em with a cane," said Phœnix. "Thank you, missy. I doesn't mind asking a nice lady to tie up my shoe when I gets out on the street."

Moving slowly and from side to side, she went into the stone building and into a tower of steps, where she walked up and around and around until her feet knew to stop.

She entered a door, and there she saw nailed up on the wall the document that had been stamped with the gold seal and framed in the gold frame which matched the dream that was hung up in her head.

"Here I be," she said. There was a fixed and ceremonial stiffness over her body.

"A charity case, I suppose," said an attendant who sat at the desk before her.

But Phœnix only looked above her head. There was sweat on her face; the wrinkles shone like a bright net.

"Speak up, Grandma," the woman said. "What's your

name? We must have your history, you know. Have you been here before? What seems to be the trouble with you?"

Old Phœnix only gave a twitch to her face as if a fly were bothering her.

"Are you deaf?" cried the attendant.

But then the nurse came in.

"Oh, that's just old Aunt Phœnix," she said. "She doesn't come for herself; she has a little grandson. She makes these trips just as regular as clockwork—she lives away back off the Old Natchez Trace." She bent down. "Well, Aunt Phœnix, why don't you just take a seat? We won't keep you standing after your long trip." She pointed.

The old woman sat down, bolt upright in the chair.

"Now, how is the boy?" asked the nurse.

Old Phœnix did not speak.

"I said, how is the boy?"

But Phœnix only waited and stared straight ahead, her face very solemn and withdrawn into rigidity.

"Is his throat any better?" asked the nurse. "Aunt Phœnix, don't you hear me? Is your grandson's throat any better since the last time you came for the medicine?"

With her hands on her knees, the old woman waited, silent, erect, and motionless, just as if she were in armor.

"You mustn't take up our time this way, Aunt Phœnix," the nurse said. "Tell us quickly about your grandson, and get it over. He isn't dead, is he?"

At last there came a flicker and then a flame of comprehension across her face, and she spoke.

"My grandson. It was my memory had left me. There I sat and forgot why I made my long trip."

"Forgot?" The nurse frowned. "After you came so far?"

Then Phœnix was like an old woman begging a dignified forgiveness for waking up frightened in the night. "I never did go to school—I was too old at the Surrender," she said in a soft voice. "I'm an old woman without an education. It was my memory fail me. My little grandson, he is just the same, and I forgot it in the coming."

"Throat never heals, does it?" said the nurse, speaking in a loud, sure voice to Old Phœnix. By now she had a card with something written on it, a little list. "Yes. Swallowed lye. When was it—January—two—three years ago——"

Phœnix spoke unasked now. "No, missy, he not dead, he just the same. Every little while his throat begin to close up again, and he not able to swallow. He not get his breath. He not able to help himself. So the time come around, and I go on another trip for the soothing-medicine."

"All right. The doctor said as long as you came to get it you could have it," said the nurse. "But it's an obstinate case."

"My little grandson, he sit up there in the house all wrapped up, waiting by himself," Phœnix went on. "We is the only two left in the world. He suffer and it don't seem to put him back at all. He got a sweet look. He going to last. He wear a little patch quilt and peep out, holding his mouth open like a little bird. I remembers so plain now. I not going to forget him again, no, the whole enduring time. I could tell him from all the others in creation."

"All right." The nurse was trying to hush her now. She brought her a bottle of medicine. "Charity," she said, making a check mark in a book.

Old Phœnix held the bottle close to her eyes and then carefully put it into her pocket.

"I thank you," she said.

"It's Christmas time, Grandma," said the attendant. "Could I give you a few pennies out of my purse?"

"Five pennies is a nickel," said Phœnix stiffly.

"Here's a nickel," said the attendant.

Phœnix rose carefully and held out her hand. She received the nickel and then fished the other nickel out of her pocket and laid it beside the new one. She stared at her palm closely, with her head on one side.

Then she gave a tap with her cane on the floor. "This is what come to me to do," she said. "I going to the store and buy my child a little windmill they sells, made out of paper. He going to find it hard to believe there such a thing in the world. I'll march myself back where he waiting, holding it straight up in this hand."

She lifted her free hand, gave a little nod, turned around, and walked out of the doctor's office. Then her slow step began on the stairs, going down.

EIGHTEENTH SUMMER
By Hallie Southgate Abbett
From *Story*

HALLIE SOUTHGATE ABBETT

was born in St. Louis, Missouri, and married at an early age. She has traveled extensively with her husband, who has taught civil engineering in various colleges. He is now a lieutenant in the Naval Reserve, and they live in Washington, D.C. They have one son who is fourteen. Mrs. Abbett has contributed articles and short stories for the past six years to the Junior League Magazine. "Eighteenth Summer" is her first story to appear elsewhere.

T̲ʜᴇʏ ᴛɪᴇᴅ ᴛʜᴇɪʀ ʙᴏᴀᴛs to the dock and the four of them began walking, single file, up the narrow path leading from the lake. The sky was still a twilight color, but it was quite dark along the path so that they could only dimly see their own light-colored slacks and tennis shoes as they looked down. The boys were ahead and the two girls followed close behind.

They had gone a few hundred feet when the sound of someone playing a piano, and playing it badly, came to them from the cabin in the clearing just ahead. Hearing it, they laughed and pushed on a little faster, ducking their heads under the leafy branches that spread out over the path and brushed against their faces.

"D'you hear it?" cried Jean, trying to see over Pudgy's fat shoulder, jumping straight up in the air like a dancer. "Sound's like a party, huh?"

"That's just Ted at the piano," Brad, her brother, answered. "That's no party, yet."

The path widened here, and the way was lighter.

"Oh, hurry, Pudgy, *can't* you move faster?" Jean put her hands against his broad back and tried to push him, but he was moving as fast as she was, and her hands slipped down. "We're hours late!"

The other girl, Katy, caught up with her. They could walk in twos now.

"Not really, Jean, you're just in love. That makes it seem like hours," said Katy.

They came nearer and could now see the whole outline of the house against the sky and trees.

"Look, the sunroom's dark again! I'll bet that's not an accident. . . . Remember last time, Jean?" Katy's voice rose teasingly at the end of her sentence.

"Ah, cut it out, Katy," said Brad.

Reaching the clearing, they locked arms and marched, four abreast, up the broad steps to the porch. As they reached the door Jean dropped their arms and stepped ahead of them into the room, her narrow, fine-boned face rounded with eagerness, her slender and articulate hands held slightly forward.

"Ted, hello! Here we are!"

The boy at the piano stopped playing and swung lazily around on the old-fashioned stool. A part of straight blond hair had fallen across his forehead and he tossed it back with a quick movement of his head as he got up, standing tall and a little awkwardly before them.

"Well, well, so you are," he said, the suggestion of a smile on the corners of his young mouth. The light came up from the table and outlined its full, boyish shape. It looks spoiled, Jean thought fleetingly, but really he's not; it's just that boys' mouths are so young somehow. Younger than girls'.

"Oh. . . ."

The four of them saw the girl in the same instant, and each stopped what he had been about to say, and looked at her. Back in the shadows near the sunroom she sat, one foot curled under her in the chair, the other, in a high-heeled pump, dangled over the chair arm. As they watched, she brought both down to the floor and sat, primly upright, smoothing her red silk skirt down over her knees.

"Oh yes, this is Marie. She's . . . ah, she's staying at the hotel."

The silence remained with them for a moment or two, not a rude silence, but still not a friendly one. The four looked at her and then at Ted, their eyes a little cold. We're part of a crowd, they seemed to say, reproaching him; she's not one of us. Why have you brought in someone like this?

Then Jean, seeing the stubborn, nervous look on Ted's face—he was standing beside the girl now—crossed the room and held out her hand.

"Hello. I didn't know anyone as young as you ever stayed in that old barn. Having a dance up there tonight, aren't they?"

"Yes, they are," answered the girl in a soft colorless voice, putting her hand in Jean's. Her hand was soft, too, and small.

"Hello," the others said, following Jean's example. Ted stood watching them, less defiantly.

After this the girl said nothing, but sat back as though finished, done with speech. Jean, looking down at her, saw the small lips closed, as in a picture, but then she met the girl's eyes and saw that they, at least, were alive. Alive in a way that suggested the high-heeled slippers she wore, the red skirt and the thin white blouse, but how this was Jean did not know. There was still the touch of that listless hand in hers, and the sound of that tired little voice in her ears, but neither of those things was in the girl's eyes.

Jean tried to talk to the girl, saying anything that came into her head, noticing also that Marie was thin and pretty in a way, with light brown hair and a white rounded forehead. Ted stood by, but he did not talk, and he did not explain why the girl was there.

The others turned to different things. Brad put a record on the phonograph, Katy ran upstairs to change her sneaks for dancing shoes, and Pudgy went out in the kitchen for a drink of water.

"Pudgy's forever drinking water," Jean chattered to the girl. "We tell him that's what makes him so fat."

"Is he?" said the girl.

"He's such a clown, though, I think we'd all hate to see him reduce. I can't imagine Pudgy thin, can you?"

"No, I guess I can't."

"I'd hate to have him changed in any way, I guess. In fact, I'd hate to have any of us change, probably. We've all been together so many summers. . . ." She glanced over at Ted. He was pretending to yawn and would not look at her. The girl listened politely. I won't get any place that way, thought Jean. "How is the food at the hotel this year? Some years it's good, and some it isn't."

"It's all right, I guess," said the girl.

The conversation stopped between the three of them. I won't just go on and on, thought Jean, suddenly feeling cross about the girl. Let her say something. He asked her here, let *him* talk. But she was restless, and it was easier to go on talking than to be silent. One moment they had been a crowd, one unit, and now they were a set of individuals, Ted there, and she here, this girl between them.

"Ted . . ."

"Huh . . . What?"

She had wanted him to speak to her, it did not matter what he said.

"Where's your mother? Over at the club?" She smiled at him, letting her feeling for him show in her eyes. It was all right, he knew anyhow. Nothing had been said, but the things that had meaning were not the ones to be put into words, could not very easily be spoken in the casual language they used. For in the middle of a sentence their eyes would meet and as soon as they could they would get away by themselves and start kissing. That was the way it had been this summer. A year ago it had been different, and only half in earnest, but now she had to hold him back, had to be careful they were not too much alone; had to pretend she felt less than she did. But it wasn't as if he did not really know. Last week, dancing in the sunroom, she hadn't bothered to pretend.

"Mother went to town this afternoon."

For a moment Jean did not take this in. The crowd had never really been chaperoned, still, a mother or someone was always there in the background. Ted's mother was such an anxious little woman too. When they were children she had made such a fuss about things; she'd been so afraid that something would happen to Ted that she could prevent, and so she kept as close to him as she could. Even after he had become the best swimmer in the crowd, she put on her suit each time that he did and came down to the lake among them, never obtrusive because she was sweet and they liked her, but staying with them because Ted was there. It was only after those few times when Ted was rude to her that she finally stopped coming. I didn't like Ted then, Jean remembered suddenly.

"But you told her we'd be here, didn't you?"

"Oh, Jean, good Lord! No. I didn't tell her. She left in a hurry, and I didn't think to tell her. She had to go in town, and I didn't see any reason why she shouldn't. Of course, if you think she *ought* to know...."

Startled, she looked at him on the other side of Marie. The girl sat in a tight closed silence between them, not taking part in this, but making them aware of her. It's her, thought Jean suddenly; he knew what his mother would think of her. But what about me? I don't like her, either, why didn't he think of that? Then seeing the stubborn, angry look on his face, she thought, He's in a mood, that's all, and she's just part of it. Well, let her be. I wish his mother *was* here, though.

There was a burst of laughter outside in the clearing and a moment later more boys and girls came in the door, dressed in casual bright sports clothes, their faces tanned, their eyes young.

Ted turned away from Jean and hurried over to greet them, loud and talkative now, full of nervous energy. But the moment came when they all saw Marie, and with each there was a silence until she was introduced. They would nod briefly and then turn back to one another, silently asking questions. What on earth? they were saying with their eyes. *She* doesn't belong here.

Doggedly Jean stayed beside the girl, doing it because of Ted. Doing it as his mother would have done with any guest in her house, even this one. But she was angry, and almost, but not quite, jealous. It was the hint of jealousy, though, that made her keep trying. So she stayed by the girl, although none of the others came near, and Ted was busy, oh, very busy now, with his guests.

Maybe she'll leave early, Jean thought. She'll have to see she's not wanted. She can't be that dumb.

There was a sudden burst of laughter from across the room, and she saw Katy stare over at them, then duck her head and stuff a handkerchief against her mouth. She looked at Katy and then she looked down at Marie, and saw that the girl was lighting a cigarette fitted into a long bright green holder, a holder almost as long as the length of her face. They were all looking at her now, wanting to laugh, too, but restraining themselves, until suddenly Katy pointed to Pudgy Leonard's tie which was pulled up under one side of his collar. "Pudgy's tie!" she gasped, and started off again.

Now they could all laugh, all seem to be laughing at Pudgy, but really were laughing at Marie sitting there in her red silk dress, holding her long cigarette holder like an imitation movie actress. But Ted's face was flushed and angry, and Jean, looking at him, felt the party mood die in her like a young bird falling from a high place.

Abruptly she turned from Marie and walked to the open door. Outside the wind brushed the leaves back and forth across a clear sky, and a new moon was rising just over the lake, its reflection streaking across the ripples into the tops of the trees. Around the rim of the lake the lights of other cottages had come on and Jean could see her own on a point of land just opposite. The voices of people fishing from a rowboat came out of the silence and a flashlight was turned on for an instant, showing their position in the center of the lake and outlining the side of their boat; then it was turned off, leaving the lake rippling softly again in the pale moonlight. It's all so pretty, Jean thought wistfully, such a wonderful, lovely night for a party. . . .

Inside they were pushing back the light summer furniture, bending down over the arms of the chairs and rushing them off into a corner, everyone nimble and quick in their sports clothes. Pudgy was whirling foolishly about the room without a partner, and when couples came out to dance he would bump into them, draw back, and elaborately apologize. Everyone was laughing at him. Everything seemed now to be as it had always been.

"Come in and dance, sis." Brad came through the screen door and took her arm. "Let's remind them how good we are." Dancing, he whispered in her ear, "For Pete's sake, sis, don't take it so hard. She's nothing to him."

Jean smiled, and felt better. Brad was a swell brother.

"That's better. Gosh, I don't know why he brought her."

"Have you ever seen her before?"

For an instant he looked away, and she tugged on his arm. "You have, haven't you? Come on, Brad, where?"

"Oh, I saw her once, a couple of nights ago, with a couple of other fellows."

Then he whirled her around and around until they were both laughing, while the others danced past them, smiling because it was nice to see a brother and sister having fun together. When it was over Jean dropped into a wicker chair near Marie, laughing weakly.

"Oh gosh," she said, while the strange girl looked at her. "He's such a nut!"

And then Ted appeared at the door from the kitchen carrying a tray of glasses, the soda water bubbling up in spurts above the glasses and down into the tray.

"What have we here?" cried Pudgy, leaning over and sniffing at them. He jumped back sneezing, and they all laughed. "Scotch!" he exclaimed, as soon as he was able. "Where'd you get that, boy?"

Ted did not answer for a minute or two, not until all but the last two glasses had been taken. Then he leaned over and held the tray before the new girl. "It's your scotch. I hope you like it," he said, while they all stopped drinking and looked at her.

"I like it," was all she said, but Jean, seeing the way she looked at Ted, took a drink quickly and turned away. But not soon enough to miss the flush on Ted's fair skin as he continued to lean over the girl, even after she had taken her glass, his hair fallen, as it always fell, over his forehead.

They changed the records on the phonograph and began dancing again, but the scotch had changed things. It was not that they weren't used to drinking—although most of them drank beer rather than scotch—but now there was so much of it, so many drinks brought in again and again from the kitchen that they drank without knowing how much. They had never before seen such a supply. At club dances they had scotch and rum, but their allowances were seldom adequate to cover many drinks, no matter how reckless they felt. Now it was there without being asked for, and even Jean, who always had the most sense, drank indifferently. It gave her something to do so she would not have to look at Ted.

Early in the evening he asked her to dance. She got up very brightly, she tried very hard to act natural. They did not dance close together, but the feeling was there. He would like to be dancing with her in the sunroom, where it was dark, she knew. But he was still a little angry, still on the defensive. Toward the end of the dance, though, everything was so nearly all right she forgot to act a part and said to him,

"How *did* you happen to ask her, Ted? You must have known how they'd all feel about it. She's not like us. . . ." It was so natural to have that feeling of possessiveness about him. There had been other times when she knew he had not liked it, and she had tried to shake it off, but it was the natural thing when they had been paired off together for so long. It was hard to stop doing the natural thing.

But it made him angry, and he answered rudely, the way he used to answer his mother, "Maybe that's our loss, then," he said.

The dance ended and he excused himself at once and went over to the girl, dropping on the floor by her feet. Jean tried to cover up by talking to Pudgy, but it was no good. She could have bitten her tongue off. That's not the way to handle him, she thought unhappily; I mustn't criticize. Now I've driven him to her.

He stayed beside the girl for a while and then went out to the kitchen to return with more drinks. But he kept going back to her as though trying to justify her being there.

As the evening wore on, as Jean watched the other girls become silly and less attractive, Marie also changed. But she did not become silly, although she laughed often, with a soft gurgling sound like the running of water over stones; she did not fade as Jean felt herself fading; she did not lose, because outwardly there had been too little of everything to start with, except in her eyes; but now a glow seemed to be upon her, and upon every movement she made. One by one the boys, who could not seem to find their way to noticing her otherwise, brought her drinks. She took them all and drank them, slowly, sitting there in her gypsy dress, her little breasts high and wide apart, smiling on them all, and saying "Thank you" in her strange, soft, stilted voice. In a way, Jean thought, she is more sure than anyone I have ever seen. And while she was thinking this, Ted seated himself in the shadows on the floor beside the girl and did not get up again.

The other girls danced and flung themselves about, sampling this new kind of fun. They were all gay, secure in their indifference, but for Jean there was no place to turn. Brad danced with her and stayed close beside until he quite suddenly had too much to drink and had to leave. Jean followed him to the steps, putting her arm through his.

"I'll take you home, Brad," she offered, but he would not hear of it. He was ashamed, and he wanted to be alone.

"I'll be all right," he said, brushing her away. "I'll go home for a while and then come back."

After he started down the path she ran out after him, but he waved her back, and she did not follow. She did not really want to stay, but she could not bring herself to leave, not while Ted sat there at the girl's feet, looking vague and drunk. Brad lurched out of sight into the shadows of the trees, and she turned back in, worrying about him. But now she wanted to stay and show Ted she wasn't really possessive, that she only seemed so because she loved him. And she wanted to get him away from that girl so that things would be lovely again, as they had been. She felt a little drunk, but she did not think she could be, because she was so unhappy.

The other girls could not remain indifferent, after all. They had to notice Marie, seeing her eyelids drop over the light eyes and the soft brown hair curling about her face. Her lips were thin, but they had fallen apart now in an odd little expression of sensuality. Now more of the boys came and brought their drinks and lingered beside her, talking to her soft face. Still she said little; only the gurgle of her laugh followed everything they said. The girls had to notice her. Once they drew off in the corner together in protest.

"What's she after?" asked Katy.

"Anything she can get," said Jean brutally, looking once more at Ted as he sat at Marie's feet, but there was nothing she could do. There was nothing any of them could do. "I'd like to kidnap Ted," she said, and none of them felt she was only jealous. They all had the same feeling about the girl, they all thought she was spoiling things.

"But what's she *got,* I'd like to know?" whispered Josy, the youngest, her full round lips pouting as she looked over at the boys. "She must have something."

They all laughed at her, half-heartedly, but Jean answered, "I don't know, Josy. It can't just be . . ." She shook her head and ran her fingers back through her short black hair. "Whew, I've been drinking too much. No more for me!"

Another record was put on the phonograph and the boys came over to them, looking strangely stimulated, their eyes evasive. They sauntered over to the girls and stood beside them, but there was something knowing in the air now that the girls could not share, some bond between the boys that kept them apart. Ted had let them know they were not wanted.

"Tell me," demanded Josy again, dancing with Terry. "What's she got that I haven't?"

He looked at her as though puzzled for a moment, then laughed unconvincingly.

"Nothing," he said. "She's just new." But he added, "I'd like to know where she's been all her life, though."

"Well, not around here, I'll bet," said Josy, and was not prepared for his burst of laughter.

One by one the girls then went up to Marie, driven by their curiosity, but she would not or could not give them anything. She had no small talk, and they felt foolish standing there doing all the talking or asking questions—questions Ted would answer for her. But her strange attraction seemed to hold, so that Ted did not move from her feet, but sat as though at watch, occasionally touching her ankle as he reached for his glass on the floor beside her chair.

They were affected by it, all of them were acting differently. They had been taught so well not to do things to excess, but now there was a recklessness in the atmosphere that affected them. Some were angrily conscious of one another, so that they quarreled, while others kept on dancing together now, through record after record, and there was less talk, less laughter.

They're different, they've never been like this before, Jean thought. She was dancing with Pudgy who had changed in the other way, becoming stiff and solemn the more he drank. He was no longer clowning, making them laugh. Instead, he was full of a tremendous solemnity, a grim earnestness about whatever he did that made him seem pathetic. And worst of all, he was trying to be amorous, trying to put his arms about the girls, and he held them too close when he danced with them.

"Y' think I'm funny 'cause I'm fat, but someday you'll see,

someday," he was muttering in Jean's ear, and then she saw Josy and Terry dance through the door out onto the porch, and stop dancing to run down the steps, out into darkness. She heard one of them stumble at the bottom step, and she heard Josy giggle, and stop suddenly, as if she were being kissed. It worried her; Josy was only sixteen, and a nice kid. To leave a party like that . . . We've all been drinking too much, she thought, we should have more sense.

But she knew it was more than this.

"You'll see, someday, all of you," Pudgy was saying in her ear, trying to hold her closer against him, his hands heavy and wet with perspiration.

For some time she had not looked at Ted, she had not looked at the girl. Numbly she had kept on dancing, waiting for something to happen to stop it all, knowing, believing desperately that it could not last. But she was tired suddenly; it was time something came to an end. It was time they all came to their senses.

"Oh, Pudgy, be yourself," she said wearily, just before she looked around.

She turned and saw Ted leaning forward, his face turned away, turned up to the girl; and at the same time she saw his hand slip around behind Marie's ankle, curve there and, like something creeping in the darkness of a dream, move up into the folds of Marie's red skirt. And all the time Marie's foolish little mouth hung loose in her soft face, but there was a faint smile about the corners now and she was moving her fingers back through Ted's hair. That yellow, fine hair that Jean had loved, lying flat and wispy along his forehead after swimming summer after summer, hair that stiffened in the wind as they played tennis together in the warm summer days. And Ted's strong, well-kept hands . . .

Suddenly she ran to the phonograph and shut it off in the

middle of a dance and stood facing the crowd, clapping her hands, her dark eyes bright and feverish. And in a loud, clear voice, she called out to them, to all these friends. (It was so simple, really, why hadn't she spoken before?)

"Let's go to the hotel to the dance. The party's dead here. Let's go where there's bright light and an orchestra!"

Instantly they seemed to wake up as though they had been waiting for this, and Josy and Terry came back in—they could not have gone very far. Everyone began talking, together again. Pudgy remained silent for a minute or two, then snatched an afghan from the end of the couch and whirled it about his shoulders, like a dancer.

"To the ball!" he cried, dipping and whirling, once more the life of the party.

Jean did not look back at Ted and the girl, did not let herself see in her mind that which had passed between them. If only none of the others had seen it, she thought, it could be forgotten. Once they had the girl out of that chair and on her feet, and Ted standing among them again, he would come to his senses and everything would be as it had been. He was acting foolish only because, secretly, he was ashamed of the girl and this was his way of showing defiance. Besides, he had been drinking too much and could not have known what he was doing. It was the same with all of them. Why, even Pudgy, look at Pudgy, now, no one would ever believe he could act the way he had.

Oh, Ted, she thought suddenly, it mustn't be too late!

The girls ran up the stairs to powder and change back to their rubber-soled shoes. In a few minutes they were down again, their hair freshly combed, their faces alive and carefree, their drunkenness nearly gone. They were all down before Jean, but she knew they would be waiting for her. She took her time, making up her face and lips very carefully, and fluffing out the dark bangs over her forehead. They're awfully curly tonight, she thought, pleased.

Coming down the stairs slowly she thought how easy it had been, how jolly and familiar they all were after all; and thinking, too, she understood Ted as she never had before. Probably as no one ever had understood him, she thought, very seriously.

It was not until she was on the bottom step that she looked —brightly, for she knew their eyes were on her—at the corner where Ted and Marie had been sitting.

But they were no longer there, neither the girl nor Ted was sitting there now. Quickly Jean looked away and then she had to turn back to verify what she had seen. Where they had been sitting was Marie's last glass knocked over, its contents emptied into a dark pattern on the floor; but the corner that had seemed too full all evening was deserted, had been deserted suddenly, she knew, because of that glass beside the chair.

"Ted and Marie just stepped into the sunroom," someone volunteered with a short laugh. "I guess they don't know we're leaving."

Awkwardly they stood there, ready to leave, but none making any move. Then Terry took a step toward the door of the sunroom, and they waited, silent and watchful.

"Ted," Terry called into the darkness. "Come on, we're going now."

There was no answer although the door was only carelessly closed, and a dark streak of the room showed along the edge of the door. But they could not see in, nor could they hear any sound; there was just that dark silent frame of darkness around the door. Terry took another step while they watched, and once more before he got there called "Ted!"

Then a strange voice, strange to them all, although it was

one they knew so well, came back in answer. "Get out!" it said, its harshness like a claw thrust out, and bared.

Stupefied, they did not move.

Suddenly with a sharp clear command Jean darted past them and out the front door. "Let's go!" she cried, and they followed behind as she ran blindly across the clearing away from the house.

"Jeannie," called Katy, trying to catch up with her, but Jean did not hesitate.

"See you at the hotel," she called back, racing down the wooded path to the lake, her feet sure, knowing the way.

Her boat was bobbing gently on the edge of the lake beside the others; Brad had not taken it, after all. Then she saw his shape dimly outlined in the boat, curled up in the bottom, his head resting on the seat.

"Brad. Oh, Brad," she said, getting in the boat. Balancing herself and leaning down, she shook him by the shoulder. "Brad, are you all right? How do you feel now?"

"Huh?" He twisted his long body around and opened his eyes. "Oh, it's you, sis! Sure, I'm all right." He stared up at her for a minute or two, then yawned and pushed the leather cushion into place under his head, and turned away. In a few moments he was breathing deeply again, his face white and relaxed in the moonlight.

Climbing over him, Jean knelt down to start the motor. But she stopped, looked at Brad, and instead lifted the oars from the sides of the boat and fitted them into place. Then cautiously, so as not to awaken him, she dipped the silent oars into the water and rowed the boat toward home.

THE VISIT
By Andy Logan
From *Redbook*
Originally published in the Swarthmore *Dodo*

ANDY LOGAN

was born February 6, 1921, in Cleveland, Ohio, and her real name is Isabel but she likes Andy better. She now lives in Candler, North Carolina, near Asheville. All her family until her father were farmers. He was a lawyer and later had his own aviation company. Miss Logan went to school in Shaker Heights, Ohio, and has never studied writing or short-story technique. She is a senior at Swarthmore College, Pennsylvania this year, where she first began writing. "The Visit" was awarded the $750 prize offered by Redbook Magazine *for the best story written by an undergraduate and published in a college magazine.* The Dodo, *which Miss Logan helped to found, received $250, and Miss Logan $500. The story was reprinted in the March 1941 issue of* Redbook.

"Ned's people live there," said Jane, suddenly lifting her hand from the wheel and waving widely at two figures moving about one of the fields they passed. "It's a big farm. I don't know anybody who's got more land or who's better thought of around here than Mr. Kleith."

"Really?" said Dan. He crooked his elbow in the air and groped about in his pocket for cigarettes. "Have one?"

"Oh no!" She looked at him quickly and turned away. He liked the look of her hands as they drove. They were small and brown and full of strength. Funny, he thought, she used to smoke.

"Did you have an interesting time in China?" asked Jane politely.

You might call it that, thought Dan. His best friend had had his head blown off. And one day when he came home from a walk around the block, his trouser-cuffs were reddish brown around the edges. He remembered sending the suit to the cleaner's.

"Rather interesting," he said. "You're very nice to let me spend the night like this."

"Don't be silly," said Jane, slowing up to let a hen run squawking to the other side of the road. "There was no sense in your making that long trip down from New York just for a couple of hours. We've got loads of room."

They were quiet for a while, driving through the autumn sunshine, past a church and some gray farmhouses and a big, raw brick school building which Jane proudly called to his attention.

"The county's had to work hard for that," she said. "Ned's father made speeches, and Ned, too, and we finally got it. It's only been finished since August."

Dan had forgotten that there were things like schools which were important and which people fought for and took pride in. He looked back at the ugly building with its red clay front yard. Probably Jane belonged to the Parents' Association. He imagined her presiding at meetings: "I think Mrs. Thatcher is quite right. I think the third-grade room needs curtains very badly."

"Are the children—— How old are they now, Jane?"

She glanced at him briefly, disapproval hovering around her mouth.

"Margaret was seven in July, Dan, and Hugh will be six next March."

"Oh." He had thought of them as older. He had thought of them, he realized suddenly, as somewhere between ten and twelve, with long brown legs and old faces. He seemed to have been away so long.

"You never call them Maggie and the General any more?" he asked, after a moment.

"Oh no," said Jane, "just Hugh and Margaret. Ned doesn't care much for nicknames," she added as she turned into the driveway.

The low bulk of the house lay awkwardly among the brown autumn leaves like a thin, sleeping hound. It was an undistinguished old place, but Dan saw nothing pathetic about it, as he had half-expected. "I wouldn't be ashamed to point it out to anyone," he thought; and he had a sudden picture of himself driving along with a carful of men in top hats, and saying casually: "Oh, by the way, that white house there is where my wife and children live. My former wife, I mean," he would have to add, and that would be awkward. He was glad it was only a silly idea.

After Jane had taken him upstairs, and he had set his bag and the presents for the children on the floor by the bed, and washed his hands in the dark bathroom, Dan went out into the garden where his son and daughter were playing, and was formally introduced to him. Their clothes were rather nicer now, he suspected, than everyday; there was something odd about a little boy playing around a farmyard garden in pleated linen. "I'd put you in khaki shorts if you were mine," thought Dan, and then stopped suddenly, because it was such a strange thing to say.

After a while Jane went back into the house to see about supper, and the two children stood there before him in the late-afternoon sun—a little girl with bows in her hair and a thin-nosed boy; and they kicked the garden dirt with their shining shoes and called him "Father," but there was no conviction in their voices.

"Do you go to school?" he asked them politely.

"I do," said Margaret. "But Hugh's too little. You have to be six."

He tried to tell them about China and Spain and Ethiopia, but they were too young to be very interested. They showed him their playhouse, ostentatiously, and as if it had been suggested beforehand.

"Did you come on a boat?" Margaret wanted to know, and he told them about that for a while, but soon they were making little bored jabs at each other and quarreling sharply. He stood watching them uncomfortably, like a stage father who couldn't remember his lines.

"Are you really our papa?" Hugh asked him when the dinner bell had rung at last, and they were hurrying up the walk toward the house.

"Of course," said Dan, but he had a quick, guilty feeling that he was lying.

It was just before dinner that Dan met Jane's husband. As he climbed up the steps to the back porch he saw Ned and Jane standing there together, talking in low voices. Jane was running the dark opal ring up and down her finger, and Dan knew she was upset about something. Ned stood beside her and smiled quietly at Dan. He was in overalls. Dan saw the way the children were dressed, and how careful they had been in the garden about how they played and where they sat. He remembered them wiping off their shoes with light fingers before coming up to dinner. He understood why Jane's face was flushed. She had wanted him to see them all at their best, and here was Ned in dirty, manure-green overalls.

"How do you do," said Ned. "I'm Ned Kleith. Glad to have you here." There was no embarrassment in his face as he looked at Dan, or in his large hand as it shook Dan's strongly. "Sorry I'm dressed this way, but my prize mare just foaled, and I had to see to her." Dan saw that the tip of the man's red nose was peeling a little. He smiled back uneasily.

The children, who had been standing shyly in the background, ran forward now and threw their arms around Ned, jerking at his sleeves and grabbing his knees and looking up at him happily.

"Is't a big colt, Ned?"

"Is't black, Ned?"

"How soon can I ride it—ever, maybe?"

"We'd have come down to see it, Ned, if——"

"Hugh," said Jane, "come, let me wash your face."

Dinner was good, although the hired girl served it awkwardly and a little resentfully. Dan suspected that on ordinary evenings she sat down to eat with the family. He ate briskly as the others did, and tried to be intelligent about seed and threshing and the breeding of cattle. The children's eyes were big and watchful.

Once Jane broke in sharply: "Let's not talk about farming all the time, Ned." She turned her spoon over and over on the table as she spoke. She didn't look at either of them.

"O.K., honey." And Ned smacked Hugh's hand lightly as it darted out for a second chicken leg. "Wait till you're asked, son! You know," he said to Dan, "we had more trouble getting that child to eat for a while, and then all at once about a year ago he turned hollow to his toes. Awfully funny thing." Ned reached over and pulled the little boy's hair playfully.

"Margaret," said Jane, "please don't dunk your bread."

"But Ned does, Mother."

"Say," said Ned, struggling up from the table a little later and stretching his arms in the air. "I'll put the kids to bed now if you two have some business you want to talk over. Take him out and show him your garden, Jane." He grinned at Dan. "Here—kiss your dad good night, kids."

"Good night, Dad."

"Good night, Dad."

And they pecked Dan lightly on the chin.

He felt foolish and thwarted as he took a walk around the yard with his ex-wife. She had led him into the living room first, and then, after a strange look about her, had hurried out through the side door into the garden.

"The yellow roses are beautiful at this time of year, don't you think?" she said, waving her hand toward them in the half-light.

He came closer, to see them, and she moved away from him, her heels biting sharply at the stone walk. "We have loads of baby's-breath too. It's lovely in July and August."

"Jane," said Dan, "do you ever write any more?"

"No," she answered. He thought of the dirty old typewriter they both had used, and of the table it sat on. Jane would kick the table leg whenever she got to the exciting parts, and that day they sold the furniture to a dealer, the fellow had called the little mahogany thing kindling wood and gave them only seventy-five cents for it.

"I saw Chuck the other day," said Dan. "He and Helen broke up, you know, and he's living with a little Polish girl down on the waterfront some place."

"Oh," said Jane.

"It was just the same," he went on after a moment, leaning against the fence. "The old gang at the table by the window—most of them—a few new ones. We sat and argued and sang at each other nearly all night—just like we used to. Molly's a little fatter," he said, "and Joe's gone over to another paper. Sal's written another novel—but they haven't changed much." He crushed out a cigarette, and watched her carefully. "The phonograph was whining in the corner, and we all sat there and sort of shouted over it through the smoke. They played old ones mostly—'Whispering'——"

"Do you like the house?" Jane asked him. "We've done a lot with it, you know. It was just an old rundown cottage in the first place, and we've built on and painted. I papered a whole bedroom myself."

"Do you ever get up to New York, Jane?" asked Dan, breaking in.

"No." She hesitated. "There's not much time, you know—I have the children and the house, and in the mornings I usually work in the garden." She looked around her. "And there's church every Sunday, and prayer meeting Wednesday nights. That's fun, you know. Things go on at school, and there's a missionary society that I'm treasurer of, which means keeping accounts. Lots of things happen all the time—maybe you wouldn't think so." She turned away from him. "Why, tomorrow night the first-grade mothers are giving a bazaar at the Methodist Church. And next week our Sunday-school class is having a big picnic at the amusement park——"

Suddenly Jane wasn't talking any more. The buzz of the evening throbbed in Dan's ears. "Oh, it's great fun, you know," she said, and when he turned to look at her, she was crying quietly, leaning against the garden fence with her hands over her face.

"Hey, you two," called Ned from the other side of the garden, and his footsteps squashed down the walk toward them. "Look, honey, I got dressed up for you. I'm not a dirty old farmer any more." His hair was slicked back now, and a neat blue suit hung on him loosely.

"Come on," he said, reaching for Jane's hand, "let's go down and take a look at this new colt. He'll make a fine horse someday."

In the morning Dan took his children off for a walk in the woods. Things were better now—he had given them their presents at breakfast, and they had those to talk about. He sat on a stump and let them build tunnels around him. He studied their faces and the way they played, and tried to remember himself as a child.

"Look at the ants, Marg—should I step on them?"

"Don't you dare, Hugh! It'll rain sure as anything."

Once during the morning, after Margaret had taken a fall on the pine needles, she climbed blindly into Dan's lap to be comforted. Dan sat there for some time on the sharp stump with his daughter warm in his arms, and thought of many things.

On the way home Hugh suddenly threw his shoulders back and spat widely, for no good reason.

"I wouldn't do that," said Dan. He would, of course, but it seemed natural to protest.

"Ned does," said Hugh firmly and finally, and they walked on.

It was decided after some argument that the children might go with them when Ned drove Dan to the station. They were very happy about it, and sat waiting patiently in the back seat while Dan said good-by to Jane.

"I'm glad you could come down and see the children," she said.

"I'm glad too," said Dan, looking at Ned. He hesitated a moment.

"I don't know how long I'll be in New York, but when I come back or when they're a little older I'd like to have them on a visit some time."

"That would be lovely," said Jane vaguely.

"Good-by." He climbed into the car and waved at her. "I'll be seeing you," he called tritely. He wanted to make her meet his eyes, to show him the truth. But she had turned and was going quickly up the front steps.

"There's something I think I ought to tell you," said Ned, when they were out on the highway with the wind blowing through the windows and the children quarreling casually on the back seat. "You know that money you send every month for the kids? Well, a couple of years ago, when there was a big corn surplus on the market, I borrowed some of it." He stopped, waiting.

"I'm glad it came in handy," Dan told him.

"Oh, it's all paid back now," said Ned quickly. *"With* interest. It'll be mighty nice to have," he added, "when it comes time for us to send these kids to college."

Dan took out a cigarette and lit it. "Alfalfa," he thought; "I'll bet that's alfalfa in that field."

The Visit

"Did Jane tell you our news?" Ned asked him a little shyly as they drove up to the station a while later.

"No." It was odd—it hadn't struck him before, but that was it, of course.

"We're planning on a child of our own in the spring," said Ned; he climbed out of the car and beamed with proud eyes at the handful of people on the platform.

When Dan was on the train he put his bag up right away so that he'd have plenty of time to wave at the two little figures standing fondly watching the big wheels and the smoke and the fat engine. But when he looked out, they were already trotting away with Ned. Each of them held one of his hands, and Margaret's mouth was going very fast. As Dan watched them Hugh suddenly took a few steps ahead and hopped into the car in front of the others.

Dan sat back in his seat and looked about him at the other passengers. He saw that their cool eyes were following the little boy and girl, and wanted suddenly to tell one or two of them that these were his children. Perhaps he could manage it a little later. In the meantime he bought a package of mints and a *New Yorker* from the candy butcher and stretched his feet comfortably in front of him. As he spread the magazine out in his lap he looked down at his knee, and finding a ring of brown sand where Margaret's feet had lain against him, he brushed it carefully clean.

HELLO, TIB
By Conrad Aiken
From *Mademoiselle*

CONRAD POTTER AIKEN

was born August 5, 1889, in Savannah, Georgia. His father and mother were New Englanders, and after his childhood he attended schools in Massachusetts. He was graduated from Harvard in 1912, where he was president of the Advocate *and class poet. He traveled extensively in Europe, and settled in Sussex in 1923, where he lived until the war. In* New Poems *(1940), he writes: "I am permanently settled in an old farmhouse in Brewster, Cape Cod, with my wife Mary Hoover, the painter." He was awarded the Pulitzer Prize for his* Selected Poems *(1929), and has had some twenty volumes of poetry published. He has also written five novels, the most recent being* Conversation *(1940), and three volumes of his short stories have been published. He has received the Shelley Memorial Award, and in 1934 was given a Guggenheim Fellowship. His story, "Impulse," from* Story, *appeared in the* O. Henry Memorial Award Prize Stories *of 1933.*

THE QUARREL had amounted to very little, to practically nothing, and yet it had cast its shadow over the evening. They had gone to bed without speaking and—more disturbing still—she did not get up to make his breakfast; and this although she knew he was going to town, and by the early train. He had had to forage in the dark kitchen by himself, attended only by Squidge, the cat; hunting among innumerable unlabeled cans for the coffee, spilling the sugar, and in general allowing himself the luxury of feeling pretty annoyed. A silly business, altogether—damned silly. And he mustn't let it spoil his day in town.

And what a day it was, what a day it was going to be! A lovely spring morning—yes, a perfect spring morning if there ever was one. Blue as a baby's eye. The apple blossoms just getting ready to pop, the song sparrows shouting in the lilac bushes, the robins—there seemed to be hundreds of them everywhere—saying over and over their loud and all-too-contented "Cheerio, cheerio, cheerilee!"—or was it jubilee? Well, yes, perhaps it was jubilee. And why not indeed? The whole world seemed to be bursting with good will.

The little local train which would take him as far as Appledore came clanking and hissing round the bend, under the crazy foot bridge, and he climbed aboard, deferring the reading of the morning paper till the longer run from Appledore to town. Besides, the marsh on a morning like this was too good to miss. Bathed in sunlight, the last of the night mist just curling away in the creeks and shadows, it looked wonderfully peaceful. Crows were quarreling over some shapeless white object in a ditch; a blue heron stood poised and arrowlike beside a pool, as still as his own image. What a morning, what a morning! And the little train rattling and clanking through it, as if only to keep the whole thing from being too precious, too lonely.

Well, it was a pity she hadn't got up and come down to see him off, for she would have enjoyed it. And it served her right. And all because he had said—— What was it he had said? That he was more perceptive—yes, that was it, perceptive. Good heavens, the word perceptive had been like a red rag to a bull! Had that been so outrageous? To claim that women weren't by any means as perceptive as they were supposed to be, and that he himself was a devil of a lot more perceptive than most? Well, you never knew when you were going to injure a woman's vanity, and that was, of course, what he had done. It had been tactless. He ought to have shied off, changed the subject when he saw that she was upset about it. But then she had been so damned positive, so damned certain of herself, so conceited, in fact, about her perceptiveness, and so incredulous about his, that he became suddenly mad, and the fat was in the fire. Extraordinary how quickly a quarrel can blaze up out of nothing, absolutely nothing! One minute everybody perfectly serene and happy, in the best and most serene of all possible worlds, and then —bingo, one little word or look blows the whole thing to smithereens. And there you are, glaring at each other like a couple of starved hyenas. And in a state of smoldering fury, moreover, that seems unlikely ever to come to an end.

Just the same, he had been perfectly right—it was perfectly true. All nonsense, this notion that women had a sort of sixth sense, or a superhuman kind of clairvoyance. What rubbish! True enough, of course, that a woman might understand a child—but did she always? Even that was debatable. And as for her understanding of other women, or men—— No, most of the time she was just thinking about herself, thinking of her own feelings and, above all, of the impression she was making. She was only perceptive when it was somehow useful to her, that was it—and very seldom perceptive merely because she had to be. No.

He was pleased with his little analysis, and smiled out of the train window as they crossed the red-iron bridge. The tide was out; mud banks were showing, channeled and raw; a rowboat hung down the muddy slope at a steep angle, as if caught in the act of falling; and further down, by the bend of the river, the old dredger was at work. How peaceful, how eternal it all seemed! It would go on forever exactly like this, there was no doubt of it. Mud, sun, and tide, day after day, the bridge rotting, the marsh rotting, the old dredger rotting, and the sun calmly blazing down on everything—world without end. And a good thing, too. . . . The train was stopping. He got to his feet without thinking, and followed the others toward the platform of Appledore Station.

He walked the length of the platform and back, tapping the rolled newspaper against his knee, and looked at the early-morning people. Early-morning people—exactly! What was it that gave them so definitely an early-morning look? Not merely the somewhat orange-colored light of the early sun on their faces and hands—though no doubt that played a part in it. No, it was something in their half-sleepy, half-awake indifference, as if—though refreshed—they were not yet quite aware. The young married couple, sitting against the station wall on their upturned suitcases, were leaning a little forward, faintly smiling to themselves, but not saying a thing. It was almost indecent to catch them like that—they were actually, at this very minute, in the act of waking up, and totally incapable of thinking of anything but their own delicious well-being. The tall man beyond them, standing with his paper held up before him, was only pretending to read. Every now and then he looked up over the edge of the paper, looked away over the living marsh, as if that tide of reality out there was much too strong for him, much too strong for anything so pallid as the printed word. But the three schoolgirls, with their strapped books and lunch-boxes —there was certainly nothing sleepy about them! They teased each other, giggled, became suddenly serious; started to play tag, and stopped as unpremeditatedly as they had begun; and then ran up the ramp to the raised platform at the end where freight cars were loaded, and ran down the smooth cement surface, screaming with delight. Energy—good heavens, what it was to have all that energy! He had to step aside quickly to avoid being run into by one of them, the smallest—the swung lunch box slapped his hand, the blue eyes looked up at him abashed but laughing, and then abruptly all three were gone, vanished, round the corner of the station, but of course only to be back again in no time.

It was in that small interval, as he himself turned round, smiling, to walk back again, that the little cat appeared. Tail in air, she advanced serenely and happily along the platform, putting down one white paw in front of the other, and if she came tentatively, the reason for that was at once obvious: the little creature was so manifestly delighted, so simply delighted, with everything and everyone she saw that she really didn't know where to begin. So many wonderful people and things to investigate! You could positively see her feeling that as she turned, first one way and then another. She had to go and rub her cheek against the delicious shoes and suitcases and ankles of the young married couple, making a lovely loop of her tail for their benefit, though they scarcely noticed her, truth to tell, so lost were they in their own world; and then she had to stroll back to a wooden box which lay on the platform, and sniff it daintily and distantly; and then rub her smile against one of its pointed corners. A kitten, rather than a cat—not half-grown—an ordinary, perfectly ordinary, gray-striped tabby with yellow eyes—but, good gracious, there had never been a creature so bursting, absolutely bursting, with love and good will!

He watched her coming toward him in her slow and intermittent progress, drawn every which way by distractions. She rubbed her sides against the tall man's legs, she revisited the married couple, she went to the station door and looked in, meanwhile kneading her paws against the platform floor in ecstasy; she turned back, she turned forward—the little creature would obviously go anywhere, do anything, out of sheer love. He stooped and snapped his fingers, once, twice—and sure enough, she came at an eager trot, she came running, as if only too delighted to receive an express invitation, but nevertheless not in the least surprised. After all, that was what life was, wasn't it? . . . Love, nothing but love! She twined about his outstretched forefinger, butted his knuckles, rearing up like a little goat to do so, all the while keeping up a continuous purring, an absolute uproar—and then, of course, she saw the three little girls, and they had to be attended to. Away she went, once more at a trot, and once more she was a huge success. And what more natural?

"Hello, Tib!"

"Hello, Tib!"

"Hello, Tib!"

All three cried their greeting, all three began stroking her and patting her. For a moment cat and children became inextricable; and then the smallest girl, the one who had bumped into him, or almost, took it into her head to begin jumping over the little cat. To and fro she jumped, back and forth, the other girls laughing; and so close, too, that he thought of intervening. But no, she never quite struck the cat, and the cat, although a little surprised by so much violence, remained quite self-possessed, sat quite still, watching the strange antics with complete trust.

Complete trust—yes! Good heavens, yes! And suddenly he was looking at the little cat with fascination. For this, he now recognized, was one of those rare creatures who are so essentially innocent, and good, and loving, as to be totally defenseless. This little creature, with her tremendous love, was already doomed, by her own wonderful simplicity—that entire trustfulness was nothing but an embodied invitation to death. In a world dominated everywhere by violence and evil she could not possibly live, or not for very long, and wasn't it precisely this obvious impossibility that made her pathetic openness and innocence so bewitching?

And there was more to it than that, even. For as he turned and looked across the tracks toward the marsh—turning away, as a matter of fact, so that if the cat should be struck or hurt he would not see it—he became aware of the fact that he and the cat had now, together, constituted a unique and extraordinary relationship. The cat was innocence, or love, or both: the fundamentally innocent thing; and he himself, with his brilliant perception of the cat's nature and need, was knowledge, godlike knowledge, with all its latent powers for good or evil. For was he not the only person here, on this early-morning platform, who had really seen and loved this little cat, and foreseen her tragic destiny? The others had been perhaps for a moment amused, or touched, but they had seen nothing of all this; for them the cat was simply another cat. Perceptiveness! Good heavens, yes—this was a case in point, it was indeed *the* case. It was the fundamental instance of the all-embracing, all-cherishing, all-sustaining power of perceptiveness. In this sense, the little cat's life was in his hands. . . .

What an extraordinary thing! And how extraordinarily delightful!

He was still feeling pleased with the whole idea, and with himself, when the train came swiftly and silently toward the station. And turning then for a last look at the cat he saw that she had left the three little girls, and had gone up the sloping ramp of concrete at the end of the platform. There she sat, at the very edge of the raised platform, looking down at the tracks—not fifteen feet away from him—and then she began putting her white paws down the wall, preparing to jump, and just as the heat and shadow of the engine passed him, she jumped. Straight into the middle of the tracks, and the engine had gone over without touching her—but then he saw the agonized darting of the small body from side to side, seeking escape, the frightened back and head darting from side to side, and through an obstruction of wheel or truck the flash of an outstretched convulsive hind leg, white, and upside down; and then nothing. The train had stopped; the three little girls were clambering up the steep steps at one end, the married couple at another; the tall man had disappeared. No one had seen it but he—no one. It was as if nothing had happened.

But as he moved toward the steps *he* saw her again. The eyes closed, the meek upturned face meeker than ever, she lay quite still. And as he sat down in the train, trembling and sick, with all that dreadful action still horribly vivid before him, and as if still in action, he felt like a murderer. He alone knew that she was dead. He alone could have saved her.

She had lived, and died, for *him*.

A BOTTLE OF MILK FOR MOTHER
By Nelson Algren
From the *Southern Review* under the title of "Biceps"

NELSON ALGREN

is thirty-one years old, and began trying to write while working as a migratory laborer throughout northern Mexico. He explains: "I obtained a half interest in an abandoned Sinclair gasoline station in the Rio Grande Valley in 1933, which furnished me with a place in which I could remain seated long enough to write a couple of short stories. One of the stories thus written was reprinted in the O. Henry Memorial Award Prize Stories of 1935." *The title was "The Brothers' House," and it was published first in* Story. *Mr. Algren's work has also appeared in* The American Mercury, New Masses, Anvil, Partisan Review, New Republic, *and other magazines. He is the author of one novel,* Somebody in Boots, *and is under contract for a novel to be called* White Hope, *which deals with the same area touched upon in "A Bottle of Milk for Mother." Mr. Algren lives in Chicago, where he is employed on the Illinois Writers' Project.*

Two months after the Polish Warriors S.A.C. had had their heads shaved Bruno Lefty Bicek got into his final difficulty with the Racine Street police. The arresting officers and a reporter from the *Dziennik Chicagoski* were grouped about the captain's desk when the boy was urged forward into the room by Sergeant Adamovitch, with two fingers wrapped about the boy's broad belt: a full-bodied boy wearing a worn and sleeveless blue work shirt grown too tight across the shoulders; and the shoulders themselves with a loose swing to them. His skull and face were shining from a recent scrubbing, so that the little bridgeless nose glistened between the protective points of the cheekbones. Behind the desk sat Kozak, eleven years on the force and brother to an alderman. The reporter stuck a cigarette behind one ear like a pencil.

"We spotted him followin' the drunk down Chicago . . ." Sergeant Comiskey began. Captain Kozak interrupted.

"Let the jackroller tell us how he done it hisself."

"I ain't no jackroller."

"What you doin' here then?"

Bicek folded his naked arms.

"Answer me. If you ain't here for jackrollin' it must be for strong-arm robb'ry—'r are you one of them Chicago Av'noo moll-buzzers?"

"I ain't that either."

"C'mon, c'mon, I seen you in here before—what were you up to, followin' that poor old man?"

"I ain't been in here before."

Neither Sergeant Milano, Comiskey, nor old Adamovitch

moved an inch; yet the boy felt the semicircle about him drawing closer. Out of the corner of his eye he watched the reporter undoing the top button of his mangy raccoon coat, as though the barren little query room were already growing too warm for him.

"What were you doin' on Chicago Av'noo in the first place when you live up around Division? Ain't your own ward big enough you have to come down here to get in trouble? What do you *think* you're here for?"

"Well, I was just walkin' down Chicago like I said, to get a bottle of milk for Mother, when the officers jumped me. I didn't even see 'em drive up, they wouldn't let me say a word, I got no idea what I'm here for. I was just doin' a errand for Mother 'n . . ."

"All right, son, you want us to book you as a pickup 'n hold you overnight, is that it?"

"Yes sir."

"What about this then?"

Kozak flipped a springblade knife with an eight-inch blade onto the police blotter; the boy resisted the impulse to lean forward and take it. His own double-edged double-jointed springblade cuts-all genuine Filipino twisty-handled All-American gut-ripper.

"Is it yours or ain't it?"

"Never seen it before, Captain."

Kozak pulled a billy out of his belt, spread the blade across the bend of the blotter before him, and with the deftness of experience clubbed the blade off two inches from the handle. The boy winced as though he himself received the blow. Kozak threw the broken blade into a basket and the knife into a drawer.

"Know why I did that, son?"

"Yes sir."

"Tell me."

" 'Cause it's three inches to the heart."

"No. 'Cause it's against the law to carry more than three inches of knife. C'mon, Lefty, tell us about it. 'N it better be good."

The boy began slowly, secretly gratified that Kozak appeared to know he was the Warriors' first-string lefthander: maybe he'd been out at that game against the Knothole Boys the Sunday he'd finished his own game and then had relieved Dropkick Kodadek in the sixth in the second. Why hadn't anyone called him "Iron-man Bicek" or "Fireball Bruno" for that one?

"Everythin' you say can be used against you," Kozak warned earnestly. "Don't talk unless you want to." His lips formed each syllable precisely.

Then he added absently, as though talking to someone unseen, "We'll just hold you on an open charge till you do."

And his lips hadn't moved at all.

The boy licked his own lips, feeling a dryness coming into his throat and a tightening in his stomach. "We seen this boobatch with his collar turned inside out cashin' his check by Konstanty Stachula's Tonsorial Palace of Art on *Div*ision. So I followed him a way, that was all. Just breakin' the old monotony was all. Just a notion, you might say, that come over me. I'm just a neighborhood kid, Captain."

He stopped as though he had finished the story. Kozak glanced over the boy's shoulder at the arresting officers and Bicek began again hurriedly.

"Ever' once in a while he'd pull a little single-shot of scotch out of his pocket, stop a second t' toss it down 'n toss the bottle at the car tracks. I picked up a bottle that didn't bust but there wasn't a spider left in 'er, the boobatch'd drunk her dry. 'N do you know, he had his pockets *full* of them little bottles? 'Stead of buyin' hisself a fifth in the first place. Can't understand a man who'll buy liquor that way. Right before the corner of Walton 'n Noble he popped into a hallway. That was Chiney-Eye-the-Precinct-Captain's-Hallway, so I popped right in after him. Me'n Chiney-Eye 'r just like that." The boy crossed two fingers of his left hand and asked innocently, "Has the alderman been in to straighten this out, Captain?"

"What time was all this, Lefty?"

"Well, some of the street lamps was lit awready 'n I didn't see nobody either way down Noble. It'd just started spittin' a little snow 'n I couldn't see clear down Walton account of Wojciechowski's Tavern bein' in the way. He was a old guy, a dino you. He couldn't speak a word of English. But he started in cryin' about every time he gets a little drunk the same old thing happens to him 'n he's gettin' fed up, he lost his last three checks in the very same hallway 'n it's gettin' so his family don't believe him no more."

Bicek paused, realizing that his tongue was going faster than his brain. He unfolded his arms and shoved them down his pants pockets; the pants were turned up at the cuffs and the cuffs were frayed. He drew a colorless cap from his hip pocket and stood clutching it in his left hand.

"I didn't take him them other times, Captain," he anticipated Kozak.

"Who did?"

Silence.

"What's Benkowski doin' for a living these days, Lefty?"

"Just nutsin' around."

"What's Nowogrodski up to?"

"Goes wolfin' on roller skates by Riverview. The rink's open all year 'round."

"Does he have much luck?"

"Never turns up a hair. They go by too fast."
"What's that evil eye up to?"
Silence.
"You know who I mean. Idzikowski."
"The Finger?"
"You know who I mean. Don't stall."
"He's hexin' fights I heard."
"Seen Kodadek lately?"
"I guess. A week 'r two 'r a month ago."
"What was *he* up to?"
"Sir?"
"What was Kodadek doin' the last time you seen him?"
"You mean Dropkick? He was nutsin' around."
"Does he nuts around drunks in hallways?"
Somewhere in the room a small clock or wrist watch began ticking distinctly.
"Nutsin' around ain't jackrollin'."
"You mean Dropkick ain't a jackroller but you are."
The boy's blond lashes shuttered his eyes.
"All right, get ahead with your lyin' a little faster."
Kozak's head came down almost neckless onto his shoulders, and his face was molded like a flatiron: the temples narrow and the jaws rounded. Between the jaws and the open collar, against the graying hair of the chest, hung a tiny crucifix, slender and golden, a shade lighter than his tunic's golden buttons.
"I told him I wasn't gonna take his check, I just needed a little change, I'd pay it back someday. But maybe he didn't understand. He kept hollerin' how he lost his last check, please to let him keep this one. 'Why you drinkin' it all up then?' I put it to him, 'if you're that anxious to hold onto it?' He gimme a foxy grin then 'n pulls out four of them little

bottles from four different pockets, 'n each one was a different kind of liquor. I could have one, he tells me in Polish, which do I want, 'n I slapped all four out of his hands. All four. I don't like to see no full-grown man drinkin' that way. A Polack hillbilly he was, 'n certainly no citizen.

" 'Now let me have that change,' I asked him, 'n that wasn't so much t' ask. I don't go around just lookin' fer trouble, Captain. 'N my feet was slop full of water 'n snow. I'm just a neighborhood fella. But he acted like I was gonna kill him 'r somethin'. I got one hand over his mouth 'n a half-nelson behind him 'n talked polite-like in Polish in his ear, 'n he begun sweatin' 'n tryin' t' wrench away on me. 'Take it easy,' I asked him. 'Be reas'nable. We're both in this up to our necks now.' 'N he wasn't drunk no more then, 'n he was plenty t' hold onto. You wouldn't think a old boobatch like that'd have so much stren'th left in him, boozin' down *Div*ision night after night, year after year, like he didn't have no home to go to. He pulled my hand off his mouth 'n started hollerin' *'Mlody Bandyta! Mlody Bandyta!"* 'n I could feel him slippin'. He was just too strong fer a kid like me to hold . . ."

"Because you were reachin' for his wallet with the other hand?"

"Oh no. The reason I couldn't hold him was my right hand had the nelson 'n I'm not so strong there like in my left 'n even my left ain't what it was before I thrun it out pitchin' that doubleheader."

"So you kept the rod in your left hand?"

The boy hesitated. Then: "Yes sir." And felt a single drop of sweat slide down his side from under his armpit. Stop and slide again down to the belt.

"What did you get off him?"

"I tell you, I had my hands too full to get *anythin'*—that's just what I been tryin' to tell you. I didn't get so much as one of them little single-shots for all my trouble."

"How many slugs did you fire?"

"Just one, Captain. That was all there was in 'er. I didn't really fire though. Just at his feet. T' scare him so's he wouldn't jump me. I fired in self-defense. I just wanted to get out of there." He glanced helplessly around at Comiskey and Adamovitch. "You do crazy things sometimes, fellas— well, that's all I was doin'."

The boy caught his tongue and stood mute. In the silence of the query room there was only the scraping of the reporter's pencil and the ticking of the unseen wrist watch. "I'll ask Chiney-Eye if it's legal, a reporter takin' down a confession, that's my out," the boy thought desperately, and added aloud, before he could stop himself: " 'N beside I had to show him . . ."

"Show him what, son?"

Silence.

"Show him what, Lefthander?"

"That I wasn't just another greenhorn sprout like he thought."

"Did he say you were just a sprout?"

"No. But I c'd tell. Lots of people think I'm just a green kid. I show 'em. I guess I showed 'em now all right." He felt he should be apologizing for something and couldn't tell whether it was for strongarming a man or for failing to strongarm him.

"I'm just a neighborhood kid. I belonged to the Keep-Our-City-Clean Club at St. John Cant'us. I told him polite-like, like a Polish-American citizen, this was Chiney-Eye-A-Friend-of-Mine's hallway. 'No more after this one,' I told him. 'This is your last time gettin' rolled, old man. After this I'm per-tectin' you, I'm seein' to it nobody touches you—but the people who live here don't like this sort of thing goin' on any more'n you 'r I do. There's gotta be a stop to it, old man—'n we all gotta live, don't we?' That's what I told him in English."

Kozak exchanged glances with the prim-faced reporter from the *Chicagoski,* who began cleaning his black tortoise-shell spectacles hurriedly yet delicately with the fringed tip of his cravat. They depended from a black ribbon: he snapped them back onto his beak.

"You shot him in the groin, Lefty. He's dead."

The reporter leaned slightly forward, but perceived no especial reaction and so relaxed. A pretty comfy old chair for a dirty old police station, he thought lifelessly. Kozak shaded his eyes with his gloved hand and looked down at his charge sheet. The night lamp on the desk was still lit, as though he had been working all night; as the morning grew lighter behind him lines came out below his eyes, black as though packed with soot, and a curious droop came to the Saint Bernard mouth.

"You shot him through the groin—*zip.*" Kozak's voice came suddenly flat and unemphatic, reading from the charge sheet as though without understanding. "Five children. Stella, Mary, Grosha, Wanda, Vincent. 13, 10, 6, 6, and one two months. So he wasn't so old after all. Mother invalided since last birth, name of Rose. W.P.A. fifty-five dollars. You told the truth about *that* at least."

Bicek's voice came in a shout: "You know *what?* That bullet must of bounced, that's what!"

"Who was along?"

"I was singlin'. Lone-wolf stuff." His voice possessed the first faint touch of fear.

"You said *'we* seen the man.' Was he a big man? How big a man was he?"

"I'd judge two-hunerd-twenty pounds," Comiskey offered, "at least. Fifty pounds heavier 'n this boy, just about. 'N half a head taller."

"Who's 'we,' Lefthander?"

"Captain, I said 'we seen.' Lots of people, fellas, seen him is all I meant, cashin' his check by Stachula's when the place was crowded. Konstanty cashes checks if he knows you. Say, I even know the project that old man was on far as that goes, because my old lady wanted we should give up the store so's I c'd get on it. But it was just me done it, Captain."

The raccoon coat readjusted his glasses. He would say something under a by-line like, "This correspondent has never seen a colder gray than that in the eye of the wanton killer who arrogantly styles himself *the lone wolf of Potomac Street*." He shifted uncomfortably, wanting to get farther from the wall radiator but disliking to rise and push the heavy chair.

"Where was that baldheaded pal of yours all this time?"

"Don't know the fella, Captain. Nobody got hair any more around the neighborhood it seems. The whole damn Triangle went 'n got army haircuts by Stachula's."

"Just you'n Benkowski I mean. Don't be afraid, son—we're not tryin' to ring in anythin' you done afore this. Just this one you were out cowboyin' with Benkowski on; were you helpin' him 'r was he helpin' you? Did you 'r him have the rod?"

Bicek heard a Ford V-8 pull into the rear of the station, and a moment later the splash of the gas as the officers refueled. Behind him he could hear Milano's heavy breathing. He looked down at his shoes, carefully laced all the way up and tied with a double bowknot. He'd have to have new laces mighty soon or else start tying them with a single bow.

"That Benkowski's sort of a toothless monkey used to go on at the City Garden at around one hundred eighteen pounds, ain't he?"

"Don't know the fella well enough t' say."

"Just from seein' him fight though, what'd you judge he'd weigh in at?"

"I only seen him fight once 'r twice is all. 'N he wore a mouthpiece, I couldn't tell about his teeth. Seems to me he came about one thirty-three, if he's the same fella you're thinkin' of, Captain."

"I guess you fought at the City Garden once 'r twice yourself, ain't you?"

"Oh, once 'r twice."

"How'd you make out, Left'?"

"Won 'em both on K.O.'s. Stopped both fights in the first. One was against that boogie from the Savoy. If he woulda got up I woulda killed him fer life. Fer Christ I would. I didn't know I could hit like I can."

"With Benkowski in your corner both times?"

"Oh no, sir."

"That's a bloodsuckin' lie. I seen him in your corner with my own eyes the time you won off Cooney from the C. Y. O. He's your manager, jackroller."

"I didn't say he wasn't."

"You said he wasn't secondin' you."

"He don't."

"Who does?"

"The Finger."

"You told me the Finger was your hex-man. Make up your mind."

"He does both, Captain. He handles the bucket 'n sponge 'n in between he fingers the guy I'm fightin', 'n if it's close he fingers the ref 'n judges. Finger, he never losed a fight. He waited for the boogie outside the dressin' room 'n pointed him clear to the ring. He win that one for me awright." The boy spun the frayed greenish cap in his hand in a concentric circle about his index finger, remembering a time when the cap was new and had earlaps. The bright checks were all faded now to the color of worn pavement, and the earlaps were tatters.

"What possessed your mob to get their heads shaved, Lefty?"

"I strongarmed him myself, I'm rugged as a bull." The boy began to swell his chest imperceptibly; when his lungs were quite full he shut his eyes, like swimming under water at the Oak Street beach, and let his breath out slowly, ounce by ounce.

"I didn't ask you that. I asked you what happened to your hair."

Bicek's capricious mind returned abruptly to the word "possessed" that Kozak had employed. That had a randy ring, sort of: "What *possessed* you boys?"

"I fergot what you just asked me."

"I asked you why you didn't realize it'd be easier for us to catch up with your mob when all of you had your heads shaved."

"I guess we figured there'd be so many guys with heads shaved it'd be harder to catch a finger than if we all had hair. But that was some accident, all the same. A fella was gonna lend Ma a barber chair 'n go fifty-fifty with her shavin' all the Polacks on P'tom'c Street right back of the store, for relief tickets. So she started on me, just to show the fellas, but the hair made her sicker 'n ever 'n back of the store's the only place she got to lie down 'n I hadda finish the job myself. The fellas begun givin' me a Christ-awful razzin' then, ever' day. God, oh, God, wherever I went around the

Triangle, all the neighborhood fellas 'n little niducks 'n old-time hoods by The Broken Knuckle, whenever they seen me they was pointin' 'n laughin' 'n sayin', 'Hi, Baldy Bicek!' So I went home 'n got the clippers 'n the first guy I seen was Bibleback Watrobinski, you wouldn't know him. I jumps him 'n pushes the clip right through the middle of his hair—he ain't had a haircut since the alderman got indicted you—'n then he took one look at what I done in the drugstore window 'n we both bust out laughin' 'n laughin', 'n fin'lly Bible says I better finish what I started. So he set down on the curb 'n I finished him. When I got all I could off that way I took him back of the store 'n heated water 'n shaved him close 'n Ma couldn't see the point at all.

"Me'n Bible prowled around a couple days 'n here come Cat Nowogrodski from Fry Street you, out of Stachula's with a spanty-new sideburner haircut 'n a green tie. I grabbed his arms 'n let Bible run it through the middle just like I done him. Then it was Catfoot's turn, 'n we caught Chester Chekhovka fer *him,* 'n fer Chester we got Cowboy Okulanis from by the Nort'western Viaduct you, 'n fer *him* we got Mustang, 'n fer Mustang we got John from the Joint, 'n fer John we got Snake Baranowski, 'n we kep' right on goin' that way till we was doin' guys we never seen before even, Wallios 'n Greeks 'n a Flip from Clark Street he musta been, walkin' with a white girl we done it to. 'N fin'lly all the sprouts in the Triangle start comin' around with their heads shaved, they want to join up with the Baldheads A.C. they called it. They thought it was a club you.

"It got so a kid with his head shaved could beat up on a bigger kid because the big one'd be a-scared to fight back hard, he thought the Baldheads'd get him. So that's why we changed our name then, that's why we're not the Warriors any more, we're the Baldhead True American Social 'n Athletic Club.

"I played first for the Warriors when I wasn't on the mound," he added cautiously, "'n I'm enterin' the Gold'n Gloves next year 'less I go to collitch instead. I went to St. John Cant'us all the way through. Eight' grade that is. If I keep on gainin' weight I'll be a hunerd ninety-eight this time next year 'n be five-foot-ten—I'm a fair-size light-heavy right this minute. That's what in England they call a cruiser-weight you."

He shuffled a step and made as though to unbutton his shirt to show his proportions. But Adamovitch put one hand on his shoulder and slapped the boy's hand down. He didn't like this kid. This was a low-class Polack. He himself was a high-class Polack because his name was Adamovitch and not Adamowski. This sort of kid kept spoiling things for the high-class Polacks by always showing off instead of just being good citizens like the Irish. That was why the Irish ran the City Hall and the Police Department and the Board of Education and the Post Office while the Polacks stayed on relief and got drunk and never got anywhere and had everybody down on them. All they could do like the Irish, old Adamovitch reflected bitterly, was to fight under Irish names and get their ears knocked off at the City Garden.

"That's why I want to get out of this jam," this one was saying beside him, "so's it don't ruin my career in the rope' arena. I'm goin' straight. This has sure been one good lesson fer me. Now I'll go to a big-ten collitch 'n make good you."

Now, if the college coat asked him "What big-ten college?" he'd answer something screwy like "The Boozological Stoodent-collitch." That ought to set Kozak back awhile, they might even send him to a bug doc. He'd have to be careful—not *too* screwy. Just screwy enough to get by without involving Benkowski.

He scuffed his shoes and there was no sound in the close little room save his uneasy scuffling; square-toed boy's shoes, laced with a buttonhook. He wanted to look more closely at the reporter but every time he caught the glint of the fellow's glasses he felt awed and would have to drop his eyes; he'd never seen glasses on a string like that before and would have given a great deal to wear them a moment. He took to looking steadily out of the barred window behind Kozak's head, where the January sun was glowing sullenly, like a flame held steadily in a fog. Heard an empty truck clattering east on Chicago, sounding like either a '38 Chevvie or a '37 Ford dragging its safety chain against the car tracks; closed his eyes and imagined sparks flashing from the tracks as the iron struck, bounced, and struck again. The bullet had bounced too. Wow.

"What do you think we ought to do with a man like you, Bicek?"

The boy heard the change from the familiar "Lefty" to "Bicek" with a pang; and the dryness began in his throat again.

"One to fourteen is all I can catch fer manslaughter." He appraised Kozak as coolly as he could.

"You like farm work the next fourteen years? Is that okay with you?"

"I said that's all I could get, at the most. This is a first offense 'n self-defense too. I'll plead the unwritten law."

"Who give you *that* idea?"

"Thought of it myself. Just now. You ain't got a chance to send me over the road 'n you know it."

"We can send you to St. Charles, Bicek. 'N transfer you when you come of age."

The boy paused at that possibility, then feigned to feel better about it immediately.

"Why, a few years on a farm'd true me up fine. I planned t' cut out cigarettes 'n whisky anyhow before I turn pro—a farm'd be just the place to do that."

"By the time you're released you'll be thirty-two, Bicek—too late to turn pro then, ain't it?"

"I wouldn't wait that long. Hungry Piontek-From-By-The-Warehouse you, he lammed twice from that St. Charles farm. 'N Hungry don't have all his marbles even. He ain't even a citizen."

"Let's talk about somethin' else, Bicek. You know, somethin' you couldn't lam out of so fast 'n easy. Like the chair. Did you know that Bogatski from Noble Street, Bicek? The boy that burned last summer, I mean."

A plain-clothes man stuck his head in the door and called confidently, "That's the man, Captain. That's the man."

Bicek forced himself to grin good-naturedly. He was getting pretty good, these last couple days, at grinning under pressure. When a fellow got sore he couldn't think straight, he reflected anxiously. And so he yawned in Kozak's face with deliberateness, stretching himself as effortlessly as a cat.

"Captain, I ain't been in serious trouble like this before," he acknowledged, and paused dramatically. He'd let them have it straight from the shoulder now: "So I'm mighty glad to be so close to the alderman. Even if he is indicted."

There. Now they knew. He'd told them.

"You talkin' about my brother, Bicek?"

The boy nodded solemnly. Now they knew who they had hold of at last.

The reporter took the cigarette off his ear and hung it on his lower lip. And Adamovitch guffawed.

The boy jerked toward the officer: Adamovitch was laughing openly at him. Then they were all laughing openly at him. He heard their derision, and a red rain danced one moment before his eyes; when the red rain was past Kozak was sitting back easily, regarding him with the expression of a man who has just been swung at and missed and plans to use the provocation without undue haste. The captain's nickname rang in the boy's brain and touched his tongue without being spoken: *King Kong! King Kong!* King Kong didn't look like the sort who'd swing back wildly or hurriedly. He didn't look like the sort who missed. His complacency for a moment was as unbearable to the boy as Adamovitch's guffaw had been. He heard his tongue going, trying to regain his lost composure by provoking them all.

"Hey, Stingywhiskers"—he turned on the reporter—"get your eversharp goin' there, write down I plugged the old rumpot, write down Bicek carries a rod night 'n day 'n don't care where he points it—You, I go around slappin' the crap out of whoever I feel like . . ."

But they all remained mild, calm, and unmoved; for a moment he feared Adamovitch was going to pat him on the head and say something fatherly in Polish.

"Take it easy, lad," Adamovitch suggested. "You're in the query room. We're here to help you, boy. We want to see you through this thing so's you can get back to pugging. You ain't letting us help you, son."

Kozak blew his nose as though that were an achievement in itself, and spoke with the false friendliness of the insurance man urging a fleeced customer toward the door.

"Want to tell us where you got that rod now, Lefty?"

"I don't want to tell you anything." His mind was setting hard now, against them all. Against them all in here and all like them outside. And the harder it set the more things seemed to be all right with Kozak; he dropped his eyes to his charge sheet now and everything was all right with everybody. The reporter shoved his notebook in his pocket and buttoned the top button of his coat as though the questioning were over.

It was all too easy. They weren't going to ask him anything more, and he stood wanting them to. He stood wishing for them to threaten, to shake their heads ominously, wheedle and cajole and promise him mercy if he'd just talk about the rod.

"I ain't mad, Captain. I don't blame you men either. It's your job, it's your bread 'n butter to talk tough to us neighborhood fellas—ever'body got to have a racket 'n yours is talkin' tough." He directed this last at the captain, for Comiskey and Milano had left quietly. But Kozak was studying the charge sheet as though Bruno Lefty Bicek were no longer in the room. Nor anywhere at all.

"I'm still here," the boy said wryly, his lip twisting into a dry and bitter grin.

Kozak looked up, his big, windbeaten, impassive face looking suddenly to the boy like an autographed pitcher's mitt he had once owned. His glance went past the boy and no light of recognition came into his eyes. Bicek felt a panic rising in him: a desperate fear that they weren't going to press him about the rod, about the old man, about his feelings. "Don't look at me like I ain't *nowheres*," he asked. And his voice was struck flat by fear.

Something else! The time he and Dropkick had broken into a slot machine! The time he and Casey had played the attention racket and made four dollars! Something! Anything else!

The reporter lit his cigarette.

"Your case is well disposed of," Kozak said, and his eyes dropped to the charge sheet forever.

"I'm born in this country, I'm educated here . . ."

But no one was listening to Bruno Lefty Bicek any more.

He watched the reporter leaving with regret—at least the guy could have offered him a drag—and stood waiting for someone to tell him to go somewhere now, shifting uneasily from one foot to the other. Then he started slowly, backward, toward the door; he'd make King Kong call him back or tell Adamovitch to grab him. Halfway to the door he turned his back on Kozak.

There was no voice behind him. Was this what "well disposed of" meant? He turned the knob and stepped confidently into the corridor: at the end of the corridor he saw the door that opened into the courtroom, and his heart began shaking his whole body with the impulse to make a run for it. He glanced back and Adamovitch was five yards behind, coming up catfooted like only an old man who has been a citizen-dress man can come up catfooted, just far enough behind and just casual enough to make it appear unimportant whether the boy made a run for it or not.

The Lone Wolf of Potomac Street waited miserably, in the long, unlovely corridor, for the sergeant to thrust two fingers through the back of his belt. Didn't they realize that he might have Dropkick and Catfoot and Benkowski with a submachine gun in a streamlined cream-colored roadster right down front, that he'd zigzag through the courtroom onto the courtroom fire escape and—*swish*—down off the courtroom roof three stories with the chopper still under his arm and through the car's roof and into the driver's seat? Like that George Raft did that time he was innocent at the Chopin, and cops like Adamovitch had better start ducking when Lefty Bicek began making a run for it. He felt the fingers thrust over-familiarly between his shirt and his belt.

A cold draft came down the corridor when the door at the

far end opened: with the opening of the door came the smell of disinfectant from the basement cells. Outside, far overhead, the bells of St. John Cantius were beginning. The boy felt the winding steel of the staircase to the basement beneath his feet and heard the whining screech of a Chicago Avenue streetcar as it paused on Ogden for the traffic lights and then screeched on again, as though a cat were caught beneath its back wheels. Would it be snowing out there still? He wondered, seeing the whitewashed basement walls.

"Feel all right, son?" Adamovitch asked in his most fatherly voice, closing the cell door while thinking to himself: The kid don't *feel* guilty is the whole trouble. You got to make them *feel* guilty or they'll never go to church at all. A man who goes to church without feeling guilty for *something* is wasting his time, I say. Inside the cell he saw the boy pause and go down on his knees in the cell's gray light. The boy's head turned slowly toward him, a pious oval in the dimness. Old Adamovitch took off his hat.

"This place'll rot down 'n mold over before Lefty Bicek starts prayin', Boobatch. Prays, squeals, 'r bawls. So run along 'n I'll see you in hell with yer back broke. I'm lookin' for my cap I dropped is all."

Adamovitch watched him crawling forward on all fours, groping for the pavement-colored cap; when he saw Bicek find it he put his own hat back on and left, feeling vaguely dissatisfied.

He did not stay to see the boy, still on his knees, put his hands across his mouth and stare at the shadowed wall.

Shadows were there within shadows.

Shadows within shadows, all down the shadowed wall.

RETREAT
By Sally Benson
From the *New Yorker*

SALLY BENSON

was born Smith in St. Louis, Missouri in 1900, and named Sara Mahala Redway. She lived successively in New York City and Houston, Texas, but during the World War her family returned to New York. When she was nearly seventeen she got a job in the National City Bank, and two years later she married Reynolds Benson, at present director of athletics at Columbia University. She has one child, a daughter. Mrs. Benson was represented in the O. Henry Memorial Award Prize Stories of 1936 *with "Suite 2049," which appeared in the* New Yorker, *where most of her work has been published. That magazine not only accepted the first manuscript she sent them, which was her first story, but told her it was the best one they had ever received from an unknown author. She has had three collections of short stories published,* People Are Fascinating *(1936),* Emily *(1939), and* Junior Miss, *a Book-of-the-Month Club selection (1941).*

Although the sign on the stone gateway read "Maplewood Farm," the place was obviously not a farm. There were no fields of corn or wheat, no outbuildings, and, more particularly, no comforting smell of cattle and hay in the air. The main house was of stucco and stone, and a driveway ran from the gates to the rear, where it circled and widened to form a parking space. Beyond this a wide lawn stretched to the edge of the woods straight ahead, to a group of stucco cottages on the right and to a flower garden on the left, where rusty chrysanthemums and a few late pansies still bloomed. The trees on the lawn were large and well cared for. No dead branches showed through their bright, thin autumn leaves, and the cavities that time and disease had worn in their trunks had been treated and filled. Small tables, gay, striped-canvas chairs, and swings were arranged about the lawn, but they were unoccupied, and an atmosphere of futility hung over the entire place.

In her bedroom on the second floor of the main house Marion Douglas took a soft-green cardigan sweater from the bottom drawer of her bureau and slipped it on. Her room was small and cheerful, with pink-and-white flowered paper on the walls and a dressing table that she had brought from home. The dressing table had gay, ruffled skirts of dotted swiss, and its top was crowded with perfumes, creams, bath and face powders, six or seven small bottles containing various shades of nail polish, and a complete jade-handled manicure set.

Her window was open and she could see, more plainly now

that most of the leaves had fallen, the dirt road that curved sharply downhill. In the field beyond she caught a glimpse of scarlet sumac, fading clumps of yellow goldenrod, and deep-purple asters. She was smiling as she left her room and, catching sight of her face in the mirror, she noticed with satisfaction how well she was looking. She had allowed her straight, fine hair to grow and wore it brushed back from her forehead to a knot at the nape of her neck. She was thinner than she had been when she had come to Maplewood Farm, almost five months before, and her eyes were clear and not swollen from crying. Her skin showed a faint touch of powder and she used lipstick. There were fine, purplish-red veins high on her cheekbones.

In the hall a middle-aged woman in a printed silk dress sat reading a book. "Good morning, Miss Davis," Mrs. Douglas said.

The woman looked up from her book and smiled. "Why, *good* morning, Mrs. Douglas," she answered. "Don't we look well this beautiful day! On your way to the studio, I suppose?" The tone of her voice had an upward lilt and carried a note of determined optimism.

"Yes, I thought I might as well."

"Now then, you can't fool me!" Miss Davis exclaimed. "I just bet you can't wait to finish the little Madonna. How is she coming?"

Mrs. Douglas frowned and shook her head. "I'm having trouble with the blue in her robe. I'm terribly afraid it will turn darker when it's baked."

"Oh, I'm sure it won't!" Miss Davis said. "And if it does, you can try again. Try, try again, you know." She resumed reading. Her smile vanished abruptly and her face settled.

Mrs. Douglas walked down the wide, carpeted stairs to the hall. The door of Dr. Scott's office was open, and she saw that he was sitting at his desk, looking absent-mindedly out of the window.

"Good morning," she said.

He turned his head quickly. "Oh, good morning, good morning, Mrs. Douglas. Beautiful day, isn't it? Good to be alive a day like today."

"Yes, indeed it is," she said.

"On your way to the studio? How's the Madonna coming?"

"I'm a little worried about her," Mrs. Douglas said.

"She'll turn out all right," he said. "Just you wait and see. Why, yesterday Mrs. MacLaren was about ready to give up doing her rug, and today she told me she'd fixed it. Rome wasn't built in a day, you know."

"Yes, I know," Mrs. Douglas said.

"That's good! That's fine!" His gaze wandered once more toward the window.

Mrs. Douglas walked through the cool, dark sitting room with its comfortable couches and open fireplace to a passage-way that led to a side door. To the right of the door a dark, competent-looking young man sat at a switchboard.

"Hello, Harry," she said.

"Morning. One swell day, isn't it?"

"Beautiful," she agreed. She stopped for a moment to look at the announcements that had been thumbtacked on the bulletin board. The guests of Maplewood Farm were informed that a group of Negro singers would entertain them in the Recreation Room on Wednesday, October 30; that there would be a fancy-dress ball in the Recreation Room Saturday, November 2, from eight to eleven; that guests wishing to play contract from four to six on weekdays would kindly hand in their names to Mrs. Tennant before noon each day.

Although she had read the same announcements for the

last week, she reread them leisurely. Then, pushing the screen door open, she stepped out onto the path. The late October sun was almost hot as she walked down past the group of stucco cottages. She was later than usual and the cottages were deserted. There were four bedrooms, a bath, and a small sitting room in each cottage, and some people preferred them to the main house, when they were allowed a choice. Far back in the woods she could see Bardwell Hall, where she had been placed on her arrival at the farm. She remembered her narrow room—a hospital room, really—and the quiet ruthlessness of Miss Frank, her nurse. In Bardwell Hall the nurses wore uniforms. It was only in the main house and in the cottages that they wore their everyday clothes. Dr. Scott had told her the reason for it the day he told her that she must not think of herself as a patient any more. "You are our guest, Mrs. Douglas," he had said. "And we want you to feel at home. We want you to feel free to come and go as you please around the grounds, and if you would like to drive to the village to have your hair done or do a little shopping, just let Mrs. Tennant know, and she will arrange for a taxi and ride in with you." He laughed pleasantly. "Ladies have their vanity, you know."

He studied her sharply. "Miss Davis is in charge of your floor."

"Oh," Mrs. Douglas said. "But she——"

"I know. We found that so many of our guests felt that uniforms were unnecessary that we decided not to use them. Besides, we don't want you to think of Miss Davis as a nurse. Just believe that she is there to make you more comfortable. Now, this afternoon Dr. Andrews will have a little talk with you, and then we'll have an idea of what you like to do. Have you any hobbies?"

"No," Mrs. Douglas answered.

"That's too bad. We all should have a hobby. We'll see if we can't interest you in one."

No, Mrs. Douglas thought, hurrying past the path that led to Bardwell Hall, she had never had a hobby, unless you could count running a big house in Scarsdale a hobby, or driving young Pete and Larry and Jeanie to school every morning. Such things were not like collecting stamps or knitting socks for the Red Cross, but they took one's time just the same. After the marketing was done for the day you found you'd spent the entire morning at the A. & P. Then there was Jeanie home for lunch, and the afternoons that flew by, there was so much to do: golf or bridge at the club, lunches and matinees in New York, hairdressers and shopping, clothes to buy for Jeanie and the boys, and her own clothes to attend to. Then there were the evenings with big Pete, who was tireless in his search for things to do. She had been busy, rushed, and important. Leaving it all had made her hate the farm at first, and although she assured herself that she felt perfectly well physically she had cried for two whole weeks.

At the end of the row of cottages there was a path that led through the woods to the studio. Miss Dodge was in charge of the studio. She was a slender, blonde girl who wore a smock, and she helped those guests of Maplewood Farm who felt inclined to model small figures, animals, ash trays, or book ends out of clay. Mrs. Douglas had been at the farm three weeks before she visited the studio, and she still remembered how strange it had looked to her; there had been the statues of girls with leaves in their hair, their fingers and toes turning into branches, that sad, dark-eyed Carter Jones had done; there had been the dozens of horses and the minute ash trays made by Mrs. MacLaren. There had also been paintings, mostly half-finished, of sunsets, sunrises, still lifes, and others that merely expressed an emotion. They had made Mrs. Douglas laugh. "I could do better than that myself," she said, "and I've never had a lesson in my life."

"Why don't you?" Miss Dodge asked.

Before Mrs. Douglas knew what she was doing she had started on a still life—a pewter vase filled with forsythia. It turned out far better than she expected, in fact was so good that Dr. Andrews asked if he might have it to hang in his sitting room. The night she finished it she slept really well for the first time in weeks. After that she painted fifteen more pictures, and everyone agreed that she had a definite style. Then she took up modeling, starting with a pair of modernistic book ends and gradually working up to figures. She found she rather liked doing them, and, after all, it was better than sitting all day long in a canvas chair on the lawn, thinking of home, worrying about Jeanie, who was only eight, until the tears started and her eyes ached.

She became scornful of the less talented guests who spent their days in the weaving shop, making scarves and rugs on the hand looms. "It's all right, I suppose, if you can't do anything else," she confided to Miss Dodge. "But it does seem as though almost anyone could push threads in and out of those things. Why, my Jeanie did things every bit as good in kindergarten."

The studio door was open and Miss Dodge was poking at the fire in the kiln. Mrs. Douglas could see Carter Jones' legs below the edge of a screen that stood in one corner. He always worked behind a screen. She took her smock from its hook and walked over to the table where she had left her Madonna. The Madonna's hands were lifted in prayer, but her body was bent in submission.

"I've been looking at her all morning," Miss Dodge said. "She's quite the best thing you've done. I would have put her in myself, but I thought you'd like to be here at the ceremony."

"She isn't too bad," Mrs. Douglas said carelessly. But when she looked at the figure her heart raced and her cheeks flushed with excitement.

When the oven was ready Miss Dodge lifted the Madonna in and closed the door.

"I don't suppose there's much use in my hanging around," Mrs. Douglas said. She lit a cigarette, her eyes anxious. "I may go back for the mail and stop around here just before lunchtime."

"Why don't you?" Miss Dodge agreed. "It's such a heavenly day."

As Marion Douglas walked through the woods toward the main house she remembered that tonight was the night for Pete to call. He called just once a week, because, as Dr. Scott had explained, sometimes one needed a rest even from one's own family. Failing to realize that, he added, would be unfair to the family as well as to herself, as he hoped she would see. He was referring, she knew, to the scene she had made the night they had moved her from Bardwell Hall to the main house. There was a telephone in every room in the main house, and she had thought her heart would burst when she saw the one on the table by her bed. By lifting the receiver, she could call Pete and talk to little Pete and Larry and Jeanie. She closed the door of her room and lifted the phone. Harry at the switchboard answered and she gave him her home number. There was a long silence while she waited, and her hands shook so that she had to rest her elbows on the table. After a few minutes she clicked the hook sharply up and down, and Harry's voice answered again. "I'm sorry, Mrs. Douglas, but I have orders that you are to have no outside calls for a while."

"Listen," she said, "I am just calling my home. I just want to know if they are all right. I just want to speak to them for a minute. I'm not going to tell them anything. Why, I wasn't even going to ask them to come get me."

"I'm sorry, Mrs. Douglas," he repeated. And the telephone went dead.

She had flown into a rage and torn the telephone from the wall. With incredible speed she had rushed past Miss Davis and down the stairs and out the front door to the driveway. She was almost at the gates when they caught up with her.

The next day her phone had been connected again, and Dr. Scott had explained how things were. Her husband, he said, would call her once a week. Pete, it seemed, had agreed with them that it was better that way.

At first her talks with Pete had been stormy, but as the weeks went by they became calmer, until now it was almost as though she and Pete had nothing to say to one another.

"Oh, hello there, Pete."

"Hello there, Marion. How's every little thing?"

"Fine. How are you?"

"I'm swell."

"How are the boys?"

"Young Pete's playing tennis and Larry's caddying at the club. They said they were going to write you tonight."

"How's Jeanie?"

"She's fine. She's out somewhere. Say, I sent you some magazines and stuff."

"Oh, that's good. The library here isn't—well, *you* know."

"I can imagine. Anything else you want?"

"Well, I was thinking I might like my bed jacket. It's hanging in my closet, to the far right."

"O.K. Anything else?"

"Nothing I can think of now. If there is, I'll let you know."

"Well, be good to yourself."

"You take care of *yourself*. And give my love to the children."

"Sure thing."

"Good-by, Pete, darling."

"Good-by."

As she crossed the lawn to the house she noticed that there were a few people sitting in the canvas chairs in the sun. And seeing Mrs. Tennant coming out of one of the cottages, she called to her, "How about some bridge later?"

"Splendid!" Mrs. Tennant called back. "We were looking for a fourth. I have a grand partner for you. You haven't met her. She used to be a bridge teacher."

Mrs. Douglas went into the house. "I put your mail and a big package that came for you in your room," Harry said.

"Good! I wonder what it is."

She hurried through the living room and up the stairs. Miss Davis was not in the hall. She opened the door to her room and shut it behind her. On her bed was a huge package, with some letters and magazines lying beside it. Going to her dressing table, she picked up her manicure scissors and cut the strings. The package had been carefully wrapped, and it was some minutes before she could get it open. It was a portable victrola and enclosed with it was a record and a note from Pete. "Dear Marion," she read, "this is the only record I could think of that I was sure you would like. When you get tired of it, make a list of what you want and I'll mail more on to you. Love, Pete."

She set the victrola on the table by her bed and, stooping down, disconnected her lamp and plugged the victrola in. She took a needle from the box, screwed it in, and turned on the switch. The record was not labeled, and she waited with a pleasant sense of anticipation for the tubes to warm up. She swung the arm of the victrola to the edge of the record. Pete's voice, loud and clear, filled the room. "This is the Douglas Studio broadcasting. We are a small company, and if we make a few mistakes the audience will kindly overlook them."

There was a pause, and Marion Douglas could hear faint laughter and the sound of scuffling. Someone whispered, "Closer, Jeanie, closer." And then Jeanie's voice came, uneven and trembling.

"Hello, Mummie," she said. "This is Jeanie speaking to you. We are having a nice time, but we miss you and hope you are lots better. Come home soon, Mummie. Come home soon."

Marion Douglas snatched the wire from the socket and threw herself across the bed. For a minute she lay quiet with her hands to her ears, and then she began to cry. "Oh, my God," she sobbed, "I've got to get out of here! Oh, my God, I've got to get out of here!"

Her voice rose, and the door of her room opened. "Mrs. Douglas! Mrs. Douglas!" Miss Davis said.

"Get away from me. Get the hell away from me!"

She reached for her pillow and threw it at Miss Davis. And as she did so she could hear feet running up the stairs. For some reason the sound frightened her and she clutched her hands tightly over her mouth so that whoever was coming would not catch her screaming.

I'M GOING TO ASIA
By John Cheever
From *Harper's Bazaar*

JOHN CHEEVER

was born in 1912, in Quincy, Massachusetts. He attended Thayer Academy in Braintree, Massachusetts, and has lived since in Washington, D.C., and New York City. His stories have appeared in the New Yorker *over a period of years, as well as in* Harper's Bazaar, Mademoiselle, Collier's, Atlantic Monthly, New Republic, Yale Review, *and* Story. *At present he is working on a novel.*

It was a Sunday evening and the Towle family sat on the terrace, admiring the familiar scenery. There were Mr. and Mrs. Towle, Mr. Towle's mother, Bill and Freddy, their two sons, and Carole, Bill's fiancée. Old Mrs. Towle sat a little apart from the group. Freddy was sprawled on the floor, nursing a drink. Bill sat on the hammock, holding Carole's hand. They were listening to a news broadcast from a portable radio. The announcer was sobbing with emotion.

When the news broadcast ended and a band began to play dance music Freddy turned off the radio. "You can all thank your lucky stars that you haven't any foreign investments," old Mrs. Towle said. Then she leaned forward in her chair and asked: "Isn't that someone on our pier, don't I hear someone talking?" The sound she had heard was a boat's wash breaking on the shore. When she realized this she laughed. "I haven't been near the water for such a long time that when I hear the waves breaking I think it's somebody talking or walking around on the pier," she explained. "I got up in the middle of the night because I thought I heard someone walking around on the pier. It was just the water."

"The news makes me sick," Freddy said quietly. He put a hand to his stomach.

"You know when I get old," Carole said, "I'm going to overdress. I think old age is such a good excuse for overdressing."

"We'll all spend the rest of our lives in uniform," Freddy said.

"I wish Helen Hughes were here," old Mrs. Towle said.

"Who, Mother?"

"Helen Hughes."

"But she's dead. She's been dead a long time."

"Yes, I know, but I just wish she were here. She always enjoyed the mountain scenery so much; she always thought the Adirondacks were more beautiful than anything in Europe."

"A damned sight safer than anything in Europe," Freddy said.

The light was going off the water. The changes of light on the water and on the mountains held their interest. They were people with the city in their blood, and for them the country was like some reassuring and ingenuous imitation of the past.

"I'm going to Asia," Carole broke in, "and I'm going to take a bathtub."

"I'm going to Asia," Bill said, "and I'm going to take an anesthetic."

"Oh, is it my turn?" Mrs. Towle asked. She was knitting on a large gray sock. "I never can understand this game. Let me see. Well, I guess I'm going to Asia and I'm going to take an icebox."

"You can't go to Asia, Mother," Carole said.

"There," old Mrs. Towle said, when the wash from another boat broke among the stones. "It does sound like somebody talking, talking or walking around, doesn't it? If you're not thinking about it, that is."

"I'm going to Asia and I'm going to take a trunk," Mr. Towle said.

"Antwerp, Liége, Amiens, Beauvais," Freddy said, "I've been to all of them. They're all ruins now. When I took the bicycle trip I went to all of those places."

"Would you like to go to Asia?" Carole asked old Mrs. Towle.

"Oh yes," she said, "I'd love to go to Asia. Let me see. I'm going to Asia and I'm going to take a dress."

"Sorry," Carole said, "you can't go to Asia. Freddy?"

"What have the others taken?"

"I'm taking a bathtub and Bill took an anesthetic and Mr. Towle took a trunk."

"I'm taking a horse," Freddy said.

"You can go to Asia."

"Oh, Charles, I forgot to tell you," Mrs. Towle said to her husband, "I sent that check you gave me for the bills to the English Speaking Union to buy yarn for socks."

"You shouldn't have done that, Louise. I don't mind giving a small contribution but we can't give away that kind of money now." He dropped his arms and said sadly: "I once paid five hundred dollars for a bowl of beef stew. That was at the Waldorf, for Near East Relief."

"Want to go for a dip?" Bill whispered to Carole. She agreed, and they got up and walked down toward the boathouse. They left the hammock swinging and the rusty chains gave off a grating and regular noise. "They don't have coffee," Freddy said, "they don't have butter. They don't have whisky, they don't have homes. At one meal we eat more meat than anybody in Europe sees in six months."

"I hope this sock isn't going to be too big," Mrs. Towle said, holding up the sock. "I always imagine soldiers as having big feet, although I suppose some of them have small feet just like everybody else." She waited for the sound of Carole and Bill, closing the locker doors in the boathouse, and then she continued in a low voice: "It makes me so happy to see them together. They're so happy. The only thing I want is to see my sons happily married and to have a few grandchildren. If you were only married, Freddy, I wouldn't ask for anything more."

Freddy laughed unpleasantly. "This is a fine time to get married. This is a swell year to get married. Maybe I'll have to go to war. I'll be in the first draft. Maybe I'll be killed. This is a swell time to get married. No, thank you."

"You take it too hard, Freddy."

"That's what you think now."

"Aunt Annie used to feel like that," Mrs. Towle said quietly. "After the World War when there was all that trouble in Armenia we had her for Thanksgiving dinner and for a minute there I thought she was going to throw the turkey at your father. 'Turkey,' she said, 'turkey! You people are eating turkey and the Armenians are starving.' Why, she used to——"

"Well, she wasn't so crazy," Freddy cried suddenly and angrily. "She wasn't so dumb. She knew something was wrong. The thing that kills me is the surprise you people have coming. You just sit around here as if nothing had happened. Well, something has happened. Our world has ended. It's the end of our world. In every way. It's all over."

"Don't talk to your mother like that, Freddy," Mr. Towle said.

"I'm not telling her anything that will hurt her. I'm telling her something she ought to know. It isn't going to be like this any more. We're nice people and there isn't going to be room for nice people any more. It's ended, it's all over, it's dead. She ought to know it. She ought to realize it." He turned his back on them and took his head in his hands.

From below they heard the sound of running footsteps on the pier. "Is it freezing?" they heard Carole shout. There was no reply and she called out the question again.

"No, not very," Bill shouted. The embrace of cold water forced his voice.

"Well, here goes," they heard Carole shout, and then there was a splash.

"It's not bad, is it?" Bill shouted.

"No, it's not bad but it's not exactly like a bathtub."

"Sissy."

"Sissy yourself."

"Come over here."

"No, let go of me, let go of me, Bill."

They could still hear their voices when Carole and Bill left the water for the boathouse. "When we get married," Bill said, "I'll build you a swimming pool with hot water. I'll build you a big glassed-in swimming pool in our house in Westchester, our big house in Westchester."

"I want to live on Long Island," Carole said.

"Oh, so you want to live on Long Island. And I suppose when we have a son you'll want to name him Michael."

"Sure, that's a nice name."

"And you'll want to name our daughter Eulalie."

"Sure." There was the sound of a struggle and then Carole giggled. "Stop it, Bill. Stop it. Ouch! Stop it."

Mr. Towle slapped at a mosquito on his ankle.

"I don't see why if I took a dress I couldn't go to Asia," old Mrs. Towle said crossly. "I don't like that game. I don't understand it."

"Next year I'd like to remodel the barn," Mrs. Towle said, "so that when Carole and Bill come up here after they're married they can be near us and still have a house of their own. The Taylors remodeled their barn and when they were through with it, it was much nicer than the house. We could make a fireplace out of the old stone wall and knock some dormers into the roof. After we've gone Freddy and his wife can have the house and Carole and Bill can have the barn." She dropped her knitting tiredly. "I'd like to go to Asia," she said. "There isn't any war in Asia, is there? Or is there?"

HOOK
By Walter Van Tilburg Clark
From the *Atlantic Monthly*

WALTER VAN TILBURG CLARK

was born August 3, 1909, in a cabin on Toddy Pond, East Oreland, Maine, near Bucksport. His father was a teacher at College of the City of New York, and when Mr. Clark was four the family moved to a farm in West Nyack. When he was eight the family migrated to Reno, where his father became president of the State University of Nevada. Except for one summer at Stanford he did all his undergraduate work there, as well as graduate work in English. He received a fellowship for two years at the University of Vermont, and was married during his second year. He taught one summer at C.C.N.Y., but for the past five years has taught school in Cazenovia, New York, and coached sports and dramatics. He is on a leave of absence this year on a ranch in Nevada, with his wife, their two small children, and one large dog. At first most of his work was verse. His novel, The Ox-Bow Incident (1940), *was well received by the critics. His first published short story was "Hook." One of Mr. Clark's hobbies is watching birds and animals, wild or tame, and being in wild places.*

Hook, the hawks' child, was hatched in a dry spring among the oaks beside the seasonal river, and was struck from the nest early. In the drouth his single-willed parents had to extend their hunting ground by more than twice, for the ground creatures upon which they fed died and dried by the hundreds. The range became too great for them to wish to return and feed Hook, and when they had lost interest in each other they drove Hook down into the sand and brush and went back to solitary courses over the bleaching hills.

Unable to fly yet, Hook crept over the ground, challenging all large movements with recoiled head, erected rudimentary wings, and the small rasp of his clattering beak. It was during this time of abysmal ignorance and continual fear that his eyes took on the first quality of hawk, that of being wide, alert, and challenging. He dwelt, because of his helplessness, among the rattling brush which grew between the oaks and the river. Even in his thickets, and near the water, the white sun was the dominant presence. Except in the dawn, when the land wind stirred, or in the late afternoon, when the sea wind became strong enough to penetrate the half-mile inland to this turn in the river, the sun was the major force, and everything was dry and motionless under it. The brush, small plants and trees alike, husbanded the little moisture at their hearts; the moving creatures waited for dark, when sometimes the sea fog came over and made a fine, soundless rain which relieved them.

The two spacious sounds of his life environed Hook at this time. One was the great rustle of the slopes of yellowed wild wheat, with over it the chattering rustle of the leaves of the California oaks, already as harsh and individually tremulous as in autumn. The other was the distant whisper of the foaming edge of the Pacific, punctuated by the hollow shoring of the waves. But these Hook did not yet hear, for he was attuned by fear and hunger to the small, spasmodic rustlings of live things. Dry, shrunken, and nearly starved, and with his plumage delayed, he snatched at beetles, dragging in the sand to catch them. When swifter and stronger birds and animals did not reach them first, which was seldom, he ate the small silver fish left in the mud by the failing river. He watched, with nearly chattering beak, the quick, thin lizards pause, very alert, and raise and lower themselves, but could not catch them because he had to raise his wings to move rapidly, which startled them.

Only one sight and sound not of his world of microscopic necessity was forced upon Hook. That was the flight of the big gulls from the beaches, which sometimes, in quealing play, came spinning back over the foothills and the river bed. For some inherited reason the big, ship-bodied birds did not frighten Hook, but angered him. Small and chewed-looking, with his wide, already yellowing eyes glaring up at them, he would stand in an open place on the sand in the sun and spread his shaping wings and clatter his bill like shaken dice. Hook was furious about the swift, easy passage of gulls.

His first opportunity to leave off living like a ground owl came accidentally. He was standing in the late afternoon in the red light under the thicket, his eyes half-filmed with drowse and the stupefaction of starvation, when suddenly something beside him moved, and he struck, and killed a field mouse driven out of the wheat by thirst. It was a poor mouse, shriveled and lice-ridden, but in striking Hook had tasted blood, which raised nest memories and restored his nature. With started neck plumage and shining eyes he tore and fed. When the mouse was devoured Hook had entered hoarse adolescence. He began to seek with a conscious appetite, and move more readily out of shelter. Impelled by the blood appetite, so glorious after his long preservation upon the flaky and bitter stuff of bugs, he ventured even into the wheat in the open sun beyond the oaks, and discovered the small trails and holes among the roots. With his belly often partially filled with flesh he grew rapidly in strength and will. His eyes were taking on their final change, their yellow growing deeper and more opaque, their stare more constant, their challenge less desperate. Once during this transformation he surprised a ground squirrel, and although he was ripped and wing-bitten and could not hold his prey, he was not dismayed by the conflict, but exalted. Even while the wing was still drooping and the pinions not grown back he was excited by other ground squirrels and pursued them futilely, and was angered by their dusty escape. He realized that his world was a great arena for killing, and felt the magnificence of it.

The two major events of Hook's young life occurred in the same day. A little after dawn he made the customary essay and succeeded in flight. A little before sunset he made his first sustained flight of over two hundred yards, and at its termination struck and slew a great buck squirrel whose thrashing and terrified gnawing and squealing gave him a wild delight. When he had gorged on the strong meat, Hook stood upright, and in his eyes was the stare of the hawk, never flagging in intensity but never swelling beyond containment. After that the stare had only to grow more deeply challenging and more sternly controlled as his range and deadliness increased. There was no change in kind. Hook had mastered the first of the three hungers which are fused into the single flaming will of a hawk, and he had experienced the second.

The third and consummating hunger did not awaken in Hook until the following spring, when the exultation of space had grown slow and steady in him, so that he swept freely with the wind over the miles of the coastal foothills, circling, and ever in sight of the sea, and used without struggle the warm currents lifting from the slopes, and no longer desired to scream at the range of his vision, but intently sailed above his shadow swiftly climbing to meet him on the hillsides, sinking away and rippling across the brush-grown canyons.

That spring the rains were long, and Hook sat for hours, hunched and angry under their pelting, glaring into the fogs of the river valley, and killed only small, drenched things flooded up from their tunnels. But when the rains had dissipated, and there were sun and sea wind again, the game ran plentiful, the hills were thick and shining green, and the new river flooded about the boulders where battered turtles climbed up to shrink and sleep. Hook then was scorched by the third hunger. Ranging farther, often forgetting to kill and eat, he sailed for days with growing rage, and woke at night clattering on his dead tree limb, and struck and struck and struck at the porous wood of the trunk, tearing it away. After days, in the draft of a coastal canyon miles below his own hills, he came upon the acrid taint he did not know but had expected, and, sailing down it, felt his neck plumes rise and his wings quiver so that he swerved unsteadily. He saw the unmated female perched upon the tall and jagged stump of a tree that had been shorn by storm, and, as if upon game, he stooped. But she was older than he, and wary of the gripe of his importunity, and banked off screaming, and he screamed also at the intolerable delay.

At the head of the canyon the screaming pursuit was crossed by another male with a great wing spread and the light golden in the fringe of his plumage. But his more skillful opening played him false against the ferocity of the twice-balked Hook. His rising maneuver for position was cut short by Hook's wild upward stoop, and at the blow he raked wildly and tumbled off to the side. Dropping, Hook struck him again, struggled to clutch, but only raked and could not hold, and, diving, struck once more in passage, and then beat up, yelling triumph, and saw the crippled antagonist sideslip away, half-tumble once as the ripped wing failed to balance, then steady and glide obliquely into the cover of brush on the canyon side. Beating hard and stationary in the wind above the bush that covered his competitor, Hook waited an instant, but, when the bush was still, screamed again, and let himself go off with the current, reseeking, infuriated by the burn of his own wounds, the thin choke-thread of the acrid taint.

On a hilltop projection of stone two miles inland he struck her down, gripping her rustling body with his talons, beating her wings down with his wings, belting her head when she whimpered or thrashed, and at last clutching her neck with his hook, and, when her coy struggles had given way to stillness, succeeded.

In the early summer Hook drove the three young ones from their nest and went back to lone circling above his own range. He was complete.

II

Throughout that summer and the cool, growthless weather of the winter, when the gales blew in the river canyon and the ocean piled upon the shore, Hook was master of the sky and the hills of his range. His flight became a lovely and certain thing, so that he played with the treacherous currents of the air with a delicate ease surpassing that of the gulls. He could sail for hours searching the blanched grasses below him with telescopic eyes, gaining height against the wind, descending in mile-long, gently declining swoops when he curved and rode back, and never beating either wing. At the swift passage of his shadow within their vision gophers, ground squirrels, and rabbits froze, or plunged gibbering into their tunnels beneath matted turf. Now, when he struck, he killed easily in one hard-knuckled blow. Occasionally, in sport, he soared up over the river and drove the heavy and weaponless gulls downstream again, until they would no longer venture inland.

There was nothing which Hook feared now, and his spirit was wholly belligerent, swift, and sharp, like his gaze. Only the mixed smells and incomprehensible activities of the people at the Japanese farmer's home, inland of the coastwise highway and south of the bridge across Hook's river, troubled him. The smells were strong, unsatisfactory, and never clear, and the people, though they behaved foolishly, constantly running in and out of their built-up holes, were large, and appeared capable, with fearless eyes looking up at him, so that he instinctively swerved aside from them. He cruised over their yard, their gardens, and their bean fields, but he would not alight close to their buildings.

But this one area of doubt did not interfere with his life. He ignored it, save to look upon it curiously as he crossed, his afternoon shadow sliding in an instant over the chicken- and crate-cluttered yard, up the side of the unpainted barn, and then out again smoothly, just faintly, liquidly rippling over the furrows and then the stubble of the grazing slopes.

When the season was dry, and the dead earth blew on the fields, he extended his range to satisfy his great hunger, and again narrowed it when the fields were once more alive with the minute movements he could not only see but anticipate.

Four times in that year he was challenged by other hawks blowing up from behind the coastal hills to scud down his slopes, but two of these he slew in mid-air, and saw hurtle down to thump on the ground and lie still while he circled; and a third, whose wing he tore, he followed closely to earth and beat to death in the grass, making the crimson jet out from its breast and neck into the pale wheat. The fourth was a strong flier and experienced fighter, and theirs was a long, running battle, with brief, rising flurries of striking and screaming, from which down and plumage soared off.

Here, for the first time, Hook felt doubts, and at moments wanted to drop away from the scoring, burning talons and the twisted hammer strokes of the strong beak, drop away shrieking and take cover and be still. In the end, when Hook, having outmaneuvered his enemy and come above him, wholly in control and going with the wind, tilted and plunged for the death rap, the other, in desperation, threw over on his back and struck up. Talons locked, beaks raking, they dived earthward. The earth grew and spread under them amazingly, and they were not fifty feet above it when Hook, feeling himself turning toward the underside, tore free and beat up again on heavy, wrenched wings. The other, stroking swiftly, and so close to down that he lost wing plumes to a bush, righted himself and planed up, but flew on lumberingly between the hills and did not return. Hook screamed the triumph, and made a brief pretense of pursuit, but was glad to return, slow and victorious, to his dead tree.

In all of these encounters Hook was injured, but experienced only the fighter's pride and exultation from the sting of wounds received in successful combat. And in each of them he learned new skill. Each time the wounds healed quickly, and left him a more dangerous bird.

In the next spring, when the rains and the night chants of the little frogs were past, the third hunger returned upon Hook with a new violence. In this quest he came into the taint of a young hen. Others, too, were drawn by the unnerving perfume, but only one of them, the same with which Hook had fought his great battle, was a fit competitor. This hunter drove off two, while two others, game but neophytes, were glad enough that Hook's impatience would not permit him to follow and kill. Then the battle between the two champions fled inland and was a tactical marvel, but Hook lodged the neck-breaking blow, and struck again as they dropped past the treetops. The blood had already begun to pool on the gray, fallen foliage as Hook flapped up between branches, too spent to cry victory. Yet his hunger would not let him rest until, late in the second day, he drove the female to ground among the laurels of a strange river canyon.

When the two fledglings of this second brood had been driven from the nest, and Hook had returned to his own range, he was not only complete but supreme. He slept without concealment on his bare limb, and did not open his eyes when, in the night, the heavy-billed cranes coughed in the shallows below him.

III

The turning point of Hook's career came that autumn, when the brush in the canyons rustled dryly and the hills, mowed close by the cattle, smoked under the wind as if burning. One midafternoon, when the black clouds were torn on the rim of the sea and the surf flowered white and high on the rocks, raining in over the low cliffs, Hook rode the wind diagonally across the river mouth. His great eyes, focused for small things stirring in the dust and leaves, overlooked so large and slow a movement as that of the Japanese farmer rising from the brush and lifting the two black eyes of his shotgun. Too late Hook saw, and, startled, swerved, but wrongly. The surf muffled the reports, and nearly without sound Hook felt the minute whips of the first shot, and the astounding, breath-breaking blow of the second.

Beating his good wing, tasting the blood that quickly swelled into his beak, he tumbled off with the wind and struck into the thickets on the far side of the river mouth. The branches tore him. Wild with rage, he thrust up, clattered his beak, challenging, but, when he had twice fallen over, knew that the trailing wing would not carry, and then heard the boots of the hunter among the stones in the river bed, and, seeing him loom at the edge of the bushes, crept back amid the thickest brush, and was still. When he saw the boots stand before him he reared back, lifting his good wing and cocking his head for the serpent-like blow, his beak open but soundless, his great eyes hard and very shining. The boots passed on. The Japanese farmer, who believed that he had lost chickens, and who had cunningly observed Hook's flight for many afternoons until he could plot it, did not greatly want a dead hawk.

When Hook could hear nothing but the surf and the wind in the thicket he let the sickness and shock overcome him. The fine film of the inner lid dropped over his big eyes. His heart beat frantically, so that it made the plumage of his shot-aching breast throb. His own blood throttled his breathing. But these things were nothing compared to the lightning of pain in his left shoulder where the shot had bunched, shattering the airy bones so the pinions trailed on the ground and could not be lifted. Yet when a sparrow lit in the bush over him Hook's eyes flew open again, hard and challenging, his good wing was lifted and his beak strained open. The startled sparrow darted piping out over the river.

Throughout that night, while the long clouds blew across the stars and the wind shook the bushes about him, and throughout the next day, while the clouds still blew and massed until there was no gleam of sunlight on the sand bar, Hook remained stationary, enduring his sickness. In the second evening the rains began. First there was a long, running patter of drops upon the beach and over the dry trees and bushes. At dusk there came a heavier squall, which did not die entirely, but slacked off to a continual, spaced splashing of big drops, and then returned with the front of the storm. In long, misty curtains, gust by gust, the rain swept over the sea, beating down its heaving, and coursed up the beach. The little jets of dust ceased to rise about the drops in the fields, and the mud began to gleam. Among the boulders of the river bed darkling pools grew slowly.

Still Hook stood behind his tree from the wind, only gentle drops reaching him, falling from the upper branches and then again from the brush. His eyes remained closed, and he could still taste his own blood in his mouth though it had ceased to come up freshly. Out beyond him he heard the storm changing. As rain conquered the sea the heave of the surf became a hushed sound, often lost in the crying of the wind. Then gradually, as the night turned toward morning, the wind also was broken by the rain. The crying became fainter, the rain settled toward steadiness, and the creep of the waves could be heard again, quiet and regular upon the beach.

At dawn there was no wind and no sun, but everywhere the roaring of the vertical, relentless rain. Hook then crept among the rapid drippings of the bushes, dragging his torn sail, seeking better shelter. He stopped often, and stood with the shutters of film drawn over his eyes. At midmorning he found a little cave under a ledge at the base of the sea cliff. Here, lost without branches and leaves about him, he settled to await improvement.

When, at midday of the third day, the rain stopped altogether and the sky opened before a small, fresh wind, letting light through to glitter upon a tremulous sea, Hook was so weak that his good wing also trailed to prop him upright, and his open eyes were lusterless. But his wounds were hardened and he felt the return of hunger. Beyond his shelter he heard the gulls flying in great numbers and crying their joy at the cleared air. He could even hear, from the fringe of the river, the ecstatic and unstinted bubblings and chirpings of the small birds. The grassland, he felt, would be full of the stirring anew of the close-bound life, the undrowned insects clicking as they dried out, the snakes slithering down, heads half erect, into the grasses where the mice, gophers, and ground squirrels ran and stopped and chewed and licked themselves smoother and drier.

With the aid of this hunger, and on the crutches of his wings, Hook came down to stand in the sun beside his cave, whence he could watch the beach. Before him, in ellipses on tilting planes, the gulls flew. The surf was rearing again and beginning to shelve and hiss on the sand. Through the white foam-writing it left the long-billed pipers twinkled in bevies, escaping each wave, then racing down after it to plunge their fine drills into the minute double holes where the sand crabs bubbled. In the third row of breakers two seals lifted sleek, streaming heads and barked, and over them, trailing his spider legs, a great crane flew south. Among the stones at the foot of the cliff small red and green crabs made a little, continuous rattling and knocking. The cliff swallows glittered and twanged on aerial forays.

The afternoon began auspiciously for Hook also. One of the two gulls which came squabbling above him dropped a freshly caught fish to the sand. Quickly Hook was upon it; gripping it, he raised his good wing and cocked his head with open beak at the many gulls which had circled and come down at once toward the fall of the fish. The gulls sheered off, cursing raucously. Left alone on the sand, Hook devoured the fish, and, after resting in the sun, withdrew again to his shelter.

IV

In the succeeding days, between rains, he foraged on the beach. He learned to kill and crack the small green crabs. Along the edge of the river mouth he found the drowned bodies of mice and squirrels and even sparrows. Twice he managed to drive feeding gulls from their catch, charging upon them with buffeting wing and clattering beak. He grew stronger slowly, but the shot sail continued to drag. Often, at the choking thought of soaring and striking and the good, hot-blood kill, he strove to take off, but only the one wing came up, winnowing with a hiss, and drove him over on to his side in the sand. After these futile trials he would rage and clatter. But gradually he learned to believe that he could not fly, that his life must now be that of the discharged nestling again. Denied the joy of space, without which the joy of loneliness was lost, the joy of battle and killing, the blood lust, became his whole concentration. It was his hope, as he charged feeding gulls, that they would turn and offer battle, but they never did. The sandpipers at his approach fled peeping, or, like a quiver of arrows shot together, streamed out over the surf in a long curve. Once, pent beyond bearing, he disgraced himself by shrieking challenge at the businesslike heron which flew south every evening at the same time. The heron did not even turn his head, but flapped and glided on.

Hook's shame and anger became such that he stood awake at night. Hunger kept him awake also, for these little leavings of the gulls could not sustain his great body in its renewed violence. He became aware that the gulls slept at night in flocks on the sand, each with one leg tucked under him. He discovered also that the curlews and the pipers, often mingling, likewise slept, on the higher remnant of the bar. A sensation of evil delight filled him in the consideration of protracted striking among them.

There was only half of a sick moon in a sky of running but far-separated clouds on the night when he managed to stalk into the center of the sleeping gulls. This was light enough, but so great was his vengeful pleasure that there broke from him a shrill scream of challenge as he first struck. Without the power of flight behind it the blow was not murderous, and this newly discovered impotence made Hook crazy, so that he screamed again and again as he struck and tore at the felled gull. He slew the one, but was twice knocked over by its heavy flounderings, and all the others rose above him, weaving and screaming, protesting in the thin moonlight. Wakened by their clamor, the wading birds also took wing, startled and plaintive. When the beach was quiet again the flocks had settled elsewhere, beyond his pitiful range, and he was left alone beside the single kill. It was a disappointing victory. He fed with lowering spirit.

Thereafter he stalked silently. At sunset he would watch where the gulls settled along the miles of beach, and after dark he would come like a sharp shadow among them, and drive with his hook on all sides of him, till the beatings of a poorly struck victim sent the flock up. Then he would turn vindictively upon the fallen and finish them. In his best night he killed five from one flock. But he ate only a little from one, for the vigor resulting from occasional repletion strengthened only his ire, which became so great at such a time that food revolted him. It was not the joyous, swift, controlled hunting anger of a sane hawk, but something quite different, which made him dizzy if it continued too long, and left him unsatisfied with any kill.

Then one day, when he had very nearly struck a gull while driving it from a gasping yellowfin, the gull's wing rapped against him as it broke for its running start, and, the trailing wing failing to support him, he was knocked over. He flurried awkwardly in the sand to regain his feet, but his mastery of the beach was ended. Seeing him, in clear sunlight, struggling after the chance blow, the gulls returned about him in a flashing cloud, circling and pecking on the wing. Hook's plumage showed quick little jets of irregularity here and there. He reared back, clattering and erecting the good wing, spreading the great, rusty tail for balance. His eyes shone with a little of the old pleasure. But it died, for he could reach none of them. He was forced to turn and dance awkwardly on the sand, trying to clash bills with each tormentor. They banked up quealing and returned, weaving about him in concentric and overlapping circles. His scream was lost in their clamor, and he appeared merely to be hopping clumsily with his mouth open. Again he fell sidewards. Before he could right himself he was bowled over, and a second time, and lay on his side, twisting his neck to reach them and clappering in blind fury, and was struck three times by three successive gulls, shrieking their flock triumph.

Finally he managed to roll to his breast, and to crouch with his good wing spread wide and the other stretched nearly as far, so that he extended like a gigantic moth, only his snake head, with its now silent scimitar, erect. One great eye blazed under its level brow, but where the other had been was a shallow hole from which thin blood trickled to his russet gap.

In this crouch, by short stages, stopping to turn and drive the gulls up repeatedly, Hook dragged into the river canyon and under the stiff cover of the bitter-leafed laurel. There the gulls left him, soaring up with great clatter of their valor. Till nearly sunset Hook, broken-spirited and enduring his hardening eye socket, heard them celebrating over the waves.

When his will was somewhat replenished, and his empty eye socket had stopped the twitching and vague aching which had forced him often to roll ignominiously to rub it in the dust, Hook ventured from the protective lacings of his thicket. He knew fear again, and the challenge of his remaining eye was once more strident, as in adolescence. He dared not return to the beaches, and with a new, weak hunger, the home hunger, enticing him, made his way by short hunting journeys back to the wild wheat slopes and the crisp oaks. There was in Hook an unwonted sensation now, that of the ever-neighboring possibility of death. This sensation was beginning, after his period as a mad bird on the beach, to solidify him into his last stage of life. When, during his slow homeward passage, the gulls wafted inland over him, watching the earth with curious, miserish eyes, he did not cower, but neither did he challenge, either by opened beak or by raised shoulder. He merely watched carefully, learning his first lesson in observing the world with one eye.

At first the familiar surroundings of the bend in the river and the tree with the dead limb to which he could not ascend aggravated his humiliation, but in time, forced to live cunningly and half-starved, he lost much of his savage pride. At the first flight of a strange hawk over his realm he was wild at his helplessness, and kept twisting his head like an owl, or spinning in the grass like a small and feathered dervish, to keep the hateful beauty of the wind rider in sight. But in the succeeding weeks, as one after another coasted his beat, his resentment declined, and when one of the raiders, a haughty yearling, sighted his up-staring eye and plunged and struck him dreadfully, and only failed to kill him because he dragged under a thicket in time, the second of his great hungers was gone. He had no longer the true lust to kill, no joy of battle, but only the poor desire to fill his belly.

Then truly he lived in the wheat and the brush like a ground owl, ridden with ground lice, dusty or muddy, ever half-starved, forced to sit hours by small holes for petty and unsatisfying kills. Only once during the final months before his end did he make a kill where the breath of danger recalled his valor, and then the danger was such as a hawk with wings and eyes would scorn. Waiting beside a gopher hole, surrounded by the high yellow grass, he saw the head emerge and struck, and was amazed that there writhed in his clutch the neck and dusty coffin-skull of a rattlesnake. Holding his grip, Hook saw the great thick body slither up after, the tip an erect, strident blur, and writhe on the dirt of the gopher's mound. The weight of the snake pushed Hook about, and once threw him down, and the rising and falling whine of the rattles made the moment terrible, but the vaulted mouth, gaping from the closeness of Hook's gripe, so that the pale, envenomed sabers stood out free, could not reach him. When Hook replaced the grip of his beak with the grip of his talons, and was free to strike again and again at the base of the head, the struggle was over. Hook tore and fed on the fine, watery flesh and left the tattered armor and the long, jointed bone for the marching ants.

When the heavy rains returned he ate well during the

period of the first escapes from flooded burrows, and then well enough, in a vulture's way, on the drowned creatures. But as the rains lingered, and the burrows hung full of water, and there were no insects in the grass and no small birds sleeping in the thickets, he was constantly hungry, and finally unbearably hungry. His sodden and ground-broken plumage stood out raggedly about him, so that he looked fat, even bloated, but underneath it his skin clung to his bones. Save for his great talons and clappers, and the rain in his down, he would have been like a handful of air. He often stood for a long time under some bush or ledge, heedless of the drip, his one eye filmed over, his mind neither asleep nor awake, but between. The gurgle and swirl of the brimming river, and the sound of chunks of the bank cut away to splash and dissolve in the already muddy flood, became familiar to him, and yet a torment, as if that great, ceaselessly working power of water ridiculed his frailty, within which only the faintest spark of valor still glimmered. The last two nights before the rain ended he huddled under the floor of the bridge on the coastal highway and heard the palpitant thunder of motors swell and roar over him. The trucks shook the bridge so that Hook, even in his famished lassitude, would sometimes open his one great eye wide and startled.

v

After the rains, when things became full again, bursting with growth and sound, the trees swelling, the thickets full of song and chatter, the fields, turning green in the sun, alive with rustling passages, and the moonlit nights strained with the song of the peepers all up and down the river and in pools in the fields, Hook had to bear the return of the one hunger left him. At times this made him so wild that he forgot himself and screamed challenge from the open ground. The fretfulness of it spoiled his hunting, which was now entirely a matter of patience. Once he was in despair, and lashed himself through the grass and thickets trying to rise, when that virgin scent drifted for a few moments above the current of his own river. Then, breathless, his beak agape, he saw the strong suitor ride swiftly down on the wind over him, and heard afar the screaming fuss of the harsh wooing in the alders. For that moment even the battle heart beat in him again. The rim of his good eye was scarlet, and a little bead of new blood stood in the socket of the other. With beak and talon he ripped at a fallen log, made loam and leaves fly from about it.

But the season of love passed over to the nesting season, and Hook's love hunger, unused, shriveled in him with the others, and there remained in him only one stern quality befitting a hawk, and that the negative one, the remnant, the will to endure. He resumed his patient, plotted hunting, now along a field on the land of the Japanese farmer, but ever within reach of the river thickets.

Growing tough and dry again as the summer advanced, inured to the family of the farmer, whom he saw daily stooping and scraping with sticks in the ugly, open rows of their fields, where no lovely grass rustled and no life stirred save the shameless gulls which walked at the heels of the workers, gobbling the worms and grubs they turned up, Hook became nearly content with his shard of life. The only longing or resentment to pierce him was that he suffered occasionally when forced to hide at the edge of the mile-long bean field from the wafted cruising and the restive, down-bent gaze of one of his own kind. For the rest he was without flame, a snappish, dust-colored creature, fading into the grasses he trailed through and suited to his petty way.

At the end of that summer, for the second time in his four years, Hook underwent a drouth. The equinoctial period passed without a rain. The laurel and the rabbit brush dropped dry leaves. The foliage of the oaks shriveled and curled. Even the night fogs in the river canyon failed. The farmer's red cattle on the hillside lowed constantly, and could not feed on the dusty stubble. Grass fires broke out along the highway and ate fast in the wind, filling the hollows with the smell of smoke, and died in the dirt of the shorn hills. The river made no sound; scum grew on its vestigial pools, and turtles died and stank among the rocks. The dust rode before the wind, and ascended and flowered to nothing between the hills, and every sunset was red with the dust in the air. The people in the farmer's house quarreled, and even struck one another. Birds were silent, and only the hawks flew much. The animals lay breathing hard for very long spells, and ran and crept jerkily. Their flanks were fallen in, and their eyes were red.

At first Hook gorged at the fringe of the grass fires on the multitudes of tiny things that came running and squeaking. But thereafter there were the blackened strips on the hills, and little more in the thin, crackling grass. He found mice and rats, gophers and ground squirrels and even rabbits, dead in the stubble and under the thickets, but so dry and fleshless that only a faint smell rose from them, even on the sunny days. He starved on them. By early December he had wearily stalked the length of the eastern foothills, hunting at night to escape the voracity of his own kind, resting often upon his wings. The queer trail of his short steps and great horned toes zigzagged in the dust and was erased by the wind at dawn. He was nearly dead, and could make no sound through the horn funnels of his clappers.

Then one night the dry wind brought him, with the

familiar, lifeless dust, another familiar scent, troublesome, mingled, and unclear. In his vision-dominated brain he remembered the swift circle of his flight a year past, crossing in one segment, his shadow beneath him, a yard cluttered with crates and chickens, a gray barn, and then again the plowed land and the stubble. Traveling faster than he had for days, impatient of his shrunken sweep, Hook came down to the farm. In the dark, wisps of cloud blown among the stars over him, but no moon, he stood outside the wire of the chicken run. The scent of fat and blooded birds reached him from the shelter, and also within the enclosure was water. At the breath of the water Hook's gorge contracted and his tongue quivered and clove in its groove of horn. But there was the wire. He stalked its perimeter and found no opening. He beat it with his good wing, and felt it cut but not give. He wrenched at it with his beak in many places, but could not tear it. Finally, in a fury which drove the thin blood through him, he leaped repeatedly against it, beating and clawing. He was thrown back from the last leap as from the first, but in it he had risen so high as to clutch with his beak at the top wire. While he lay on his breast on the ground the significance of this came upon him.

Again he leapt, clawed up the wire, and as he would have fallen, made even the dead wing bear a little. He grasped the top and tumbled within. There again he rested flat, searching the dark with quick-turning head. There was no sound or motion but the throb of his own body. First he drank at the chill metal trough hung for the chickens. The water was cold, and loosened his tongue and his tight throat, but it also made him drunk and dizzy, so that he had to rest again, his claws spread wide to brace him. Then he walked stiffly, to stalk down the scent. He trailed it up the runway. Then there was the stuffy, body-warm air, acrid with droppings, full of soft rustlings as his talons clicked on the board floor. The thick white shapes showed faintly in the darkness. Hook struck quickly, driving a hen to the floor with one blow, its neck broken and stretched out stringily. He leaped the still pulsing body and tore it. The rich, streaming blood was overpowering to his dried senses, his starved, leathery body. After a few swallows the flesh choked him. In his rage he struck down another hen. The urge to kill took him again, insanely, as in those nights on the beach. He could let nothing go; balked of feeding, he was compelled to slaughter. Clattering, he struck again and again. The henhouse was suddenly filled with the squawking and helpless rushing and buffeting of the terrified, brainless fowls.

Hook reveled in mastery. Here was game big enough to offer weight against a strike, and yet unable to soar away from his blows. Turning in the midst of the turmoil, cannily, his fury caught at the perfect pitch, he struck unceasingly. When the hens finally discovered the outlet and streamed into the yard to run around the fence, beating and squawking, Hook followed them, scraping down the incline, clumsy and joyous. In the yard the cock, a bird as large as he and much heavier, found him out and gave valiant battle. In the dark, and both earth-bound, there was little skill, but blow upon blow and only chance parry. The still squawking hens pressed into one corner of the yard. While the duel went on a dog, excited by the sustained scuffling, began to bark. He continued to bark, running back and forth along the fence on one side. A light flashed on in an uncurtained window of the farmhouse and streamed whitely over the crates littering the ground.

Enthralled by his old battle joy, Hook knew only the burly cock before him. Now in the farthest reach of the window light they could see each other dimly. The Japanese farmer, with his gun and his lantern, was already at the gate when the finish came. The great cock leapt to jab with his spurs, and, toppling forward with extended neck as he fell, was struck and extinguished. Blood had loosened Hook's throat. Shrilly he cried his triumph. It was a thin and exhausted cry, but within him as good as when he shrilled in mid-air over the plummeting descent of a fine foe in his best spring.

The light from the lantern partially blinded Hook. He first turned and ran directly from it, into the corner where the hens were huddled. They fled apart before his charge. He essayed the fence, and on the second try, in his desperation, was out. But in the open dust the dog was on him, circling, dashing in, snapping. The farmer, who at first had not fired because of the chickens, now did not fire because of the dog, and, when he saw that the hawk was unable to fly, relinquished the sport to the dog, holding the lantern up in order to see better. The light showed his own flat, broad, dark face as sunken also, the cheekbones very prominent, and showed the torn-off sleeves of his shirt and the holes in the knees of his overalls. His wife, in a stained wrapper and barefooted, heavy black hair hanging around a young, passionless face, joined him hesitantly, but watched, fascinated and a little horrified. His son joined them, too, encouraging the dog, but quickly grew silent. Courageous and cruel death, however it may afterward sicken the one who has watched it, is impossible to look away from.

In the circle of the light Hook turned to keep the dog in front of him. His one eye gleamed with malevolence. The dog was an Airedale, and large. Each time he pounced Hook stood ground, raising his good wing, the pinions torn by the fence, opening his beak soundlessly, and at the closest approach hissed furiously and at once struck. Hit and ripped twice by the whetted horn, the dog recoiled more quickly on several subsequent jumps, and, infuriated by his own cowardice, began to bark wildly. Hook maneuvered to watch him, keeping his head turned to avoid losing the foe on the blind side. When the dog paused, safely away, Hook watched him quietly, wing partially lowered, beak closed, but at the first move again lifted the wing and gaped. The dog whined, and the man spoke to him encouragingly. The awful sound of his voice made Hook for an instant twist his head to stare up at the immense figures behind the light. The dog again sallied, barking, and Hook's head spun back. His wing was bitten this time, and with a furious side blow he caught the dog's nose. The dog dropped him with a yelp, then, smarting, came on more warily as Hook propped himself up from the ground again between his wings. Hook's artificial strength was waning, but his heart still stood to the battle, sustained by a fear of such dimension as he had never known before, but only anticipated when the arrogant young hawk had driven him to cover. The dog, unable to find any point at which the merciless, unwinking eye was not watching him, the parted beak waiting, paused and whimpered again.

"Oh, kill the poor thing," the woman begged.

The man, though, encouraged the dog again, saying, "Sick him, sick him."

The dog rushed bodily. Unable to avoid him, Hook was bowled down, snapping and raking. He left long slashes, as from the blade of a knife, on the dog's flank, but before he could right himself and assume guard again was caught by the good wing and dragged, clattering and seeking to make a good stroke from his back. The man followed them to keep the light on them, and the boy went with him, wetting his lips with his tongue and keeping his fists closed tightly. The woman remained behind, but could not help watching the diminished conclusion.

In the little palely shining arena the dog repeated his successful maneuver three times, growling but not barking, and when Hook thrashed up from the third blow both wings were trailing and dark, shining streams crept on his black-fretted breast from the shoulders. The great eye flashed more furiously than it ever had in victorious battle, and the beak still gaped, but there was no more clatter. He faltered when turning to keep front; the broken wings played him false even as props. He could not rise to use his talons.

The man had tired of holding the lantern up, and put it down to rub his arm. In the low, horizontal light the dog charged again, this time throwing the weight on his forepaws against Hook's shoulder, so that Hook was crushed as he struck. With his talons up, Hook raked at the dog's belly, but the dog conceived the finish, and furiously worried the feathered bulk. Hook's neck went limp, and between his gaping clappers came only a faint chittering, as from some small kill of his own in the grasses.

In this last conflict there had been some minutes of the supreme fire of the hawk whose three hungers are perfectly fused in the one will; enough to burn off a year of shame.

Between the great sails the light body lay caved and perfectly still. The dog, smarting from his cuts, came to the master and was praised. The woman, joining them slowly, looked at the great wingspread, her husband raising the lantern that she might see it better.

"Oh, the brave bird," she said.

SEVEN BOYS TAKE A HILL
By David Cornel DeJong
From *Virginia Quarterly Review*

DAVID CORNEL DeJONG

was born in 1905 in Blija, Friesland, Holland. He came to the United States with his family when he was thirteen, and settled in Grand Rapids. Instead of becoming a minister he worked in a bank, in a cemetery, and as soda jerker in a drugstore. He was graduated from Calvin College, in Grand Rapids, and also studied at the University of Michigan and the University of Wisconsin. His poetry was printed in Pagany, *the* American Caravan, Midland, *and other magazines. He taught in high school, and then obtained a scholarship at Duke University, where he took his Master of Arts degree in two years. After this he had a fellowship at Brown University. He won third prize in the* O. Henry Memorial Award Prize Stories of 1939 *with his story "Calves," from* Esquire. *He has had published the novels* Belly Fulla Straw *(1934),* Old Haven *(1938), written on a Houghton, Mifflin fellowship,* Light Sons and Dark *(1940) and* Day of the Trumpet *(1941). He lives in Providence, Rhode Island, in the winter, and West Barrington, Rhode Island, in the summer.*

Though it was an unexpected school holiday, he had gone dutifully home to see if his uncle and aunt had anything for him to do. Immediately they had put their heads together, their voices rising and falling somewhat querulously beneath the chinaberry tree and blurred a little by the subdued zooming of flies and little bees. Evidently they couldn't come to any conclusion but kept bickering futilely as they separated. Aunt Morine scuffled into the house, and Uncle Steve stood looking out toward the hills, seeming actually to stand there half-tilted against the lushly swelling spring day with its rising tide of clean green and cloying odors, into which even the birds seemed to be flying lethargically. "Well, I dunno, Bram," his uncle said to him at last. "All the necessary work is done. . . ." He left the sentence unfinished, and poked with his shoe at the heavy-leaved weeds on which the fallen tree blossoms lay like supine stars.

"There's nothing?" he asked hopefully.

"No," his uncle answered, turning slowly. "Nothing, but that don't mean you're gonna go wandering off all alone over the hills, moping, keeping everything to yourself, even your breath, like your aunt says. I don't know why your father brought you up that way. But he was always a lone-goer too," he added almost wistfully. And then with more authority in his voice: "It ain't good for you, Bramford."

The boy nodded his head, unconvinced, but making that polite gesture of submission they expected of him here. All grownups expected it, perhaps because they wouldn't or couldn't understand simple ways and desires. As his father had. "Yes," he said then, making his submission final.

"You a growin' lad of fourteen," his uncle continued, again leaving all the significance in the unfinished part of his sentence, as if his purpose had floated away on the air like pollen. "A growin' lad . . ."

It was at that moment the six boys came shouting down the road and then came storming the fence behind which they had spied him and his uncle. "Come on, Bram," they yelled. "We're goin' exploring. He can come, can't he, Mr. Pearcefield?"

The man turned on them pleasantly, grimacing at the ringleader, Mose Cameron's boy. "Take 'im with you, kids," he said. "Take 'im off my hands."

Aside to Bram he added: "Now at least you won't be skulking around alone in the midst of snakes and lizards. Upsettin' your aunt. Now go and have fun with the boys."

Bram stood studying the boys. They were his own age, except Dizzy Cameron. So he didn't mind them. They wouldn't talk dirt, except Dizzy Cameron again. And they'd leave him alone, if he wanted that, all except Dizzy. "Thanks," he said to his uncle, joining the boys.

They went bouncing up the old wagon path that led into the hills. Jostling each other and making wild sallies for no reason at all upon a flowering Judas in full bloom, shaking petals off the dogwoods, scaring up a turkey buzzard from the carcass of a rabbit, they continued their way. But it was already warm, and their busy scurrying waned in the slow murmuring midmorning. Half a mile up they straggled off the wagon track and started singing "Carolina Moon" together.

Dizzy Cameron, poking Bram, asked suddenly: "Sounded like the old man was scared lettin' you go off alone. Why?"

"Snakes and lizards," he said, interrupting his singing.

"Aw, go on. You can't tell me that stuff," Dizzy jeered.

"Then I won't," he answered indifferently, singing again.

They weren't so bad, any of them, not even Dizzy. And Dizzy's whole trouble was getting grown-up too fast. That's why he'd rather talk dirt, why he kept his mind glued on dirt rather than on birds, snakes, and salamanders, all small living things. Grownups didn't, unless they grew up as his father must have. . . . He started stalking ahead, as if to escape from thinking about his father. Whenever he did, loneliness closed in around him like a fog, even when he was in crowds. He marched ahead with three of the boys, all four falling silent in the warm sun and the slow, all-enclosing perfume of the wild honeysuckle which covered the entire swamp here like a sweet mat.

He didn't mind them when they were quiet like this. But that wouldn't last. Now, having crossed a creek four times and traversed two hills and having reached the rocky ledges that protruded like black, humped beasts from the jungle-like undergrowth, he realized that he had actually led them where he had intended to go all the time. Of course they didn't know he was leading them. To them it was a desultory trek through swamps, woods, and open spaces, a trek that had no particular direction, that would eventually tire them out, whereupon they'd lie on the grass to rest and then go back home, sweaty and hungry. Only Dizzy was noisy, drumming a stick on an old bucket he had found. But none of them was really intent on what they were doing. It was a holiday; it was endless; it extended far beyond their immediate thoughts.

They were far past all houses here. The wild honeysuckle was draped wantonly even over high pines and tamaracks. Birds swooped languorously. Plunging into sudden heavy shade, the boys grew noisy again, unconsciously combating the vast and jealous silence of the trees. Bram stopped them before a brook widening shallowly between weed jungles. "Take off your shoes and stockings," he commanded, without intending it as a command.

Obediently three followed his example, two murmured and hesitated, and only Dizzy was raucous, yelling: "Gee, you ain't gonna make us wade through no snake holes, are you?"

"You don't have to," Bram said calmly.

"Think I'm scared, don't you?" Dizzy shouted.

"I don't know," he said, wading out into the shallow brook, letting the cool water slide past his ankles, feeling the black sediment, softer than velvet, beneath his feet. He sucked in his breath from the pleasure of it, not caring if Dizzy followed or not. Glad now he was the first, so his feet could leave slow blue-black clouds in their wake, before the others muddied it all up. They'd come close around him soon, scared of snakes and what not. They'd yell and muddle and then in a few minutes they'd go back on dry land, relieved. . . .

He was right. They came shouting behind him, jubilantly noisy, tagging closer as he waded farther under the dark undergrowth from which things darted and rustled. "Sure there's no water moccasins here, is there, Bram?" they asked anxiously.

"Guess not," he said with studied indifference, aware that they were becoming more quiet and wary as the water deepened. It was Dizzy who was closest behind him now, sloshing noisily, poking at the shore with a stick. He waded on, not looking back. It was dark here, the honeysuckle making a black cavern of the brook. Crows cawed at them to make it all the more cavernous and mysterious. They had fallen completely silent behind him now, and when he turned he saw that only Dizzy was following him still. All the others had climbed stealthily ashore. Dizzy, seeing him turn, said: "Thought I was scared, didn't you?"

"I don't know," he said.

Dizzy came abreast him, thrashing the water with his stick. Bram restrained him. "Look." He pointed at a large snake making a leisurely getaway, dignity in its marvelous undulations.

"Bram, it's a moccasin," Dizzy whispered, clutching his arm in fascinated terror.

"Naw," he started to protest. "Can't you see the markings? It's a king snake——" But then, solemnly looking at Dizzy, he added: "Well, supposin' it is a moccasin? It's going away from us, isn't it?"

"It's a moccasin," Dizzy gasped, leaping noisily toward shore. "You're crazy, Bram. You're as crazy as a coot." He danced frantically through the tangled weeds toward higher ground, bellowing terror with his young changed voice.

From safe higher ground he looked back at Bram. "Honest, no wonder your uncle thinks you're batty. No wonder . . ."

"Aw, there ain't no moccasins in this neck of Carolina," Bram said derisively. "Aw, go on. . . ." Losing interest in Dizzy, he started following the snake, keeping pace with it, till it disappeared under the roots of a tree. When he looked back Dizzy was no longer there. The voices of the others sounded subdued behind the trees. Then they became louder, Dizzy's raucous barks among them. He smiled. He was alone.

Slowly he trod through the velvety sediment, stepping high to keep the water clear. It was very dark and still here, so that the rustling of the fleeing lizards seemed like greater stillness, and the fanning of birds was a quietness that had somehow gotten wings. He came upon a small eddy with a whole colony of black water snakes, lifting their pensile heads from the slush to watch him, their eyes cobalt-blue scintillations in the deep shadows. "Moccasins," he murmured in disgust, watching the black snakes. "As if they'd ever seen one . . ."

The voices of the other boys sounded farther away. They were climbing the hill now, he figured. From time to time they shouted his name, half urgent, half lost. He didn't answer. It made his aloneness more complete that his name sounded in the distance, as if he had left it there behind him. He stooped and scooped up a small wriggling salamander and then let it swim on in clearer water, watching its flight. The black snakes moved lazily, each a few inches away from the others, watching him from slightly different places, the farthest with their heads lifted highest. A turtle dragged itself from the mud, its head like a banner over its glossy shell. Silent birds flitted away. One invisible bird shouted mischievously at him with a solemnly benign voice: "Ahweeh, ahweeh."

Again they shouted his name from the hidden hill. First six voices at once, then six voices separately. Someone drummed discordantly on the old bucket. Dizzy. All of them scared of snakes. Like grownups, ready to kill them, from sheer fear. Like his uncle clubbing that seven-foot chicken snake that had been in the henhouse since March, doing no harm, just lying there beautiful and calm on the shelf. His uncle clubbing it, till it was ten times dead . . . his aunt running around, yelling and shrieking: "It's that boy. You, Bramford Pearcefield, you. Practically living with rats and snakes and lizards. Tell you, Steve, it ain't good for the boy to have been with his father so long alone. . . ." with so much silly terror in both their faces that they'd better have worn masks.

Contentedly he waded on. Not to grow up. Not in that

fashion, he corrected himself, remembering his father. Not to fear, not to make unnecessary noises, unless you had to because they simply welled up in you. Hear and see small things, know them. Know that they watched you, too, thinking you clumsier and bigger than themselves. That's all. Have dignity like them, his father had said. "Then my heart stood still on that distant hill." He sang his father's song under his breath, his voice no louder than the water's gurgling. Judas trees showered blossoms; a mocking bird was tediously sonorous. No snakes here; only shoals of fine bright fishes darting everywhere. Then came a dense tangle of honeysuckle and creepers again, and the brook beneath went singing along the black rock ledges from which ferns dangled and spiders hung suspended like grotesque jewels. Far up the hill, accompanied by the drumming on the old bucket, the boys were still shouting his name, as if they were now simply in the habit of doing it, as if they had half forgotten him.

Then the silence had no bird voices contesting it, he realized. He heard only the cantankerous whining of one catbird from among the trees. Lizards made their whispering forages from beneath dead leaves and darted under them again, and here and there the head of a black snake or a turtle watched him. He knew then that everything was poised to an awareness for something alien. Not for him. Not for anything that now indented the silence. Certainly not for the drum's thudding and the distant cries of the boys, already nostalgically far: "Bram, hey, Bram . . ."

And then looking up to the ledge, between the trees curtained with creepers, he saw them. The man was sitting up and looking at him. Of the woman only a pair of run-down heels and soles were visible, silly spindly heels and worn soles. He came to a stop in the middle of the brook, staring up at the man. Now the woman was slowly rising too. He didn't like their red, shiny faces. Above all he hated them for being there. There were plenty of other places for couples like that, easier to reach, near roads; they needn't have come here to do their ridiculous mauling.

"What're you sneaking around here for, kid?" the man demanded.

"What's he want, anyway?" the woman said thickly, pushing at her hair.

"Damned kid, come sneaking up on us," the man growled, getting to his feet threateningly.

Slowly Bram waded on. "It ain't none of your business," he said under his breath. And louder: "And what are you doing here?"

"Come here, and I'll push your face in," the man shouted.

"Come here and try it," he said, not turning till he knew he was far beyond them. For a while longer he heard their voices. Then they fell silent. This had spoiled everything, however. Just the thing Dizzy would have liked to come upon and talk about for days after. Just the thing fools like that would be carrying out in a spot like this, with millions of other places in which to do their dirty work. He was indignant now and sulkily he started up the weedy bank of the creek, startling a ground bird. He sat down, letting his bare toes grovel in the soft black silt and then seeing something move on the opposite bank, he crossed over and found a sluggish toad hiding ridiculously beneath an altogether too small plantain leaf. Far away the boys were still shouting his name, more intermittently now. Eventually he'd have to go and retrieve his shoes. Eventually, too, he'd have to go back to the boys. He looked up at the sweet gum towering over him with honeysuckle shrouding its stem like a spread skirt.

Seven Boys Take a Hill

It wasn't that he actually wanted to know what they were doing. Certainly he would never talk about it. But there was that strange curiosity nagging at the periphery of his consciousness. To it his thoughts seemed to give very little heed, but his body was already obeying, as he started climbing the gum tree with noiseless dexterity. He went as silently as a savage, his actions actually beating his intentions. At first the tangles of honeysuckle obscured his view; then climbing higher, he could see the dark sheen of the brook, and there, but alone, the woman was lying on her back, her arm across her face and beside her, in the gleam of sunless light, an empty bottle.

"Fools," he breathed to himself. But where was the man? He did not hear the sound of feet snapping twigs or brushing through undergrowth. The woman was now straightening her skirts and fingering the bottle furtively. Then she yawned, and the light caught on her teeth and lipstick-smeared lips. Near him the catbird scolded. And directly beneath him he saw only the mat of honeysuckle and ivy above which the bees hummed with a great abstract noise that could easily swallow all sounds beneath it. Where was that man?

With sudden clairvoyant apprehension he seemed to know he was in danger. One last look at the woman, who seemed to have fallen asleep, and he stealthily climbed down the tree, sliding as noiselessly as a honey bear. He looked sharply around him as he neared the ground but saw nothing. Then just as he dropped himself from the lowest branch, as his feet touched the weeds, the man was upon him.

He made no sound. The man pinned his shoulders back against the tree stem and pushed his red face so close that Bram seemed to inhale the sour liquor breath. "What'd I tell you," the man growled, so low that his voice was hardly more than a whisper. "So you had to see what was going on. Well, what did you see?"

He didn't answer. He didn't even shake his head. They were there curtained by the honeysuckle, in fearful dusklike privacy.

"Well, you know what I said I'd do to you?" the fellow threatened. "I could"—he made his voice come insidiously low and lifted one knee and pressed it hard against the boy's stomach—"I could squeeze your guts out. You sneaking pup. . . ."

Then Bram's words come slowly, pushed out by violent anger, as he stared up at the fellow: "You just try. You . . ."

"And you'll what?" the man taunted, pressing his knee harder. But he tottered a little, unsteady on his one leg in his drunkenness. His lips stayed curled away from his stained teeth, and his breath fanned hotly as he added: "You sneaking cur. . . ."

But those were the last words he said, and they became a cutoff croak, not human, choking in his throat, as he lunged backward. The man's tottering on his one leg had given the boy a cue. Pushing himself violently away from the tree, so that the fellow lost his balance completely, he added a well-aimed kick at the man's belly. Too hard, because the fellow fell, a lump of impotent flesh, loose arms flaying, now stumbling backward over the algaed rock ledge flanking the brook and incongruously over it. Then the water splashed, and all that remained visible of him was one foot in a ridiculous canvas shoe, pointing upward from the rock. That foot twitched once or twice and then lay still. Then silence . . .

Bram breathed hard. He remained standing with his back against the gum tree, staring only at the protruding foot. Not till the catbird scolded again did he step forward to see what had happened. The man lay with his back in the water, which rippled very slowly against him, almost touching the corners of his open mouth. The one foot lay fantastically on the rock ledge; the other was caught behind a tough ivy creeper. With horrified fascination the boy kept staring down. "Serves you right, you fool," he said tensely, not knowing what to do. He kept watching, tense with terror. The fellow must be dead. Mechanically he moved to free the entangled foot but he stopped.

The woman was approaching, thrashing through the undergrowth, shouting querulously: "Hank, where the hell are you? I tole you to leave that kid alone. . . . Hank! Hank!" In the pauses, very distantly, he could still hear the boys shouting: "Oh, Bram. Oh, Bram." The thudding on the bucket continued, like the sound of a tribal drum. The woman came shouting: "Hank, Hank, you damned fool. Don't you go sneakin' out on me. . . ."

From the dusk-dark shadows he watched her come closer, a pink print dress through the leaves. He heard her grumble and stand still. His hand still lay two inches away from the man's caught foot. Below him the slow water eddied against the stupid red face, the mouth fallen open, the tongue curled.

The boy sat taut in wordless terror. The woman passed by, cursing: "Can't go sneakin' out on me, you . . . you lousy drunkard, you. . . ." She stumbled drunkenly on, then started yelling in a piercing voice: "Hank! Hank!"

The catbird above him scolded back at the woman. In the water black snakes curiously watched the half-submerged man. Then he saw the man's lips move slightly along a gray flickering of teeth. He wasn't dead! Not yet. The woman went on, shouting the man's name. Then in mad haste the boy pulled the man's foot free from the creeper. He sat hunched back in terror watching the fellow's legs gather themselves onto the fallen torso, as if they were inanimate. His breath stood still. The water churned darkly; the snakes slid away. The knees sank for a while against the body, folded incongruously back. Then the man started groveling, turning, his face stuck deep in the sediment now; but gradually he lifted himself on hands and knees. Then Bram saw where the back of his head must have struck against the rock. He ran.

Scurrying madly through the tangled growth, he dashed in the woman's direction first. She turned, hearing him. "You, you," she cried, shaking her finger loosely at him. "You . . ."

"Better get him," he yelled hoarsely, pointing back at the creek.

As she came stumbling toward him he ran again, dashing away from her and far around her to the spot where he had left his shoes and stockings. Tucking them beneath his arm, he continued running. His breath pounded the words out of him: "You did. You did. You made me. You could have made me kill you. You did. You fools. . . ."

At last, halfway up the slope, he came to a stop. Below him meandered the brook through the tropical, lush foliage. That fool woman was no doubt tugging the man out of the water by now. The fools, the stupid grown-up fools. He started pulling on his stockings, watching the far hill with a nigger cabin and a man walking behind a mule and over them four buzzards keeling. There was nothing else in the warm blue sky. He put his shoes on then, his eyes riveted unseeingly on the toadstools and boletes around him. Miserably he cried a little, pulling angrily at his shoestrings. His thoughts came madly, tripping over each other, leaving no sense or succor. "And they say, don't be alone," he murmured bitterly. "Then they say, you've gotta grow up; you've gotta associate with people. Then they say, quit hanging around with snakes and rats, and . . ."

Suddenly he jumped to his feet. Far in the distance the boys shouted his name again. The drum thudded, thudded, thudded. Madly he raced now, up one slope, down another, up a still higher one, and from that hill with its small pin oaks he looked down on the boys straggling desultorily among the trees, with Dizzy thudding two sticks on the old bucket. One of them shouted his name again. And at that moment he simply had to outrace his mad feelings, outrace his blood and the pounding of his heart, outrace everything that was cautious and planned and sane. . . .

He leaped, while they were shouting his name again, unaware that he was there. He charged down like a wild beast and he was practically upon them before they realized anything. Then five of them stared at him in dumb amazement, while Dizzy kept drumming on his bucket. He roared, as if his voice had suddenly changed, and pounced upon Dizzy, hurtling him to the ground, sending the bucket flying against a tree. "The enemy is upon you," he bellowed. "Fight or perish! Fight!"

Startled and indignant, Dizzy lay pinned beneath him, his face slowly contorting with fear. "Bram," he gasped, "for gosh sakes!"

"Gosh, look at Bram!" the others shouted.

He was going to pound the living breath out of Dizzy. He was going to tear him limb from limb. "You, you," he barked ineptly, and then he jumped to his feet. Dizzy kept lying on the ground, pale and disheveled.

"Gosh, Bram," one of the youngest boys gasped.

Suddenly he roared with mirthless laughter. Then, shouting madly, he pointed to the highest hill, a bare boulder-studded hill. "Take the hill, boys!" he shouted. "Take the hill. This is war. This is our last stand. Follow me!"

His wild voice and fierce eyes were contagious. They stared at him with unalloyed fascination. Then they started shouting too. "Get ready! Come on! Charge the hill!" he commanded.

"Come on!" they shouted, storming after him. Even Dizzy leaped to his feet and followed. The hill was steep and difficult, but madly, as if they had taken leave of their senses, they followed Bram. He got to the top first, but they were not far behind. They clustered around him as he raised his arm to the sky, proclaiming: "This hill we claim forever and ever. This hill is for boys only. No grownup shall ever take it from us."

"No grownup shall ever take it from us," they repeated in solemn intoxication. Even Dizzy joined in with his cracked adolescent voice. They looked at Bram's face for understanding, for further words.

Then they looked, too, where Bram was looking, down into the lush valley where they had been earlier, where now very distantly two figures were walking through the dark green, one a woman in pink. "They shan't take it from us," Bram repeated solemnly.

They repeated it in singsong incantation.

THE OLD PEOPLE
By William Faulkner
From *Harper's Magazine*

WILLIAM FAULKNER

is a native Mississippian who served as an aviator with the Canadian forces in World War I. His first novel, Soldier's Pay, *published in 1926, won him immediate recognition, and since then he has published many novels and short stories centering around the imaginary town of Jefferson, which closely resembles his place of residence, Oxford. He has made several appearances in this collection, the most recent being in 1940, when his "Hand upon the Waters" was included. In 1939 he was awarded the first prize for a story called "Barn Burning." He is a recognized master of the short narrative, even among people who find most of his novels difficult reading.*

At first there was nothing but the faint, cold, steady rain, the gray and constant light of the late November dawn, and the voices of the dogs converging somewhere in it. Then Sam Fathers, standing just behind me, as he had been standing when I shot my first running rabbit four years ago, touched me, and I began to shake, not with any cold, and then the buck was there. He did not come into sight; he was just there, looking not like a ghost but as if all of light were condensed in him and he were the source of it, not only moving in it but disseminating it, already running, seen first as you always see the deer, in that split second after he has already seen you, already slanting away in that first soaring bound, the antlers even in that dim light looking like a small rocking chair balanced on his head.

"Now," Sam said, "shoot quick and slow."

I don't remember that shot at all. I don't even remember what I did with the gun afterward. I was running, then I was standing over him where he lay on the wet ground still in the attitude of running and not looking at all dead. I was shaking and jerking again, and Sam was beside me, and I had his knife in my hand.

"Don't walk up to him in front," Sam said. "If he ain't dead he will cut you all to pieces with his feet. Walk up to him from behind and take him by the horn."

And I did that—drew the throat taut by one of the antlers and drew Sam's knife across it, and Sam stooped and dipped his hands in the hot blood and wiped them back and forth across my face. Then he blew his horn, and there was a moiling of dogs about us with Jimbo and Boon Hogganbeck driving them back after they had all had a taste of the blood. Then Father and Major de Spain sitting the horses, and Walter Ewell with his rifle which never missed, from the barrel of which all the bluing had long since been worn away, were looking down at us—at the old man of seventy who had been a Negro for two generations now but whose face and bearing were still those of the Chickasaw chief, and the white boy of twelve with the prints of the bloody hands across his face, who now had nothing to do but stand straight and not let the shaking show.

"Did he do all right, Sam?" Father said.

"He done all right," Sam Fathers said.

We were the white boy, not yet a man, whose grandfather had lived in the same country and in almost the same manner as the boy himself would grow up to live, leaving his descendants in the land in his turn, and the old man past seventy whose grandfathers had owned the land long before the white men ever saw it and who had vanished from it now with all their kind, what of blood they had left behind them running now in another race and for a while even in bondage and now drawing toward the end of its alien course, barren. Because Sam Fathers had no children.

His grandfather was Ikkemotubbe himself, who had named himself Doom. Sam told me about that—how Ikkemotubbe, old Issetibbeha's sister's son, had run away to New Orleans in his youth and returned seven years later to the plantation in north Mississippi, with a French companion called the Chevalier Soeur-Blonde de Vitry, who must have been the Ikkemotubbe of his family, too, and who was already addressing Ikkemotubbe as *Du Homme,* and the slave woman who was to be Sam's grandmother, and a gold-laced hat and coat and a wicker basket containing a litter of puppies and a gold snuffbox of white powder. And how he was met at the river by two or three companions of his bachelor youth, and with the light of a smoking torch glinting on the gold-laced hat and coat, Doom took one of the puppies from the basket and put a pinch of the white powder from the gold box on its tongue, and at once the puppy ceased to be a puppy. And how the next day the eight-year-old son of Doom's cousin, Moketubbe, who was now hereditary head of the clan (Issetibbeha was now dead) died suddenly, and that afternoon Doom, in the presence of Moketubbe and most of the others (the People, Sam always called them), took another puppy from the basket and put a pinch of the powder on its tongue, and so Moketubbe abdicated, and Doom became in fact the Man which his French friend already called him. And how Doom married the slave woman, already pregnant, to one of the slaves which he had just inherited—hence Sam Fathers' name, which in Chickasaw had been Had-Two-Fathers—and later sold them both and the child, too (his own son), to my great-grandfather almost a hundred years ago.

Up to three years ago he had lived on our farm four miles from Jefferson, though all he ever did was what blacksmithing and carpentering was needed. And he lived among Negroes, in a cabin among the other cabins; he consorted with them and dressed like them and talked like them and went to a Negro church now and then. But for all that, he was still the grandson of that Indian chief, and the Negroes knew it. Boon Hogganbeck's grandmother had been a Chickasaw woman, too, and although the blood had run white since and Boon was a white man, it was not a chief's blood. You could see the difference at once when you saw them together, and even Boon seemed to know that the difference was there —even Boon, to whom in his tradition it had never occurred that anyone might be better born than himself. A man might be smarter, he admitted that, or richer (luckier, he called it) but not better born. He was a mastiff, absolutely faithful to Father and Major de Spain, absolutely dependent upon them for his very bread, hardy, courageous enough, a slave to all the appetites and almost unrational. It was Sam Fathers who bore himself, not only toward Father but toward all white men, with gravity and dignity and without servility or recourse to that impenetrable wall of ready and easy mirth which Negroes sustain between themselves and white men, bearing himself toward Father not only as one man to another but as an older man to a younger one.

He taught me the woods, to hunt, when to shoot and when not to shoot, when to kill and when not to kill, and better, what to do with it afterward. Then he would talk to me, the two of us sitting under the close fierce stars on a summer hilltop while we waited for the dogs to return within hearing behind the red or gray fox they ran, or beside a fire in the November or December woods while the dogs worked out a coon's trail along the creek, or fireless in the pitch dark and the heavy dew of April mornings while we waited for daylight beneath a turkey roost. I would not question him; he did not react to questions. I would just wait and then listen, and he would begin, talking about the old days and the People whom he had never known and so could not remember himself, and in place of whom the other race into which his blood had run had supplied him with no substitute.

And as he talked about those old times and those dead and vanished men of another race from either that I knew, gradually those old times would cease to be old times and would become the present, now, not only as if they had happened yesterday but as if they were still happening, and some of them had not even happened yet but would occur tomorrow, so that at last it would seem as if I myself had not come into existence yet, that none of my race nor the other race which we had brought into the land with us had come here yet; that although it had been my grandfather's and was now my father's and someday would be my land which we hunted over and now rested upon, our hold upon it actually was as trivial and without reality as that now faded and archaic script in one of the chancery clerk's books in the courthouse in town, and that it was I who was the guest here and Sam Fathers' voice the mouthpiece of the host.

Until three years ago there had been two of them, the other a fullblood Chickasaw, in a sense even more astonishingly lost than Sam Fathers. He called himself Jobaker, as if it were one word. Nobody knew his history at all. He was a hermit; he lived in a foul little shack at the forks of the creek four or five miles from our farm and about that far from any other habitation. He was a market hunter and fisherman and he consorted with nobody, black or white; no Negro would even cross his path, and no man dared approach his hut except Sam, and perhaps once a month I would find the two of them in Sam's shop—two old men squatting on their heels on the dirt floor, talking in a mixture of Negroid English and flat hill dialect and now and then a phrase of that old tongue which, as time went on and I squatted there, too, listening, I began to learn. Then he died. That is, nobody had seen him in some time. Then one morning Sam Fathers was missing; none of the Negroes knew when nor where until that night when some Negroes, possum hunting, saw the sudden burst of flames and approached them. It was Joe Baker's hut, but before they got anywhere near it someone shot toward them. It was Sam, but nobody ever found Joe Baker's grave.

Two days after that Sam walked to town and came to Father's office. I was there when he walked in without knocking and stood there—the Indian, with the Indian face for all the nigger clothes.

"I want to go," he said. "I want to go to the big bottom to live."

"To live?" Father said.

"You can fix it with Major de Spain," Sam said. "I could live in the camp and take care of it for you all. Or I could build me a little house." For a little while they both looked at each other, he and Father. Then Father said:

"All right. I'll fix it." And Sam went out, and that was all.

I was nine then; it seemed perfectly natural to me that nobody, not even Father, would argue with Sam any more than I would. But I could not understand it.

"If Joe Baker's dead like they say," I said, "and Sam hasn't got anybody any more at all kin to him, why does he want to go into the big bottom where he won't ever see anybody except us for a few days in the fall while we are hunting?"

Father looked at me. It was not a curious look; it was just thoughtful. I didn't notice it then. I did not remember it until later. Then he quit looking at me.

"Maybe that's what he wants," he said.

So Sam moved. He owned so little that he could carry it. He walked. He would neither let Father send him in the wagon nor would he take one of the mules. He was just gone one morning, the cabin vacant in which he had lived for years yet in which there never had been very much, the shop standing idle now in which there never had been very much to do. Each November we would go into the big bottom, to the camp—Major de Spain and Father and Walter Ewell and Boon and Uncle Ike McCaslin and two or three others, with Jimbo and Uncle Ash to cook, and the dogs.

Sam would be there; if he was glad to see us he did not show it. If he regretted to see us depart again he did not show that. Each morning he would go out to my stand with me before the dogs were cast. It would be one of the poorer stands, of course, since I was only nine and ten and eleven and I had never even seen a deer running yet. But we would stand there, Sam a little behind me and without a gun himself, as he had stood when I shot the running rabbit when I was eight years old; we would stand there in the November dawns and after a while we would hear the dogs. Sometimes they would sweep up and past, close, belling and invisible; once we heard the five heavy reports of Boon's old pump gun with which he had never killed anything larger than a rabbit or a squirrel, and that sitting, and twice we heard from our stand the flat unreverberant clap of Walter Ewell's rifle which never missed, so that you did not even wait to hear his horn.

"I'll never get a shot," I said. "I'll never kill one."

"Yes, you will," Sam said. "You wait. You'll be a hunter. You'll be a man."

And we would leave him there. He would go out to the road where the surrey would be waiting in order to take the horses and mules back; for now that he lived at the camp all the time, Father and Major de Spain left the horses and the dogs there. They would go on ahead on the horses, and Uncle Ash and Jimbo and I would follow in the wagon with Sam, with the guns and the bedding and the meat and the heads, the antlers, the good ones, the wagon winding on among the tremendous gums and cypresses and oaks where no ax had ever sounded, between the impenetrable brakes of cane and brier—the two changing yet constant walls just beyond which the wilderness seemed to lean, stooping a little, watching us and listening; not quite inimical because we were too small, our sojourn too brief and too harmless to excite to that, just brooding, secret, almost inattentive. Then we would emerge; we would be out of it, the line as sharp as the demarcation of a doored wall. Suddenly skeletoned cotton- and corn-fields would flow away on either hand, gaunt and motionless beneath the gray rain; there would be a house, barns, where the hand of man had clawed for an instant, holding, the wall of the wilderness behind us now, tremendous and still and seemingly impenetrable in the gray and fading light. The surrey would be waiting, Father and Major de Spain and Uncle Ike dismounted beside it. Then Sam would get down from the wagon and mount one of the horses, and, with the others at lead behind him, he would turn back. I would watch him for a while against that tall and secret wall, growing smaller and smaller against it. He would not look back. Then he would enter it, returning to what I believed, and thought that Father believed, was his loneliness and solitude.

So the instant came; I pulled trigger and ceased to be a child forever and became a hunter and a man. It was the last day. We broke camp that afternoon and went out, Father and Major de Spain and Uncle Ike and Boon on the horses and mules, Walter Ewell and old Ash and Jimbo and I in the wagon with Sam and the duffel and my hide and antlers. There could have been other trophies in the wagon, too, but I should not have known it, just as for all practical purposes Sam Fathers and I were still alone together as we had been that morning, the wagon winding and jolting on between those shifting yet constant walls from beyond which the wilderness watched us passing, less than inimical now and never inimical again since my buck still and forever leaped, the shaking gun barrels coming constantly and forever steady at last, crashing, and still out of his moment of mortality the buck sprang, forever immortal, that moment of the buck, the shot, Sam Fathers, and myself, and the blood with which he had marked me forever, one with the wilderness which had now accepted me because Sam had said that I had done all right; the wagon winding on, when suddenly Sam checked it, and we all heard that unforgettable and unmistakable sound of a deer breaking cover.

Then Boon shouted from beyond the bend of the trail, and while we all sat motionless in the halted wagon, Walter and I already reaching for our guns, Boon came galloping back, flogging his mule with his hat, his face wild and amazed as he shouted down at us. Then Father and the others came round the bend.

"Get the dogs!" Boon cried. "Get the dogs! If he had a nub on his head he had fourteen points! Laying right there in that pawpaw thicket! If I'd a knowed he was there I could a cut his throat with my pocketknife!"

"Maybe that's why he run," Walter said. "He saw you never had your gun." He was already out of the wagon with his rifle. Then I was out, too, with my gun, and Father and Major de Spain and Uncle Ike had come up, and Boon got off his mule somehow and was scrabbling among the duffel for his gun, still shouting, "Get the dogs! Get the dogs!" And it seemed to me, too, that it would take them forever to decide what to do—the old men in whom the blood ran cold and slow, in whom, during the intervening years between us, the blood had become a different and colder substance from that which ran in me and even in Boon and Walter.

"What about it, Sam?" Father said. "Could the dogs bring him back?"

"We won't need the dogs," Sam said. "If he don't hear

dogs behind him he will circle back in here about sundown to bed."

"All right," Major de Spain said. "You boys take the horses. We'll go on out to the road in the wagon and wait there." So he and Father and Uncle Ike got into the wagon, and Boon and Walter and Sam and I took the horses and turned back and out of the trail. We rode for about an hour, through the gray and unmarked afternoon whose light was little different from what it had been at dawn and which would become darkness without any graduation. Then Sam stopped us.

"This is far enough," he said. "He'll be coming upwind and he don't want to smell the mules."

So we dismounted and tied them and followed Sam on foot through the markless afternoon through the unpathed woods.

"You got time," Sam said to me once. "We'll get there before he does."

So I tried to go slower. That is, I tried to slow, decelerate, the dizzy rush of time in which the buck which I had not even seen was moving, which it seemed to me was carrying him farther and farther and more and more irretrievably away from us even though there were no dogs behind him to make him run yet. So we went on; it seemed to me that it was for another hour. Then suddenly we were on a ridge. I had never been in there before, and you could not see the ridge; you just knew that the earth had risen slightly because the undergrowth had thinned a little and the ground which you could not see slanted, sloping away toward a dense brake of cane.

"This is it," Sam said. "You all follow the ridge and you will come to two crossings. You can see the tracks."

Boon and Walter went on. Soon they had disappeared, and

once more Sam and I were standing motionless in a clump of switchlike bushes against the trunk of a pin oak, and again there was nothing, as in the morning. There was the soaring and somber solitude in the dim light; there was the thin whisper of the faint cold rain which had not ceased all day; then, as if it had waited for us to find our positions and become still, the wilderness breathed again. It seemed to lean inward above us, above Walter and Boon and Sam and me in our separate lurking places, tremendous, attentive, impartial, and omniscient, the buck moving in it, too, somewhere, not running since he had not been pursued, not frightened and never fearsome but just alert, too, as we were alert, perhaps already circling back, perhaps quite near, conscious, too, of the eye of the ancient immortal Umpire. Because I was just twelve then, and that morning something had happened to me, in less than a second I had ceased forever to be the child I was yesterday. Or perhaps this made no difference, perhaps even a city-bred man, let alone a child, could not have understood it; perhaps only a country-bred one could comprehend loving the life he spills. I began to shake again.

"I'm glad it's started now," I whispered. "Then it will be gone when I raise the gun——"

"Hush," Sam said.

"Is he that near?" I whispered. We did not move to speak: only our lips shaping the expiring words. "Do you think——"

"Hush," Sam said. So I hushed. But I could not stop the shaking. I did not try because I knew that it would go away when I needed the steadiness, since Sam Fathers had already made me a hunter. So we stood there, motionless, scarcely breathing. If there had been any sun it would be near to setting now; there was a condensing, a densifying, of what I thought was the gray and unchanging light until I realized it was my own breathing, my heart, my blood—something, and that Sam had marked me indeed with something he had had of his vanished and forgotten people. Then I stopped breathing; there was only my heart, my blood, and in the following silence the wilderness ceased to breathe, too, leaning, stooping overhead with held breath, tremendous and impartial and waiting. Then the shaking stopped, too, as I had known it would, and I slipped the safety off the gun.

Then it had passed. It was over. The solitude did not breathe again yet; it had merely stopped watching me and was looking somewhere else, and I knew as well as if I had seen him that the buck had come to the edge of the cane and had either seen or scented us and had faded back into it. But still the solitude was not breathing; it was merely looking somewhere else. So I did not move yet, and then, a second after I realized what I was listening for, we heard it —the flat single clap of Walter Ewell's rifle following which you did not need to wait for the horn. Then the sound of the horn itself came down the ridge, and something went out of me, too, and I knew then that I had never really believed that I should get the shot.

"I reckon that's all," I said. "Walter got him."

I had shifted the gun forward, my thumb on the safety again, and I was already moving out of the thicket when Sam said:

"Wait." And I remember how I turned upon him in the truculence of a boy's grief over the missed chance, the missed luck.

"Wait?" I said. "What for? Don't you hear that horn?"

And I remember how he was standing. He had not moved. He was not tall; he was rather squat and broad, and I had been growing fast for the past year or so, and there was not much difference between us, yet he was looking over my head. He was looking across me and up the ridge toward the sound of Walter's horn and he did not see me; he just knew I was there; he did not see me. And then I saw the buck. He was coming down the ridge; it was as if he were walking out of the very sound of the horn which signified a kill. He was not running; he was walking, tremendous, unhurried, slanting and tilting his head to pass his antlers through the undergrowth, and I standing there with Sam beside me now instead of behind me as he always stood and the gun which I knew I was not going to use already slanted forward and the safety already off.

Then he saw us. And still he did not begin to flee. He just stopped for an instant, taller than any man, looking at us, then his muscles suppled, gathered. He did not even alter his course, not fleeing, not even running, just moving with that winged and effortless ease with which deer move, passing within twenty feet of us, his head high and the eye not proud and not haughty but just full and wild and unafraid, and Sam standing beside me now, his right arm lifted at full length and the hand turned palm-outward and speaking in that tongue which I had learned from listening to him and Joe Baker, while up the ridge Walter Ewell's horn was still blowing us in to a dead buck.

"Oleh, Chief," he said. "Grandfather."

When he reached Walter he was standing with his back toward us, looking down at the deer. He didn't look up at all.

"Come here, Sam," he said quietly. When we reached him he still did not look up, standing there over a little spike buck which even last spring had still been a fawn. "He was so little I pretty near let him go," Walter said. "But just look at the track he was making. It's pretty near big as a cow's.

If there were any more tracks here besides the ones he is laying in I would swear there was another buck that I never even saw."

It was after dark when we reached the road where the surrey was waiting. It was turning cold; the rain had stopped, and the sky was beginning to blow clear. Father and Major de Spain and Uncle Ike had a fire going. "Did you get him?" Father said.

"Got a good-sized swamp rabbit with spike horns," Walter said, sliding the little buck down from his mule.

"Nobody saw the big one?" Father said.

"I don't even believe Boon saw it," Walter said. "He probably jumped a stray cow back there."

Then Boon started cursing, swearing at Walter and at Sam for not getting the dogs to begin with and at the buck and all.

"Never mind," Father said. "He'll be here for us next fall. Let's get started home now."

And it was after midnight when he let Walter out at his gate two miles from town, and it was later still when we put Major de Spain and Uncle Ike down at Major de Spain's. It was cold; the sky was clear now; there would be a heavy frost by sunup, and the ground was frozen beneath the horses' feet and beneath the wheels. I had slept a little but not much and not because of the cold. And then suddenly I was telling Father, the surrey moving on toward home over the frozen ground, the horses trotting again, sensing the stable. He listened quite quietly.

"Why not?" he said. "Think of all that has happened here on this earth. All the blood hot and fierce and strong for living, pleasuring. Grieving and suffering, too, of course, but still getting something out of it for all that, getting a lot out of it, because after all you don't have to continue to bear what you believe is suffering; you can always stop that. And even suffering and grieving is better than nothing; there is nothing worse than not being alive. But you can't be alive forever and you always wear out life before you have completely exhausted the possibilities of living. And all that must be somewhere. And the earth is shallow; there is not a great deal of it before you come to the rock. And even that does not want to keep things. Look at the seed, the acorns, at what happens even to carrion when you try to bury it: it refuses, too, seethes and struggles, too, until it reaches light and air again, hunting the sun still. And they"—he lifted his hand for an instant toward the sky where the scoured and icy stars glittered—"they don't want it, need it. Besides, what would it want, knocking about out there, when it never had enough time about the earth as it was, when there is plenty of room about the earth, plenty of places still unchanged from what they were when the blood used and pleasured in them while it was still blood?"

"But we want them," I said. "We still want them. There is plenty of room among us for them."

"That's right," Father said. "Suppose they don't have substance, can't cast a shadow——"

"But I saw it!" I cried. "I saw it!"

"Steady," Father said. For an instant his hand rested upon my knee. "Steady. I know you did. So did I. Sam took me in there once after I killed my first deer."

THE SNOW GOOSE
By Paul Gallico
From the *Saturday Evening Post*

PAUL WILLIAM GALLICO

was born in New York City in 1897. He was the highest-paid sports writer in Manhattan when he resigned his job in 1936 to write fiction, and also to take a reporting job on the city desk of his newspaper, the New York Daily News. *In the fourteen years up to that time he had been movie critic, sports writer, sports editor, columnist, and sports promoter, but he had never written a story from the news angle. He loves the English sea and countryside and spent three summers in South Devonshire, just above Plymouth, in England. This accounts for the locale of "The Snow Goose." He has also lived in Mexico and the Southwest, as well as the West Coast. His hobbies are fencing, flying, deep-sea fishing, and collecting symphonic recorded music, as well as cooking spaghetti. He loves ocean travel. Among his books are* Farewell to Sport *(1938),* Adventures of Hiram Holliday *(1939), and* Secret Front *(1940). "The Snow Goose" has also been published by Alfred A. Knopf as a separate volume.*

The great marsh lies on the Essex coast between the village of Chelmbury and the ancient Saxon oyster-fishing hamlet of Wickaeldroth. It is one of the last of the wild places of England, a low, far-reaching expanse of grass and reeds and half-submerged meadowlands ending in the great saltings and mud flats and tidal pools near the restless sea.

Tidal creeks and estuaries and the crooked, meandering arms of many little rivers whose mouths lap at the edge of the ocean cut through the sodden land that seems to rise and fall and breathe with the recurrence of the daily tides. It is desolate, utterly lonely, and made lonelier by the calls and cries of the wild fowl that make their homes in the marshlands and saltings—the wild geese and the gulls, the teal and widgeon, the redshanks and curlews that pick their way through the tidal pools. Of human habitants there are none, and none are seen, with the occasional exception of a wildfowler or native oyster fishermen, who still ply a trade already ancient when the Normans came to Hastings.

Grays and blues and soft greens are the colors, for when the skies are dark in the long winters the many waters of the beaches and marshes reflect the cold and somber color. But sometimes, with sunrise and sunset, sky and land are aflame with red and golden fire.

Hard by one of the winding arms of the little River Aelder runs the embankment of an old sea wall, smooth and solid, without a break, a bulwark to the land against the encroaching sea. Deep into a salting some three miles from the English Channel it runs, and there turns north. At that corner its face is gouged, broken, and shattered. It has been breached, and at the breach the hungry sea has already entered and taken for its own the land, the wall, and all that stood there.

At low water the blackened and ruptured stones of the ruins of an abandoned lighthouse show above the surface, with here and there, like buoy markers, the top of a sagging fence post. Once this lighthouse abutted the sea and was a beacon on the Essex coast. Time shifted land and water, and its usefulness came to an end.

Lately it served again as a human habitation. In it there lived a strange and lonely man. His body was warped, but his heart was filled with love for wild and hunted things. He was ugly to look upon but he created great beauty. It is about him and a girl who came to know him and see beyond the grotesque form that housed him to what lay within that this story is told.

It is not a story that falls easily and smoothly into sequence. It has been garnered and gathered from many sources and from many people. Some of it comes in the form of fragments from men who looked upon strange and violent scenes. For the sea has claimed its own and spreads its rippled blanket over the site, and the great white bird with the black-tipped pinions that saw it all from the beginning to the end has returned to the dark, frozen silences of the northlands whence it came.

In the late spring of 1930 Philip Rhayader came to the abandoned lighthouse at the mouth of the Aelder. He bought the light and many acres of marshland and salting surrounding it.

He lived and worked there alone the year round. He was a painter of birds and of Nature, who, for reasons, had withdrawn from all human society. Some of the reasons were apparent on his fortnightly visits to the little village of Chelmbury for supplies, where the natives looked askance at his misshapen body and dark visage. For he was a hunchback, and his left arm was crippled, thin and bent at the wrist, like the claw of a bird.

They soon became used to his queer figure, small but powerful, the massive, dark, bearded head set just slightly below the mysterious mound on his back, the glowing eyes and the clawed hand, and marked him off as "that queer painter chap that lives down to lighthouse."

Physical deformity often breeds hatred of humanity in men. Rhayader did not hate; he loved very greatly, man, the animal kingdom, and all Nature. His heart was filled with pity and understanding. He had mastered his handicap but he could not master the rebuffs he suffered due to his appearance. The thing that drove him into seclusion was his failure to find anywhere a return of the warmth that flowed from him. He repelled women. Men would have warmed to him had they got to know him. But the mere fact that an effort was being made hurt Rhayader and drove him to avoid the person making it.

He was twenty-seven when he came to the Great Marsh. He had traveled much and fought valiantly before he made the decision to withdraw from a world in which he could not take part as other men. For all of the artist's sensitivity and woman's tenderness locked in his barrel breast, he was very much a man.

In his retreat he had his birds, his painting, and his boat. He owned a sixteen-footer, which he sailed with wonderful skill. Alone, with no eyes to watch him, he managed well with his deformed hand and he often used his strong teeth to handle the sheets of his billowing sails in a tricky blow.

He would sail the tidal creeks and estuaries and out to

sea and would be gone for days at a time, looking for new species of birds to photograph or sketch, and he became an adept at netting them to add to his collection of tamed wild fowl in the pen near his studio that formed the nucleus of a sanctuary.

He never shot over a bird, and wild-fowlers were not welcome near his premises. He was a friend to all things wild, and the wild things repaid him with their friendship.

Tamed in his enclosures were the geese that came winging down the coast from Iceland and Spitsbergen each October, in great skeins that darkened the sky and filled the air with the rushing noise of their passage—the brown-bodied pink feet, white-breasted barnacles with their dark necks and clowns' masks, the wild white fronts with black-barred breasts, and many species of wild ducks—widgeon, mallard, pintails, teal, and shovelers.

Some were pinioned, so that they would remain there as a sign and signal to the wild ones that came down at each winter's beginning that here were food and sanctuary.

Many hundreds came and remained with him all through the cold weather from October to the early spring, when they migrated north again to their breeding grounds below the ice rim.

Rhayader was happy in the knowledge that when storms blew, or it was bitter cold and food was scarce, or the big punt guns of the distant bag hunters roared, his birds were safe; that he had gathered to the sanctuary and security of his own arms and heart these many wild and beautiful creatures who knew and trusted him.

They would answer the call of the north in the spring but in the fall they would come back, barking and whooping and honking in the autumn sky, to circle the landmark of the old light and drop to earth near by to be his guests again—

birds that he well remembered and recognized from the previous year.

And this made Rhayader happy, because he knew that implanted somewhere in their beings was the germ knowledge of his existence and his safe haven, that this knowledge had become a part of them and, with the coming of the gray skies and the winds from the north, would send them unerringly back to him.

For the rest, his heart and soul went into the painting of the country in which he lived and its creatures. There are not many Rhayaders extant, because he hoarded them jealously, piling them up in his lighthouse and the storerooms above by the hundreds. He was not satisfied with them because as an artist he was uncompromising.

But the few that have reached the market are masterpieces, filled with the glow and colors of marsh-reflected light, the feel of flight, the push of birds breasting a morning wind bending the tall flag reeds. He painted the loneliness and the smell of the salt-laden cold, the eternity and agelessness of marshes, the wild, living creatures, dawn flights, and frightened things taking to the air, and winged shadows at night hiding from the moon.

One November afternoon, three years after Rhayader had come to the Great Marsh, a child approached the lighthouse studio by means of the sea wall. In her arms she carried a burden.

She was no more than twelve, slender, dirty, nervous, and timid as a bird, but beneath the grime as eerily beautiful as a marsh fairy. She was pure Saxon, large-boned, fair, with a head to which her body was yet to grow, and deep-set, violet-colored eyes.

She was desperately frightened of the ugly man she had come to see, for legend had already begun to gather about

Rhayader, and the native wild-fowlers hated him for interfering with their sport.

But greater than her fear was the need of that which she bore. For locked in her child's heart was the knowledge, picked up somewhere in the swampland, that this ogre who lived in the lighthouse had magic that could heal injured things.

She had never seen Rhayader before and was close to fleeing in panic at the dark apparition that appeared at the studio door, drawn by her footsteps—the black head and beard, the sinister hump and the crooked claw.

She stood there staring, poised like a disturbed marsh bird for instant flight.

But his voice was deep and kind when he spoke to her. "What is it, child?"

She stood her ground and then edged timidly forward. The thing she carried in her arms was a large white bird, and it was quite still. There were stains of blood on its whiteness and on her kirtle where she had held it to her.

The girl placed it in his arms. "I found it, sir. It's hurted. Is it still alive?"

"Yes. Yes, I think so. Come in, child, come in."

Rhayader went inside, bearing the bird, which he placed upon a table, where it moved feebly. Curiosity overcame fear. The girl followed and found herself in a room warmed by a coal fire, shining with many colored pictures that covered the walls, and full of a strange but pleasant smell.

The bird fluttered. With his good hand Rhayader spread one of its immense white pinions. The end was beautifully tipped with black.

Rhayader looked and marveled, and said, "Child, where did you find it?"

"In t' marsh, sir, where fowlers had been. What—what is it, sir?"

"It's a snow goose from Canada. But how in all heaven came it here?"

The name seemed to mean nothing to the little girl. Her deep violet eyes, shining out of the dirt on her thin face, were fixed with concern on the injured bird.

She said, "Can 'ee heal it, sir?"

"Yes, yes," said Rhayader. "We will try. Come, you shall help me."

There were scissors and bandages and splints on a shelf, and he was marvelously deft, even with the crooked claw that managed to hold things.

He said, "Ah, she has been shot, poor thing. Her leg is broken, and the wing tip, but not badly. See, we will clip her primaries, so that we can bandage it, but in the spring the feathers will grow and she will be able to fly again. We'll bandage it close to her body, so that she cannot move it until it has set, and then make a splint for the poor leg."

Her fears forgotten, the child watched, fascinated, as he worked, and all the more so because while he fixed a fine splint to the shattered leg he told her the most wonderful story.

The bird was a young one, no more than a year old. She was born in a northern land far, far across the seas, a land belonging to England. Flying to the south to escape the snow and ice and bitter cold, a great storm had seized her and whirled and buffeted her about. It was a truly terrible storm, stronger than her great wings, stronger than anything. For days and nights it held her in its grip, and there was nothing she could do but fly before it. When finally it had blown itself out and her sure instincts took her south again she was over a different land and surrounded by strange birds that she had never seen before. At last, exhausted by her ordeal, she had sunk to rest in a friendly green marsh, only to be met by the blast from the hunter's gun.

"A bitter reception for a visiting princess," concluded Rhayader. "We will call her *La Princesse Perdue,* the lost princess. And in a few days she will be feeling much better. See?" He reached into his pocket and produced a handful of grain. The snow goose opened its round yellow eyes and nibbled at it.

The child laughed with delight and then suddenly caught her breath with alarm as the full import of where she was pressed in upon her, and without a word she turned and fled out of the door.

"Wait, wait!" cried Rhayader and went to the entrance, where he stopped so that it framed his dark bulk. The girl was already fleeing down the sea wall, but she paused at his voice and looked back.

"What is your name, child?"

"Frith."

"Eh?" said Rhayader. "Fritha, I suppose. Where do you live?"

"Wi' t' fisherfolk at Wickaeldroth." She gave the name the old Saxon pronunciation.

"Will you come back tomorrow, or the next day, to see how the princess is getting along?"

She paused, and again Rhayader must have thought of the wild water birds caught motionless in that split second of alarm before they took to flight.

But her thin voice came back to him, "Aye!"

And then she was gone, with her fair hair streaming out behind her.

The snow goose mended rapidly and by midwinter was already limping about the inclosure with the wild pink-footed geese with which it associated, rather than the barnacles, and had learned to come to be fed at Rhayader's call. And the child, Fritha, or Frith, was a frequent visitor. She had overcome her fear of Rhayader. Her imagination was captured by the presence of this strange white princess from a land far over the sea, a land that was all pink, as she knew from the map that Rhayader showed her, and on which they traced the stormy path of the lost bird from its home in Canada, to the Great Marsh of Essex.

Then one June morning a group of late pink feet, fat and well-fed from the winter at the lighthouse, answered the stronger call of the breeding grounds, and rose lazily, climbing into the sky in ever-widening circles. With them, her white body and black-tipped pinions shining in the spring sun, was the snow goose. It so happened that Frith was at the lighthouse. Her cry brought Rhayader running from the studio.

"Look! Look! The princess! Be she going away?"

Rhayader stared into the sky at the climbing specks. "Aye," he said, unconsciously dropping into her manner of speech. "The princess is going home. Listen! She is bidding us farewell."

Out of the clear sky came the mournful barking of the pink feet, and above it the higher, clearer note of the snow goose. The specks drifted northward, formed into a tiny v, diminished and vanished.

With the departure of the snow goose ended the visits of Frith to the lighthouse. Rhayader learned all over again the meaning of the word "loneliness." That summer, out of his memory, he painted a picture of a slender, grime-covered child, her fair hair blown by a November storm, who bore in her arms a wounded white bird.

In mid-October the miracle occurred. Rhayader was in his

inclosure, feeding his birds. A gray northeast wind was blowing, and the land was sighing beneath the incoming tide. Above the sea and the wind noises he heard a clear, high note. He turned his eyes upward to the evening sky in time to see first an infinite speck, then a black-and-white-pinioned dream that circled the lighthouse once, and finally a reality that dropped to earth in the pen and came waddling forward importantly to be fed, as though she had never been away. It was the snow goose. There was no mistaking her. Tears of joy came to Rhayader's eyes. Where had she been? Surely not home to Canada. No, she must have summered in Greenland or Spitsbergen with the pink feet. She had remembered and had returned.

When next Rhayader went in to Chelmbury for supplies he left a message with the postmistress—one that must have caused her much bewilderment. He said, "Tell Frith, who lives with the fisherfolk at Wickaeldroth, that the lost princess has returned."

Three days later Frith, taller, still tousled and unkempt, came shyly to the lighthouse to visit *La Princesse Perdue*.

Time passed. On the Great Marsh it was marked by the height of the tides, the slow march of the seasons, the passage of the birds, and, for Rhayader, by the arrival and departure of the snow goose.

The world outside boiled and seethed and rumbled with the eruption that was soon to break forth and come close to marking its destruction. But not yet did it touch upon Rhayader, or, for that matter, Frith. They had fallen into a curious, natural rhythm, even as the child grew older. When the snow goose was at the lighthouse, then she came, too, to visit and learn many things from Rhayader. They sailed together in his speedy boat, that he handled so skillfully. They caught wild fowl for the ever-increasing colony, and built new pens and inclosures for them. From him she learned the lore of every wild bird, from gull to gyrfalcon, that flew the marshes. She cooked for him sometimes and even learned to mix his paints.

But when the snow goose returned to its summer home it was as though some kind of bar was up between them, and she did not come to the lighthouse. One year the bird did not return, and Rhayader was heartbroken. All things seemed to have ended for him. He painted furiously through the winter and the next summer and never once saw the child. But in the fall the familiar cry once more rang from the sky, and the huge white bird, now at its full growth, dropped from the skies as mysteriously as it had departed. Joyously Rhayader sailed his boat into Chelmbury and left his message with the postmistress.

Curiously, it was more than a month after he had left the message before Frith reappeared at the lighthouse, and Rhayader, with a shock, realized that she was a child no longer.

After the year in which the bird had remained away its periods of absence grew shorter and shorter. It had grown so tame that it followed Rhayader about and even came into the studio while he was working.

In the spring of 1940 the birds migrated early from the Great Marsh. The world was on fire. The whine and roar of the bombers and the thudding explosions frightened them. The first day of May Frith and Rhayader stood shoulder to shoulder on the sea wall and watched the last of the unpinioned pink feet and barnacle geese rise from their sanctuary; she, tall, slender, free as air and hauntingly beautiful; he, dark, grotesque, his massive bearded head raised to the sky, his glowing dark eyes watching the geese form their flight tracery.

"Look, Philip," Frith said.

Rhayader followed her eyes. The snow goose had taken flight, her giant wings spread, but she was flying low and once came quite close to them, so that for a moment the spreading black-tipped, white pinions seemed to caress them, and they felt the rush of the bird's swift passage. Once, twice, she circled the lighthouse, then dropped to earth again in the enclosure with the pinion geese and commenced to feed.

"She isn't going," said Frith with marvel in her voice. The bird in its close passage seemed to have woven a kind of magic about her. "The princess be goin' t' stay."

"Aye," said Rhayader, and his voice was shaken too. "She'll stay. She will never go away again. The lost princess is lost no more. This is her home now—of her own free will."

The spell the bird had girt about her was broken, and Frith was suddenly conscious of the fact that she was frightened, and the things that frightened her were in Rhayader's eyes— the longing and the loneliness and the deep, welling, unspoken things that lay in and behind them as he turned them upon her.

His last words were repeating themselves in her head as though he had said them again, "This is her home now—of her own free will." The delicate tendrils of her instincts reached to him and carried to her the message of the things he could not speak, because of what he felt himself to be, misshapen and grotesque. And where his voice might have soothed her, her fright grew greater at his silence and the power of the unspoken things between them. The woman in her bade her take flight from something that she was not yet capable of understanding.

Frith said, "I—I must go. Good-by. I be glad the—the princess will stay. You'll not be so alone now."

She turned and walked swiftly away, and his sadly spoken "Good-by, Frith" was only a half-heard ghost of a sound borne to her ears above the rustling of the marsh grass. She was far away before she dared turn for a backward glance. He was still standing on the sea wall, a dark speck against the sky.

Her fear had stilled now. It had been replaced by something else, a queer sense of loss that made her stand quite still for a moment, so sharp was it. Then, more slowly, she continued on, away from the skyward-pointing finger of the lighthouse and the man beneath it.

It was a little more than three weeks before Frith returned to the lighthouse. May was at its end, and the day, too, in a long golden twilight that was giving way to the silver of the moon already hanging in the eastern sky.

She told herself, as her steps took her thither, that she must know whether the snow goose had really stayed, as Rhayader said it would. Perhaps it had flown away, after all. But her firm steps on the sea wall were full of eagerness, and sometimes unconsciously she found herself hurrying.

Frith saw the yellow light of Rhayader's lantern down by his little wharf, and she found him there. His sailboat was rocking gently on a flooding tide, and he was loading supplies into her—water and food and bottles of brandy, gear, and a spare sail. When he turned to the sound of her coming she saw that he was pale but that his dark eyes, usually so kind and placid, were glowing with excitement, and he was breathing heavily from his exertions.

Sudden alarm seized Frith. The snow goose was forgotten. "Philip! Ye be goin' away?"

Rhayader paused in his work to greet her, and there was something in his face, a glow and a look that she had never seen there before.

"Frith! I am glad you came. Yes, I must go away. A little trip. I will come back." His usually kindly voice was hoarse with what was suppressed inside him.

Frith asked, "Where must ye go?"

Words came tumbling from Rhayader now. He must go to Dunkirk. A hundred miles across the Channel. A British army was trapped there on the sands, awaiting destruction at the hands of the advancing Germans. The port was in flames, the position hopeless. He had heard it in the village when he had gone for supplies. Men were putting out from Chelmbury in answer to the government's call, every tug and fishing boat or power launch that could propel itself was heading across the Channel to haul the men off the beaches to the transports and destroyers that could not reach the shallows, to rescue as many as possible from the German fire.

Frith listened and felt her heart dying within her. He was saying that he would sail the Channel in his little boat. It could take six men at a time; in a pinch, seven. He could make many trips from the beaches to the transports.

The girl was young, primitive, inarticulate. She did not understand war or what had happened in France or the meaning of the trapped army, but the blood within her told her that here was danger.

"Philip! Must 'ee go? You'll not come back. Why must it be you?"

The fever seemed to have gone from Rhayader's soul with the first rush of words, and he explained it to her in terms that she could understand.

He said, "Men are huddled on the beaches like hunted birds, Frith, like the wounded and hunted birds we used to find and bring to sanctuary. Over them fly the steel peregrines, hawks and gyrfalcons, and they have no shelter from these iron birds of prey. They are lost and storm-driven and harried, like the *Princesse Perdue* you found and brought to me out of the marshes many years ago, and we healed her.

They need help, my dear, as our wild creatures have needed help, and that is why I must go. It is something that I can do. Yes, I can. For once—for once, I can be a man and play my part."

Frith stared at Rhayader. He had changed so. For the first time she saw that he was no longer ugly or misshapen or grotesque, but very beautiful. Things were turmoiling in her own soul, crying to be said, and she did not know how to say them.

"I'll come with 'ee, Philip."

Rhayader shook his head. "Your place in the boat would cause a soldier to be left behind, and another and another. I must go alone."

He donned rubber coat and boots and took to his boat. He waved and called back, "Good-by! Will you look after the birds until I return, Frith?"

Frith's hand came up, but only half, to wave too. "God speed you," she said, but gave it the Saxon turn. "I will take care of t' birds. Godspeed, Philip."

It was night now, bright with moon fragment and stars and northern glow. Frith stood on the sea wall and watched the sail gliding down the swollen estuary. Suddenly from the darkness behind her there came a rush of wings, and something swept past her into the air. In the night light she saw the flash of white wings, black-tipped, and the thrust-forward head of the snow goose.

It rose and cruised over the lighthouse once and then headed down the winding creek where Rhayader's sail was slanting in the gaining breeze and flew above him in slow, wide circles.

White sail and white bird were visible for a long time.

"Watch o'er him. Watch o'er him," Fritha whispered.

When they were both out of sight at last she turned and walked slowly, with bent head, back to the empty lighthouse.

Now the story becomes fragmentary, and one of these fragments is in the words of the men on leave who told it in the public room of the Crown and Arrow, an East Chapel pub.

"A goose, a bloomin' goose, so 'elp me," said Private Potton, of His Majesty's London Rifles.

"Garn," said a bandy-legged artilleryman.

"'A goose it was. Jock, 'ere, seed it same as me. It come flyin' down outa the muck an' stink an' smoke of Dunkirk that was over'ead. It was white, wiv black on its wings, an' it circles us like a bloomin' dive bomber. Jock, 'ere, 'e sez, 'We're done for. It's the angel of death a-come for us.'

"'Garn,' Hi sez, 'it's a ruddy goose, come over from 'ome wiv a message from Churchill, an' 'ow are we henjoying the bloomin' bathing. It's a omen, that's what it is, a bloody omen. We'll get out of this yet, me lad.'

"We was roostin' on the beach between Dunkirk an' Lapanny, like a lot o' bloomin' pigeons on Victoria Hembankment, waitin' for Jerry to pot us. 'E potted us good too. 'E was be'ind us an' flankin' us an' above us. 'E give us shrapnel and 'e give us H. E., an' 'e peppers us from the bloomin' hatmosphere with Gittersmiths.

"An' offshore is the *Kentish Maid,* a ruddy hexcursion scow wot Hi've taken many a trip on out of Margate in the summer, for two-and-six, waiting to take us off, 'arf a mile out from the bloomin' shallows.

"While we are lyin' there on the beach, done in an' cursin' becos there ain't no way to get out to the boat, a Stuka dives on 'er, an' 'is bombs drop alongside of 'er, throwin' up water like the bloomin' fountains in the palace gardens; a reg'lar display it was.

"Then a destroyer come up an' says 'No, ye don't' to the Stuka with ack-acks and pom-poms, but another Jerry dives on the destroyer, an' 'its 'er. Coo, did she go up! She burned before she sunk, an' the smoke an' the stink come driftin' inshore, all yellow an' black, an' out of it comes this bloomin' goose, a-circlin' around us trapped on the beach.

"An' then around a bend 'e comes in a bloody little sailboat, sailing along as cool as you please, like a bloomin' toff out for a pleasure spin on a Sunday hafternoon at 'Enley."

" 'Oo comes?" inquired a civilian.

" 'Im! 'Im that saved a lot of us. 'E sailed clean through a boil of machine-gun bullets from a Jerry in a Gittersmith wot was strafin'—a Ramsgate motorboat wot 'ad tried to take us off 'ad been sunk there 'arf an hour ago—the water was all frothin' with shell splashes an' bullets, but 'e didn't give it no mind, 'e didn't. 'E didn't 'ave no petrol to burn or hexplode an' he sailed in between the shells.

"Into the shallows 'e come out of the black smoke of the burning destroyer, a little dark man wiv a beard, a bloomin' claw for a 'and, an' a 'ump on 'is back.

" 'E 'ad a rope in 'is teeth that was shinin' white out of 'is black beard, 'is good 'and on the tiller, an' the crooked one beckonin' to us to come. An' over'ead, around and around, flies the ruddy goose.

"Jock, 'ere, says, 'Lawk, it's all over now. It's the bloody devil come for us 'imself. Hi must 'ave been struck an' don't know it.'

" 'Garn,' I sez, 'it's more like the good Lord, 'e looks to me, than any bloomin' devil.' 'E did, too, like the pictures from the Sunday-school books, wiv 'is white face and dark eyes an' beard an' all and 'is bloomin' boat.

"'Hi can take seven at a time,' 'e sings out when 'e's in close.

"Our horfficer shouts, 'Good, man! . . . You seven nearest, get in.'

"We waded out to where 'e was. Hi was that weary Hi couldn't clumb over the side, but 'e takes me by the collar of me tunic an' pulls, wiv a 'In ye go, lad. Come on. Next man.'

"An' in Hi went. Coo, 'e was strong, 'e was. Then 'e sets 'is sail, part of wot looks like a bloomin' sieve from machine-gun bullets, shouts, 'Keep down in the bottom of the boat, boys, in case we meet any of yer friends,' and we're off, 'im sittin' in the stern wiv 'is rope in 'is teeth, another in 'is crooked claw, an 'is right hand on the tiller, a-steerin' an' sailin' through the spray of the shells thrown by a land battery somewhere back of the coast. An' the bloomin' goose is flyin' around and around, 'onking above the wind and the row Jerry was makin', like a bloomin' Morris autermobile on Winchester by-pass.

"'Hi told you yon goose was a omen,' Hi sez to Jock. 'Look at 'im there, a bloomin' hangel of mercy.'

"'Im at the tiller just looks up at the goose, wiv the rope in 'is teeth, an' grins at 'er like 'e knows 'er a lifetime.

"'E brung us out to the *Kentish Maid* and turns around and goes back for another load. 'E made trips all afternoon an' all night, too, because the bloody light of Dunkirk burning was bright enough to see by. Hi don't know 'ow many trips 'e made, but 'im an' a nobby Thames Yacht Club motorboat an' a big lifeboat from Poole that come along brought off all there was of us on that particular stretch of hell, without the loss of a man.

"We sailed when the last man was off, an' there was more than seven hunder' of us haboard a boat built to take two hunder'. 'E was still there when we left an' 'e waved us good-by and sails off toward Dunkirk, and the bird wiv 'im. Blyme, it was queer to see that ruddy big goose flyin' around 'is boat, lit up by the fires like a white hangel against the smoke.

"A Stuka 'ad another go at us, 'arfway across, but 'e'd been stayin' up late nights an' missed. By mornin' we was safe 'ome.

"Hi never did find out what become of 'im or 'oo 'e was. 'Im wiv the 'ump an' 'is little sailboat. A bloody good man 'e was, that chap."

"Coo," said the artilleryman. "A ruddy big goose. Watcher know?"

In an officers' club on Brook Street a retired naval officer sixty-five years old, Com. Keith Brill-Oudener, was telling of his experiences during the evacuation of Dunkirk. Called out of bed at four o'clock in the morning, he had captained a lopsided Limehouse tug across the Channel, towing a string of Thames barges, which he brought back four times loaded with soldiers. On his last trip he came in with her funnel shot away and a hole in her side. But he got her back to Dover.

A naval-reserve officer, who had two Brixham trawlers and a Yarmouth drifter blasted out from under him in the last four days of the evacuation, said, "Did you run across that queer sort of legend about a wild goose? It was all up and down the beaches. You know how those things spring up. Some of the men I brought back were talking about it. It was supposed to have appeared at intervals the last days between Dunkirk and La Panne. If you saw it you were eventually saved. That sort of thing."

"H'm'm'm," said Brill-Oudener, "a wild goose. I saw a tame one. Dashed strange experience. Tragic, in a way, too. And lucky for us. Tell you about it. Third trip back. Toward six o'clock we sighted a derelict small boat. Seemed to be a chap or a body in her. And a bird sitting up on the edge.

"We changed our course when we got nearer and went over for a look-see. By Gad, it was a chap. Or had been, poor fellow. Machine-gunned, you know. Badly. Face down in the water. Bird was a goose, a tame one.

"We drifted close, but when one of our chaps reached over the bird hissed at him and struck at him with her wings. Couldn't drive it off. Suddenly, young Kettering, who was with me, let out a yell and pointed to starboard. Big mine floating by. One of Jerry's beauties. If we'd kept on our course we'd have piled right into it. Ugh! Head on. We let it get a hundred yards astern of the last barge, and the men blew it up with rifle fire.

"When we turned our attention to the derelict again she was gone. Sunk. Concussion, you know. Chap with her. He must have been lashed to her. The bird had got up and was circling. Three times, like a plane saluting. Dashed queer feeling. Then she flew off to the west. Lucky thing for us we went over to have a look, eh? Odd that you should mention a goose."

Fritha remained alone at the little lighthouse on the Great Marsh, taking care of the pinioned birds, waiting for she knew not what. The first days she haunted the sea wall, watching, though she knew it was useless. Later she roamed through the storerooms of the lighthouse building with their stacks of canvases on which Rhayader had captured every mood and light of the desolate country and the wondrous, graceful, feathered things that inhabited it.

Among them she found the picture that Rhayader had painted of her from memory so many years ago, when she was still a child and had stood, wind-blown and timid, at his threshold, hugging an injured bird to her.

The picture and the things she saw in it stirred her as nothing ever had before, for much of Rhayader's soul had gone into it. Strangely, it was the only time he had painted the snow goose, the lost wild creature, storm-driven from another land, that to each had brought a friend, and which, in the end, returned to her with the message that she would never see him again.

Long before the snow goose had come dropping out of a crimsoned eastern sky to circle the lighthouse in a last farewell Fritha, from the ancient powers of the blood that was in her, knew that Rhayader would not return.

And so, when one sunset she heard the high-pitched, well-remembered note cried from the heavens it brought no instant of false hope to her heart. This moment, it seemed, she had lived before many times.

She came running to the sea wall and turned her eyes, not toward the distant channel whence a sail might come, but to the sky from whose flaming arches plummeted the snow goose. Then the sight, the sound, and the solitude surrounding broke the dam within her and released the surging, overwhelming truth of her love, let it well forth in tears.

Wild spirit called to wild spirit, and she seemed to be flying with the great bird, soaring with it in the evening sky and hearkening to Rhayader's message.

Sky and earth were trembling with it and filled her beyond the bearing of it. "Frith! Fritha! Frith, my love. Good-by, my love." The white pinions, black-tipped, were beating it out upon her heart, and her heart was answering, "Philip, I love 'ee."

For a moment Frith thought the snow goose was going to land in the old inclosure, as the pinioned geese set up a welcoming gabble. But it only skimmed low, then soared up again, flew in a wide, graceful spiral once around the old light, and then began to climb.

Watching it, Frith saw no longer the snow goose but the soul of Rhayader taking farewell of her before departing forever.

She was no longer flying with it, but earthbound. She stretched her arms up into the sky and stood on tiptoes, reaching, and cried, "Godspeed! Godspeed, Philip!"

Frith's tears were stilled. She stood watching silently long after the goose had vanished. Then she went into the lighthouse and secured the picture that Rhayader had painted of her. Hugging it to her breast, she wended her way homeward along the old sea wall.

Each night, for many weeks thereafter, Frith came to the lighthouse and fed the pinioned birds. Then one early morning a German pilot on a dawn raid mistook the old abandoned light for an active military objective, dived onto it, a screaming steel hawk, and blew it and all it contained into oblivion.

That evening, when Fritha came, the sea had moved in through the breached walls and covered it over. Nothing was left to break the utter desolation. No marsh fowl had dared to return. Only the frightless gulls wheeled and soared and mewed their plaint over the place where it had been.

THOSE ARE AS BROTHERS
By Nancy Hale
From *Mademoiselle*

NANCY HALE

was born in Boston in 1909, the daughter of Philip Hale, the painter, and a granddaughter of Edward Everett Hale. She was an associate editor of Vogue, *but now lives in Virginia. She appeared in the* O. Henry Memorial Award Prize Stories *of 1933, winning third prize with her story, "To the Invader," from* Modern Youth. *She was a judge for the 1936 volume, and has been represented successively in 1937 with "To the North," which appeared in* Redbook Magazine *under the title "All He Ever Wanted"; in 1938 with "Always Afternoon," from* Redbook; *and in 1940 with "That Woman," from* Harper's Magazine. *Her novels,* The Young Die Good, *appeared in 1932,* Never Any More *in 1934, and a collection of her short stories,* The Earliest Dreams, *in 1936. She is now at work on another novel.*

THE LONG, clear American summer passed slowly, dreaming over the Connecticut Valley and the sound, square houses under the elms and the broad living fields, and over the people there that came and went and lay and sat still, with purpose and without, but free, moving in and out of their houses of their own free will, free to perceive the passage of the days through the different summer months and the smells and the sun and the rain and the high days and the brooding days, as was their right; without fear and without apprehension.

On the front lawn of the white house on the river bank the two little boys came out every morning and dug holes and hammered nails into boards and pushed the express wagon around filled with rocks. Their skins were filled with the sun, with the season, and they played all day, humming tuneless songs under their breath.

Up the road at the gardener's cottage of the big house where nobody lived, the gardener, who was unmarried, a short stout man who was a Jewish refugee, tended the borders of the garden and painted the long white fence and worked on the driveway; in the summer-morning sun he sang, too, in German, as he did his slow, neat work.

In the evenings after supper when it was dusk and the only light was left in the red sky on the other side of the river he would come walking down the road to the house on the river bank, to call on the German governess who took care of the two little boys. His footsteps could be heard walking, hard and quick, down the road. Fräulein would be sitting on the stone front steps. He would stop short in the road in front of her, dressed in his clean clothes, his body round and compact and his black hair brushed down, and bow. "Good evening," he said. Fräulein said, "How are you?" Then he would come and sit beside her on the steps and the conversation would continue in German, because although he could understand sufficient English, Mr. Loeb could talk hardly any.

Fräulein was friendly to him because she was a friendly woman, but always a little superior because he was a Jew and she belonged to a family of small merchants in Cologne. She was sorry for him because he was a refugee and because he had been in a concentration camp in Germany, and it was necessary to be kind to those who had suffered under that Hitler, but a Jew was a Jew; there were right German names and wrong German names; Fräulein's name was Strasser. She did not mind speaking her mind to him on the subject of the Nazis who were ruining Germany. There were no other Germans about, in this place, as there were in the winter in New York, who might be on the other side; to them she had only praise to speak of Hitler, for her family was still in Cologne and people suffered at home for what was said by their relatives in America—if it came to the wrong ears. But Mr. Loeb was a Jew and safe to talk to, to tell exactly what she thought of those people, those Nazis. He never said anything much back, just listened and nodded; his face was round and florid.

In the evenings Mrs. Mason, the children's mother, sat in a garden chair out on the lawn and listened to the crickets in the marshes and watched the red fade beyond the river. Or, if it was one of the nights when she could not enjoy the evening sounds, the smells, when a little of the tension and fear clung to her mind and twisted it about, she would sit inside the living room, on one of the chintz-covered chairs under a light with a book. She read all sorts of books—novels, detective stories, and the papers and magazines that were full of the news about Europe. On the bad nights, the nights when peace was not quite at her command, she noticed that whatever she read seemed curiously to be written about her . . . to fit her situation, no matter what it was meant to be about. And especially all the books, the articles, about the Nazis. She did not know if it was morbid of her, but she could not help feeling he had stood for the thing that was the Nazis, that spirit, and she had been a country being conquered, a country dominated by those methods. It was so like; so very like. When she read of those tortured in concentration camps, of those dispossessed and smashed to the Nazi will, she knew she felt as those people felt. She had been through a thing that was the same in microcosm. Her life was a tiny scale model of the thing that was happening in Europe: the ruthless swallowing the helpless. By a miracle, by an overlooked shred of courage, she had escaped and was free here. She was a refugee like that man out there talking to Fräulein who had escaped, too, by another miracle, for only miracles saved people from that spirit. In refuge, peace and assurance were coming back slowly like strength to a sick body, and the fear, the terror that was once everything, was draining away drop by drop with the days of safety. The same thing must be happening to him, the man out there; confidence and a quietly beating heart, in this calm summer country where there was nothing any more to fear.

Only the habit of fear, only the uncontrollably quickened pulse for no reason, the fear that came out of nothing because fear was a poison in the blood and passed in and out of the heart again and again and again before it was finally worked out, if it ever was. Perhaps, she thought, it never was. If you were infected virulently enough with that poison perhaps it never left you but recurred forever like some tropical fevers, forever part of you and in your blood though you were a thousand miles away from the source. He was nearly a thousand miles away, too, and there would be no reason, no need, ever to see him again; but perhaps the fear would stay with her though there was nothing left to fear.

As the summer wandered by, the young man from across the river came over more and more often to see Mrs. Mason. He had a boat with an outboard motor; she would hear it buzzing across the water, and the sound of the motor cut as he drew near to the dock; there would be silence while he tied up, and then he would come walking up the lawn, very tall with his fair hair cut short all over, catching the light from the sunset in the quiet dusk.

"Hello, Fräulein," he would say as he came up the steps. "Hello, Mr. Loeb."

Mr. Loeb always got to his feet and bowed smartly. Fräulein said "Good evening, Mr. Worthington." Then the screen door would slam and the sound of German being spoken quietly would begin again and he would walk into the living room and grin at Mrs. Mason.

He used to sit in the chintz-covered chairs with his long legs stuck out in front of him, smoking cigarettes. Sometimes he took her out on the smooth dark river in his boat. Once they struck a log in the darkness on the water and she started violently and cried out. "What are you afraid of?" he asked her. "You're so lovely; I don't see why you should ever be afraid of anything." It was impossible to explain to him that she was not afraid of the log, nor of the water, nor of anything; that it was only a reflex which she was helpless to control, without reason; just fear. "You know I'd take care of you, if anything ever happened, don't you?" he said. "If you'd just let me." And she knew he would, but that did not make any difference. Nobody could help because nobody could possibly understand the irrationality, the uncontrollability, of fear when it was like this, in the blood. Any help had to come from within, the self-learning through days, perhaps years, of peace: that nothing of all which was over would ever happen again. Talking to it was no good; no young man's protectiveness penetrated to it; it had to learn slowly by itself.

The young man was falling in love with Mrs. Mason through that long summer. But it was inconceivable that she should fall in love with him. No matter how kind and strong he was, no matter how much more each day she saw him—how good he was, how there was none of that spirit in him—it was inconceivable that her muscles could ever grow slack enough for her to look at him quietly, a man, and fall in love with him. She had been naked once, and vulnerable to everything that had happened to her; now, and perhaps forever, something in her clutched the coverings of tension, of reserve, of aloneness, having learned what happened when they were dropped. Her mind could say that it would not happen with this young man, who was all gentleness and generosity; but the inner thing did not believe that; it believed nothing except what it had learned.

When they sat on the lawn smoking in the twilight, or inside in the big cool living room, the German talk went on quietly on the front steps. Mr. Loeb was a quiet man, and Fräulein did most of the talking. When she had said her say about the Nazis, Fräulein told him about the children— how Hugh was as good as an angel and Dicky was just so different, a sweet child but always up to something. The big June bugs and the moths banged against the screen door, and the light from the house came soft and yellow through the door and lay upon the stone slabs of the steps.

After a while, when she knew him pretty well, Fräulein told him about that Mr. Mason, what a bad man he was and how glad she was that they did not live with him any more.

"That poor lady," she said. "She took plenty of unhappiness from him, I can tell you. My, what a place! I can't tell you what a man he was. You wouldn't believe it. She never said anything, but I knew what went on. I don't mean maybe beating her; I know husbands get mad sometimes and beat their wives; that's all right, but that man! I tried to keep my babies from seeing the things that used to happen, and she helped me to do it. Not that I ever discussed it with her. She's that kind of lady, very proud, and I never saw her cry, only heard her sometimes, nights when he was very bad. She had such a look in her eyes in those days; she doesn't have it any more. I can tell you I'm glad she got rid of him. In this country it's very easy to divorce, you know."

"Yes," Mr. Loeb said quietly in the darkness.

"Well, she's got rid of him now and I'm glad. It would have killed her, a life like that. And my poor babies, what would have happened to them? She's got rid of him, thank God, and now she can just forget about him and be happy."

Mr. Loeb said nothing. He didn't smoke because he was saving money out of what he earned as a gardener. He just sat there in the darkness, and he smelled a little of sweat. Fräulein made allowances for his smell, knowing that he was a laborer and a Jew.

In the middle of the summer Hugh had a birthday and there was a big cake with seven candles, and one to grow on. Mr. Worthington came across the river for the little party, and both children were allowed to sit up till ten. After supper Mr. Loeb came walking down the road as usual, and Mrs. Mason called him in.

"Won't you have a piece of cake?" she said, holding out a plate to him. "Here's a piece with a candle."

Mr. Loeb made his bow and took the plate. Mrs. Mason smiled at him and he smiled at her and they did not say anything.

"We're going to play games in the living room," Mrs. Mason said. "Do you know any games, Mr. Loeb?"

The children were wild with excitement and ran round and round the room. Mr. Worthington showed Hugh a game with a piece of paper and a pencil, where he could guess any number of a total if he knew the right-hand numbers of the other lines. It was very mysterious. Dicky didn't understand it at all, and stamped and yelled to make them stop and do something else.

"I show you," Mr. Loeb said and hesitated. He asked Fräulein how to say something in English.

"He shows you a card trick," Fräulein said. Mr. Loeb's face was round and red and smiling. He took the pack of cards Mrs. Mason held out to him and drew out two aces.

"You see," he said to Hugh. "This is the farmer's cow." He pointed to the ace of hearts. "And this is Mrs. Sisson's cow." Mrs. Sisson owned the big place where Mr. Loeb was gardener. The card was the ace of clubs.

"Now I put them back again," Mr. Loeb said, shuffling the pack. "Now. Which cow you want to see? The farmer's cow? Mrs. Sisson's cow?"

Hugh deliberated, standing on one leg.

"Mrs. Sisson's cow," he decided.

"Then go to the barn and look for it!" cried Mr. Loeb.

The children were enchanted. They screamed and rolled

on the floor; Dicky kept crying, "Go to the barn and look for it!" Everybody was laughing.

"That was a very nice trick," Mrs. Mason said.

The children, after a while, fell to playing with the cards in a corner on the floor. Their two little round butts stuck up in the air, and their two little boys' heads were close together. From time to time they would break apart and shout about something, then go back to their game.

Mr. Loeb finished his cake and took out a folded handkerchief and wiped his mouth. He put the plate down carefully on the desk near him.

"Thank you very much," he said to Mrs. Mason. He was still standing up politely. Now he moved toward the door.

"Don't go away," she said. "Stay and talk. Sit down, please. You're part of the party."

"Thank you very much," he said.

"Understand you had a bad time with those Nazi fellows," Mr. Worthington said, being very friendly. "Were you really in one of the concentration camps?"

"Yes, I was. It was very bad."

"I was in Germany once," Mr. Worthington said. "The thing I kept noticing was, they were such damned bad losers. One night I went out drinking beer with a lot of fellows, me and a Frenchman I knew. They seemed all-right guys. But about two in the morning when we'd all drunk a lot of beer one of them said, 'Let's have a foot race.' Down the main street there, it was all quiet. Well, we started, and in a minute or two the Frenchman was way in front, and I was just behind. They just quit. Started walking along. Wouldn't admit they'd been racing. But if they'd been ahead you can bet they'd have rubbed it in. They want to be on top, that's it, and they take it out on the fellow underneath. If *they* get licked, they won't admit they were playing at all."

"Yes," said Mr. Loeb.

"You'd see fellows pick fights all the time, late at night, but you never saw them pick a fight unless they thought they could win. I played a lot of tennis over there and, of course, you know, American tennis. . . . They just wouldn't play again. Fellow over here would say, 'Let's play a return match and I'll lick you.' Not them."

"Yes," said Mr. Loeb.

"Those concentration camps, now. Just the fellows on top doing it to the fellows underneath. . . . It must have been a job keeping your courage up."

"I did not keep my courage up," Mr. Loeb said.

Mr. Worthington looked embarrassed.

"I don't blame you," he said. "The things you hear about those places; they break your spirit, I guess."

"Yes," Mr. Loeb said.

Fräulein sat under the light with her hair parted smoothly from the middle. She looked from Mr. Worthington to Mr. Loeb with self-assured eyes, not entirely understanding nor especially interested. Mr. Worthington twisted his long legs around one side of his chair.

"Anyway," he said, "it's all over for you, and I bet you're damned glad. You can just forget about all that stuff. This is a free country and you can do what you please and nobody can hurt you. It's all over and finished for you."

"For many it is not," Mr. Loeb said after a minute.

"Yeah, that's right. Poor devils."

"But," Mr. Loeb said hesitantly, "I have thought—I do not know how you say it—the more and more that are all the time—surrendered?"

"How do you mean?"

"He means oppressed," Mrs. Mason said. Mr. Loeb bowed to her.

"The more and more that are oppressed all the time, the more there are who know together the same thing, who have it together. When it is time and something happens to make it possible, there is something that all of these have had together and that will make them fight together. And now Frenchmen, too, Belgians, too, Flemings. If you have been in a concentration camp it is more together than that you might be of different countries. I speak very badly," Mr. Loeb said.

"No," Mrs. Mason said. "A common cause."

"Please?" Mr. Loeb asked. Fräulein spoke to him in German.

"I do not think that it is what you call cause, just. But knowing the concentration camps together. And what happens. That they were all crying together and no—courage. It makes them love."

"I don't see what you mean, exactly," Mr. Worthington said.

"I do," said Mrs. Mason. "They all remember the same thing together."

"Yes," Mr. Loeb said.

It seemed to her for a minute that she saw a sea of faces upturned, with the same look in all the thousands of them, the anguish, the terrible humiliation, the fear. It was a vast and growing sea, a great host of the tortured and the outcast, who had known ultimate fear instead of death and had been together in the valley of living hell. Separately each of them had known fear, had felt it burning in their veins, but now that they were all together the common fear became something else, larger, because there were so many millions of them, because they were not alone; it was set in dignity like a brand of brotherhood upon their lifted faces. And there were more of them, and more of them; if there were any more they would be the largest part of all the people on earth; this part would be strong by its numbers, and unshakable because of its suffering shared. This was something that she had never thought of before.

The children were sent off to bed at last, and Mrs. Mason went up to say good night to them. They lay in the two cot beds holding still while they said their prayers and then releasing into a last wild activity before the light should be turned out on them. She pushed them back under their sheets and kissed them. When she came downstairs again Mr. Worthington was sitting alone in the living room and the German voices were coming in softly through the screen door, from the warm darkness outside.

"Hello," Mr. Worthington said.

"Hello," she said. He reached out and took her hand as she passed where he sat, and kissed it. She stood still for a minute and smiled at him.

"I love you from now," he said. She went on looking at his face, bent over her hand but with his eyes looking up at her. After a minute the consciousness of what he said, where she was, the consciousness of herself came back over her and she drew away her hand. But for a moment she had lived in freedom, without watching herself.

In August Mrs. Sisson came back from California and opened the big house, and Mr. Loeb was much busier, doing all the things that Mrs. Sisson wanted done. Mrs. Sisson was a woman of fifty with black hair and a tall strong figure, who was very particular and liked her big place tended to perfection. Mrs. Mason knew her only slightly—to wave to when Mrs. Sisson drove along the road in her black car with her initials on the Connecticut license plate, and to speak to in a neighborly way when they met in the village. Sometimes now Fräulein started to tell her things about Mrs.

Sisson, how badly she treated all her servants, that she didn't even feed them properly, and had had three different waitresses in just the time she had been back.

"Nobody wants to work for a woman like that," Fräulein said.

But Mrs. Mason thought she ought not to listen to gossip and did not let Fräulein talk about it much.

One afternoon when she came out of the house Mr. Loeb was standing at the gate, talking to Fräulein. The two little boys were playing at the end of the lawn. Mr. Loeb was talking very fast in German, his voice much higher than usual, and Fräulein was looking at him and from time to time saying something calmly. Mrs. Mason walked down to the gate.

"Hello, Mr. Loeb," she said.

Mr. Loeb made his bow, but he seemed distracted. His eyes were tense and his face was even redder than usual. Mrs. Mason thought he looked almost as if he were going to cry. He turned to her and began to speak in English but stumbled and was silent.

"That Mrs. Sisson," Fräulein said. "She says to him she will report him to the Refugee Committee in New York so that he will never be able to get a job again."

"What did he do?"

"Nothing! She talked to him the way she talks to all the people who work for her; she bawled him out; he doesn't paint the fence quick enough; she says he's too slow. He's a foolish man; he pays attention to what she says. I tell him he ought to shrug his shoulders. What does he care, as long as he gets his pay?"

"I cannot have her speak to me that way!" Mr. Loeb broke out. "I cannot have her call me those things she says. I cannot...."

"He pays attention," Fräulein said. "He gets his feelings hurt too easy. I tell him, what does he care what she says? She's nothing. But he says to her, she can't speak to him that way; he cannot have her speak to him that way; he cannot stay and work for her if she talks like that. So she says all right, she's going to report him to the Refugee Committee."

"What can she say?"

"She was terrible angry," Mr. Loeb said. "She will say I do not work. She will say I am a no-good worker. She will say I speak to her fresh."

He looked at Mrs. Mason with his frightened eyes, and she nodded at him. Their eyes met and she nodded again, but slowly this time.

"I'll go up and talk to her," Mrs. Mason said. She did not feel at all afraid to do that, suddenly. She was not thinking about how she felt.

Fräulein shrugged.

"I don't think it makes any difference; you excuse me, Mrs. Mason. That Mrs. Sisson, she doesn't want Mr. Loeb to work for her any more because he talks back to her, and she writes the letter anyway."

"I'll write to the Refugee Committee, too," she said. "I'll tell them that I know all about Mr. Loeb and he's a good worker and a nice man. But I'll go up and talk to her now anyway."

Mr. Loeb leaned against the fence and looked at her. She came out of the gate into the road.

"Thank you very much," Mr. Loeb said in his foreign, formal voice.

She smiled at him. The tension had gone away from his eyes, the look of fear that she recognized had gone.

"You don't have to worry, you know," she said. "I wouldn't ever let anything happen to you."

I'D GIVE IT ALL UP FOR TAHITI
By Paul Kunasz
From *Story*

PAUL KUNASZ

was born in Denver, Colorado, thirty-one years ago, the son of a traveling evangelist. He was educated in Chicago, and has been many things, to quote Story: "telephone repairman, marine radio operator, assistant director of a New York men's club, gravedigger, salesman, actor, butler, publicity man for the first Byrd Antarctic Expedition, and most of the early transatlantic fliers, dude-ranch publicist, publicity man for MGM's glamour girls, scenarist, beachcomber, amateur swimmer, and deep-sea fisherman."

H<small>E CAME</small> down the aisle small and smiling and very dapper. His eyes, tie, and checked sport coat were bright blue, and he had a little pointed mustache like the late Douglas Fairbanks'. He looked a little like Fairbanks—he had the same jauntiness but he was smaller and on the chubby side. He was the last one aboard before we pulled out of Los Angeles and he found the seat, which he was to share with me, without fumbling all over the car. He threw his handbag and topcoat on the rack and sat down. "Damn near missed it," he said.

"How far you going?"

"Turkey," he said.

"*Where?*"

He grinned a Fairbanks grin. "Turkey. By way of Kansas City."

I thought he was one of those jokers and I wanted to get it over.

"Why Kansas City?" I said, like a straight man.

He was trying to get a clear look at a girl at the far end of the car but he was too short. "I'm ferrying a bomber across. New batch going to France."

"France? I thought you said——"

He tore his eyes away from the girl. "I'm not going to France; the ships are. I ferry one to New York, for dough, then I go to Turkey."

"You're a flier?"

"A bomber," he nodded, smiling.

He had just flown in, delivering a private plane from the factory at Kansas City, because he wanted to see a friend in

Los Angeles. His friend was up testing a new Douglas when he landed about an hour ago, and he almost missed the train waiting for him. "He's my pal," he said. "I wanted to see him before I left the States."

There was nothing to do but ask questions. I asked him what he was going to do in Turkey.

"Fly," he said. "England's hiring, but that's supposed to be on the q.t." He looked at me sharply. "You're not a government man, are you? I didn't think so. You alone? Let's have a beer." We got up. "That's something you can't get in China any more."

So I puzzled over that, following him through the train, noticing again how small he was. He led the way, glancing all around, smiling. Whenever he saw a girl he would look back at me and nod. We found seats in the club car, ordered beer, and I asked him what about China.

"A lousy place," he said. "Stay away from it." He glanced up the aisle, and I saw that an attractive girl was coming through the car. As she passed he hooked his thumbs under his coat and, blue eyes beaming up at her, he began to whistle, very loud. The girl frowned at us, annoyed. He looked hurt. "No soap," he said sadly. "Even here in my own country."

"Maybe it's the technique," I suggested.

"I don't know." He really looked depressed. Then he brightened. "My pal can get them, though. That's the one in L.A. now. You should see him. A Texan. You think you're tall? He's six foot four in his socks. We were buddies in China. He's just a kid, only twenty-five, but what a boy! I could never fight for beans, always got the hell kicked out of me, but you should see him. I wish he'd come along to Turkey." He fumbled through his pockets, found a small bottle, shook out two black pills, and washed them down with beer. "For tiger," he said. "Got tiger for belly."

I'd Give It All Up for Tahiti

We had pulled out of Pasadena and were racing along the open stretch between the Santa Anita track and San Bernardino. The palm trees were whipping around in the wind out here. "How was the trip coming this way?" I asked.

"From K.C.? Bad. Rain. Lightning. Wind. Everything. Got turned on my back coming through the Cajon Pass. Damn little puddle jumper. Forgot it wasn't a bomber. Scared the pants off me. Thought I never would get right side up again."

I was surprised. "You've been flying a long time, haven't you?"

"Well, let's see, I'm forty now. About twenty-two years. I've been scared lots of times too." He glanced out the window. "Boy, look at this thing go! We're doing a hundred easy. I don't like larruping this fast on the ground. Sure wish I had enough dough to fly back."

"Were you flying in China?"

He nodded. "Against the Japs. Bombing. Just got back."

"How's the war going?"

"Damned if I know." He seemed surprised at the question. "Give and take a year where I was. Back and forth. I don't know about anywhere else. Never asked. It didn't matter to me who won, just so they paid me. And they did, every week on the line; I've got to give 'em that. Good money too. Thirty-five bucks a day, American, whether we went up or not. How we loved to see it rain!

"But they get it away from you. Twenty bucks for a woman. Two bits to a Chink, twenty bucks to me." He shook his head. "That's how it is for me anywhere. I don't understand it. And even then they act like they're doing you a favor. You should see them, flat as sticks. No intellested." He made the face of profound boredom. "They think Americans are nuts, all the excitement. Dumb? Boy! In lots of ways. When you come in from a raid, for instance. Half the time they start belting at you with anti-aircraft. Their own ships. They get scared and can't tell the difference. Of course they can't hit you very often, but it gets in your hair. They did shoot my pal's landing gear off once, though. He got sore and threw his weight around, but they didn't know what he was saying, and he didn't know what they were, so it didn't do much good. They let us have it again next day. How about a whisky this time?"

"This is mine," I said.

"No, I like to buy drinks. I really like to; I don't know why. Don't let me talk you to death. It's just this being back in the States for a few days. What a language that Chinee is. But then I couldn't even learn French when I was flying over there. Not that it would have done me any good, with my luck, even in Paris. Jap is just as bad, but they're better people. I mean the girls are better than Chink girls. They're expensive, to me anyway, but you get something for your money. We always took our leaves in Japan."

"After bombing them in China?" I just wanted to be sure.

"Oh, they didn't know that," he said earnestly. "They just thought we were tourists, and anyway we had money to spend, so it was all right. The Jap girls are kind of cute. I like them even if they did roll me."

He grinned and rubbed his face, and I waited for him to go on.

"It was my own fault for getting stiff. I mean when my pal wasn't there. He had a girl, and I was wandering around Tokyo. We weren't sailing till next morning, and this was the night before. That was only, let's see, about two weeks ago. Well, I guess I just passed out in that joint, and they rolled me. It's all right; they always do if they can, but like a sucker

I had all my dough on me for Tahiti. American money too."

"Tahiti?" I was getting mixed up again.

"Two more of these," he said to the waiter. He put a half dollar on the tray, as he had twice before.

"This one's mine," I said. "That's a pretty big tip for each round, isn't it?"

He shrugged. "It makes him smile. I like to see people smile."

"Okay. So what about Tahiti?"

"Yes, well, you see my whole idea has been to get enough together to go and settle down there. They tell me it's a pretty good life, warm and peaceful and nice and no clothes or anything to worry about. After all, I'm not getting any younger, and you get tired banging around and getting shot at all the time and paying twenty bucks for a girl who don't give a damn about you. So. I've been trying to get down there for quite a while now. Thought if I had three or four grand I could go down and marry a native girl and take it easy the rest of my life. They say some of them aren't bad at all and that they like white men, really like them, I mean. That'd be all right, huh, having somebody really like you? I might even have some kids, just for the hell of it."

He paused to light a fresh cigarette off the stub of the old one. Somehow in that gesture he looked for a moment a full forty years.

"Well," he went on, "my pal used to hide part of my salary every week, and finally I had the money, or almost enough. Anyway I was going. I had passage for Hawaii where I'd lay over for Tahiti and then like a damn fool I got stinko and passed out in that place."

He stared into his glass. I couldn't think of anything to say. Then suddenly he laughed.

"My pal like to killed me when he found me next morning. First he kicked me around, then he kicked a couple of Japs on their can, then we had a free-for-all that sounded like a fire in a monkey house, and then the cops came." The smile faded. "So now I go to Turkey and try it again. Turkey, for God's sake. I been to Turkey."

I asked him if he knew yet just what the fight would be.

"Something the British are cooking up," he said. "I'll let them worry about it."

The car door nearest us opened, and two girls came in. Instantly the gloom was gone, and he was smiling that Fairbanks smile, looking up at them with concentrated interest. Just as they passed he compressed his lips and let loose a whistle that must have been heard in Los Angeles. The two girls jumped and turned. Everyone looked at us, startled. The girls glared, then continued in short, angry steps to the far door.

"See?" he said.

"I still think it's the technique," I said. "Maybe you shouldn't whistle."

"If I don't they won't even look at me."

"I see your point," I said.

"Well, anyway, let's have a drink." He pulled out the bottle of pills. "Time to feed tiger again."

A question had been forming in my mind, but I hesitated to ask it. I had read, as we all have, of the reticence with which men like fliers meet any question of their real feelings in war. So I led up to it tentatively by asking about the routine of aerial operations, and he told me how it was in China, how the American pilots waited until the racks were loaded before climbing into the ships, because "those dumb Chinks get so excited they're always tripping over something with a bomb in their hand and blowing up half the field."

Then how they flew two or three hours to their objective, a town or railroad or garrison, dropped their bombs, and hiked for home, sometimes with enemy pursuit ships after them, sometimes not.

"But they don't worry you," he said. "They can't fly any better than the Chinks, and we had fast American ships. The only danger is ramming into one of them in the dark."

He was sitting back in the big chair, his blue eyes smiling, his short, dapper legs crossed. We had another drink and were feeling pretty good, and I took a chance.

"On the level," I said, "how does it feel to bomb a town full of people, especially when they're people you like?"

He put his glass down and looked at me. For the first time he hesitated.

"Kid," he said after a moment, "you don't know. You just don't know." His eyes were very bright. "Look," he said. "You're up there say four thousand feet. It's night. You're carrying six twenty-four-pound bombs and four fifty-pounders. The town is pitch-dark below you; everybody's asleep, not a single light, just blackness, but you know from your charts you're right over it. You go into a turn and pull the release levers, one at a time, and drop your load. The twenty-four's, the fifty's. Then," he said, and stopped. "Well, it's beautiful, that's all. It's like fireworks. All those greens and yellows and reds blossoming out down there. It's the most beautiful thing you've ever seen in your life. But even so, I'd give it all up for Tahiti."

AFTERNOON IN THE JUNGLE
By Albert Maltz
From the *New Yorker*

ALBERT MALTZ

was born in 1908, in Brooklyn, New York. He was graduated from Columbia University in 1930 and attended the Yale School of the Drama under Professor George Pierce Baker. He wrote "Merry-Go-Round," and "Peace on Earth," both in collaboration with George Sklar, and "The Black Pit." He won the New Theater League contest for one-act plays with "Private Hicks." He won first prize in the O. Henry Memorial Award Prize Stories of 1938 *with "The Happiest Man on Earth," from* Harper's Magazine. *His stories are included in numerous anthologies. He worked during the summer of 1932 for Paramount Pictures, and was an instructor in playwriting at the Writers' Conference in the Rocky Mountains, at Boulder, Colorado, in 1939 and 1940. His novel,* The Underground Stream (1940), *was warmly received by the critics.*

Charles Fallon, aged thirteen, jiggled a hand grenade in his palm and waited for the traffic lights to change. When the Eighth Avenue bus moved off he took cover behind a snow pile. At twenty yards he looped the deadly missile high into the air. It exploded squarely on top of the bus. Charlie smiled with satisfaction and scooped up snow for another grenade.

He progressed slowly up Hudson Street, killing time, a smallish, wiry, rather white-faced boy with tight lips. At the corner of Perry he found an envelope containing one million two hundred and thirty-four dollars. He dropped his grenade and crossed the avenue to a pawnshop. It was Sunday, and there was a steel-mesh gate in front of the door, but Charlie made a wish and got inside. He helped himself to a flashlight, a pair of ice skates, a Boy Scout knife, binoculars, a picture of Mary in the Manger, and a lot of other things. He left a hundred-thousand-dollar bill in payment.

At Twelfth Street he crossed the avenue again. He wandered down Greenwich, stopping to gaze at the pictures in the lobby of a movie house. He decided that Anita Louise was nicer-looking than a stuck-up like Norma Shearer. He kissed Anita Louise. They sat on the edge of her million-dollar swimming pool, and he kissed her again. She was about to tell him how swell he was when the ticket-taker came over and said, "Beat it, kid." He scuffed away.

At Eleventh Street and Seventh Avenue he planted himself before the window of a bakery. In rapid succession he ate a chocolate cake, a napoleon, a charlotte russe, and two twenty-five-cent peach cakes with whipped cream. He was just about to buy the whole bakery when a lady came out and told him to stop leaning against the glass and move along.

Bored, he turned down Seventh Avenue and started home. Between Commerce and Morton he went into a candy store where he occasionally traded. The stout proprietress wheezed over to the counter.

"How much is the caramels?" Charlie asked.

"Two for a penny."

"And these?"

"Four for a penny."

"And the lollipops?"

"A penny apiece. Which do you want?"

"I'm going home and get some money. I'll be back in eight minutes."

He crossed the street again and walked down to Houston, wishing he could buy some candy. He knew a way to make one caramel last half an hour. You put it on your tongue and sucked it. It took will power not to chew it right down, but the sweet taste stayed with you longer. And you avoided the toothache. He took off his soaking mittens and blew on his hands. He wished it weren't Sunday. His neighborhood was like a cemetery on Sunday because the factories were closed.

A bus approached, going south. Old Man Sheehy and his wife, who lived in Charlie's house, ran across Varick to catch it. The bus stopped. The old couple hurried forward, and as Mr. Sheehy took his hand from his pocket, a fifty-cent piece dropped to the sidewalk. He made a frantic grab for it, but the coin rolled onto the subway grille and dropped to the bottom of the pit. Muttering, the old man stepped up into the bus. He held the door back with his hand and shouted

Afternoon in the Jungle

out to Charlie, who had run over to the grille, "If you find it, Charlie, I'll give you a dime!"

"Sure," said Charlie.

The bus moved off, and Charlie raced away. He would need chewing gum and a string to do the lifting. Fifty cents! He had retrieved pennies from subway grilles—once even a dime—but this was the first chance he had ever had at so much money. It would be the simplest thing in the world, of course, to tell Old Man Sheehy that he had not been able to find it.

He covered the distance to his house on Downing Street at a run. He was too excited to remember the broken step on the second flight of stairs, and his right foot slipped through, flinging him headlong and giving him a terrible crack on the shin. He limped up the remaining three flights with tears in his eyes.

His mother was sitting at the window, darning.

"Ma, can I *please* have three pennies?" he asked. Phrased as a question, his words expressed a command. He had learned long ago that his mother always yielded to bullying.

"Hush, for goodness!" she said. "Your father's asleep. Now, why do you come in here with your wet rubbers and filthy the floor?"

"I'm going right out again. Just give me the pennies, Ma."

"I can't give you pennies. You had a penny for candy on Tuesday."

"Ma, I got to have them. Look, there's a dime that fell down in the subway place. If I had some chewing gum I could get it up."

"So that's it? You were trying to hold out on me, weren't you?" She laughed softly. "I'll give you one penny, not three, and you'll have to give it back."

"One's no good. I gotta have three. I can't do anything

with one. It doesn't make a big enough piece of gum, don't you see, Ma?"

Mrs. Fallon went into the kitchen and came back with her change purse. "I only have two pennies," she said. "Beside a dime for church tonight."

"Well, give me that. I'll——" He stopped to sneeze. "I'll change it. You'll get it all back, honest."

"No. I can't risk it." She gave him the two pennies.

Glumly Charlie accepted them. This would make his task harder, but he knew that his mother was inflexible about church money as about nothing else.

"And I expect the two pennies back," she said.

"O.K." He was already busy in the kitchen, searching for a string.

"Ah, yes," his mother said, in the long-suffering whine he knew so well, "in the old days if you'd come to your father or me for a penny we'd given you a nickel. If you'd asked for a nickel you'd get a dime."

Charlie found a ball of heavy cord, cut off a ten-foot length, and stuffed it quickly into his pocket.

"But now your father's a cripple, poor man," his mother went on. "Limping where other men walk, working at night when other men work at day, he's grateful for the little he has."

"O.K., Ma, I'm going," said Charlie. Without waiting for an answer, he banged out. He told himself that all mothers were a pain and fathers worse. Catch the old man giving up a glass of beer to buy his kid a chocolate bar.

He ran down the block and around the corner to the candy store on Carmine Street. He bought two boxes of Chiclets and emptied them both into his mouth. The gum had to be moist and pliable or else the coin wouldn't stick to it. He trotted across Varick, chewing hard but on the right side of his mouth only, so that he wouldn't get a toothache. Near the bus sign he lay down full length on the icy grille. The concrete base at the bottom of the pit was covered with debris and snow and little puddles of water. Methodically he began to search for the coin, inching himself along from one spot to another on the grille. His heart pumped with excitement, and an image of the bakery window danced in his head.

Ten minutes passed with no result, and he stopped to blow on his hands. Then he returned to his task.

He located the coin. It lay half in a puddle of water, half on the concrete base—a difficult target. With a tight little smile on his lips he knotted the end of his cord several times and wound the chewing gum around the knot, giving it a broad, flat base. A wrist loop at the other end of the cord prevented his losing it. Then, after thrusting the wad of gum into his mouth for a last moistening, he lowered it carefully to the bottom.

Working intently, he did not notice the man who had come up behind him, a small, shabby man of about forty-five whose thin face was reddened by the wind but was liverish gray beneath the surface color.

Charlie heard him before he saw him; the man's breathing was labored, as though he were straining at a heavy burden. The boy looked up briefly and went back to his work. He was concentrating upon the most difficult part of his job. The wad of gum was not sufficiently heavy to make a plumb line, yet he must drop it with some force on the coin in order to make it take hold. It might take a hundred trials to achieve one accurate strike.

The man watched in silence for a moment. Then he dropped to his knees by Charlie's side, exclaiming in a hoarse tone, "Fifty cents, eh?" He peered down at the swaying length of cord above the coin. "Ah, it's hard that way, isn't it?" he asked softly.

Charlie didn't answer.

The man peered down to watch another trial. "Sure, the gum gets solid right away in this cold," he commented. "It don't look to me like you'll make it, kid. And it's getting dark. You need real tools for this job. You'll never get it this way."

Without looking up, Charlie said loudly, "Who's asking you?"

The man got to his feet. Quickly he glanced all around. There was no one in sight. He stepped back a few paces and unbuttoned his overcoat. Secured to the inside of his coat by leather straps were four lengths of broom handle, whittled to reduce their thickness, each about three feet long, each fitted at one end with a rubber socket by which it could be joined to another length. With practiced efficiency he connected them. At the tip of the final length there was a small rubber suction cup. He stepped forward, fitted the end of his pole neatly into the grate, and, dropping to his knees, thrust it to the bottom. "I'll show you how a professional does it," he said lightly. He kept his eyes averted from the boy's face. "Now, this is one method. Another is cup grease. With cup grease you can pick up a bracelet. But when you spot some change a suction cup is——"

"What's the idea?" Charlie cried out in fury. "What do you think you're doing?"

"I'll show you how a professional does it, kid."

"Get out of here!" With his left hand Charlie tugged savagely at the man's arm. "Get out of here!"

The man fended him off, laughing in a hoarse tone that had no humor in it. "What's the difference? You wouldn't get it," he said. "Why let it lay there for somebody else?"

"The hell I won't get it!" Charlie cried. "You leave it alone. It's mine. Please, mista."

"I'll give you a nickel," said the man.

Charlie pulled up his string with decision and crammed it into his pocket. Then, rising, he stepped behind the man and kicked him viciously in the small of his back. The man cried out in pain. Instantly Charlie retreated a dozen feet.

"That's a hell of a thing to do," the man groaned, holding his back. "I'll break your neck, you little rat. You almost made me drop my pole." They glared at each other for a moment, motionless and undecided. There were thirty years between them, yet in a way they looked startlingly alike. Both were small, the boy as boy, the man as man; both were drawn, hard-bitten.

The man knelt down again, watching Charlie carefully. He lowered the pole but kept his head raised. Charlie stood indecisively. Then he ran to a snow pile by the curbstone. The man shifted to face him. "You come near me, and I'll break your neck," he said. "I'm telling you. Beat it. I won't even give you the nickel now. I'm mad."

Charlie grabbed a chunk of ice from the snow pile. He flung it with all his strength. It missed by a foot, but the man was frightened and jumped to his feet, pulling up the pole. Charlie retreated behind the snow pile. Trembling, eyes fixed on his enemy, he clawed under the crust of ice.

"You're looking for trouble, ain't you?" the man said bitterly. He glanced up and down the deserted, darkening avenue. "You think I like this?" he asked suddenly. "Do you think I like to fight with a kid like you over fifty cents?"

A snowball struck his knee, just below the protection of his frayed overcoat. He shook his fist, his voice swelling with anger. "I'll give you trouble if you want it, you kid!" He stopped, panting for breath. Then he dropped the pole and hurled himself forward. Charlie darted out of reach. A snowball, almost pure ice, struck the man full in the forehead. He clapped a hand to his head, half sobbing in rage and pain.

"How do you like that, you skunk?" the boy cried.

The man chased him, but Charlie was twice as agile and kept the snow barrier between them. Within a minute the man stopped, his mouth open, a hand pressed to his heaving chest. Without uttering a word, he went back to the grille and crouched down, lowering his pole.

Frantic, the boy varied his attack. He came past at an angling run, from behind, and slammed down a piece of loose ice. It struck the man at the base of his neck. His body quivered, but he didn't turn. He was raising the pole to slip it through another opening in the grille. Charlie made another rush, this time determined to use his feet. Swearing, the man leaped up to meet him, catching the boy's arm as he veered off in terror and swinging him in. He had him, gripped by both arms. The pole lay on the grille between them.

"I ought to break your neck!" he cried, shaking him. "I ought to break your ratty little neck! But I'm not going to, see? You're a kid. But you listen——"

Charlie twisted hard, broke free, and at the same moment stamped on the man's foot. He ran to the security of the snow pile. The man stood looking at him blankly, his face twisted in pain. "Oh, my Jesus," he said, "what a little gutter rat! Did I hurt you? Did I do anything to you when I had the chance? I was going to make you a proposition." A snowball struck him in the chest. "All right," he said. "I can't get it if you don't let me. You can't get it if I don't let you. We're both going to lose it. It's getting dark. I'll split with you. I'll give you twenty-five cents."

"No!" Charlie cried. "It's mine!" His whole body was shaking.

"Don't you see you can't get it without real tools?" The man was pleading now. "Your gum ain't no good in this cold weather."

"It's mine."

"Jesus, you found it, I'll admit it," the man said. "But I got a suction cup. I can get it for both of us."

"No."

"Jesus Christ, I got to have some of it!" the man cried, his voice corroded by shame and bitterness. "This is my *business,* kid. It's all I do. Can't you understand? I been walking all day. I ain't found a thing. You got to let me have some of it. You got to!"

"No."

The man flung out his hands. "Oh, you kid, you kid!" he cried despairingly. "If you was ten years older you'd understand. Do you think I like to do this? If you was ten years older I could talk to you. You'd understand."

Charlie's lips tightened. His white face, spotted by the cold, was filled with rage. "If I was ten years older I'd beat your face in," he said.

The man bent painfully and picked up the pole. Limping slightly, his hand pressed to the small of his back, he walked away. He was crying.

Charlie stood trembling in triumph, his face turned to stone.

It had become dark.

CAPUT MORTUUM
By Edita Morris
From *Harper's Bazaar*, New York

EDITA MORRIS

was born in Sweden, but has lived in a number of countries. She is married to I. V. Morris, an American, also a writer, and since the outbreak of the war has lived in Mexico. She writes in Swedish and English, and her stories have appeared in anthologies, including the O'Brien collection. Her book of short stories, Birth of an Old Lady, *was published simultaneously in London and Stockholm, and was well received. She is at work on a novel with a Swedish background.*

When Father's wife went shopping, he used to tell us about Mother. My, but they must have had it cozy! Cozy as cozy can be! Winter or summer, it was always warm and snug. In winter Father used to sit before a sizzling fire in a little room with carpets on both floor and walls, while Mother stood in a warm velvet dress laying out the brandy glasses on the woolly pouf by his feet. In summer they would stay on the balcony, and Father would lie fanning himself and laughing because of the beautiful pearls of sweat on Mother's brow. Before them would be an ice bucket, and Mother would stand twirling about the punch bottle in the ice to get it cool.

"Was it always time to put out drinks?" asked Elsa.

"What?" said Father. "Oh no—no, of course not," he said, and looked quickly toward the door. When he saw that it was properly shut he put his hand over his eyes; it looked white against his dark nose. When he took it away he was smiling at us. "There was an orange-colored lamp above the dining table," he said. "It made the schnapps decanter glow like a rose! Your mother would pour us out two little glasses the moment that she heard my key in the lock, and I'd march straight in with fur coat and cap and snow and all, and we'd toss off our glasses—just like that! When we had filled them again we would walk about with our arms around each other and glasses in our hands. Round and round the table we would walk, singing, 'Drink, drink, the golden drop, the joyful drop. La, la, la—la, la, la.' Oh, children, her waist was thin as a wasp's. And it was just as silky as a silk worm's waist."

"Weren't you hungry?" Elsa said. "Didn't you want your dinner?"

"Eh?" said Father. "Dinner? B'r. Don't speak of dinner." But then he said quickly, putting his arm around both of us, "Of course *you* must eat—big growing girls like you! You must eat great hunks of meat and bread and such things. But Mother and I—why, we just used to nibble." He sat and laughed, and his laughter had a rustling sound, as if he were crumbling up tissue paper inside him. "We would find a fork and sit on the edge of the table to peck at things," he said. "Pickled and salted and soused things that just beg for schnapps and make beer seem like a river breaking through parched earth. My word but we used to have our fill of schnapps! The room simply stood on end."

"And then Mother would bring out the brandy. She would put it on the pouf, wouldn't she?" I asked Father.

"Yes, yes," Father answered, laughing, and he leaned back in the sofa and drew up his knees with his hands. "Yes, she'd bring in the brandy. I'd get myself safely installed in the big chair, and then she'd dance out and come back slowly— slowly, balancing the bottle on her head, just like an Italian girl balances a pitcher. Her arms would be raised up high, like two long lily stalks, and her hands would hold the gleaming bottle on her head, red with the color of *caput mortuum*——"

"Of what?" Elsa asked.

"Of blood that has been tinged by death. Dark and frightening is the color of brandy grown old in cellars."

Soon afterward, Father told us, Mother would go to fetch another beautiful bottle, and then later they would go to sleep beside the fire. Then little gilt hairpins would drop out of Mother's hair—one by one they would drop upon the carpet. Often they would sleep there in the big chair the whole night through. How lovely it must have been! How wonderful! It was only the maid who spoiled things. Father said that she used to get furious when she found them there, so when he woke up toward dawn he would carry Mother to their bed in her long crumpled velvet dress. She would be quite limp, and her velvet arms fell down his back like lily stalks that had been broken. They would sit on the bed and try to get undressed, and giggle and giggle because it was so difficult. Almost impossible it used to be to get undressed, and in the end they sometimes had to cut Mother's ribbons and fastenings with a knife!

"Why was it so difficult?" Elsa asked.

"Well, have you ever tried to get undressed, my little Elsa, when you were a bit—that is to say when you were . . ." He didn't finish, and sat and laughed until he rattled. It sounded as if there was something broken loose inside him. "No, I don't suppose you ever have," he answered himself. "Buttons stick in their holes and won't come out when one's—when one's—sleepy," he said, and all at once he looked as if he were terribly bored with Elsa.

Apart from the maid's not letting them sleep in the big chair, they didn't like her anyway. She used to stand and sigh while she sponged the front of Mother's velvet dress, for the dried punch used to get as stiff as sugar. She looked disgusted and superior as she did it. She gave Mother the shivers, too, because of her spying on them. When she brought in Grandma's weekly letter, she used to watch Mother with a sneer while she read it aloud to Father, though pretending to be dusting the whole time. Once when Grandma wrote about Elsa and me and about how happy we were with her in the country the maid gave a sort of a snort and walked right out of the room! After that they sacked her.

It was ever so much nicer without a maid. They soon found

out that they hadn't really needed her because they didn't want to eat much anyway, and it was terribly hot, so they just lived out on their little balcony. They used to bring all the punch bottles out at once, so that they wouldn't have to keep trotting back and forth all the time. "The bottles lay and pitched about in the ice pail and got white as snow men from the cooking salt," said Father.

But there were other people just as silly as the maid. They stood on the street and stared up at them as Mother sat singing on the balcony with her head against the creeper roses, and roses stuck in her hair. "People can't bear you when you're happy," Father said—at least not when you're always happy, as he and Mother were. "How can they expect the Kingdom of God to come when they won't even let happiness come?" said Father.

One day a policeman came up to see them. He wasn't really nasty but just stood about smelling sweaty and talking in a haw-haw way. The trouble was that Mother had emptied her glass of punch over the balcony railing, right onto the hat of an old gentleman who was walking by. The whole time that the policeman talked Father kept his arm about Mother's waist, and Mother laughed and laughed and told the policeman that there were roses growing on the gentleman's hat and that she only had wanted to water them for him. She said that she was going to do that every time he passed underneath their balcony. "Every time—every single time," Mother promised him. Then she took all the flowers from her hair and hung them on the policeman's saber belt, and he wasn't angry about the whole thing at all. Only after that they weren't so fond of the balcony any more. There always seemed to be a crowd of people by the lamppost staring up at them.

Anyway, it got to be winter soon, and it was terribly cozy

indoors, with no maid to worry them. Mother always had thought it silly to fuss so much about being dressed or not being dressed and to make such a difference between day and night. Now she began to think it even sillier, so she brought her playing cards and all sorts of things to bed with her. She had a basket with skeins of colored silk—burgundy and emerald and milky gray—and she used to sit and play with them, loving their lovely colors.

Oh, how Father hated to leave her and go down to the hard icy street, where heaps of people, blue from the cold, ran in one direction and heaps ran in the other, all staring straight ahead! "And where did they think that they were going?" Father said. "As if one ever got anywhere by tearing about!"

Mother called their poster bed "our little house with the thatched roof," and Father began to stay in their little house the whole day too. They got awfully angry with him at his office because of that and told him that he needn't come back. But a lot Father cared! It wasn't as if Mother and he wanted to buy big roast beefs all the time, costing lots of money, or legs of mutton. They ate hardly a thing and didn't need any money. They stayed in their little house with the thatched roof all day long, and Father would just kick all the playing cards and the spools of silk and the brandy glasses onto the floor when they wanted to go to sleep.

Sometimes he got up and made a fire in the sitting room, and then Mother's bare feet would come pattering after him. They would fetch a nice bottle and sit in their big chair for a change, Mother with just her Angora shawl on. It felt like a kitten's ear to touch, and Mother loved it like a live animal, even though it was in rags with bits of wool sticking out of it.

Much of the trouble began with that shawl, Father told us.

It was in February or thereabouts, and they had forgotten to answer Grandma's letters ever since the autumn. "Happy people never bother about writing letters," Father said. Finally Grandma sent her housekeeper up to town. She came marching in one day and began to open all the windows and to tidy up. She even tried to coax Mother to get out of bed and dress. She got out a pair of shoes and made Mother put her feet in them. Through it all Mother sat as still as a flower growing in a pot, but when that awful woman started pulling off the shawl, then she went wild. She ripped off everything that the housekeeper had put on her, and the clothes flew about the room like birds. The moment the housekeeper was gone, they were back in bed again! They jumped right back into bed and took a lovely red bottle of brandy with them to celebrate. They were so happy to be alone again they didn't know what to do and they finished up the whole bottle before you could say knife. My, but they must have had it cozy! Cozy as cozy can be!

But that housekeeper was a cunning one! She sneaked out to make a telephone call to Grandma and then she took the night train back to the country and sat talking Grandma full of nonsense. In two days Grandma herself was in town, and then all sorts of things began to happen. Father wasn't able to remember them exactly, but he said that all at once life went limp. It must have been early spring, for there always seemed to be rain washing down the windowpanes, and inside the flat there was plenty of water, too, for a hag was scrubbing floors. Yes, there was water everywhere—and tears. Grandma sat weeping. Tears and the hag's scrubbing brush and rain on the windowpanes! "Oh Lord!" Father said, and he rocked back and forth shivering between Elsa and me. He got all cold, just thinking back on it. The pores in his nose looked as big as the holes in the top of a pepper box.

He remembered also a strange female in white being about during those awful days. She had worn a badge saying that she was a nurse or something and had had on such a blinding white apron that Father had to blink his eyes and screw up his face when he passed her in the hall. Maybe it was because she was ugly that he simply had to make faces at her when he talked to her—such awful faces that she used to get scared and run off screaming. Of course he had been spoiled, always having Mother's delicious little face so close to his, with her funny nose and warm mouth and silky cheeks. He said that he used to find himself doing the queerest things, like wiggling his ears or twitching his nose, whenever he had to look at an ugly woman.

But though there were strangers in their flat, there was one thing no one dared do, and that was rout Mother out of bed. The doctor said no. She wasn't at all well, poor little love, Father told us. She was ill, ill. And the worst of it was that they wouldn't let him nurse her. Think of it! He, who knew exactly what she wanted and needed, wasn't allowed to look after her. One little glass or two would have set her right, but the idiots told him that that was just what she shouldn't have! If he wanted to kill himself he should go ahead, only he had to leave Mother alone. They wouldn't even let him in her room, for fear that he might sneak her something. Oh, wasn't it cruel! When Father and Mother were just aching for each other, and Mother lay calling for him and screaming so loud that the neighbors got furious. It was the wickedest thing.

"Don't you think I could have taken care of Mother, children?" Father asked us, his face wet from crying. "Don't you?" And I answered, "Of course, darling. Of course you could have!" We sat, all three of us, with our arms around each other and we held each other hard.

Father told us that the people in the other flats kept on complaining, and that that was the reason they made Mother go to that place, whatever it was called, where they teach people to get well. But when they wouldn't let Mother take her shawl along with her because it was so dirty and wouldn't even let her tie funny ribbons in her hair to look pretty for the journey, then Father saw red. He gave that awful nurse such a whack on her stony chest that she screamed and toppled over, and then Father ran into Mother's room. Oh, how he and Mother held on to each other! How they squeezed one another!

"Oh, oh, children!!" said Father weeping. "Oh, it's as if it was yesterday. It hurts like a red-hot iron stuck in here—here! And I didn't even have time to sneak her a little something to comfort her before those ambulance men came clamp-clamping up the stairs. Oh! Oh!" He sat and wept and he was so thin for Elsa and me to hug. He scarcely could hold himself upright. His tears fell into our hair and felt just like rain, and we kept listening for the front door, so scared that Father's wife would come back and find him like that again.

"Was the hospital terrible?" Elsa said. She knew that she shouldn't ask that but she never could stop herself.

"Eh?" said Father. "The what? Oh, the hospital. Yes, it was ghastly—it was a dreadful place, children. And to think of Mother in her hard white bed, seeing snakes and tigers with me not there to help her! To think of her straining backward when they hissed and breathed their hot breath on her! That's what finished me off—sitting in our empty flat thinking of my darling. In the end I only wanted to crow like a cock. Do you know, children, that's the only thing I wanted to do. I don't know why, but it helped me when I stood on one leg and crowed really hard."

Oh, what awful days Father had! And later when they locked him in the hospital, too, it was worse. They used to jump on him if he even sneezed, and not a drop of anything could he squeeze out of them.

"I needed something—I needed something terribly to make me feel close to her again," said Father. "The tiniest little drop would have helped me along after my darling was . . . I mean after my darling wasn't any more. Oh, I was so alone, so cold! All day I sat hunched up on a little chair behind the barred window and thought of how cold I was. I couldn't think of anything else. And I'm frozen now, children! My teeth are chattering, even though I'm cured. They won't stop chattering till I get a little something to remember Mother by. Just a little something warming—a little glassful . . ."

Elsa and I lay across Father's knees and cried. We knew that we'd have to grow up and earn money quickly so as to get him a little something warming. Elsa asked, "What was the color of the stuff in the bottle that Mother carried on her head that day—that day you were so awfully happy?"

"Caput mortuum," Father said. "The color of blood that has been tinged by death. Oh, children, I can't wait much longer. My legs are getting icy—that's the end. I must shout. I must!" And he opened his mouth. But we clapped our hands over it, for there were the steps of Father's wife coming down the passage, click-click. She had finished with her shopping.

MY FRIEND FLICKA
By Mary O'Hara
From *Story*

MARY O'HARA

was born in Brooklyn, New York, on the Heights, the daughter of an Episcopalian clergyman, and the great-granddaughter of Gardiner Spring, pastor of the Brick Church, New York, and for whom Spring Street in Manhattan is named. On her father's side the family were Philadelphia Quakers, and William Penn and Jonathan Edwards are among her forebears. She was educated in Brooklyn and at a New England finishing school, and spent two years in Europe learning languages and studying music. She is also a composer, and has had a number of musical compositions published. Her first marriage took her to California, where she began writing for the screen. Among her notable successful screen adaptations were the first version of "The Prisoner of Zenda," "Peg o' My Heart," and "Black Oxen." Since 1930 she has lived on a horse ranch in Wyoming. She has made the short story reprinted here into a full-length novel under the same title, which was published during the summer of 1941 by J. B. Lippincott Company.

Report cards for the second semester were sent out soon after school closed in mid-June.

Kennie's was a shock to the whole family.

"If I could have a colt all for my own," said Kennie, "I might do better."

Rob McLaughlin glared at his son. "Just as a matter of curiosity," he said, "how do you go about it to get a *zero* in an examination? Forty in arithmetic; seventeen in history! But a *zero*? Just as one man to another, what goes on in your head?"

"Yes, tell us how you do it, Ken," chirped Howard.

"Eat your breakfast, Howard," snapped his mother.

Kennie's blond head bent over his plate until his face was almost hidden. His cheeks burned.

McLaughlin finished his coffee and pushed his chair back. "You'll do an hour a day on your lessons all through the summer."

Nell McLaughlin saw Kennie wince as if something had actually hurt him.

Lessons and study in the summertime, when the long winter was just over and there weren't hours enough in the day for all the things he wanted to do!

Kennie took things hard. His eyes turned to the wide-open window with a look almost of despair.

The hill opposite the house, covered with arrow-straight jack pines, was sharply etched in the thin air of the eight-thousand-foot altitude. Where it fell away, vivid green grass ran up to meet it; and over range and upland poured the strong Wyoming sunlight that stung everything into burning color. A big jack rabbit sat under one of the pines, waving his long ears back and forth.

Ken had to look at his plate and blink back tears before he could turn to his father and say carelessly, "Can I help you in the corral with the horses this morning, Dad?"

"You'll do your study every morning before you do anything else." And McLaughlin's scarred boots and heavy spurs clattered across the kitchen floor. "I'm disgusted with you. Come, Howard."

Howard strode after his father, nobly refraining from looking at Kennie.

"Help me with the dishes, Kennie," said Nell McLaughlin as she rose, tied on a big apron, and began to clear the table.

Kennie looked at her in despair. She poured steaming water into the dishpan and sent him for the soap powder.

"If I could have a colt," he muttered again.

"Now get busy with that dish towel, Ken. It's eight o'clock. You can study till nine and then go up to the corral. They'll still be there."

At supper that night Kennie said, "But Dad, Howard had a colt all of his own when he was only eight. And he trained it and schooled it all himself; and now he's eleven, and Highboy is three, and he's riding him. I'm nine now and even if you did give me a colt now I couldn't catch up to Howard because I couldn't ride it till it was a three-year-old and then I'd be twelve."

Nell laughed. "Nothing wrong with that arithmetic."

But Rob said, "Howard never gets less than seventy-five average at school, and hasn't disgraced himself and his family by getting more demerits than any other boy in his class."

Kennie didn't answer. He couldn't figure it out. He tried hard; he spent hours poring over his books. That was supposed to get you good marks, but it never did. Everyone said he was bright. Why was it that when he studied he didn't learn? He had a vague feeling that perhaps he looked out the window too much, or looked through the walls to see clouds and sky and hills and wonder what was happening out there. Sometimes it wasn't even a wonder, but just a pleasant drifting feeling of nothing at all, as if nothing mattered, as if there was always plenty of time, as if the lessons would get done of themselves. And then the bell would ring, and study period was over.

If he had a colt . . .

When the boys had gone to bed that night Nell McLaughlin sat down with her overflowing mending basket and glanced at her husband.

He was at his desk as usual, working on account books and inventories.

Nell threaded a darning needle and thought, "It's either that whacking big bill from the vet for the mare that died or the last half of the tax bill."

It didn't seem just the auspicious moment to plead Kennie's cause. But then, these days, there was always a line between Rob's eyes and a harsh note in his voice.

"Rob," she began.

He flung down his pencil and turned around.

"Damn that law!" he exclaimed.

"What law?"

"The state law that puts high taxes on pedigreed stock. I'll have to do as the rest of 'em do—drop the papers."

"Drop the papers! But you'll never get decent prices if you don't have registered horses."

"I don't get decent prices now."

"But you will someday if you don't drop the papers."

"Maybe." He bent again over the desk.

Rob, thought Nell, was a lot like Kennie himself. He set his heart. Oh, how stubbornly he set his heart on just some one thing he wanted above everything else. He had set his heart on horses and ranching way back when he had been a crack rider at West Point; and he had resigned and thrown away his army career just for the horses. Well, he'd got what he wanted. . . .

She drew a deep breath, snipped her thread, laid down the sock, and again looked across at her husband as she unrolled another length of darning cotton.

To get what you want is one thing, she was thinking. The three-thousand-acre ranch and the hundred head of horses. But to make it pay—for a dozen or more years they had been trying to make it pay. People said ranching hadn't paid since the beef barons ran their herds on public land; people said the only prosperous ranchers in Wyoming were the dude ranchers; people said . . .

But suddenly she gave her head a little rebellious, gallant shake. Rob would always be fighting and struggling against something, like Kennie; perhaps like herself too. Even those first years when there was no water piped into the house, when every day brought a new difficulty or danger, how she had loved it! How she still loved it!

She ran the darning ball into the toe of a sock, Kennie's sock. The length of it gave her a shock. Yes, the boys were growing up fast, and now Kennie—Kennie and the colt . . .

After a while she said, "Give Kennie a colt, Rob."

"He doesn't deserve it." The answer was short. Rob pushed away his papers and took out his pipe.

"Howard's too far ahead of him, older and bigger and quicker, and his wits about him, and——"

"Ken doesn't half try, doesn't stick at anything."

She put down her sewing. "He's crazy for a colt of his own. He hasn't had another idea in his head since you gave Highboy to Howard."

"I don't believe in bribing children to do their duty."

"Not a bribe." She hesitated.

"No? What would you call it?"

She tried to think it out. "I just have the feeling Ken isn't going to pull anything off, and"—her eyes sought Rob's—"it's time he did. It isn't the school marks alone, but I just don't want things to go on any longer with Ken never coming out at the right end of anything."

"I'm beginning to think he's just dumb."

"He's not dumb. Maybe a little thing like this—if he had a colt of his own, trained him, rode him——"

Rob interrupted. "But it isn't a little thing, nor an easy thing to break and school a colt the way Howard has schooled Highboy. I'm not going to have a good horse spoiled by Ken's careless ways. He goes woolgathering. He never knows what he's doing."

"But he'd *love* a colt of his own, Rob. If he could do it, it might make a big difference in him."

"*If* he could do it! But that's a big if."

At breakfast next morning Kennie's father said to him, "When you've done your study come out to the barn. I'm going in the car up to section twenty-one this morning to look over the brood mares. You can go with me."

"Can I go, too, Dad?" cried Howard.

McLaughlin frowned at Howard. "You turned Highboy out last evening with dirty legs."

Howard wriggled. "I groomed him——"

"Yes, down to his knees."

"He kicks."

"And whose fault is that? You don't get on his back again until I see his legs clean."

The two boys eyed each other, Kennie secretly triumphant and Howard chagrined. McLaughlin turned at the door, "And, Ken, a week from today I'll give you a colt. Between now and then you can decide what one you want."

Kennie shot out of his chair and stared at his father. "A—a—spring colt, Dad, or a yearling?"

McLaughlin was somewhat taken aback, but his wife concealed a smile. If Kennie got a yearling colt he would be even up with Howard.

"A yearling colt, your father means, Ken," she said smoothly. "Now hurry with your lessons. Howard will wipe."

Kennie found himself the most important personage on the ranch. Prestige lifted his head, gave him an inch more of height and a bold stare, and made him feel different all the way through. Even Gus and Tim Murphy, the ranch hands, were more interested in Kennie's choice of a colt than anything else.

Howard was fidgety with suspense. "Who'll you pick, Ken? Say—pick Doughboy, why don't you? Then when he grows up he'll be sort of twins with mine, in his name anyway. Doughboy, Highboy, see?"

The boys were sitting on the worn wooden step of the door which led from the tack room into the corral, busy with rags and polish, shining their bridles.

Ken looked at his brother with scorn. Doughboy would never have half of Highboy's speed.

"Lassie, then," suggested Howard. "She's black as ink, like mine. And she'll be fast——"

"Dad says Lassie'll never go over fifteen hands."

Nell McLaughlin saw the change in Kennie, and her hopes

rose. He went to his books in the morning with determination and really studied. A new alertness took the place of the daydreaming. Examples in arithmetic were neatly written out, and as she passed his door before breakfast she often heard the monotonous drone of his voice as he read his American history aloud.

Each night, when he kissed her, he flung his arms around her and held her fiercely for a moment, then, with a winsome and blissful smile into her eyes, turned away to bed.

He spent days inspecting the different bands of horses and colts. He sat for hours on the corral fence, very important, chewing straws. He rode off on one of the ponies for half the day, wandering through the mile-square pastures that ran down toward the Colorado border.

And when the week was up he announced his decision. "I'll take that yearling filly of Rocket's. The sorrel with the cream tail and mane."

His father looked at him in surprise. "The one that got tangled in the barbed wire? that's never been named?"

In a second all Kennie's new pride was gone. He hung his head defensively. "Yes."

"You've made a bad choice, son. You couldn't have picked a worse."

"She's fast, Dad. And Rocket's fast——"

"It's the worst line of horses I've got. There's never one amongst them with real sense. The mares are hellions and the stallions outlaws; they're untamable."

"I'll tame her."

Rob guffawed. "Not I, nor anyone, has ever been able to really tame any one of them."

Kennie's chest heaved.

"Better change your mind, Ken. You want a horse that'll be a real friend to you, don't you?"

"Yes." Kennie's voice was unsteady.

"Well, you'll never make a friend of that filly. She's all cut and scarred up already with tearing through barbed wire after that bitch of a mother of hers. No fence'll hold 'em——"

"I know," said Kennie, still more faintly.

"Change your mind?" asked Howard briskly.

"No."

Rob was grim and put out. He couldn't go back on his word. The boy had to have a reasonable amount of help in breaking and taming the filly, and he could envision precious hours, whole days, wasted in the struggle.

Nell McLaughlin despaired. Once again Ken seemed to have taken the wrong turn and was back where he had begun; stoical, silent, defensive.

But there was a difference that only Ken could know. The way he felt about his colt. The way his heart sang. The pride and joy that filled him so full that sometimes he hung his head so they wouldn't see it shining out of his eyes.

He had known from the very first that he would choose that particular yearling because he was in love with her.

The year before, he had been out working with Gus, the big Swedish ranch hand, on the irrigation ditch, when they had noticed Rocket standing in a gully on the hillside, quiet for once, and eying them cautiously.

"Ay bet she got a colt," said Gus, and they walked carefully up the draw. Rocket gave a wild snort, thrust her feet out, shook her head wickedly, then fled away. And as they reached the spot they saw standing there the wavering, pinkish colt, barely able to keep its feet. It gave a little squeak and started after its mother on crooked, wobbling legs.

"Yee whiz! Luk at de little *flicka!*" said Gus.

"What does *flicka* mean, Gus?"

"Swedish for little gurl, Ken——"

Ken announced at supper, "You said she'd never been named. I've named her. Her name is Flicka."

The first thing to do was to get her in. She was running with a band of yearlings on the saddleback, cut with ravines and gullies, on section twenty.

They all went out after her, Ken, as owner, on old Rob Roy, the wisest horse on the ranch.

Ken was entranced to watch Flicka when the wild band of youngsters discovered that they were being pursued and took off across the mountain. Footing made no difference to her. She floated across the ravines, always two lengths ahead of the others. Her pink mane and tail whipped in the wind. Her long delicate legs had only to aim, it seemed, at a particular spot, for her to reach it and sail on. She seemed to Ken a fairy horse.

He sat motionless, just watching and holding Rob Roy in, when his father thundered past on Sultan and shouted, "Well, what's the matter? Why didn't you turn 'em?"

Kennie woke up and galloped after.

Rob Roy brought in the whole band. The corral gates were closed, and an hour was spent shunting the ponies in and out and through the chutes, until Flicka was left alone in the small round corral in which the baby colts were branded. Gus drove the others away, out the gate, and up the saddleback.

But Flicka did not intend to be left. She hurled herself against the poles which walled the corral. She tried to jump them. They were seven feet high. She caught her front feet over the top rung, clung, scrambled, while Kennie held his breath for fear the slender legs would be caught between the bars and snapped. Her hold broke; she fell over backward, rolled, screamed, tore around the corral. Kennie had a sick feeling in the pit of his stomach, and his father looked disgusted.

One of the bars broke. She hurled herself again. Another went. She saw the opening and, as neatly as a dog crawls through a fence, inserted her head and forefeet, scrambled through, and fled away, bleeding in a dozen places.

As Gus was coming back, just about to close the gate to the upper range, the sorrel whipped through it, sailed across the road and ditch with her inimitable floating leap, and went up the side of the saddleback like a jack rabbit.

From way up the mountain Gus heard excited whinnies, as she joined the band he had just driven up, and the last he saw of them they were strung out along the crest running like deer.

"Yee whiz!" said Gus, and stood motionless and staring until the ponies had disappeared over the ridge. Then he closed the gate, remounted Rob Roy, and rode back to the corral.

Rob McLaughlin gave Kennie one more chance to change his mind. "Last chance, son. Better pick a horse that you have some hope of riding one day. I'd have got rid of this whole line of stock if they weren't so damned fast that I've had the fool idea that someday there might turn out one gentle one in the lot—and I'd have a race horse. But there's never been one so far, and it's not going to be Flicka."

"It's not going to be Flicka," chanted Howard.

"Perhaps she *might* be gentled," said Kennie; and Nell, watching, saw that although his lips quivered, there was fanatical determination in his eye.

"Ken," said Rob, "it's up to you. If you say you want her we'll get her. But she wouldn't be the first of that line to die rather than give in. They're beautiful and they're fast, but let me tell you this, young man, they're *loco!*"

Kennie flinched under his father's direct glance.

"If I go after her again I'll not give up whatever comes; understand what I mean by that?"

"Yes."

"What do you say?"

"I want her."

They brought her in again. They had better luck this time. She jumped over the Dutch half door of the stable and crashed inside. The men slammed the upper half of the door shut, and she was caught.

The rest of the band were driven away, and Kennie stood outside of the stable, listening to the wild hoofs beating, the screams, the crashes. His Flicka inside there! He was drenched with perspiration.

"We'll leave her to think it over," said Rob, when dinnertime came. "Afterward we'll go up and feed and water her."

But when they went up afterward there was no Flicka in the barn. One of the windows, higher than the mangers, was broken.

The window opened into a pasture an eighth of a mile square, fenced in barbed wire six feet high. Near the stable stood a wagonload of hay. When they went around the back of the stable to see where Flicka had hidden herself they found her between the stable and the hay wagon, eating.

At their approach she leaped away, then headed east across the pasture.

"If she's like her mother," said Rob, "she'll go right through the wire."

"Ay bet she'll go over," said Gus. "She yumps like a deer."

"No horse can jump that," said McLaughlin.

Kennie said nothing because he could not speak. It was, perhaps, the most terrible moment of his life. He watched Flicka racing toward the eastern wire.

A few yards from it she swerved, turned, and raced diagonally south.

"It turned her! It turned her!" cried Kennie, almost sobbing. It was the first sign of hope for Flicka. "Oh, Dad! She has got sense. She has! She has!"

Flicka turned again as she met the southern boundary of the pasture; again at the northern; she avoided the barn. Without abating anything of her whirlwind speed, following a precise, accurate calculation and turning each time on a dime, she investigated every possibility. Then, seeing that there was no hope, she raced south toward the range where she had spent her life, gathered herself, and shot into the air.

Each of the three men watching had the impulse to cover his eyes, and Kennie gave a sort of a howl of despair.

Twenty yards of fence came down with her as she hurled herself through. Caught on the upper strands, she turned a complete somersault, landing on her back, her four legs dragging the wires down on top of her, and tangling herself in them beyond hope of escape.

"Damn the wire!" cursed McLaughlin. "If I could afford decent fences——"

Kennie followed the men miserably as they walked to the filly. They stood in a circle watching, while she kicked and fought and thrashed until the wire was tightly wound and knotted about her, cutting, piercing, and tearing great three-cornered pieces of flesh and hide. At last she was unconscious, streams of blood running on her golden coat, and pools of crimson widening and spreading on the grass beneath her.

With the wire cutter which Gus always carried in the hip pocket of his overalls he cut all the wire away, and they drew her into the pasture, repaired the fence, placed hay, a box of oats, and a tub of water near her, and called it a day.

"I don't think she'll pull out of it," said McLaughlin.

Next morning Kennie was up at five, doing his lessons. At six he went out to Flicka.

She had not moved. Food and water were untouched. She was no longer bleeding, but the wounds were swollen and caked over.

Kennie got a bucket of fresh water and poured it over her mouth. Then he leaped away, for Flicka came to life, scrambled up, got her balance, and stood swaying.

Kennie went a few feet away and sat down to watch her. When he went in to breakfast she had drunk deeply of the water and was mouthing the oats.

There began then a sort of recovery. She ate, drank, limped about the pasture, stood for hours with hanging head and weakly splayed out legs, under the clump of cottonwood trees. The swollen wounds scabbed and began to heal.

Kennie lived in the pasture too. He followed her around; he talked to her. He, too, lay snoozing or sat under the cottonwoods; and often, coaxing her with hand outstretched, he walked very quietly toward her. But she would not let him come near her.

Often she stood with her head at the south fence, looking off to the mountain. It made the tears come to Kennie's eyes to see the way she longed to get away.

Still Rob said she wouldn't pull out of it. There was no use putting a halter on her. She had no strength.

One morning, as Ken came out of the house, Gus met him and said, "De filly's down."

Kennie ran to the pasture, Howard close behind him. The right hind leg which had been badly swollen at the knee joint had opened in a festering wound, and Flicka lay flat and motionless, with staring eyes.

"Don't you wish now you'd chosen Doughboy?" asked Howard.

"Go away!" shouted Ken.

Howard stood watching while Kennie sat down on the ground and took Flicka's head on his lap. Though she was conscious and moved a little she did not struggle nor seem frightened. Tears rolled down Kennie's cheeks as he talked to her and petted her. After a few moments Howard walked away.

"Mother, what do you do for an infection when it's a horse?" asked Kennie.

"Just what you'd do if it was a person. Wet dressings. I'll help you, Ken. We mustn't let those wounds close or scab over until they're clean. I'll make a poultice for that hind leg and help you put it on. Now that she'll let us get close to her, we can help her a lot."

"The thing to do is see that she eats," said Rob. "Keep up her strength."

But he himself would not go near her. "She won't pull out of it," he said. "I don't want to see her or think about her."

Kennie and his mother nursed the filly. The big poultice was bandaged on the hind leg. It drew out much poisoned matter, and Flicka felt better and was able to stand again.

She watched for Kennie now and followed him like a dog, hopping on three legs, holding up the right hind leg with its huge knob of a bandage in comical fashion.

"Dad, Flicka's my friend now; she likes me," said Ken.

His father looked at him. "I'm glad of that, son. It's a fine thing to have a horse for a friend."

Kennie found a nicer place for her. In the lower pasture the brook ran over cool stones. There was a grassy bank, the size of a corral, almost on a level with the water. Here she could lie softly, eat grass, drink fresh running water. From the grass, a twenty-foot hill sloped up, crested with overhanging trees. She was enclosed, as it were, in a green, open-air nursery.

Kennie carried her oats morning and evening. She would watch for him to come, eyes and ears pointed to the hill. And one evening Ken, still some distance off, came to a stop and a wide grin spread over his face. He had heard her nicker. She had caught sight of him coming and was calling to him!

He placed the box of oats under her nose, and she ate while he stood beside her, his hand smoothing the satin-soft skin under her mane. It had a nap as deep as plush. He played with her long, cream-colored tresses, arranged her forelock neatly between her eyes. She was a bit dish-faced, like an Arab, with eyes set far apart. He lightly groomed and brushed her while she stood turning her head to him whichever way he went.

He spoiled her. Soon she would not step to the stream to drink but he must hold a bucket for her. And she would drink, then lift her dripping muzzle, rest it on the shoulder of his blue chambray shirt, her golden eyes dreaming off into the distance, then daintily dip her mouth and drink again.

When she turned her head to the south and pricked her ears and stood tense and listening, Ken knew she heard the other colts galloping on the upland.

"You'll go back there someday, Flicka," he whispered. "You'll be three, and I'll be eleven. You'll be so strong you won't know I'm on your back, and we'll fly like the wind. We'll stand on the very top where we can look over the whole world and smell the snow from the Neversummer Range. Maybe we'll see antelope——"

This was the happiest month of Kennie's life.

With the morning Flicka always had new strength and would hop three-legged up the hill to stand broadside to the early sun, as horses love to do.

The moment Ken woke he'd go to the window and see her

there; and when he was dressed and at his table studying he sat so that he could raise his head and see Flicka.

After breakfast she would be waiting for him and the box of oats at the gate; and for Nell McLaughlin with fresh bandages and buckets of disinfectant; and all three would go together to the brook, Flicka hopping along ahead of them, as if she was leading the way.

But Rob McLaughlin would not look at her.

One day all the wounds were swollen again. Presently they opened, one by one; and Kennie and his mother made more poultices.

Still the little filly climbed the hill in the early morning and ran about on three legs. Then she began to go down in flesh and almost overnight wasted away to nothing. Every rib showed; the glossy hide was dull and brittle and was pulled over the skeleton as if she was a dead horse.

Gus said, "It's de fever. It burns up her flesh. If you could stop de fever she might get vell."

McLaughlin was standing in his window one morning and saw the little skeleton hopping about three-legged in the sunshine, and he said, "That's the end. I won't have a thing like that on my place."

Kennie had to understand that Flicka had not been getting well all this time; she had been slowly dying.

"She still eats her oats," he said mechanically.

They were all sorry for Ken. Nell McLaughlin stopped disinfecting and dressing the wounds. "It's no use, Ken," she said gently, "you know Flicka's going to die, don't you?"

"Yes, Mother."

Ken stopped eating. Howard said, "Ken doesn't eat anything any more. Don't he have to eat his dinner, Mother?"

But Nell answered, "Leave him alone."

Because the shooting of wounded animals is all in the

day's work on the western plains, and sickening to everyone, Rob's voice, when he gave the order to have Flicka shot, was as flat as if he had been telling Gus to kill a chicken for dinner.

"Here's the Marlin, Gus. Pick out a time when Ken's not around and put the filly out of her misery."

Gus took the rifle. *"Ja,* boss——"

Ever since Ken had known that Flicka was to be shot he had kept his eye on the rack which held the firearms. His father allowed no firearms in the bunkhouse. The gun rack was in the dining room of the ranch house; and, going through it to the kitchen three times a day for meals, Ken's eye scanned the weapons to make sure that they were all there.

That night they were not all there. The Marlin rifle was missing.

When Kennie saw that he stopped walking. He felt dizzy. He kept staring at the gun rack, telling himself that it surely was there—he counted again and again—he couldn't see clearly. . . .

Then he felt an arm across his shoulders and heard his father's voice.

"I know, son. Some things are awful hard to take. We just have to take 'em. I have to too."

Kennie got hold of his father's hand and held on. It helped steady him.

Finally he looked up. Rob looked down and smiled at him and gave him a little shake and squeeze. Ken managed a smile too.

"All right now?"

"All right, Dad."

They walked in to supper together.

Ken even ate a little. But Nell looked thoughtfully at the

ashen color of his face and at the little pulse that was beating in the side of his neck.

After supper he carried Flicka her oats but he had to coax her, and she would only eat a little. She stood with her head hanging but when he stroked it and talked to her she pressed her face into his chest and was content. He could feel the burning heat of her body. It didn't seem possible that anything so thin could be alive.

Presently Kennie saw Gus come into the pasture carrying the Marlin. When he saw Ken he changed his direction and sauntered along as if he was out to shoot some cottontails.

Ken ran to him. "When are you going to do it, Gus?"

"Ay was goin' down soon now, before it got dark——"

"Gus, don't do it tonight. Wait till morning. Just one more night, Gus."

"Vell, in de morning den, but it got to be done, Ken. Yer fader gives de order."

"I know. I won't say anything more."

An hour after the family had gone to bed Ken got up and put on his clothes. It was a warm moonlit night. He ran down to the brook, calling softly. "Flicka! Flicka!"

But Flicka did not answer with a little nicker; and she was not in the nursery nor hopping about the pasture. Ken hunted for an hour.

At last he found her down the creek, lying in the water. Her head had been on the bank, but as she lay there the current of the stream had sucked and pulled at her, and she had had no strength to resist; and little by little her head had slipped down until when Ken got there only the muzzle was resting on the bank, and the body and legs were swinging in the stream.

Kennie slid into the water, sitting on the bank, and he hauled at her head. But she was heavy, and the current dragged like a weight; and he began to sob because he had no strength to draw her out.

Then he found a leverage for his heels against some rocks in the bed of the stream and he braced himself against these and pulled with all his might; and her head came up onto his knees, and he held it cradled in his arms.

He was glad that she had died of her own accord, in the cool water, under the moon, instead of being shot by Gus. Then, putting his face close to hers, and looking searchingly into her eyes, he saw that she was alive and looking back at him.

And then he burst out crying and hugged her and said, "Oh, my little Flicka, my little Flicka."

The long night passed.

The moon slid slowly across the heavens.

The water rippled over Kennie's legs and over Flicka's body. And gradually the heat and fever went out of her. And the cool running water washed and washed her wounds.

When Gus went down in the morning with the rifle they hadn't moved. There they were, Kennie sitting in water over his thighs and hips, with Flicka's head in his arms.

Gus seized Flicka by the head and hauled her out on the grassy bank and then, seeing that Kennie couldn't move, cold and stiff and half-paralyzed as he was, lifted him in his arms and carried him to the house.

"Gus," said Ken through chattering teeth, "don't shoot her, Gus."

"It ain't fur me to say, Ken. You know dat."

"But the fever's left her, Gus."

"Ay wait a little, Ken——"

Rob McLaughlin drove to Laramie to get the doctor, for Ken was in violent chills that would not stop. His mother had him in bed wrapped in hot blankets when they got back.

He looked at his father imploringly as the doctor shook down the thermometer.

"She might get well now, Dad. The fever's left her. It went out of her when the moon went down."

"All right, son. Don't worry. Gus'll feed her, morning and night, as long as she's——"

"As long as I can't do it," finished Kennie happily.

The doctor put the thermometer in his mouth and told him to keep it shut.

All day Gus went about his work, thinking of Flicka. He had not been back to look at her. He had been given no more orders. If she was alive the order to shoot her was still in effect. But Kennie was ill, McLaughlin making his second trip to town taking the doctor home, and would not be back till long after dark.

After their supper in the bunkhouse Gus and Tim walked down to the brook. They did not speak as they approached the filly, lying stretched out flat on the grassy bank, but their eyes were straining at her to see if she was dead or alive.

She raised her head as they reached her.

"By the powers!" exclaimed Tim. "There she is!"

She dropped her head, raised it again, and moved her legs and became tense as if struggling to rise. But to do so she must use her right hind leg to brace herself against the earth. That was the damaged leg, and at the first bit of pressure with it she gave up and fell back.

"We'll swing her on to the other side," said Tim. "Then she can help herself."

"*Ja*——"

Standing behind her, they leaned over, grabbed hold of her left legs, front and back, and gently hauled her over.

Flicka was as lax and willing as a puppy. But the moment she found herself lying on her right side, she began to scramble, braced herself with her good left leg, and tried to rise.

"Yee whiz!" said Gus. "She got plenty strength yet."

"Hi!" cheered Tim. "She's up!"

But Flicka wavered, slid down again, and lay flat. This time she gave notice that she would not try again by heaving a deep sigh and closing her eyes.

Gus took his pipe out of his mouth and thought it over. Orders or no orders, he would try to save the filly. Ken had gone too far to be let down.

"Ay'm goin' to rig a blanket sling fur her, Tim, and get her on her feet, and keep her up."

There was bright moonlight to work by. They brought down the posthole digger and set two aspen poles deep into the ground either side of the filly, then, with ropes attached to the blanket, hoisted her by a pulley.

Not at all disconcerted, she rested comfortably in the blanket under her belly, touched her feet on the ground, and reached for the bucket of water Gus held for her.

Kennie was sick a long time. He nearly died. But Flicka picked up. Every day Gus passed the word to Nell, who carried it to Ken. "She's cleaning up her oats." "She's out of the sling." "She bears a little weight on the bad leg."

Tim declared it was a real miracle. They argued about it, eating their supper.

"Na," said Gus. "It was de cold water, washin' de fever outa her. And more dan dot—it was Ken—you tink it don't count? All night dot boy sits dere and says, 'Hold on, Flicka, Ay'm here wid you. Ay'm standin' by, two of us togedder'——"

Tim stared at Gus without answering, while he thought it over. In the silence a coyote yapped far off on the plains; and the wind made a rushing sound high up in the jack pines on the hill.

Gus filled his pipe.

"Sure," said Tim finally. "Sure. That's it."

Then came the day when Rob McLaughlin stood smiling at the foot of Kennie's bed and said, "Listen! Hear your friend?"

Ken listened and heard Flicka's high, eager whinny.

"She don't spend much time by the brook any more. She's up at the gate of the corral half the time, nickering for you."

"For me!"

Rob wrapped a blanket around the boy and carried him out to the corral gate.

Kennie gazed at Flicka. There was a look of marveling in his eyes. He felt as if he had been living in a world where everything was dreadful and hurting but awfully real; and *this* couldn't be real; this was all soft and happy, nothing to struggle over or worry about or fight for any more. Even his father was proud of him! He could feel it in the way Rob's big arms held him. It was all like a dream and far away. He couldn't, yet, get close to anything.

But Flicka—Flicka—alive, well, pressing up to him, recognizing him, nickering . . .

Kennie put out a hand—weak and white—and laid it on her face. His thin little fingers straightened her forelock the way he used to do, while Rob looked at the two with a strange expression about his mouth and a glow in his eyes that was not often there.

"She's still poor, Dad, but she's on four legs now."

"She's picking up."

Ken turned his face up, suddenly remembering. "Dad! She did get gentled, didn't she?"

"Gentle—as—a kitten——"

They put a cot down by the brook for Ken, and boy and filly got well together.

THE CONQUEROR
By Vincent Sheean
From *Redbook*

VINCENT SHEEAN

was born December 5, 1899, at Pana, Illinois, and was educated privately and at the University of Chicago. He became a foreign correspondent at twenty-one and served in this capacity in many parts of the world. He began writing magazine fiction in 1927, and has also published two books of travel and three novels, the most recent of which is The Bird of the Wilderness, *which appeared in the late summer of this year. He is married and has two small daughters. At present he is in England as war correspondent for the* Saturday Evening Post.

W<small>HEN</small> the general asked Marie-Honorée to dinner the first time she ignored the invitation. On the second occasion, two or three weeks later, she sent a frigidly polite note to say that she was no longer dining out. After another month had passed he asked her again, and this time she felt constrained to accept. "After all," she reflected, "I am to all intents and purposes a prisoner: it is a kind of duty that I owe my jailers." So she wrote another note to the general, informing him that she would dine with him at half-past eight.

The circumstances were, to say the least, peculiar. There she was, living in a maid's room at the top of her own house, with the general and nineteen other officers in occupation of all the rest. They had not molested her in any way: they had simply taken possession, and she had been given not quite a full day to move her personal belongings and papers. It had all been done very efficiently by a severe young officer from the Kommandantur, working on a list of householders and living quarters, and she had not even seen the general or his officers. And in all these weeks she had still never seen them. She took good care of that—slipping out by the back way whenever she had to leave the house, never going even into the hall at the head of the marble stairs, and of course never setting foot on the marble stairs themselves. One of the maids in the house helped her settle into her new quarters, and after that she fended for herself. Her servants (those who had not left Paris before the Germans arrived) were much too busy now to do anything for her.

But Marie-Honorée was perfectly able to take care of

herself. Gentle and exquisite as she always seemed to be, she was in fact a woman of intelligence with considerable business acumen and practical common sense in all the affairs of life. It used to be said that she had a harder and better head for such things than her husband Paul, who was now a prisoner somewhere in Germany. Before the war Marie-Honorée had conducted negotiations in the wine business with more than usual success—always in the name of her husband and in his presence—and had also done very tidily indeed in a small, very smart perfumery establishment out by the Place Victor Hugo. People who saw in her merely the lovely Marquise de Quiberon, passing gracefully across the scene of culture and society—such as these were—in the 1930s, had an incomplete notion of her character and gifts. Her better friends knew better: they tended to say with a laugh: "Oh, the thing's bound to go well if Marie-Honorée is running it. That girl can do anything."

She had taken hold of the Quiberon estates down in the Bordeaux wine country and worked them into a better imitation of solvency than they had been able to give for a generation or two. And the house in Paris, that very house which was now the abode of the German general and nineteen other officers, had been her creation. She had always known artists and people of that kind, people of taste; she knew how to accept their work as a sort of homage, even when she paid for it. Her big salon was famous in Paris—in her kind of Paris, anyhow—for its astute combinations and arrangements of white and gray and silver, "modern" enough without being actually dangerous to life or limb and beautiful without a sense of disuse. You had no hesitation about sitting down in any of the chairs there, and the rugs were not too delicate to sustain contact with the shod human foot. The whole house was innocent of snakeskin or ostrich feathers, and there were not too many of anything—chairs, pictures, lamps, or musical instruments—in any room.

This lovely, temperate quality was the flower (one flower, at least) of a whole culture and did not betray, in the subtle simplicity of its surface, how numerous and complex were its elements. So true was this that even the German officers liked the house or said they did, in spite of the fact that it was just about the most French thing in Paris. In the German general's first note to Marie-Honorée he had written:

"*Madame la Marquise, my officers and I appreciate the use of your beautiful house and wish for the honor of your acquaintance. We hope that you will dine with us tonight at eight o'clock.*"

This was the note she ignored. It was signed General Graf von Thaunburg, with the name and number of a Hanover infantry division.

The second note was signed also with his Christian names, which appeared to be Otto Helmuth, and the military rank beneath. It said, in correct French:

"*Madame la Marquise, my officers have greatly admired your portrait in the great salon and have begged me to renew my invitation to dinner, so that we may have the honor of your acquaintance. If you agree we shall dine at half-past eight, as I believe this hour to be more in accordance with your custom. Accept the assurance of my profound esteem.*"

To this she replied in a note containing one sentence, remitted by old Annette, the maid who lived in the adjoining attic room. The sentence was: "*The Marquise de Quiberon regrets that she is unable to accept any invitations to dinner under the present circumstances.*"

The third note from the general was phrased as follows:

"*Madame la Marquise, at the risk of being importunate I should like again to renew my request for the honor of your company at dinner. I well understand your reluctance to accept and can only beg that you make an effort to overcome it, since the present circumstances have caused us to be housed under your roof. You will find my officers deeply appreciative of the honor you do us. I leave to you the choice of the day and hour. Accept the assurance of my homage and esteem.* Otto Helmuth von Thaunburg."

To this Marie-Honorée sent back a note by Annette:

"*The Marquise de Quiberon acknowledges the invitation of M. le Comte de Thaunburg and will dine with him at half-past eight on tomorrow, Wednesday, evening.*"

In writing "*will dine with him,*" she used the phrase *diner à chez lui,* as if the house belonged to him. The shade of meaning was one which she hoped would not escape him.

That evening she started to tell the story to some of her friends and found herself laughing harder than she had laughed since before May, 1940. They were gathered in a room inhabited by one of the Quiberon relations; there were six or seven of them, women who met together to knit or sew; most of them had husbands or brothers in the German prison camps, and all had seen enough human suffering in the last few months to dry up the springs of laughter; but they all laughed helplessly. Marie-Honorée had the actual notes to show them.

"*Mon Dieu, mon Dieu,*" said Louise, one of the cousins, wiping her eyes, "it's something straight out of the eighteenth century. I haven't seen such language since I used to have to write model letters in the convent."

"You should have asked him to send you a beefsteak, Marie-Honorée," another cousin pointed out. "After all, language is cheap, and if you actually go to the dinner you'll probably be unable to eat anything. I should ask for some steak or a big pot roast, sent up to your room."

"Or some of the butter and chocolate they are carting off to Germany," another said.

"Or tell them you'll compromise on a sandwich if they'll give one decent meal to your husband in the prison camp," said another.

"No," Marie-Honorée said, "I shall be just as eighteenth-century as he is. And I shall ask him for nothing, absolutely nothing. It would be no use, in any case."

"Do you mean to say you actually mean to *go?*" Louise demanded. "It's madness. You don't know what they'll do. I should be frightened to death."

"Well, I am a little frightened," Marie-Honorée admitted, "but I think I shall be able to manage. After all, they are the conquerors. They could order me out of the house altogether, and then where could I go? I have little enough money as it is without having to pay rent too."

"I wonder what they'll give you for dinner," said old Mme. de Beaupré, who had always been very fond of food. Her blue eyes were slightly dreamy. "I know what I should like: duck with orange sauce. And a soufflé afterward, made with pineapple, you know, like the ones old Joseph used to give us."

"I would have a very thick *filet mignon,*" said Louise. "Duck is no good if you're hungry. But the chances are you'll get sauerkraut."

"There have been days in these past weeks when I should have been glad to get some sauerkraut," Marie-Honorée said. "But it won't be that: it'll be the best French cooking. I know; Annette tells me about it. She even smuggles a little food upstairs now and then, but of course I don't eat it."

"Of course not," Madame de Beaupré said virtuously. "Still, what kind of food is it? Does she ever get butter?"

"Sometimes," said Marie-Honorée.

"I should never dream of eating their food," said Mme. de Beaupré, "but butter—well, butter seems a little different, somehow. I am not sure that I wouldn't accept a little butter now and then if I were in your position."

"The terrifying thing," said Marie-Honorée, "is the conversation at dinner. What on earth can I find to talk to them about?"

Louise, who was not without a trace of envy for her more brilliant cousin, settled that question.

"You've never been at a loss yet, Marie-Honorée," she said. "I think it will take more than a Hanoverian general to silence you. Now I've run out of gray wool. Is there any more in that bag over there?"

On the day of the dinner Marie-Honorée, aided from time to time by Annette, spent a great deal of time inspecting her wardrobe. She had worn no evening dress—indeed no very assertive garments—for some months, and the prospect of appearing before the conquerors filled her, at first, with alarm. But as she picked and chose, slowly piecing together the full complement of her night's requirements, confidence began to return. After all, these were beautiful clothes, acknowledged to be the best Paris could produce before the war; and in all probability General Count von Thaunburg and his officers had never seen anything like them.

Marie-Honorée had been famous, in her own world, for the clothes she wore and the way she wore them. She was a graceful, slightly insinuating figure, who seemed to slip over a floor rather than to walk; she tended to elect clinging and trailing garments of delicate color and with a minimum of ornament. Her shiny fair hair was nearly always knotted loosely at the neck, in artful simplicity, and without decoration; if she wore jewels at all it was likely to be earrings.

After hours of deliberation she determined upon her costume for the night. She would go in full regalia, as for the Elysée or the British Embassy in the old days, with the longest train she possessed. It was a dress of innumerable softly shifting hues between silver and green, with a serpentine train of silver, narrow and long, originating not at shoulder or waist but almost at her heels. She had spent weeks upon its architecture in the old days: it had been a great dress, a very important dress, the triumph of a celebrated old house in the Rue de la Paix. She had evolved it for the visit of George VI and Queen Elizabeth to Paris, in the old days, a century or two ago, in 1938. It would serve now in a different purpose, but it would serve.

Punctually at twenty-seven minutes past eight Marie-Honorée left the corridor where the maids' rooms were and opened the door to the top landing of the grand staircase. She had not been there for months. The reflections of all the lights on the marble below made her pause for a moment. The staircase was in two flights, the lower one very broad and grand, the upper less imposing: it led to the rooms which had once been Marie-Honorée's but were now occupied by General Count von Thaunburg. She took a deep breath, restrained her nervous fingers from their instinctive flutter, put out one hand to the balustrade and began to descend. She was quite well aware that she had not taken four steps before the household below became aware of her approach. Through the carved white marble of the balustrade she could see the German officers coming out of the drawing room and standing there in the great hall, waiting. For a second or two she felt slightly dizzy: it was so far down there, such a long journey, and her knees were shaking with weakness.

The last part was the most difficult. That was the grand staircase proper, the real thing: it was made of very broad, shallow steps, and from the last landing it was all in full view of the waiting officers. Marie-Honorée moved slowly, her hand just touching the balustrade, her silver train rustling softly over the stairs behind her. Only a few more steps, and she would be at the end: was it possible that her own staircase could be so strange, so cold, and so long?

An officer advanced, reached for her hand. She was at the foot of the stairs, lingering on the last step, curiously reluctant to set foot among them; she gave him her hand, and he bent low over it. His mustache brushed the soft skin, and she repressed a little involuntary movement of the shoulders.

"Madame la Marquise," the officer said, "you do us very great honor. Let me present my officers."

This, then, was General Count von Thaunburg: a tall man, stiff and uncomfortable, with decorations ranged on his breast. His eyes were a burning blue, of which she became conscious almost at once. He had a single eyeglass which he sometimes replaced in his eye and sometimes allowed to dangle on a black silk cord, but with or without it, his eyes had curious power. Marie-Honorée did not wholly dislike their intentness, but it was impossible to know what store of thought or feeling lay behind them.

The other officers bowed, each in turn, and kissed her hand. It was like a royal progress round a room. As they bowed they clicked their heels together very audibly with a resounding crack. She was afraid to speak, for fear she might laugh or cry; either would have been disastrous. She merely inclined her head and smiled, slightly bowed and smiled again, lifting her hand mechanically to the alien lips in her own house, smiling a little more or a little less, and saying nothing. The general walked beside her, repeating a list of names that crackled barbarically in her ears: *Von Glueckwald-Minneberg, Zerbstheim, Dornschuld, Windischlohn-Lanz....*

They were of all ages, two or three of them hardly more than children, with a terrifying precision in the way they clicked their heels. The louder the click of the heels, she reflected confusedly, the more candid the blue glance that followed when the hand kissing was over. She thought of Paul, her husband, and of the prison camp where he would be eating his dinner tonight. The general gave her his arm, and they passed through the great open doors from the hall to the salon, her own salon. On a table near the fireplace was the huge silver tray with the sherry things on it. My little Venetian glasses, she thought; they are using my little Venetian glasses for sherry. Well, why not? They won the war.

"Thank you, M. le Comte," she said, accepting some sherry. "I hope you and your officers are comfortable in this house? This is a rather charming room, I always thought. Some of our best artists worked on it."

The general's intent blue eyes never left her face.

"We appreciate the beauty of your house very much," he said. "We have long wished to express our appreciation. That portrait, there, which we have so much admired—permit me to say that we admire it less now, madame. It does not do you justice."

"It is rather nice, I think," said Marie-Honorée. "The painter is—well, the painter is not here any more. He was one of our best."

"I know something of the Quiberon family," the general said. "If I am not mistaken one of them married a Thaunburg in the eighteenth century."

"How delightful!" said Marie-Honorée. "Then we are, in fact, relations?"

"In a distant degree, yes," said the general. "There was a young Thaunburg countess who came here in the Prussian embassy, at one interval between wars, and she married a Quiberon. I shall have all the details investigated and forwarded to you if the subject is of interest."

"You are exceedingly kind," said Marie-Honorée. "I have an aunt, Mme. de Beaupré, who is particularly intelligent in these genealogical matters. She will no doubt be able to fit in your information to the family tradition. I confess I know very little about such things. There are some books in the library that might interest you—a history of the family, I believe."

"I have already studied it with some care," said the general. . . . "It seems that our dinner is ready. Shall we go in?"

Marie-Honorée sat at the head of her own table, as in a dream, and looked down the long double line of gray-clad officers.

Her dishes and her linen, but only her second-best silver . . . Under the surface of her mind, as she smiled and talked, she wondered if they had found the best silver yet; it was buried at the château down in Gascony, where the wine came from; all that country was occupied now by the conquerors, and perhaps they had dug up the best silver too. It was Orléans Regency, and very beautiful: she could see its slender, frail old forks now against the linen and lace of this table. They were using the Empire silver tonight, and old glasses from Bohemia and new glasses from Sweden; there were roses in a broad, low centerpiece of Lalique glass; she wondered if they had broken many dishes.

The general was talking about music. It seemed that he was fond of music and out of sheer politeness tried to dig up from his memory something good to be said of French operas and symphonies. Marie-Honorée came to his rescue with a swift, graceful babble about Salzburg and Bayreuth and Berlin: she had heard all the music that was going in the 1930s, and could talk about it with familiar affection, although as she listened to her own voice, it seemed to come from somewhere very far away. Was it possible that she had ever gone to Salzburg—or that such a place as Salzburg had ever existed? She looked down the table and saw many pairs of blue eyes steadily fixed upon her. The younger officers talked in subdued tones in German; those sitting nearest her were of higher rank and tried to talk only in French. Ten minutes on her right, ten minutes on her left: she must try to remember that this was only a dinner party, after all, and that she should talk to the men on both sides.

On her left was a heavy, sad-faced man, a colonel. When she turned to him she discovered that his French left much to be desired; they compromised on English, which he spoke almost without an accent. They talked for a few minutes about Paris, the gardens, the museums, the boulevards; but she found it the hardest thing of all, because in his heavy, elderly face and pale, overset eyes she detected the intolerable emphasis of pity. She turned with relief to her general when the opportunity came. He, at least, with all his eighteenth-century pomposity, had the reserve which was the last minimal demand of good taste in an occasion so bizarre. He was everything she would have found funny in the old days: he was good form itself; he was protocol and genealogy and we-aristocrats-are-not-like-the-others; and yet she was grateful for it because it contained no pity and no sentiment. Behind his intense blue gaze there might have lurked innumerable adverse opinions of the world they lived in, the situation forced upon them, the grotesque novelties of 1940—but she would never know. He talked of music.

The food was exceptionally good. Through the dreamlike unreality of the scene Marie-Honorée was aware of a procession of dishes such as she had never even seen, much less tasted, since June. There was a really good soup and an exquisite sole with a sauce of mussels; there were *filets mignons* and three vegetables and a salad superbly mixed in the kitchen by French hands; there was a soufflé with orange in it, and at the end there were more fresh fruits than Marie-Honorée had believed to exist in Paris. She wondered a little sadly what all these polite, disciplined officers—behaving so "well," according to their lights and their orders—would say if she asked permission to take some fruit upstairs with her. They would load her down with it; they would send orderlies upstairs with baskets of it; they would behave very "well." Why not? They had won the war, and this food was conquered food.

There was rose-pink champagne at the beginning and end of the meal, and there was Romanée-Conti with the meat. Marie-Honorée recognized the red wine: it was her own, with a small gold tab and a number toward the base of the label. She could not be sure about the pink champagne, which might have been hers or might have been requisitioned from any of the numerous stores in Paris. All this would be paid for someday, supposedly, by the French government, which was responsible for the support of the German army; but in the meanwhile Marie-Honorée thought of it in simpler and more concrete terms: *my table, my wine, my glasses.*

"Years ago," the general said, "there was a very remarkable French basso who used to sing in Germany and Austria. His name was Pol Plançon. I suppose he was before your time, madame?"

The meal came to an end; coffee was brought to the salon. Marie-Honorée sat for about ten minutes with her coffee cup. She had tasted no such coffee for a long time. Some of the younger officers who spoke French were allowed to come near and exchange a word or two with her. She finished the last drop of the coffee; it was very good, but she would have no more.

"No, thanks so much," she said. "It might keep me from sleeping, you know. . . . And I keep such early hours nowadays, I really—— Most kind . . . You have all been very kind."

The officers lined up as if on parade, all down the long salon—her room, more distinctly her own room than any other in the house, except perhaps the one upstairs which was now the general's. She passed slowly along the line, giving each one her hand to kiss. They cracked their heels together very loudly and looked up afterward with enigmatic blue eyes. The general accompanied her down the room and out into the hall. At the foot of the stairs he bowed very low over her hand and clicked his heels too. For one moment afterward his eyes looked straight into hers with almost unbearable intensity. She sustained the look and turned to go.

"*Adieu,*" she said on some impulse, wondering if he would understand the finality of it. It was different in German, wasn't it? But no matter—"*Adieu.*" He stood there while she went up the grand staircase to the first landing, with her silver train rustling gently behind her. He was standing very straight and stiff, and there was something in his posture which suggested the sense of a salute.

In her own room at the top of the house Marie-Honorée slowly undressed and put her beautiful clothes away. She would probably never wear them again. The room was small and ugly, with a single iron bed, a table and two chairs. She turned out the lights so that she could not see it. Then, in her dressing gown, with her hair loosened and the hairbrush in her hand, she sat on one of the straight-backed chairs by the window. But she did not brush her hair, and presently the brush fell to the floor unheeded. Outside the window the whole of Paris lay caught in moonlight, a thick, still moonlight that gave great ghostly shadows among the pointed roofs. The roofs and chimney pots of Paris filled the silent night down to the winding river.

Marie-Honorée could not weep now, but her heart was filled with sorrow for the living and the dead.

THE PROUD WALKERS*
By James Still
From the *Saturday Evening Post*

*From *On Troublesome Creek* by James Still. Copyright, 1941, by James Still. By permission of the Viking Press, Inc., N. Y.

JAMES STILL

was born in 1908, on Double Creek, in the hills of Alabama, one of ten children. He wanted to be a "horse doctor" like his father, but instead turned to literature. After he was graduated from Vanderbilt University he was librarian at the Hindman Settlement School, Knott County, Kentucky, for several years, but resigned in order to devote himself to writing. He lives in a small cabin which he built himself, at Dead Mare Branch, Kentucky. He first appeared in the O. Henry Memorial Award Prize Stories of 1938, with "So Large a Thing as Seven," from The Virginia Quarterly Review. *In 1937 he published a volume of verse,* Hounds on the Mountain. *He won second prize in the O. Henry collection in 1939, with "Bat Flight," which appeared in the* Saturday Evening Post, *and later was part of his novel,* River of Earth *(1940). His newest book is* On Troublesome Creek, *recently published by Viking Press.*

WE MOVED out of Houndshell mine camp in May to the homeplace Father had built on Shoal Creek, and I recollect fox grapes were blooming and there was a spring chill in the air. Fern and Lark and I ran ahead of the wagon, frightening water thrushes, shouting back at the poky mare. We broke cowcumber branches to wave at the baby, wanting to call to him, but he did not then have a name.

Only Mother forbore stretching eyes to see afar. She held the baby atop a shuck tick, her face pale with dread to look upon the house. A mort of things she had told Father before he had gone to raise the dwelling. "Ere a board is rived," she'd said, "dig a cellar. There'll be no more pokes o' victuals coming from the commissary." She had told him the pattern for the chimney, roof, and walls; she told him more than a body could keep in their head, saying at last, "Could I lend a hand, 'twould be a satisfaction."

Father had grinned. "A nail you drove would turn corkscrew. A blow sarpent couldn't quile to your saw marks. Hit's man's work. A man's got to wear the breeches." Oh, Father nearly had a laughing spell listening to Mother's talk. Mother had said, "A house proper to raise chaps in, a cellar for laying by food, and lasty neighbors. Now, that hain't asking for the moon ball."

I recollect bull bats soared overhead when we reached Shoal Creek in the late afternoon; I recollect Mother looked at the house, and all she had feared was true. The building stood windowless, board ends of walls were unsawn, and the chimney pot barely cleared the hip roof. But Fern and Lark and I were awed. We could not think why Mother dabbed her eyes with baby's dress tail.

"Hit's not finished to a square T," Father said uneasily. "After planting they'll be time in plenty. A late start I've got. Why, field corn and a garden ought to be breaking ground. Just taste a grain o' patience."

Mother glanced into the sky where bull bats hawked. She was heartsick with the mulligrubs. Her voice sounded tight and strange. "A man's notions are ontelling," she said, "but if this creek's a fitten place to bring up chaps, if good neighbors live nigh, reckon I've got no right to complain."

"The Crownover family lives yon side the ridge," Father said. "Only folks in handy walking distance. I hear they're the earth's salt. No needcessity o' lock or key on Shoal Creek."

The wagon was unloaded by dusk dark. Father lighted the lamp on coming from stabling the mare, and we hovered to a smidgen of fire. We trembled in the night chill, for it was fox-grape winter. Mother feared to heap wood on the blaze, the chimney pot being low enough to set sparks to the roof. She knelt by the hearth, frying a skillet of hominy, cooking it mortal slow.

Father saddled the baby on a knee. "Well, now," he said, buttoning his jump jacket and peeping to see what the skillet held, "reckon I've caught a glimpse o' neighbors already. I heard footsteps yon side the barn in a brushy draw, though I couldn't see for blackness till they'd topped the ridge. There walked two fellers, with heads size o' washpots."

Lark crept nearer Mother. Fern and I glanced behind us. Nailheads shone on the walls as bright as the eyes of beasts.

"I figure it to be men carrying churns or jugs on their shoulders." Mother spoke coldly.

"I saw a waterhead baby in the camps once," Fern said. "I did."

"Hit might o' been Old Bloody Tom and some'un," Lark said.

"Odd they'd go by our place," Father mused, "traveling no path." He joggled the baby on his knee, making him squeal. "But it's said them Crownovers can be trusted to Jordan River and back ag'in. I'm wanting to get acquainted the first chance."

"A man's fancy to take short cuts," Mother replied, nodding her head at the boxed room. "They're men cutting across from one place to another, taking the lazy trail."

Fern's teeth chattered. She was ever the scary one.

"I hain't a chip afraid," I bragged, rashy with curiosity. "Be they boys amongst them Crownovers? I'm a-mind to play with one."

"Gee-o," Father chuckled, "a puore bee swarm o' chaps. Stair-steppers, creepers, and climbers, biddy ones to nigh growns. Fourteen, by honest count. A sawyer at Beddo Tillett's mill says they all can whoop weeds out of a crop in one day."

"I be not to play with waterheads," Lark said.

"That sawyer says every one o' Izard Crownover's young 'uns have rhymy names," Father went on. "He spun me a few, many as he could think of. Bard, Nard, Dard, Guard, Shard—names so slick yore tongue trips up."

"Are there girls too?" Fern asked.

"Bulah, Dulah, Eulah. A string like that."

Mother stirred the hominy. "Clever neighbors I've allus wanted," she said, her voice gloomy, "and allus I've longed for a house fitten to make them welcome."

"Be-jibs!" Father spoke impatiently. "A fair homeseat we'll have once the crop's planted and they's a spare minute. Why, I raised this place off the ground in twelve days, elbow for axle. I didn't have half the proper tools; I had no help hands. I hauled lumber twelve miles from Beddo Tillett's sawmill." He grunted, untangling baby's fingers from his watch chain. "Anyhow, hit might take them Crownovers a year's thawing to visit. Hain't like the camps where folks stick noses in, the first thing. I say let time get in its lick."

We were quieted by the thought of enduring a lonesome year, of nobody coming to put their feet under our table, nobody to borrow, or heave and set and calculate weather. Oh, the camps had spoiled us with its slew of chaps and rattling coal conveyors and people's talky-talk. Dwelling there, you couldn't stretch your elbows without hitting people.

I said, sticking my lips out, "I hain't waiting till I'm crookback ere I play with some'un."

Fern bat her eyes, trying to cry. "Ruther to live on a gob heap than where no girls are."

The skillet jiggled in Mother's hand. She spoke, complaining of the house, though now it was small in her mind compared with this new anxiety. "Nary a window cut," she said. "A house blind as a mole varmint."

"Jonah's whale!" Father exclaimed angrily. His ears reddened. He galloped his knee. "A feller can't whittle window frames with a pocket knife. I reckon nothing will do but I hie at daybreak to Tillett's and 'gin making them. Two days it'll take; two I ought to be rattling clods. Why, a week's grubbing to be done before a furrow's lined. Crop's won't mature planted so late." He swallowed a great breath. "Had we the finest cellar in Americee, a partickle o' nothing there'd be for winter storing."

"I reckon I've set my bonnet too high," Mother admitted. "The cellar's got to be filled with canning, turnips, cabbages, and pickling, if we're to eat the year through. Now, windows can be put off, but the chimley's bound to have a taller stacking."

The blood hasted from Father's ears. Never could he stay angry long. He coaxed baby to latch hands on his lifted arm and swing. "Ought to fill the new barn loft so full o' corn and fodder hit's tongue will hang out," he said. He taught the baby to skin a cat, come-Andy-over, head foremost. "One thing besides frames I'm fotching, and that's a name for this tadwhacker. Long enough he's gone without."

"Hain't going to call him Beddo," Fern said. "That's the ugliest name-word ever was."

"Not to be Tillett neither," Lark said.

The hominy browned. We held plates in our laps. The yellow kernels steamed a mellow smell. It was hard not to gobble them down like an old craney crow.

Mother ate a bit, then sat watching Father. "I had a house pattern in my head," she said, "and I ached to help build, to try my hand making it according. And I'd wished for good neighbors. But house and neighbors hain't a circumstance to getting a crop and the garden planted. Hit's back to the mines for us if we don't make victuals. Them window frames can wait."

"I can't follow a woman's notions," Father said. "For peace o' mind I'd better gamble two days and get the windows in." He chuckled, his mouth crammed. "I'd give a Tennessee pearl to see you atop a twenty-foot ladder potting nails." His chuckle grew to laughter; it caught like a wind in his chest, blowing out in gusts, shaking him. He began to cough. A kernel had got in his windpipe. His jaws turned beety; he sneezed a great sneeze. We struck our doubled fists against his back, and presently the grain was dislodged. "Ah, ho," he said, swallowing, "had I'd died, 'twould been in good cause."

Mother lightened. "I'm no witty with a hammer and saw," she said, "and if that cellar's not dug to my fancy I can spade."

Father sobered. He got as restless in his chair as a cadged bird. Of a sudden he turned his head to the door, listening. "Hush-o!" he said. We pricked our ears. "Hush!"

We waited, unbreathing, hearing the harsh *peent* of bull bats.

"I heard nothing onnatural," Mother said.

Fern shivered. Lark searched under the beds. He knew boogers were abroad at night.

Father reached the baby to Mother, and got up. So sleepy baby was, his head rolled like a dropped gourd. "The mare's restless," Father decided. "She might o' heard Crownover's stally bray yon side the mountain. I'll see that she's latched in tight." He went outside.

"Let's play Old Bloody Tom," Lark said. "I be Tom, a-rambling, smoking my pipe. You all be sheeps."

"Now, no," Fern snuffed. "It'd make me scared."

We children were abed when Father returned. He shucked off his boots and dabbed tallow on them; he breathed on the leather and rubbed it fiercely with a linsey rag. He spoke, faltering, hunting words, "I've been aiming to tell about the cellar."

Mother fitted a skillet's eye to a peg. She paused.

"After I'd shingled the roof," Father said, "I put in to dig. Got three feet down and struck bottom. This house is setting on living rock. I've larnt they hain't a cellar on Shoal Creek. This vein runs under all."

And later, when the light was blown, I heard Father speak from his pillow. "I saw more fellers on the ridge a while ago, walking with heads so square I figured they hefted boxes on their shoulders. I'm a-mind to stop by the

Crownovers' tomorrow, asking a hinting question. Hit's quare folks would go a dark way no road treads."

The sun ball was eating creek fog when Mother waked me. The door stood wide upon morning. "Your father's gone to Tillett's already," she said, "and against my will and beg. He hurried off afoot, saying he'd let the mare rest, saying he'd get the window frames hauled somehow." She gazed dolesomely upon the fields where black gum, sassafras, and redbud grew as in a young forest. "I argued; I plead, yet he would to go. Oh, man judgment's like weather. Hit's onknowing."

My breeches were on in a wink. I'd thought to go feed the mare, then hie to the brushy draw to quest for signs of walkers. I went before eating, being more curious than hungry. I fed the mare ten ears of corn; I stole beyond the barn. The draw was a moggy place. Wahoos grew thick against a limerock wall, and a sprangle of water ran out. I found a nest of brogan tracks set in the mud; I saw where they printed the ridge. "If I was growed up," I spoke aloud, "I'd follow them steps, be they go to the world's end." Then I ran to the house; I ran so fast a blue-snake racer couldn't have caught me.

Mother was putting dough bread and rashers on the table when I hurried indoors. Her face was gaunt with worry. She circled the table where Fern and Lark ate. Baby threshed in his tall chair, sucking a meat rind. "It would take Adam's grands and greats to rid that ground in time for planting," she said. "I tried grubbing a pawpaw, but its roots sunk to Chiney. I'm afeared we might have to backtrack to the mines. We'll be bound to, if the crops don't bear."

"I've seen a quare thing," I said.

Mother paid me no mind. "Two days your father will be gone, and no satisfaction I'll see till he returns. Yet he can't grub by his lone. He'd not get through in time." She halted, staring at the walls, searching in her head for what to do.

"Never was a mine shack darker," she said at last, having decided. She rolled her sleeves above her elbows, like a man's. "I can't grub fitten. I can't dig a cellar through puore rock. But window holes I can saw—holes three feet by five." She fetched a hatchet and a handsaw; she marked a window by tape.

"I'd be scared of a night, with holes cut," Fern complained. "Robber men might come."

"I saw tracks," I blurted. My words were drowned under Mother's chopping. She hewed a crevice to give the saw blade lee.

"It's Father's work," Fern whined. She squeezed her eyelids, trying to cry.

I recollect Mother worked that day through, cutting four windows, true as a sawyer's. The hours crawled turkle-slow. Fern and Lark and I longed for shouting children; we longed for the busy noises of the camps. We could only mope and look at the empty road. Nobody passed upcreek or down; nobody we glimpsed from daybreak to dusk dark. Oft when Mother took a little rest she'd glance the hills over. Oh, she was lost as anyone. Loneliness swelled large as mast balls inside of us.

When night came we heard the first lorn cry of a chuck-will's-widow. The evening chill was sharp. We ate supper huddled to a mite of fire. "One spark against a shingle," Mother explained, "and we'd have to roust a fox from his cave house. That chimley begs fixing."

The dishes were washed and put away. We sat quietly, our faces yellow in the lamplight. The *peent* of bull bats came through the window holes. Spring lizards prayed for rain in the bottoms.

Mother saw how our eyes kept stealing to the window. The darkness there was black as corpse cloth. "Sing a ballad or play a game," she urged. "Then hap baby will go to sleep."

"Play Bloody Tom," Lark called. "I be Tom, coming for a coal to tetch my pipe. You be sheeps or chaps."

"Now, no," Fern said, "that 'un's scary."

"Let's do a talking song," I chose. "Let's sing 'Old Rachel,' and me do the talking."

We sang "Old Rachel"; Old Rachel nobody could do a thing with; Old Rachel going to the Bad Place with her toenails dragging and a bucket on her arm, saying, "Good morning, Mister Devil, hit's getting mighty warm"; and I spoke, after every verse, "Now, listen, Little Rachel, please be kind o' quiet."

We hushed suddenly. Beast sounds rang the hills. Crownover's stallion had trumpeted afar, and our mare had whinnied.

"Sing ahead," Mother coaxed, "the mare's stall is latched. I saw to it. Sing what the Devil done with Rachel when he couldn't handle her."

We had no heart to sing more. "I propped the stall door," I said. Fern's eyes were beaded upon the black window. "Wisht it was allus day," she said.

"Ah, now," Mother chided, trying to comfort us. "A body gets their growth of a night. I'd not want the baby a dwarf."

"I saw a low-standing man in the camps once," Fern recalled, "not nigh tall as me."

"I saw tracks in the draw——" I began, and hushed. They grew in my mind. They seemed to have been made by the largest foot a man ever had. The thought held my breath. "Wisht Poppy was here," I said.

The baby sat up, round-eyed, blinking.

Mother spoke, making talk. "I wonder what name your father's going to bring this chap. I promised him the naming."

"He'll fotch a sour 'un," Fern grudged. "Ooge, Boll, Zee. One like smut-face little 'uns wear at the mines."

"I told your father, 'Name him for an upstanding man. A man clever, with heart and pride.'"

"Hope it's a rhymer," I said. "Whoever named them fourteen Crownovers was clever. Hit tuck a head full o' sense to figure all o' them."

"Once I knew a man who had a passel o' children," Mother related. "He married two times and pappyed twenty-three. After there come sixteen he ran out o' names. Just called them numbers, according to order. Seventeen, eighteen, nineteen, twenty——" She paused, watching baby. He slept, leaned upon nothing, like a beast sleeps.

"If Poppy was here," Fern yawned, "I bet he'd laugh."

"You'll all be dozing on foot before long," Mother told us. "Time to pinch the wick."

The lamp was smothered; we crawled between covers. Once the light died the window hole turned gray. You could see the shoulders of hills through it. Fern and Lark hushed and slept. I lay quiet, listening, and my ears were large with dark, catching midges of sound. The shuck mattress ticked, ticked, ticked. A rooster crowed. Night wore.

In my sleep I heard the mare thresh in her stall, pawing the ground with a forefoot. I raised on an elbow. From behind the barn came an owly cough and a voice saying, "Hold!" Someone stood inside the window, tall, white-gowned. It was Mother. I sprang beside her, looking. Fellows topped the ridge as ants march, up and over. Their heads were like folks' heads, but their backs were humpty.

"Six walkers with pokes," Mother said, "carrying only God knows what."

I recollect waking with the sun in my face; I recollect thinking Father would come home that day, bringing the frames to set against robbers and bloom winters. Lark was asleep beside me, and Fern and the baby lay in Mother's bed with their heads on a duck pillow. I recollect glancing through the window and seeing Mother run out of the fields.

I stood in my shirttail as Mother swung the door. Her hair fell wild about her shoulders. For a moment she had no breath to speak. "The mare's gone!" she gasped. "Gone."

Fern roused, meany for being awakened with a start. Lark's eyes opened, damp and large.

"I propped the stall door," I vowed. "Hit was latched and propped too."

"Had Poppy been at home," Fern quarreled, "stealers wouldn't a-come."

"I'd have figured she broke the latch of her own free will," Mother said, "hadn't it been for where the tracks led. I followed."

"Was they brogan prints alongside?" I asked. They grew immense in my mind. "Bigger'n anything?"

"Just bare mare tracks. I followed within sight o' the Crownovers."

Of a sudden I scorned the Crownovers. I could hear blood drum my ears. I said, "If I met one o' them chaps I'd not know him from dirt. I'd not speak a howdy."

Fern twisted into her garments. "I bet them girl-chaps wear old flour-sack dresses, and you kin read print front and back." She wrinkled her nose, making to cry. "I'm wanting to move to Houndshell." She flicked her eyelids, but not a tear would come. She got angry, angry as I. "Ruther be dust in a grave box than have to do with them folks. Be my name theirs, I couldn't hold up my head for shame."

"Don't lay blame for shore," Mother warned. "The mare's tracks went straight, yet they might o' veered a bit this side. There's nothing we can settle till your father's here, and he aimed to stop by Crownovers' anyhow."

Fern stamped her feet against the floor. "I wisht this house would burn to ashes. We'd be bound to live at the mines where they's girls to play with and hain't no robbers."

"Ramshack house, a-setting on a rock," I mocked.

Mother turned hurt eyes upon us. She stood before the cold fireplace and began to lay off with hands like the Houndshell schoolteacher. "Fifteen years we lived under a rented roof, fifteen years o' eating out o' paper pokes. We were beholden to the mines, robbed o' fresh breathing air, robbed o' green victuals. Now, cellar nor neighbors we've got here, but there's clean air and ground and home. I say this house hain't going to burn. That chimley's to rise higher."

"Poppy ought to be a-coming," Lark sniffled.

"The land not grubbed," Mother lamented, "no seeds planted, the mare stolen. Oh, it's Houndshell for us another winter." She turned away, her shoulders drawn and small.

We children ate breakfast alone, one of us forever peering through the window hole toward the way Father would come. Fern held the baby, giving him tastes of mush. We scraped the pot; we sopped our plates, for Mother had gone into the far room. But she came as we pushed the chairs aside. We stared. She wore Father's breeches. The legs were rolled at the bottom. "I can't climb a ladder or straddle a roof in a dress," she said. "Allus I've wanted to take a hand with this house. Here's my chance, before your father's back. He'd tear up the patch if he knew."

"It's man's work," Fern said grumpily.

Rocks were gathered, clay batter stirred, a ladder leaned against the roof. Up Mother went with a bucket of mud. I climbed, lifting the rocks in a coffee sack, reaching the poke's neck to her on gaining the tiptop. Mother edged along the hip roof, balancing the sack and bucket. Her face went dead white. Traveling the steep of a roof was not as simple as spoken.

Fern began to whimper, and the baby cried a spasm. "Come down!" Fern called. "Come down!"

Mother buttered two rocks with clay, placing them on the chimney. They rolled off, falling inside. She was slapping mud to a third when a voice roared beside the house. A man stood agape. A stranger had come unbeknownst. Mother jerked, and the bucket slipped, and the coffee sack emptied in a clatter across the shingles. The fellow had to jump limber dodging that rock fall. He roared, laughing, "Come down, woman, afore you break yore neck!" Mother obeyed, red-faced, ashamed of the breeches she wore.

We studied the man. He was older than Father, smaller, and two hands shorter. His eyes were bright as new tenpennies. An empty pipe stuck out of his mouth, the bowl a tiny piggin carved from an oak boss. "When a woman undertakes man's gin-work," he spoke, "their fingers all turn to thumbs." He didn't stand back. He hauled rocks and a new batch of clay up the ladder; he fashioned that chimney to a fare-you-well.

Lark and Fern and I whispered together.

Fern asked, "Who be this feller?"

Lark ventured, "Hit might be Old Bloody Tom, come for a coal o' fire."

I mouthed words in their ears. "I'd vow he's not a Crownover. His feet hain't big enough."

"We're obliged," Mother said when the stranger descended. She wore a dress now, though she was still abashed.

The man bowed his arms, tipped the pipe, discounting. "A high perch I've needed to search about. A horse o' mine broke stable last night. I'm looking for him."

Lark raised on his toes, straining to tell of our mare. Mother hushed him with a glance.

"Animals are apt to go traipsing when another'n nigh," the man continued, eying the barn, "but they usually come home by feeding time. Like as not, they'll bring in a furren critter, and it's a puzzle to whom they're belongen. I allus said, men and beast air cut from the same ham." He bent his knees to glance under the house and grunted knowingly. He shuffled to go. "Yonder atop the roof I beheld you've got a sight o' grubbing to do. Hit'd take Methuselum's begats to ready that ground for seed." He started off, speaking over his shoulder, "If you had fitten neighbors they'd not fail to help." He went downhill and upcreek, and we watched him out of sight.

We set a steady lookout for Father. As the hours crept into afternoon Mother complained, her voice at the rag edge of patience, "Your father ought to come while daylight's burning."

But Father arrived when the bull bats were flying and night darkened the hollows, and he came alone and empty-handed. No window frames he brought. I recollect he smiled on seeing our glum faces in the light of the great fire Mother had built. Even baby sulled a mite.

"What bush did you get them pouts off of?" he asked.

Mother lifted her hands in defeat. "I'm a-mind we'll have to endure the camps a spell longer."

"Hark!" Father exclaimed. How strangely he looked at

Mother, at us all. The mulligrubs were writ deep upon our faces.

"The mare stolen, no chance for a crop. Oh, the sorriest of folks we've moved nigh."

"Hark-o!"

"Them Crownovers hain't fitten neighbors," Fern scoffed. "A man come a-saying it."

I spoke with scorn. "They've got rhymy chaps. Their names sound like an old rain crow hollering *'cu cu cu, cucucu.'*"

"A man come a-saying——"

"Even if the garden and crop were planted," Mother despaired, "there'd be no place earthy to store winter food."

Father grinned. "Why, we've got a cellar dug by the Man Above. Old Izard Crownover says it's yonder in that brushy draw—a cave hole in solid lime rock that'll keep stuff till Glory. Now he ought to know."

Our mouths fell open. We could scarcely believe.

"Ah, ho," Father chortled, swinging the baby onto his shoulder. "They's another thing we've got for sartin, and that's a name for this little tadwhacker. He's to be named for a feller proud as ever walked. I'm going to call him Zard, after Old Izard."

"A man come a-saying——"

"Old Izard himself," Father said. "Why, them Crownovers are so proud they dreaded telling us o' using our cave for a cellar. They called hit trespassing. Walked their stuff out in the black o' night."

"The mare might o' broke the latch," Mother admitted, "but her tracks went straight as a measure."

"Come morning," Father chuckled, "you kin look up Shoal Creek, and there'll be the mare and Crownover's stally hauling window frames in a wagon. And there'll be Old

Izard and his woman and all his rhymers a-walking, coming to help grub, plow, and seed. Such an ant bed o' folks you'll swear hit's Coxey's Army."

Father halted, remembering what Izard had told him. He eyed Mother and began to laugh. Laughter boiled inside of him. He could barely make words, so balled his tongue was. "From now on," he gulped, "thar's one thing for shore." He threshed the air, his face fiery with joy. "I'm the one wearing the breeches." He struggled for breath. He choked.

Mother struck the flat of her hands against his back. "The nature of a man is a quare thing," she said.

MY PIGEON PAIR
by Dorothy Thomas
From *Harper's Magazine*

DOROTHY THOMAS

was born in Kansas, the sixth child and second daughter in a family of ten. She is descended from generations of Welsh clergymen. When she was seven the family moved to Alberta, Canada, and homesteaded in the brush country thirty-four miles from a railroad. Her father taught her to read, and her playthings were homemade. After her father died, when she was thirteen, the family moved back to Kansas, and after two years there went to Lincoln, Nebraska. She attended Cotner College and the University of Nebraska, and taught in between, clerking in stores in the summer. She now lives in New York. Her stories have appeared regularly in the Saturday Evening Post, Harper's Magazine, *and many other periodicals. She was represented in the O. Henry Memorial Award Prize Stories of 1933 with "The Consecrated Coal Scuttle," from* Harper's Magazine, *and in 1935 she won second prize with "The Home Place," also from* Harper's Magazine. *Her book of short stories under this title was published in 1936, while her other book,* Ma Jeeter's Girls, *appeared in 1933.*

J̲ENNY HAD LEFT two folded extra blankets for me on the large chair at the foot of her bed, and the bed was turned down. The studio was very like others she had lived in, and it was strange to see her bright-colored and oddly matched furniture without her large person moving awkwardly about to make me feel at home among it. All her paintings stood in a dovetailed outlining row on the floor against the four walls of the room.

In the bathroom, above the old-fashioned oval wash basin, hung two medicine cabinets. The one with the red loop of ribbon hung from its latch would be Jenny's and the other her roomer's. I wondered if Jenny's roomer had come home and was then in the little room beyond the bath's other door.

I was tired from my trip and I had had my dinner on the train and so wanted only to get to sleep and be really rested for the morning. I reached for my pocketbook and took out and, by the student lamp that arched from the table at the end of Jenny's bed, reread the note she had sent me.

Leaving key with supt. [she had written in her generous hand]. *Have to be away but want you to use studio just the same. Ring supt. bell. Don't try to keep food. Roaches and no ice. Eat out. Sleep in studio. Bedroom rented out to girl who clerks. Has own door to hall and bath and won't bother you. Has boy friend. May be there. May not. Walls thin. If she cries at night never mind it. Hope elevated doesn't keep you awake. Have a good time. Sorry to miss you. Love, Jenny.*

I turned off the light, and the squares of the window went from dark blue to gray blue, patterned with rows of lights. The window squares threw a wavering pattern on the wall and on Jenny's haphazard pieces of furniture, and in my weariness I got a feeling as if the place had lately been under water, that the huddling chairs had been washed where they stood, and that the pictures round the room were flotsam. The elevated trains, on a level with the story below, roared like some mighty chance-timed surf. Rest, comfort even, was not easily come by in Jenny's matter-of-fact bed. I lay and tried to get used to the noise of the trains and of the cars, trucks, and busses in the street below.

After a little I heard a key turning in the lock and started up, thinking someone was trying to get into the room, and then lay back, remembering the little girl in Jenny's bedroom. The wall was very thin, for I could hear the girl's slow step and knew quite well as she moved about what she was doing.

I saw her in my imagining hanging up her coat in a mothproof cardboard cupboard like the one in the studio where I lay, laying her turban and her cotton gloves away in the top drawer of a small chest, and then turning to the kitchen end of her little room. It must be that the room was about the size of Jenny's bathroom. I heard her turning on the switch of the little electric plate: low, medium, high, and the little click of each turn. Then she filled a small teakettle with water at the bathroom tap—I heard the lid fitted on the kettle and then the grating sound of it being slid on to the burner. A spoon tapped against the side of a smaller pan. I imagined the girl with a limp organdy apron tied about her waist, an apron sent her at Christmas time from an aunt in Iowa to remind her of home. Jenny assured me that almost all New York young people were from states away. I saw her stand patiently waiting for the gray-pink coils to turn fiery red and for the water in the kettle to heat. I heard the sound of a plate thumped down on the enamel-topped table, and then knife, fork, and spoon put beside it, and lastly a heavy glass that could only be an emptied and saved jelly glass.

A little afterward the smell of coffee came to me; the girl slid a chair to the table and sat down to eat. I wondered how it was that she had come from work so late. Obviously she had not eaten out. There were places possibly where a girl who clerked could shop after work. I wondered if the friend Jenny spoke of in her note would be coming to see the girl. I hoped that he would come and lift the tiredness that was in her steps by saying they would go to a movie.

The girl shoved back her chair and for moments walked briskly and determinedly about the room. She was putting things to rights; it was plain. She took pillows from the bed against the wall, spanked them, and tossed them back. Then she went back to the table. Whatever disorder there had been in the room had annoyed her, I told myself, and she had needed to right it before she could enjoy her second cup of coffee.

There were steps in the hallway that slowed near the studio door, and then the train thundered below, and when quiet came again there were voices in the room beyond the wall. The girl was saying, "I thought you weren't coming. I waited, and you didn't come."

"I'm sorry," the man said. "I couldn't make it." Both their voices were young, the girl's tired, determinedly steady, with, I felt, kept-back reproach in it.

"I thought something must have held you up," she said. "I waited."

"I'm sorry," the boy said.

"It's all right," the girl said. "I warmed up some stew. Will you have some? I've had all I want."

"No. No, thanks," the boy said, and his voice was both tired and wary. "You go ahead and finish your supper."

"Well, some coffee then? You'll have some coffee, won't you?"

"Thanks."

"Wait! Here, let me poke a fork in the holes of this milk can. They stop up. The milk's all right though. I opened it just last night, and it's been in the shaft window all day. There! I've been meaning to go out and get a little pitcher, but I can't seem to remember it at noon."

I heard the rattle of cup and saucer on the enamel-topped table. Then the girl's voice came, tender, half afraid to ask. "You didn't find anything?"

"Nope."

"Here, take some more milk. Take some sugar."

"Thanks."

"Allen?"

"Um?"

"What's the matter?"

"Nothing."

"I haven't done anything, have I?"

"No, a-course not."

"Then why—why did you draw your hand away when I touched you?"

"I was reaching for the sugar."

"Yes—but you drew away."

"Don't imagine things, Judy!"

"I don't mean to."

"The old girl gone?"

I had been listening as you listen to a radio serial, so lost in their talk that I had forgotten I was listening, and I was startled to have them speak of Jenny.

"Yes, she's out of town. I saw her yesterday in the hall, giving Mrs. Grimes the key."

"You pay her before she left?"

"I sure did. That's what I pay first, my rent. Nobody can say anything to you, about anything, if your rent's paid." There was a sudden sharpness in her voice.

A train came.

When I heard them again the boy was up from his chair, walking the little he could walk, in the length there was in the tiny room. Then he sat down heavily on the bed, and I heard a chair being slid across the room to him, and the girl said, "There, stretch out, Allen, and rest, and please, honey, put your cigarettes in this ash tray."

"That an ash tray?" There was lightness and a trying at humor in the boy's voice.

"It may look like a saucer to you, but it better be an ash tray." How quick she was to answer his lightness with hers. I heard her bring water from the bathroom, and at the little table wash the few dishes and then set them away in the cupboard over the table. The boy lay on the bed. When she had finished she came to the bed and sat down beside him.

"Hello, Allen," she said.

"Hello, Judy," he said. He patted the round of her slender arm.

I wanted to get up, to take hold of Jenny's heavy bed and drag it to some other part of the room, as far from the thin wall and from them as possible; but I knew that they did not know that I was there, that they believed themselves alone now, after the many times of reminding each other that Jenny was there and might hear them. I tried to remove myself from them in my thoughts, to leave them to themselves and to whatever happiness their being there together could bring them. I did my best to feel as a city woman might feel, to hear without hearing, without caring; but it was not easy to a night ear tuned to snow sliding from eaves or branches and to the far barking of neighbors' dogs. I put my mind on the trains and listened for them, counted between their comings, and waited for and heard those crashings in the street below that to a city ear mean nothing at all if heard and to me are astounding.

The boy and girl talked on, and I heard every word that they said between the coming of the trains. The girl seemed so eager that they be at peace, with no difference between them, seemed ready to try to forget some hurt, some unwilling grudge she held against him.

"Allen," she said, "why don't you talk to me?"

The young man sighed and stirred. "I can't. I don't want to talk. What is there to say?"

The girl was still a while and then said, "You used to talk. You used always to have something to say, things you'd been waiting to say—saving for me."

"Did I?" There was a little tenderness, along with wonder at this old self of his she spoke of, in his voice. "What did I say?"

"You know what you said. I know; I remember every word, but I don't want to say it. You don't want me to say it for you, do you? Say it back to you? What good would that be?"

"No good, I guess, Judy. Why do we have to talk?"

"We don't have to. You're tired, aren't you?"

"Yes."

Her voice was low, so that I could hardly hear it, and very gentle. " 'You're my treasure, my sweet!' " she said. "You used always to say that to me. 'My treasure.' Now, I say it to you. 'My treasure!' " Her voice broke suddenly on the word "treasure," and I felt, more than heard, felt it through the thin wall, that he had taken her by the arms and was shaking her.

"Judy," he said, "don't be like this, honey. Can't we just be quiet? Can't I come here and we just rest, just be quiet? Why do we have to be talking? I came, didn't I?"

"Yes, but after you made me wait! You let me wait. Do you think I wasn't tired waiting there, standing there so long? I was so tired I could die! I kept saying to myself, 'Would he wait this long for me?' Would you, Allen?"

"I have, times a-plenty."

"That was long ago. That was—that was before. Would you wait that long now, Allen, and ever come to see me again if I let you down?"

Trains drowned them.

When I heard them again I knew that the boy was holding her in his arms, was caressing her. "You know what'll happen, Judy, if we go on like this," he was saying. "My God, I thought last time if we ever went through that again, if you started in talking again about being scared and what would we do, I'd go crazy. That's what we've got to think about, Judy. Do you think I don't want to love you?"

The girl laughed suddenly, like a child, and I heard her quick kisses and her voice, between laughing and crying, "Oh, Allen, why did you wait? Why didn't you say so? I don't care! I don't care about anything if you love me, if you tell me you love me. Tonight you didn't say it. You didn't come to me and kiss me and say you were sorry you made me wait. You just stood there by the door. Honey, I know I'm silly but I can't help it. If you'll just say it when you come I can stand just being quiet then, just sitting by you and not talking. I can stand our not being together or I can stand our being together. I can even stand being scared, like I was last month. I can stand anything!"

"You think you can now," the boy said, "but——"

"Honey, I don't think anything. There isn't anything I have to think about, but that you love me, that you said it——"

"I didn't say it," the boy said playfully. "I just said, honey, don't you think I *want* to love you?"

"Then say it, say it, 'My treasure,' and 'I love you, Judy. I will always love you!' Oh Allen—I know I oughtn't to talk like this; I try to hold back talking like this. I don't think a girl ought to but I love you so! I can stand on my two feet all day and smile and always be nice to people, because I know—I think I know—that when night comes I'll maybe see you and I'll hear you, and you'll hold me."

"Judy, Judy!"

I heard their kisses. I heard the boy saying doggedly, like a boy talking in sleep, who has fallen asleep trying to work a hard problem, "Judy, we haven't anything. I haven't any job. What would happen to you? . . ."

I wrapped Jenny's thick pillow about my head, not to hear, and then, under cover of the roaring of a train, slipped from the bed and went and stood by the studio window, looking down on the tracks and on the street below. I stood with my hands pressed close to my ears, jealous for those two, against myself and my own nearness to their brief and troubled love-making.

I wished for a succession of trains that would follow one another without ceasing of sound. I got cold standing there and when a later train was passing I went back to bed.

"You all right, sweet?"

"Yes."

"You're not. It wasn't right for you again. I know when you pretend. I was afraid it wouldn't be. Aw, Judy, we're too tired, too scared. There's never any peace!"

"Sh! I'm all right. I had a fine time; I really had."

"No, you didn't. It's different when you do. You just want me to feel good."

"It was my fault," the girl said. "It's just—I'm so tired, that's all. It can't always be like it is sometimes. We know that."

"You're not sorry?"

"I'm never sorry. Don't you remember, honey, how I wasn't, that first time. You said, 'My brave, good girl!'"

"Judy, you think everything's all right?"

"Yes—of course."

"You won't be scared, won't worry this time?"

"Not unless I need to. It's all right, Allen."

"Judy?"

"Yes, darling?"

"Do you care if I go to sleep?"

"No, of course not. You go to sleep."

"Will you sleep?"

"Pretty soon I will. I like it, Allen, when you sleep, when you love me and go to sleep. Next to love, that's nicest, to have you sleep. When you sleep—you know how I feel?"

His voice was distant with drowsiness. "How?"

"Married, that's how. When you sleep with your head on my shoulder and breathe—slow, like you do, fast asleep—then I'm married; we're married. There's even—don't you laugh at me, dear—a ring on my hand. I can feel it without touching it with my other hand—a plain gold band, like my grandmother's."

Between trains I fell asleep then, and when I woke the girl was crying. She was trying to cry without sound, but I heard her. Finally the boy heard her too and spoke her name. She answered with only stifled crying.

"Judy," he said, "don't cry. Please don't cry, darling!"

"I don't mean to," the girl said. "Go back to sleep, Allen."
"I can't sleep if you cry."
"I'll stop as soon as I can."
"Why are you crying?"
"Because—because I was so lonesome!"
"Pet—you're not alone. I'm here. Did you sleep? Did you dream something that made you lonesome?"

"No, I didn't sleep. I couldn't get to sleep. And for a moment, once, I thought I heard *her* in there. I thought I heard her turning in her bed, that she'd heard us, but I just imagined that. She's gone."

"You go to sleep now, Judy."

"I will; I will just as soon as I can. Allen, I was thinking about us and how it was at first, how you'd hold me, and I'd tremble so—how just to touch your hand, to look up and see you—Allen, what is it that happens? Here—it's been just this little while, just these months, and these few times really we've been together like this, and something's gone. I love you just the same; I love you awfully, and I know that you love me, but—Allen, here, all my life, I wait for love, and it comes, and it's better than I ever dreamed, and in this little time it changes. I can't bear it to change. I got so lonesome, and it made me cry."

"Judy—don't cry. I feel like a louse. I think and think about it, about us. I come here and I think we'll just talk, just rest, just be quiet together. You're so nice just to be with, Judy—in the same room, talking. I think I'll just talk with you, hold you a little——"

"Yes, yes," the girl said. "Never mind, dear, never mind me talking; go to sleep!"

"I thought tonight I wouldn't come. I started to meet you and then turned back. I thought I wouldn't come here any more. Judy—we can't go on like this!"

"It's all right, dear. There's nothing really wrong! My heavens, can't a girl cry a little? Don't ever say that, that you'll not come. I'd die. I truly should die, Allen. I'd be lonesome, like I was just now—forever!"

He was holding her, comforting her, trying to still her crying that was wild now and unrestrained, like a child's.

Somehow I got away, into sleep, away from her lessening sobs and the boy's concern.

Sleeping, I dreamed that I was lying on a pallet, along with any number of children, visiting children, I thought, cousins who had come to stay the night with us in the country. I was the only child among them awake. I raised up on my elbow and looked at the others in the moonlight, at the sleeping children on the pallets of quilts and blankets, and then I saw the two in the next room, and they were not grown boy and girl but children, like the rest of us. The girl was still crying a little in her sleep. Near, above me and to one side, was a huge canopied bed, and in it slept my father. But he, too, had wakened. He was resting on his elbow, looking down and round at all the sleeping children. I saw his beard moving and I felt his voice more than heard it, reverberating through the posts of the high bed and along the floor under me. I heard him talking to himself, in the night, saying a poem, and his poem was one that I half remembered, and I felt his voice and the poem coming down to us on our pallets. I woke and said all that I could remember of the poem to myself, lying there in Jenny's too hard bed, looking up at the tall empty windows and waiting for the morning to come:

> *My little children twain, my pigeon pair,*
> *How will men deem you?*

> *As eye-delighting as I find you now?*
> *As full of joy? As passionate as bees*
> *Battling with flowers?*
> *Or will a slough of blossomless time engulf you?*
> *Oh, little sweetings, whereto were ye born?*
> *How can I save you?*

Wide-eyed I waited for the morning. Only once I heard the girl sigh in her sleep and mumble something. When it was not yet light I heard her getting up, heard her moving from the little room to the bath, walking on tiptoe. Then I heard the tapping of the kettle lid and, after a while, smelled the coffee and heard her setting dishes on the table.

There was no sound from the boy. At last the girl spoke to him, and I knew that she was sitting for an instant on the edge of the bed.

"Allen," she said. "Allen, honey."

"What?" he asked, from sleep.

"I want to tell you something. Are you awake?"

"Yes, I guess so."

"Allen, I've fixed your breakfast, honey. You just warm up the coffee a little when you get up. But don't get up yet. It's early."

"I'll get up."

"No, there's no sense in it. No place you'll want to go will be open for hours yet. You rest a while."

"You going now?"

"Yes. There's a quarter under the cup in your saucer. I'm telling you—so you'll be sure to get it."

"No, you take it—you'll need it."

"No, tomorrow's payday."

"Well—I wish you wouldn't. Thanks, Judy. Gosh—you look pale."

"Do I? It's just this light. I'm all right. Honey, I think your luck'll turn. I think you'll find something today! Will you miss me?"

"Yes, Judy. I wish I could come and not make you cry!"

"You didn't make me cry, honey. I told you—it was just I got lonesome. A body does sometimes. You'll come soon again?"

"I ought not. Aw, Judy——"

"I've got to go now, sweet. You heat the coffee, and first you sleep, just as long as you can. A good day to you, Allen!"

I heard her kiss, not like a lover's, but a quick, firm, family kiss, that said, "Be good now. Look after things! Good luck!"

Then the door closed after her, and I heard her feet walking swiftly along the hall, then running, on the stairs.

In the growing light I made out Jenny's paintings lined along the floor, against the walls. Sharp pictures they were, Village doorways, back yards with clotheslines sagging over cement courts, lampposts with gray snow falling through the wheels of light round them, and each picture forced into brave colors that such places, when I had seen them, had never held for me. The girl's steps echoed in my mind, and beyond the wall I heard the boy's breathing in that troubled last sleep before the day.

APPENDIX

APPENDIX

List of American magazines publishing short stories which were consulted in choosing stories for this volume:

Accent. Box 102, Urbana, Ill.
Adventure. Kenneth S. White, ed. Popular Publications, 205 E. 42nd St., New York City.
American Magazine (The). Sumner Blossom, ed. Crowell-Collier Pub. Co., 250 Park Ave., New York City.
American Mercury (The). Eugene Lyons, ed. 570 Lexington Ave., New York City.
American Prefaces. Wilbur L. Schramm, Paul Engle, eds. University Hall, University of Iowa, Iowa City, Iowa.
Argosy. George Worthington Post, ed. The Frank A. Munsey Co., 280 Broadway, New York City.
Atlantic Monthly (The). Edward Weeks, ed. 8 Arlington St., Boston, Mass.

Blue Book. Donald Kennicott, ed. The McCall Corp., 230 Park Ave., New York City.

City of Destiny. Zella Newcomb, ed. and pub. 614 Bernice Bldg., Tacoma, Wash.
Clipper (The). The Black and White Press, Inc., 1717 N. Vine St., Hollywood, Calif.
Coast (The). The Coast Corp., 130 Bush St., San Francisco, Calif.
Collier's Weekly. William L. Chenery, ed. Crowell-Collier Pub. Co., 250 Park Ave., New York City.
Columbia. John B. Donahue, ed. Knights of Columbus, 45 Wall St., New Haven, Conn.

Columbia Review (The). 415 John Jay Hall, Columbia University, New York City.

Coronet. Arnold Gingrich, ed. 919 N. Michigan Ave., Chicago, Ill.

Cosmopolitan. Harry Payne Burton, ed. Hearst Magazines, Inc., 57th St. and 8th Ave., New York City.

Crisis (The). Roy Wilkins, ed. 69 Fifth Ave., New York City.

Decade of Short Stories. Lee Lukes, ed. 2952 Belden Ave., Chicago, Ill.

Decision. Klaus Mann, ed. Decision, Inc., 141 E. 29th St., New York City.

Direction. M. Tjader Harris, ed. Direction, Inc., Darien, Conn.

Elks' Magazine (The). Coles Phillips, managing ed. 50 E. 42nd St., New York City.

Esquire. Arnold Gingrich, ed. 919 N. Michigan Ave., Chicago, Ill.

Flamingo (The). Jess Gregg, ed. Rollins College, Winter Park, Fla.

Good Housekeeping. Herbert R. Mayes, ed. Hearst Magazines, Inc., 57th St. & 8th Ave., New York City.

Hairenik. Hairenik Association, Inc., 212 Stuart St., Boston, Mass.

Harper's Bazaar. Carmel Snow, ed. 572 Madison Ave., New York City.

Harper's Magazine. Lee F. Hartman, ed. Harper & Bros., 49 E. 33rd St., New York City.

Holland's Magazine. Miss Claude Weir, ed. Texas Farm & Ranch Co., 3306 Main St., Dallas, Texas.

Household Magazine. Nelson Antrim Crawford, ed. Arthur Capper, pub. 8th & Jackson Sts., Topeka, Kan.

Kansas Magazine (The). Russell I. Thackrey, ed. Kansas State College, Manhattan, Kan.

Appendix

Kapustkan (The). Bruce Kapustka, Stan Lee Kapustka, eds. Kapustka Literary Foundation, 5013 S. Throop St., Chicago, Ill.

Ladies' Home Journal (The). Bruce Gould, Beatrice Blackmar Gould, eds. Curtis Pub. Co., Independence Sq., Philadelphia, Pa.

Liberty. Fulton Oursler, ed. 122 E. 42nd St., New York City.

Lights Up. Frances Mazo, ed. 26 East 4th St., St. Paul, Minn.

Mademoiselle. Betsy Talbot Blackwell, ed. 1 E. 57th St., New York City.

Magnificat. Sisters of Mercy, eds. and pubs. 131 Laurel St., Manchester, N.H.

Manhattan Quarterly (The). John G. Keating, ed. Manhattan College, Spuyten Duyvil Parkway & 242nd St., New York City.

Matrix. Joseph Moskovitz, ed. 1500 W. Nedro Ave., Philadelphia, Pa.

McCall's Magazine. Otis L. Wiese, ed. The McCall Corp., 230 Park Ave., New York City.

New Anvil (The). Jack Conroy, ed. 3569 Cottage Grove Ave., Chicago, Ill.

New Horizons. Robert and Margaret Williams. Box 336, Evanston, Ill.

New Masses. Joseph North, ed. 461 Fourth Ave., New York City.

New Mexico Quarterly Review (The). (Formerly the *New Mexico Quarterly*.) Dudley Wynn, ed. The University of New Mexico, Albuquerque, N.M.

New Yorker (The). Harold Ross, ed. 25 W. 43d St., New York City.

North Georgia Review (The). Lillian E. Smith, Paula Snelling, eds. Clayton, Ga.

Opportunity: A Journal of Negro Life. Elmer Anderson Carter, ed. National Urban League, 1133 Broadway, New York City.

Pax: A Catholic Monthly. Very Rev. Dom Michael Heinlein, O.S.B., ed. Benedictine Convent, Newton, N.J.

Prairie Schooner. Lowry Charles Wimberly, ed. University of Nebraska, 12th & R Sts., Lincoln, Neb.

Pyramid. Ben and Isabel Hagglund, eds. San Benito, Texas.

Redbook Magazine. Edwin Balmer, ed. The McCall Corp., 230 Park Ave., New York City.

Rocky Mountain Review. Ray B. West, Jr., ed. Box 5, Branch Agricultural College, Cedar City, Utah.

San Francisco Quarterly. University of San Francisco, San Francisco, Calif.

Saturday Evening Post (The). Wesley Winans Stout, ed. Curtis Pub. Co., Independence Sq., Philadelphia, Pa.

Scholastic Magazine. Maurice R. Robinson, ed. 220 E. 42nd St., New York City.

Short Stories. Dorothy McIlwraith, ed. 9 Rockefeller Plaza, New York City.

Short Story Manuscripts of 1941. Sylvia Chatfield Bates, ed. Fiction Workshop, Dept. of Journalism, New York University, New York City.

Southern Literary Messenger (The). F. Meredith Dietz, ed. 109 E. Cary St., Richmond, Va.

Southern Review. Charles W. Pipkin, ed. Louisiana State University, Baton Rouge, La.

Southwest Review. John H. McGinnis, et al., eds. Southern Methodist University, pub., Dallas, Texas.

Story. Whit Burnett, ed. 432 Fourth Ave., New York City.

Tanager (The). Henry Alden, ed. Box 66, Grinnell College, Grinnell, Iowa.

This Week. Mrs. William Brown Meloney, ed. United Newspapers Magazine Corp., 420 Lexington Ave., New York City.

Tumbleweed. Joseph E. Shelton, ed. 201 Park Bldg., Portland, Ore.

Twice a Year. Dorothy Norman, ed. 509 Madison Ave., New York City.

University Review (The). Alexander Cappon, ed. University of Kansas City, Kansas City, Mo.

Virginia Quarterly Review. Archibald Bolling Shepperson, ed. University of Virginia, Charlottesville, Va.

Woman's Day. Eileen Tighe, ed. 19 W. 44th St., New York City.
Woman's Home Companion. Gertrude B. Lane, ed. Crowell-Collier Pub. Co., 250 Park Ave., New York City.
Writer's Forum (The). Freeman Champney, managing ed. The Antioch Press, Yellow Springs, Ohio.

Yale Literary Magazine. Yale University, New Haven, Conn.
Yale Review (The). Wilbur Cross, ed. Yale University Press, New Haven, Conn.
Yankee. Robb Sagendorph, ed. Yankee, Inc., Dublin, N.H.

List of Prize Stories in O. HENRY MEMORIAL AWARD PRIZE STORIES
1919 to 1941 Inclusive

1919—1st. ENGLAND TO AMERICA, Margaret Prescott Montague
    2nd. FOR THEY KNOW NOT WHAT THEY DO, Wilbur Daniel Steele

1920—1st. EACH IN HIS GENERATION, Maxwell Struthers Burt
    2nd. CONTACT, Frances Noyes Hart

1921—1st. THE HEART OF LITTLE SHIKARA, Edison Marshall
    2nd. THE MAN WHO CURSED THE LILIES, Charles Tenney Jackson
    (Special prize for best work in 1919, 1920, 1921)—
        THE MARRIAGE IN KAIRWAN, Wilbur Daniel Steele

1922—1st. SNAKE DOCTOR, Irvin S. Cobb
     2nd. INNOCENCE, Rose Wilder Lane
     SS. GOLD-MOUNTED GUNS, F. R. Buckley

1923—1st. PRELUDE, Edgar Valentine Smith
     2nd. A FRIEND OF NAPOLEON, Richard Connell
     SS. TOWERS OF FAME, Elizabeth Irons Folson

1924—1st. THE SPRING FLIGHT, Inez Haynes Irwin
     2nd. MARGARET BLAKE, Chester T. Crowell
     SS. RACHEL AND HER CHILDREN, Frances Newman

1925—1st. MR. BISBEE'S PRINCESS, Julian Street
     2nd. SPLENDID WITH SWORDS, Wythe Williams
     SS. PAPAGO WEDDING, Mary Austin

1926—1st. BUBBLES, Wilbur Daniel Steele
     2nd. DEATH IN THE WOODS, Sherwood Anderson
     SS. COMMAND, Albert Richard Wetjen

1927—1st. CHILD OF GOD, Roark Bradford
     2nd. THE KILLERS, Ernest Hemingway
     SS. THE SCARLET WOMAN, Louis Bromfield

1928—1st. THE PARROT, Walter Duranty
     2nd. THE PECULIAR TREASURE OF KINGS, Marjory Stoneman Douglas
     SS. BRIDAL POND, Zona Gale

1929—1st. BIG BLONDE, Dorothy Parker
     2nd. THE HOMESICK LADIES, Sidney Howard
     SS. HIM AND HER, Katharine Brush

1930—1st. DRESSING-UP, W. R. Burnett
     1st. NEITHER JEW NOR GREEK, William M. John
     2nd. THE SACRIFICE OF MAIDENS, Elizabeth Madox Roberts
     SS. CORONER'S INQUEST, Marc Connelly

Appendix

1931—1st. (no prize) CAN'T CROSS JORDAN BY MYSELF, Wilbur Daniel Steele
    2nd. (1st money) ONE HEAD WELL DONE, John D. Swain
    3rd. (2nd money) THE FIVE MINUTE GIRL, Mary Hastings Bradley
    SS. HAUNTED GROUND, Oliver La Farge

1932—1st. AN END TO DREAMS, Stephen Vincent Benét
    2nd. FAREWELL TO CUBA, James Gould Cozzens
    SS. A TRIP TO CZARDIS, Edwin Gracberry

1933—1st. GAL YOUNG UN, Marjorie Kinnan Rawlings
    2nd. THE FRILL, Pearl S. Buck
    SS. TO THE INVADER, Nancy Hale

1934—1st. NO MORE TROUBLE FOR JEDWICK, Louis Paul
    2nd. OLD RED, Caroline Gordon
    SS. THE DARING YOUNG MAN ON THE FLYING TRAPEZE, William Saroyan

1935—1st. THE WHITE HORSES OF VIENNA, Kay Boyle
    2nd. THE HOME PLACE, Dorothy Thomas
    SS. JOHN THE SIX, Josephine W. Johnson

1936—1st. TOTAL STRANGER, James Gould Cozzens
    2nd. SUITE 2049, Sally Benson
    SS. A SUM IN ADDITION, William March

1937—1st. THE DEVIL AND DANIEL WEBSTER, Stephen Vincent Benét
    2nd. TO THOSE WHO WAIT, Elick Moll
    3rd. THE FURY, Robert M. Coates

1938—1st. THE HAPPIEST MAN ON EARTH, Albert Maltz
    2nd. FIRE AND CLOUD, Richard Wright
    3rd. THE PROMISE, John Steinbeck

1939—1st. BARN BURNING, William Faulkner
2nd. BAT FLIGHT, James Still
3rd. CALVES, David Cornel De Jong

1940—1st. FREEDOM'S A HARD-BOUGHT THING, Stephen Vincent Benét
2nd. DON'T GET ME WRONG, Roderick Lull
3rd. THE KILL, Edward Havill

1941—1st. DEFEAT, Kay Boyle
2nd. A WORN PATH, Eudora Welty
3rd. EIGHTEENTH SUMMER, Hallie Southgate Abbet
Special Prize for a "First" Story. THE VISIT, Andy Logan

DATE DUE

WITHDRAWN
from
Funderburg Library